ECLIPSE OF THE TRIPLE MOONS

KENNETH BROWN

Adgitize Press

This is a work of fiction. All the characters and events portrayed in this novel are either fictitious or used fictitiously

.

Eclipse of the Triple Moons

By Kenneth Brown

Adgitize Press

First Edition: May 2018

For Mary

You've been the love of my life for 47
years. You give me the confidence to dream
big and act on my dreams.

ABOUT THE STORY

THEY WERE JUST PLAYING A GAME

Four teenagers playing a real-life fantasy game in a Montana mountain cave find a portal to another world. Alpherge, Sherry, Lily, and Erik step through the shimmering portal, and find themselves in a strange world with three moons hanging low in the sky.

As they explore this new world, they come across an ancient and powerful magical staff imbued with the ability to control elemental magic. But their adventure takes a turn for the worse when they learn that a ruthless dark sorcerer seeking to harness the power of the triple moon eclipse kidnaps their friend Lily.

Vowing to save their friend despite the dangers, the trio sets out to rescue Lily, using the magical staff to overcome the many obstacles and enemies they face along the way. As they journey through enchanted snow-capped mountains, they discover a hidden strength within themselves and the true power of friendship.

Can they rescue Lily and save the world from the darkness that threatens to consume it before the eclipse of the triple moons?

CHAPTER 1

High school junior, Erik Anderson, waited in the hallway next to his locker with his best friend, Al, a tall lanky kid.

Al explained, "I'm working on the next D&D game for this weekend. It's my best dungeon ever. You're coming over, aren't you?"

Erik's body tensed. "We'll see." His thoughts weren't on D&D as he scanned the hallway for his friend, Lily. Today, he planned to overcome his fears and ask Lily to the homecoming dance.

"I've developed two new monsters and I'm including a spectacular water feature that will blow your mind. Plus, for my birthday I received a book on adding more descriptive detail to wilderness areas and I've been working hard on my wizard character, Alpherge the Mighty."

Al's voice droned on about the game, but Erik's mind remained on Lily. Every day for the last two weeks he had stood in this same spot to talk with her about the dance, but fear and other people kept getting in the way. Well, not today. Nothing and no one would stop him. All night he had rehearsed his request, both his words and her responses. He felt ready and would not be denied.

Al said, "Sherry is coming over and bringing a girl she talks to in Physics class. That means there will be seven adventurers in the group. Are you listening?"

Erik continued his internal monologue about Lily. It felt like she had placed a spell over him at the end of the last school year when he had first noticed his blonde haired, blue-eyed friend had transformed into a beautiful woman.

"Mr. Siglar, the math teacher, said he used to play D&D as a kid and maybe one day he would play with us.

He even said they played in college using the school's heating tunnels as real dungeons. That would make it an interesting three-D experience."

Lily's transformation into a woman caused hormones to race through Erik's body. He knew today their relationship as friends would change forever. Then he saw her.

"We should get Lily to play D&D with us," Erik said.

Al said, "Are you serious? Lily? Why would she play D&D? She's too busy brushing her hair and dancing. "

"She isn't always brushing her hair. She just wants to look nice."

He thought back to the school talent show last spring, when Lily performed a ballet. Each move she made in the tights and short skirt accentuated her curves and enhanced his desire for her as a woman, not a girl.

"Ha, we've been friends since kindergarten and she's never had an interest in the Dungeon and Dragon games we play. Why would she now?"

Erik said, "I don't know, I thought it would be nice to spend more time with her. We've lost touch with our friend since we entered high school."

"Yeah, because we are taking college prep classes and she… well she isn't."

Lily approached, dressed in blue jeans and a baby-blue cable sweater, as she walked with her shorter, red-haired friend, Sherry. Lily's locker stood across the hall from Erik's and he moved toward her locker with the expectation they would meet at her locker at the exact same time. Within ten feet Lily noticed Erik and she waved and smiled.

Perfect, she's happy to see me. He waved back at her. He half-shouted, "Hi Lily."

"Oh, Erik, how are you?" she bubbled in excitement.

"Can I ask you a quick question?" Erik felt the tension rising in his throat muscles as his mind raced. *Don't back down now, be strong, be brave, you can do it.*

"Oh, let me tell you my news first. I'm going to homecoming with Billy Cutter. I'm so excited."

Erik pressed his lips tight, his shoulders slumped as he touched the lockers to steady shaking legs. Really, she's going to homecoming with the newcomer with the long, black hair, Billy Cutter? He was a muscular, good looking, exchange student with a foreign accent.

"Billy just asked me after English class." Lily's eyes sparkled. She closed her eyes and swayed side to side with an imaginary dance partner.

Erik said nothing as he thought about punching the lockers, but he took a deep breath and glanced at his locker, his mind numb. The sounds of the hallway faded into a pounding in the back of his head.

"Are you okay? What did you want to ask me?" Lily touched Erik's arm.

His muscles quivered and his body tensed; no part of his rehearsal included Lily already having plans for homecoming. He struggled to stay positive.

"Are you okay?" she asked.

"I'm, I'm, I'm, so happy for you." Sweat built on his brow. "I gotta go to class now."

Erik bolted through the hallway pushing students aside, while books flew from their hands. He wanted to punch something right now, anything, or anybody. Approaching his physics class he slowed, knowing he needed to get his emotions under control as he opened and closed his fist.

Erik pushed a student aside and stomped to the water fountain.

As Erik drank the cool water he felt better. Then a student walking past bumped him. He bolted upright and glared at the smaller freshman and yelled, "If you ever touch me again, I'll knock your block off."

The smaller student scowled at Erik and scampered to class.

Al walked up beside Erik, "Are you okay?"

Erik tensed his fist in a tight ball. "Yeah."

"Why did you run down the hall so fast? I thought you wanted to ask Lily a question or something."

"Don't worry about it."

A rich, deep voice sounded behind Erik. "Hi guys, what's going on?"

Billy Cutter stood next to Erik.

"What do you want?" His face becoming hot, Erik moved back from Billy.

Billy said, "Just seeing what you guys are doing."

"We're talking about D&D." Al said. "I'm putting together a new game and we're playing on Saturday. Do you want to come?"

"I love that game, but have you ever played it in a real cave?" Billy asked. "I know a place at the state park that is an out-of-the-way cave with only a few visitors this time of year. It makes for a way different game."

"That would be awesome."

"Would you like to play Friday after school?" Billy asked.

"We're busy on Friday, aren't we Al?" Erik grabbed Al's arm.

"No, I'm not busy." Al pointed at Billy. "Are you a dungeon master?"

"Yeah, I've put together games before, and we've done a cave once. I can shake the cobwebs off the game and have something ready for Friday."

"I'm busy on Friday, I won't be there." Erik fantasized about punching Billy in the face.

"I bet I can get Sherry to come and a couple more people." Al said.

"This quest is only built for four adventurers." Billy cleared his throat. "I'll get Lily to join—"

"Ha, Lily, she'll never play." Erik felt the heat rising in his face. How could this newcomer with the strange accent get Lily to do something he couldn't?

"Oh, she'll love it. I bet I can convince her to play."

Al said, "I don't know, she's never shown interest in the game."

Erik blurted out, "I'll play if you get Lily."

"Okay, that's four, I'll text you directions to the cave."

CHAPTER 2

Erik sat in his car at Table Rock Park in the Bitteroot Mountains in Montana with his friends, Al, Sherry and Lily. "Are you guys sure you still want to do this? It's kind of cold outside."

"I'm all in, it will be fantastic," Al said from the old hatchback's front seat. The small car didn't leave much room for the tall, lanky boy, but he always found a way to shoehorn his legs into the space.

"I don't trust Billy Cutter," Erik said. "His eyes are too close together."

"Oh, you're funny, Erik. You're just jealous." Lily said. "Did you notice how Billy's jaw looks cut from stone and ends with that cute dimple in his chin?"

He felt the heat rise to his face. Did she know how he really felt about her?

"Billy is a great kid. We've been talking on the phone the last three nights and I've really gotten to know him."

Sherry said, "He has a terrific bod." She shared a glance and a grin with Lily.

"Hey, you're going to homecoming with me you know." Al glared at Sherry.

"Where's Billy from?" Erik asked.

"He's from another country."

"Yeah, but which country? Nobody I talk to knows where he came from. It's like he's an alien just plopped down from the sky." Erik said.

"He told me he's from the mountains and lives close to volcanos. It all sounds very exciting when he talks about it." Lily said.

"Well, he's expecting us at the cave entrance at three we'd better get going."

They stepped out of the car and Lily said, "I'm so excited to be playing D&D with you guys, you've never invited me to your games, and I've always wanted to play."

Al glanced at Erik and hunched his shoulders.

"Okay, volcanos, that means maybe Guatemala, Nicaragua, or New Guinea."

"How about the Philippines?" Al chimed in.

Lily laughed, "No not the Philippines. Billy says the mountains have snow on them. He told me he grew up in a castle."

"Ha, a castle. So, he's a prince or king or something." Erik stared at Lily. How was he going to compete with a prince, a man with money, power and prestige?

"The cave is on the scenic lookout trail, right Sherry?"

"Right."

They walked the trail, ascending the steep path and five minutes later reached a sign.

Trail Closed - Bridge Out.

"Now what?" asked Al?

"We're going up the trail." replied Erik. He led the way past the sign and soon reached the damaged bridge. "This is weird. A few boards are missing from the bridge."

Sherry said, "Can we shimmy past the damage?"

"No way am I walking over that suspension bridge." Al shook his head.

Erik glanced at the distant valley floor. "I will prove it's safe or we go home. Come on, where's your sense of adventure?"

Al said, "I'm not walking across that swaying monstrosity."

"Sherry and I will go and you hang here until we get back."

Al said, "No way am I'm staying here by myself, Mom told me the mountains are dangerous and crawling with Yetis and Chupacabra."

Sherry laughed. "Bigfoot, Sasquatch and goat suckers? No such things. Not in Montana. You're watching too much late-night TV and the History Channel."

"I can't stay here alone. Sasquatch will take me to the forest and devour me piece by piece, cutting chunks of flesh each day."

"Then you're coming across," Erik took his time testing his weight on each slat before applying full pressure as he walked across the swaying bridge. The railings were in-tact with ten feet of missing slats. He held to the upper railing and scooted his feet along the lower railing to safety. He felt drops of water splashing from the waterfall nearby. "Al this is secure."

Lily followed Erik across safely, taking more time. She smiled at Erik when she reached him on the other side.

Sherry pushed Al. "Move Brainiac, visualize yourself on the opposite side."

"That's easy for you. I see my corpse at the base of this chasm and Mom yelling at me."

"Make an effort, please?" said Sherry. "Assuming you fall to your death, you won't have to agonize over what your mom says.

Al grasped the handrail and shuffled to the missing section, his entire body trembling.

"Do you need help?" asked Erik.

"No, it won't hold us both at the same time."

Erik jumped on the bridge forcing it to sway where Al traversed.

Al froze and closed his eyes. "Stop it."

"I'm joking. Come on, I'll stay off."

Al reached the broken section and placed his right hand on the railing and attempted to put his left foot on the support rail. Shaking his head and changing direction, he put his left hand on the railing and his right foot on the support rail. "I can't do it."

"Come on Brainiac, we're doing this." Sherry grabbed his hand. "Put your right hand here." She placed his hand on the railing. "Now put your right foot on the bottom rail."

"I can't, I'll fall into the ravine."

Erik yelled, "Al don't look down. You can do this."

Sherry edged up next to Al on the bridge. "Come on Al. You can do it. You are the wizard, Alpherge the Mighty. Do you have a magic spell for this task? What are the words? Shoes light as feathers make me a bird. Or maybe a bravery spell."

Al chided her, "This isn't Dungeons & Dragons. That's a game not real life."

"Maybe this is part of the D&D game by Billy. This is a true adventure." Sherry pushed on Al and he moved his right foot along the bottom railing. He held the railing with both hands and had both feet on the lower railing where the boards were missing. Al froze for half a minute before moving more, and after a number of small moves, he stepped onto the boards on the other side. Al said, "I did it," and ran to Erik.

Erik gave Al a high five. Then he watched Sherry for a moment then she disappeared in a flash as her scream echoed off the mountain ridges. Adrenaline coursed through his veins. He didn't see her. "Sherry!" He studied the ravine for a sign of his friend.

"Help me!"

Erik ran to the broken section. Sherry grasped the bottom railing on the damaged section of the bridge. "What happened?"

"It doesn't matter. Help!"

Erik kneeled on a loose board. He wasn't strong and questioned if he had strength to lift his friend. "Can you get closer?" He asked.

"Hurry! My hands are slipping."

The bridge swayed side-to-side.

Erik grabbed an arm and said, "Okay, I have your arm."

She released her grip on the railing with her left hand and grabbed one of Erik's arms. "Don't drop me." Her body swung over the ravine.

Lily lay on her belly and held Erik's legs.

Sherry's legs dangled in space with her life depending on Erik, "I have you." His arms were failing fast. How long could he hold her with the water from the falls splashing soaking his hands? He pulled her but the water made her skin slippery.

Sherry released Erik's hand, pulled on the railing and grabbed a board on the bridge. Erik grasped a leg and dragged her over the rest of the way. They both lay on the bridge gasping for breath.

Erik, Lily and Sherry caught up with Al on the path, Sherry said to Al, "Why didn't you help me?"

"No way am I going back onto the bridge."

"You would watch me plummet to my death?" She hit Al on the arm and stalked down the path.

# # # #

They walked for eight minutes and Erik said, "The cave is up there; Billy should be there." He didn't see anyone near the cave, but maybe they just needed to get closer.

"Yes, this is the cave where Billy told us to meet." Al said.

Erik edged closer to the cavern in the deciduous forest. The park got its name from the exposed granite rock that resembled a huge table. A small stream of water came down off the mountain and fed into a huge clay pipe running underneath the trail. The trees were bare and orange, brown and yellow leaves covered the forest path. He felt cold in the late afternoon wind. A rustling noise on the path startled him, and a squirrel ran up a tree.

The cave was a small hole in the rock that dropped back maybe ten feet. As a kid the first time he had visited, the cave seemed a huge wilderness cavern, but he was older now, and the cave's capacity of four or five adults appeared small.

He grabbed a large stick as he came to the cave entrance. No one stood at the cave or around it. Where was Billy?

At the cave entrance, Erik shined his phone's flashlight into the cave but saw nothing but rock and shadows.

Al said, "Where's Billy?"

"Look around, there's a logical explanation." said Erik. "Maybe this is part of the Dungeon plan."

"What should we do?" asked Sherry? "Do you need us to search for him?"

"I want to go into the cave, maybe he's in there."

CHAPTER 3

Erik got on his knees to enter the small cave entrance but once inside straightened. "I can stand in here. Not much light though." He brushed the leaves off his jeans.

"Any bears preparing for a long winter with you," Al asked?

"No, it seems different from the last time I explored this section. It's weird to say this, but the size of the cave has changed. The cave stretches for a few feet with plenty of room. Come on in."

Tall Al had trouble getting into the cave, "I don't want to get my new jeans dirty crawling on the ground."

They crowded into the opening. The natural light didn't extend far from the entrance.

They turned their phones on flashlight mode.

Erik remarked, "The cave is larger than I remember, and what is that trail over there? That wasn't there the other times I've been in this cave. What's the deal?"

Sherry said, "Mom and I came here a couple of times, but you're right, I don't remember an offshoot trail."

Lily said, "Maybe you're thinking about a different cave."

Erik glanced at Sherry and shook his head. "It's the same cave, just different."

Sherry nodded. "Weird. Like a geological event happened and opened up sections in the cave. Do we continue searching the cavern for Billy?"

Al said, "No, I don't want to get trapped in the cave. I saw a show on TV where people entered a cave. Then an earthquake happened and the ceiling collapsed blocking the people into the cave where they all died."

"This isn't TV, and I doubt we need to worry about earthquakes." Erik pushed Al in the back to get him moving farther into the cave system.

"Oh, I'm not leading us into this death trap, you go first." Al stepped aside and Erik moved in front.

As Erik walked with caution through the cave he thought of Lily. What could he do to get her to tell Billy to get lost and then agree to go to homecoming with him?

With his mind on Lily, he missed the looming shadow. A man dressed all in black wearing a cape stepped from the wall.

"Hello adventurers."

Erik jumped. "What?"

They all laughed, and Lily said, "Billy there you are." She hugged him and gave him a quick peck on the lips.

"I'm not Billy, today, I'm Kestrel the Falcon Prince."

Erik shined his phone flash light on Billy and the boy twirled his cape embroidered with an image of an exploding volcano on the back and a flying falcon imprinted on the cape's left breast.

"Excellent!" laughed Al. "Let the game begin."

"Oh brother, nice outfit." Erik rolled his eyes and stared at the cavern ceiling.

Water dripped in whispering plip-plops from the ceiling to a stalagmite on the cave floor. A stale musty odor filled their nostrils.

Al said, "Is there gold and silver in this cave?"

"Great treasures are hidden throughout the cave, but be careful. Dangerous animals, like orcs, dragons and dwarves guard the treasures."

"I check the wall for silver and gold." Al shone his flashlight on a portion of the wall.

Billy rolled a twelve-sided dice and checked his phone. "Shiny objects are on the wall."

Erik said, "I pull a pick axe from my pack. I hit the wall a couple of times with the axe."

"The shiny objects fall from the wall and land on the floor of the cave."

"I examine the shiny objects." Sherry mimed at examining something in her hands.

"Oh, we've already found gold, this is so much fun." Lily said.

"It may be gold; it has hard edges and glistens." Billy said.

"I rub the object against a small copper plate I keep in my backpack."

"The object scratches the copper plate."

"Oh, pyrite, fool's gold." Sherry said.

"It's not real gold?" Lily asked. "You're tricking us, Billy."

"Remember, I'm Kestrel."

"Oh right, we're pretending you're the Falcon Prince."

They walked for twenty minutes, playing the game, the adventurers earning virtual treasures found during their quest while losing life points against orcs and monsters.

The cave became narrow and cramped forcing Erik to bend over to keep from hitting his head.

After a series of curves to the left and right, they heard a rustling in the cave. Bats flew everywhere brushing their hair, arms and faces.

Sherry let out a scream, "I hate bats!"

Al lay on the cavern floor covering his head.

Lily screamed and Erik covered her with his body and arms, a pleasant experience as he inhaled her fresh scent.

They waited for the bats to leave and then traveled two minutes more in the cramped cave before entering a huge cavern.

"I can stand up full height now. My back is killing me," Al knuckled his back.

Sherry's breathing was heavy and rapid, "Even I ducked those last ten feet. Any chance someone brought water?"

"No," Erik regretted the lack of planning, knowing he had no idea where they were going. "Are you guys okay?"

"Falcon Prince, can you get us out of this cave?" Sherry asked. "It isn't smart to get disoriented in this cave without water. Can we get back to the cave entrance without getting lost?"

Billy said, "We aren't lost yet. Let's go for another fifteen minutes. Then we go home. Are you okay with that idea?"

Al gestured above his head, "Hey guys, isn't this cavern ginormous?"

"It's beautiful." Sherry's phone flashed as she took a photo. "Those stalactites hanging in that roof section require thousands of years to grow that large. Why haven't we seen this part of the cave in previous hikes?"

They wandered in the large cavern playing the game. Billy brought a number of monsters into the D&D scenario. The cavern extended another hundred feet and then came to a section where the cave split into three separate tunnels.

"Now where to, O Great Leader?" asked Sherry?

"We explore the different paths." Erik said.

Al stood in front of one tunnel and said, "We should go here."

"Okay, I'll lead," Erik walked into the tunnel.

Al followed close behind.

Sherry followed Al into the yellow tunnel offshoot.

Billy rolled a couple of die. "You are hit with an electrical CME, a coronal mass ejection, from the sun, and your phones and all electrical devices you own are disabled for ten minutes. To add realism to the game you must turn off all your devices so you will be in darkness for ten minutes."

"Oh no, my phone's flash light stopped working," Al turned off his phone.

"What's happening to my electronic device," Erik deactivated his phone, and darkness crept closer in the dank little corridor.

"Has a CME hit? I heard there was a large sunspot on the sun this morning and it released a coronal mass ejection." Sherry extinguished the light from her phone, and they waited in the dim light from Billy's phone.

Billy said, "I'm going to take Lily into another part of the cavern. While you were plunged into darkness, she is kidnapped by foreign beings in the cave. You can search for her, but you can't turn on your lights for ten minutes. Lily, go ahead and scream."

Lily screamed as good as any B movie actress ever has.

Then the teens were plunged into darkness when Billy and Lily walked away.

"Lily? Are you okay?" Erik asked.

Lily's voice moved away from the teens, "Help me, Erik."

"Lily!"

Her voice rose in distress. "Help me!"

Sherry said, "Lily are you all right?"

No response.

"Lily."

Drip, drip, drip of water.

Erik said, "Should we go after her?"

"In the dark?" Sherry asked.

"What if we all end up in different tunnels? Or if we go into a tunnel and find a huge hole that plunges you one-hundred feet into a former coal mine?" Al asked.

"We have to wait here the ten minutes." Erik said. "Is he kidnapping her?"

"I bet they're in some nook of the cavern making out."

"That's even worse." Erik wanted to activate his light and find Lily, but knew this was a game with no actual danger to Lily. He put the phone in his jeans' back pocket.

"How will we know when ten minutes have elapsed?"

"Billy will tell us the CME has passed and to turn on our lights at the appropriate time."

They waited in the darkness planning strategies to create a torch if they really did lose their phones.

CHAPTER 4

The three stood in the darkness for what seemed an eternity to Erik. The dripping of water and Al's shallow breathing grew louder in the claustrophobic darkness. Even in his house at night there were lights from electric devices like clocks, the stove and the porch light shining through the window. There was never total, oppressive darkness.

Sherry spoke, "Ten minutes is up. What do you say we find Billy and Lily?"

"Let's do it." Erik said.

"Lily and Billy didn't come by us in this tunnel, so let's check out the next tunnel." Al shone his flashlight toward the entrance.

They traveled down the second cavern tunnel which became smaller as the ceiling dropped lower until the cave ended with water gurgling through a small hole in the rock.

"Guess they didn't come this way." Sherry turned back to the tunnel entrance.

Erik stomped after her. "If that jerk is hurting Lily he's going to be in big trouble."

"Relax, this is a game, I'm sure Lily is fine. Keep your anger under control." Sherry said.

They backtracked to the cavern and walked to the third offshoot tunnel where a blue light emanated.

Al said, "They must have gone this way, light is coming from this cave."

"This looks carved with human machinery instead of a natural cave formation." Erik rubbed his hand on the smooth surface of the tunnel.

Erik proceeded into the man-made tunnel. Why had someone hollowed this path and not the rest of the cave?

He approached the glowing rock. The blue light came from the ceiling and had a strange movement like water cascading over falls. The phone's flashlight wasn't needed here. Putting the phone in his pocket, he watched for Billy and Lily hiding in holes carved into the tunnel walls, but found no one. The blue light flowed from the ceiling. Erik had no description for the phenomenon. The light extended the width of the tunnel and forty feet ahead. He could discern no natural or man-made sources of light.

The teens stood side by side in the tunnel viewing the phenomenon. "You guys are smarter than me," said Erik. "What is it?"

Al said, "A portal where you're transported to another dimension or another world."

"Come on Brainiac, not a portal but a light source causing the effect. Sun is shining through a crack in the rocks and bouncing off a blue bottle that someone discarded. Tree branches blowing above the bottle is causing the rippling effect."

"I'm not walking through to have my skin burned off and disfigured for life. Send Sherry first, she's already disfigured."

Sherry whacked Al. "I'll disfigure you right now." She pounded his arm with her fist. "I'm not going to homecoming with you anymore after that comment."

"Stop. That hurts," said Al.

"Stop it, both of you, we aren't sending anybody through until we comprehend what's happening. Let's experiment." Erik thrust a stick through the blue beam. He watched the cascading light flow around the stick then drew the stick from the light and examined it. "No damage."

"Last time I checked a stick doesn't have flesh." Al rubbed his arm. "Did the stick pull toward an abnormal other world?"

"Nope."

Sherry handed Erik a rock. "Throw this through the light."

He heaved the rock and observed it slow, but not lose momentum. It continued in a straight trajectory and then dropped to the cavern floor on the opposite side of the illuminated space.

Al said, "I've never seen a rock act that way. Did it slow near the middle? I expected it would fall to the floor, but instead it sped up. Like gravity stopped working."

Erik said, "If gravity disappeared, wouldn't the object have floated upwards?"

"No, the rock continued at the same velocity and trajectory with no resisting force." Sherry said. "But why slow and then accelerate?"

Al said, "Are forces acting in the middle like solar wind preventing forward momentum?"

Sherry said, "Yeah, but the speed increased after passing the middle section. What caused that?"

"Passing the mid-point, the wind applies the force behind the object."

"Okay, we need to decide as a group," said Erik. "Go through the light or turn back? I wished we had a sign Lily headed this direction; I'm not comfortable."

Al said, "Let's return to the cave entrance. I bet Billy and Lily are making out and laughing at us. I bet this is booby trapped like in the Indiana Jones movie. Poison arrows will come out of the stone wall, or the tunnel ceiling collapses."

"Those are possibilities," said Erik. "Sherry? Did Billy take Lily through here?"

"I agree with Al."

"That's a miracle!" said Al.

Sherry high-fived Al. "Yeah that never happens."

Erik persisted. "I'm going through the light."

"Are you crazy? That light will kill you, or make you sterile or who knows what?" Al waved his hand at the light,

"I will stay here and wait for you to come back. Do we want to subject ourselves to this?"

"Where's your scientific curiosity," asked Erik? "Don't you crave to learn more? We might make a groundbreaking discovery."

"I'll study it on the web. What's producing this light? Can you see the other side? Will our faces melt or our skin age?"

Erik stared at his running shoes and massaged the back of his neck. It would be wrong to force his friends to continue this journey. "You two should go home."

"I'm not traveling over that bridge by myself," said Al.

Sherry grabbed Al's arm. "Then come with us, Brainiac, because I'm examining this phenomenon and you will starve and get attacked by bats while waiting here."

"Quit talking about bats."

"Let's go through one at a time," said Erik. "I'll lead."

He stepped into the glow and felt an intense winter wind. The light changed colors as he advanced. Forward, the light appeared blue, but looking toward his friends, the hue shifted to yellow. A prism of colors surrounded him. Sometimes the wind came from behind and other times from above, below or in front. Little dots of light cascading from the ceiling bounced off his clothing and exploded into colors like fireworks on the fourth of July.

Reaching the mid-section felt like he had plunged into a cold lake in late August. The winds stopped and Erik experienced an eerie silence. He walked, afraid to peer at his hands or arms for fear they were being destroyed in some fashion. The winds, colors and rainbows resumed as he walked. Upon reaching the other side, out of the light, a heavy weight pressed upon his body.

Erik watched Al and Sherry step into the illuminated section together. When they reached the middle Al glanced at the ceiling and pointed. His feet lifted off the floor. Sherry grabbed his right leg as he floated toward the ceiling in slow motion. Sherry's movement caused her to fall to the ground and Al fell on top of her with the fulcrum where Sherry held his leg. They tumbled to the floor laughing and pointing at the ceiling. Five minutes later they reached Erik.

Erik asked, "What happened?"

Al grabbed Erik's forearm and in one breath said, "The center of light is like gazing at a thousand stars in the Milky Way on a cloudless winter's night. I didn't recognize the constellations. When I pointed up to show Sherry Berry, I became weightless. Sherry tripped and reversed my direction. Let's go back, it's awesome."

Sherry stared wide-eyed, "Ten thousand stars and a spiral galaxy. It felt like drifting in a spacecraft with a porthole to the universe."

Al took a handful of Sherry's sleeve. "And the light bubbles exploding on your clothing? What is this phenomenon? Examining them from this angle, they glow yellow and the bubbles rise."

Erik stared at the yellow bubbles breaking the force of gravity flowing to the ceiling. *Where were they?*

CHAPTER 5

After they passed the strange light, the path ascended and Erik said, "It's getting steeper, where does this tunnel go?"

"And colder," Sherry said. "If we were still playing D&D Billy should have found us by now. This isn't right."

Al pointed to unlit torches hung on the walls, "Do these torches mean we're getting out of this cave or does the tunnel lead into a castle dungeon?"

"Signs of civilization." Sherry grabbed a torch. "I can get this torch lighted, because we trained in Girl Scouts rubbing two twigs together to produce fire." Sherry seized the stick from Erik and rolled the stick between her palms as it rubbed against the torch.

Erik watched Sherry work the stick and torch for five minutes producing no smoke.

Al said, "Come on Sherry Berry, you camped with your mom, show your great fire making skills."

"This takes time. If you don't want to wait, then you make fire." She heaved the torch at Al.

"Ha, with magical abilities, I will cast a spell and produce fire." Al caught the torch.

"Earth to Al, real life is not a fantasy game. Show us Alpherge the Mighty Wizard, how to make fire." Sherry laughed.

Erik watched his two friends with amusement. They fought over silly semantics and word play every day, but their current situation was beginning to feel dangerously unlike a game.

"You want magic and fire, prepare to be spellbound with magic and fire," Al waved his hands over the torch.

"Quiet everybody. I have to free my brain of distractions, and I demand absolute quiet."

"Come on you two, stop horsing around, we're going." Erik walked up the ascending cave floor.

Al chanted behind him, "We need warmth, we require light, we want heat our desire is dire, where I point place this fire."

"Where's the fire, Wizard Boy?"

"I sensed something. I'm trying again. Sherry hold the torch."

Erik spurred them forward. "Come on."

Al pointed to the torch with both hands raised. "We need warmth, we require light, we want heat our desire is dire, where I point place this fire."

Smoke shimmered off the top of the torch.

"Woo-hoo, a hint of magic, it surged through my fingers. Watch."

He said with confidence. "We need warmth, we require light, we want heat our desire is dire, where I point place this fire." The torch burst into flame. "Woohoo, I did it. I'm a first level magician. No, change that. I'm a spellcaster and someday I'll be a—"

"You did nothing," Sherry interrupted. "When you were speaking to the torch, you added oxygen to a spark I gave birth to, and that caused the torch to flame."

"Wait, I'll do it again. There's another torch on the wall." Al pointed fingers at the torch on the wall and said the same phrase. After repeated attempts, no fire materialized and Al gave up, his shoulders slumping.

"Told you." Sherry held her torch to a second torch on the wall, and fire lighted more of the cavern.

"How far have we traveled through this mountain?"

"We've been going through this cave for an hour," Al said. "That's at least two miles. What are we doing? This is crazy, even if we find Lily what're we gonna do?"

"I'm beginning to—Look, a light," Erik pointed to light coming from a cave entrance in the distance.

"Is this another one of those portals?" Al said. "Will we go from universe to universe until we die of starvation?"

"Stop the histrionics, Brainiac."

The others moved closer, and as Erik walked, the cavern became larger. "Look snow, we reached the end of the cave." Large icicles hung from the ceiling and a rush of winter air blew through his jacket.

Sherry said, "We've climbed above the snow line."

At the cave entrance, Al broke off an icicle and licked it. "No way we traveled four-thousand vertical feet to the snow line. The cave path inclined, but it doesn't account for this large change in altitude. The temperature dropped when we left the house. A storm has come in bringing snow."

Sharp icicles dangled from the ceiling, Erik pointed to the snow on the ground, "Footprints in the snow, we're on the right path, see Billy's large footprints and the smaller ones must be Lily's."

Erik headed off following the footprints. "Yeah, we're near, I'm sure of it. We'll follow the footprints and find Lily before sunset." Erik knew they were still in the Bitterroot mountains. Outside the cave, huge rocks rose one hundred feet on the right side with a steep drop-off on the left. Erik's sneakers were not the best footwear to be plowing through snow. "Stay together and move fast. There must be a cabin somewhere close where Billy and Lily are keeping warm and laughing at us."

They trudged upward beside the granite wall which seemed to shrink until the land plateaued.

Al was leading, and said, "Wow."

"What is it?" Sherry crested the top and stopped.

Erik stepped beside his friends. A thousand soldiers stood in formation in a clearing one hundred yards away. The soldiers were in attack mode with bows and arrows nocked ready for flight. Spears were held ready to thrust toward the enemy.

Al said, "They haven't moved since I got here. Are they dangerous?" The footprints led straight to the soldiers. "This must be where Billy took Lily. But check out the clothing."

"It's not right," Erik said, "snow is piled on their shoulders, what soldier allows that? They're not alive."

"You're right, but why put statues of soldiers in the mountains?" Al brushed snow off his jacket as if to prove Erik's point. "Who are these guys, and who do they represent?"

The three moved toward the soldiers and Sherry said, "Each statue is different like pictures on the web of the terracotta warriors in China. This reminds me of that."

Erik examined a soldier. "The clothing is old-fashioned not modern. The weapons are swords and spears with nothing modern. There are no guns. Is this a monument to a battle?"

Erik thought the uniforms resembled pictures of the American Revolutionary war. They wore tri-cornered hats, breeches that buckled just below their knees, jackets with rows of buttons on both sides of the chest, and a vest. The soldiers wore small backpacks, and canteens and a foodstuff bag dangled from striped material running across their fronts.

"I know," said Al. "These guys fought the native Americans two hundred years ago. They aren't stone. They froze to death in a flash freeze or an avalanche from those mountain peaks over there. The earth has warmed up since the Little Ice Age, and they are becoming un-frozen."

Sherry responded, "They aren't frozen, they're stone. Their expressions show that whatever happened they weren't expecting to be changed to stone. The detail in their faces is amazing." She tapped the figure with her fingernail. "Definitely not plastic, they're stone."

Erik followed the footprints while examining the soldiers he passed. "This guy's important based on his uniform. Is he a sergeant, commander or general?"

"This soldier with the big, bulbous nose has his eyes shut." Al rubbed the statue's nose.

The statue spoke in a nasal voice, "Hey don't touch me."

The teens stopped and Al asked. "Who said that?"

"I did." said the soldier.

"You guys talk? This is awesome. They must put electronics into the statues. Hey buddy, can you tell us what you're doing here?" Al stepped back from the statue.

The soldier replied,

"Six thousand strong marched to stop the suffering
The people screamed, souls died, the slaves shackled,
the wizard, angered, created chaos in his path.
Six thousand strong marched day and night
the Kalluri people cried out in pain.
The wizard made the people wish to die
Six thousand strong climbed the mountain
the battle plan hatched.
Pin the wizard against the gate to cavern evil.
Six thousand strong met at the gate;
their spears and arrows launched straight and true.
Six thousand strong turned to stone
to live eternity as statues.
The wizard laughed; the plan failed."

The soldier standing next to the one that recited the poem said, "Worst poem ever."

Other soldiers spoke, "Gentry, take up another hobby, poetry isn't your forte."

"Gentry, you have the education of an eight-year-old; why are you making poetry?"

"Go back and sharpen the swords."

"Somebody put a spear in that guy. That's horrible."

Gentry said, "You try to tell our story in a poem. I've been working on that for eight years."

The commander figure said, "Quiet! Thank you, Gentry, that will do. We came to this place to fight the wizard, the mountain king. He defeated us with great magic by hiding magical objects in the mountains. We weren't trapping him, he lured us to a lifetime of being living statues. Our army tried hitting him with spears and arrows. Then we felt a huge explosion with wave after wave of aftershocks. We were knocked out and woke as statues. According to the soothsayer we will be here, forever."

"What nation's army do you represent?" Erik asked.

"We are the proud nation of Kalluri." said the commander. "Why are you here?"

Erik said, "We're searching for our friend Lily. Have two teenagers passed this way? A long black-haired boy and a girl with blonde hair?"

The commander said, "This land is dangerous for you. Go home and never come back."

Al spoke, "If magic changed you into stone, then magic can change you back."

Gentry said, "The soothsayer said the Crystal—"

"Quiet Gentry." The commander spoke.

"We're trying to find our friends."

"Yes, they passed us, but go home," responded the commander. "You aren't safe in this land."

"We appreciate your concern, but we need to keep going. Our friend is in danger and we're here to rescue her—" Erik pushed Al on the back, "Come on guys, we need to find them, they must have an hour's lead or more by now."

"This is an amazing, realistic D&D game." Al said. "Bet you didn't expect these guys when you left the house."

"This is crazy cool, but we gotta find Lily and get back before dark."

The commander said, "The path you choose is dangerous. I command you, go home. People in this land fear you and will kill you. Go Home!"

The teens followed Erik through the snow as he plodded forward tracking Lily's footprints.

CHAPTER 6

A few minutes later they found a small farming village of four stone buildings with steep roofs. One of the buildings had a hanging sign with an image of a man holding a large chicken leg to his mouth.

Al said, "All right a restaurant, someplace to get something to eat."

"We don't have time to eat; we gotta find Lily and go home." Erik said.

A woman about their age exited the building her head facing the ground.

"Hi," Erik raised his hand, "can you help us?"

The woman appraised Erik and his friends, and her posture perked up as if surprised.

She walked around the teens in slow cautious steps looking at them with narrowed eyes and her head cocked to one side.

"Is something wrong?" Erik asked.

She stopped walking, pressed her lips together and bit her lower lip.

"Can you help us?" Erik wondered if the woman couldn't hear.

The woman, her black hair flowing from the cowl of the green scarf wrapped over her head, stared back at Erik, her emerald eyes sparkling in the mid-day sun.

Sherry said, "Let's go inside, someone can help us in there."

"No." The woman raised her hand to stop Sherry's movements. "I can help you."

"Have you seen my friends, Billy and Lily? We lost them in the mountains. She has blonde hair, she's about your size, and Billy is maybe six feet with long black hair."

"I saw a strange blonde woman, but she wasn't with anyone named Billy. She was with a man known around here as Kestrel the Falcon Prince."

"Yeah, that's him," Al chimed in. "We're playing a game and Billy is going by the Falcon Prince. This is an awesome game it's like we have stumbled upon a real-life D&D adventure."

"Do you know where we can find them?" Erik asked, his mind racing to make sense of it all. Did Billy set up this huge D&D adventure all in a couple of days? Was he dreaming all this?

"The couple is on their way to the Velidred Castle."

"Are we far behind? Can we catch up if we hurry? How far is it to the castle?"

"You're at least an hour behind, I'm Zita." She smiled at Erik.

He returned the smile as a light hearted palpation filled him, "I'm Erik and these are my friends, Sherry and Al."

"Can you give us directions to the castle?"

"Hmmm, it's pretty far away and I can't tell you how to get there. But, I'm willing to take you if you don't mind company."

Erik glanced at his friends who all bobbed their heads in agreement, "Okay show us the way."

"Wait," Al said, "I'm not going another step until I get something to eat."

"We don't have time to eat." Erik said.

"Yeah, we do, because I need to eat."

"It's getting late," Sherry said, "let's eat now and then we'll catch up later."

"The time is like six thirty and the sun is high in the sky like noon. Strange." Al opened the building door.

Zita led the way into the tavern.

Erik stepped through the doorway of the little village tavern, a dilapidated building with stones missing from the walls of the fireplace.

They sat at a table, and the chair Erik sat in wobbled on uneven legs. A man with long hair and a long black beard wiped the table. "I'm Carl, what can I get you?"

Sherry said, "Two hamburgers and a Pepsi."

"Two hamburgers, fries and a Mountain Dew." Al said.

The man taking the order, dressed in a white tunic and a green apron, appeared confused. "Where you from?"

Erik said, "Cullerton, Montana."

"Montana," the waiter said and drawled the word like chewing a piece of fat. "Never heard of it."

"What village is this?" Al said.

"The Village of the Stone Warriors."

"Yeah, the stone warriors, they're cool. Can we get a brochure on the statues and how they operate? And the commander said, 'you shouldn't be here, go home;' it was awesome. How are the electronics wired? Is there an optical lens on the statues? Are they controlled from this village?"

Carl walked to the kitchen where the cook stood preparing food. Carl whispered to the overweight cook, and she threw on a coat and left the building.

Zita said, "Carl might be out of 'hamburgers' try the Pink Anouora instead. Carl doesn't use enough spices, and it's early in the season, but they're okay."

Carl returned to the table and Zita said, "Bring a plateful of Pink Anouora and try adding spices this time and hot tea, my friends are frozen."

"Yes ma'am."

A large man stood, wobbled a moment, then approached the teens' table, got in Zita's face and said, "Listen lady. I don't like you. Carl and I plan to ride you out of town tonight. What will the great mountain king do then?" He spit on the floor next to Zita.

Zita pushed her chair back, stood before the larger man and poked her finger at his chest. "Think the stone warriors have problems. Touch me and you'll wish you were a stone warrior."

Carl stepped in between the two and pushed on the large guy, "Arthur, go home, don't cause problems." Then Carl whispered something to the man.

Erik watched until the man sat, and Carl headed to the kitchen. "Why don't these people like you Zita?"

Zita smirked at Erik. "The locals don't like the mountain king. He's trying to bring peace to this land, but the Kalluri people refuse peace." She put her hand on Erik's arm and yelled toward the kitchen, "These kids are freezing, Carl, stoke the fire."

Carl served four large legs of an animal to the teens and a basket of bread. Walking back from the stove, he returned with a hot pot and poured tea into wooden cups on the table.

"This smells delicious." Al took a huge bite and mumbled. "Tastes like barbecued chicken wings."

"Large birds," Sherry wiped her mouth.

"These aren't birds." Zita said. "They're frog legs."

Erik said, "Frog legs? They're the size of my thigh."

Zita laughed. "Never eaten Anouora? It's a great delicacy in the Velidred Kingdom. The frogs populate the swampy areas near the valleys."

The front door burst open and the cook came in breathing hard, and two men entered the tavern. "There," the cook pointed to the table where the teens sat.

The small guy had a goatee and a pointed nose. The other, a swarthy larger man, wore a tattoo of color dots across his nose.

Goatee man came to the table, "It can't be these kids, because they're nothing more than teenagers."

The large guy at the next table wobbled over. "You're wrong Marvin. They aren't from here, check their clothing. They're the ones."

Erik spoke, "What?"

"The prophecy. Tell him Marvin. How they'll save us from the mountain king."

Al stood, "Erik, they're brilliant. Our high school plays could learn from this village."

Marvin said, "The prophecy might not come true."

"They're kids," said Carl. "They're supposed to be princesses, warriors, and wizards. Not kids. This can't be right."

The big man grabbed the collar of the smaller Marvin, "Tell the prophecy."

Marvin began in a hushed voice and got louder as he spoke,

> *"By night they reach our land*
> *four friends fast a helping hand.*
> *From three kings they are born*
> *To raise the flags of kingdom's home.*
> *The wizard fears them and will use*
> *Golden-hair's life to defuse*
> *a time of fear from land to land.*
> *The warrior's son will lead them brave*
> *king's daughter will help them save,*
> *young wizard with fear will tremble*
> *as the volcano shakes and rumbles.*
> *The virgin princess beats the fire*
> *of volcano's eternal funeral pyre.*
> *To save us all as we embrace*
> *lands of glory and homeland grace"*

Al clapped, "Brilliant!"

"You have the wrong people." Erik said. "We aren't wizards, warriors or princesses. High school kids from

Montana trying to find our friend, Lily. There's no royalty in Montana nor in the USA except for Michael Jackson and Elvis Presley."

Marvin shook his head. "The kid's right, they aren't the ones. Eight years been drinking in this tavern to see the ones. Not supposed to be teens."

"Erik, why so serious? This is play acting, D&D; it's still the game; get into the role." Al stood to his full size, "I'm a great wizard, Alpherge the Mighty, and I will slay the mountain king and bring peace to the kingdom."

Sherry jumped on Al and spoke through clinched teeth. "Sit down and stop talking. These people are serious. They aren't acting a part. They believe what they're saying. We traveled too long without water and we're confused and disoriented. Shut-up."

Zita said, "Who taught you magic? You're young to be a great wizard."

Al said, "I've been studying magic since I was twelve-years-old. I study magic books from the master wizards of D&D in Wisconsin. I have mastered hundreds of spells."

Sherry bopped him on the arm. "Stop."

"Go with the flow, Sherry Berry."

"It's not a skit, play acting or a tourist event. I don't know where we are, Brainiac, but keep talking and we'll be in trouble."

Marvin said to Al, "Who's your Papa?"

"I'm Al, from the family of Greystone, grandson of Alpherge."

The men stepped back, and the cook ran out of the building yelling, "They're here."

Zita stumbled back from the table.

Marvin said, "Carl, let me pay for these children's meal."

Zita spoke, "Al, grandson of Alpherge the Great, use magic to warm the fire for us."

"No, I'm tired and have traveled a great distance to defeat the mountain king. I must rest and conserve my magic—"

"Oh, please, great one, warming a fire shouldn't take much magic."

Al whispered to Sherry, "Watch this, all part of the skit. The fire will go poof and appear to grow stronger."

Al raised his voice to fill the entire room, "Watch my great magic." Pointing at the fire with both hands he proclaimed, "We need warmth, we need light, we want heat our need is dire, where I point place this fire."

Nothing happened.

Al changed his stance, rubbed his brow and tried again. "We need warmth, we need light, we want heat our need is dire, where I point place this fire." Nothing happened.

Zita said, "You're tired, sit, eat and rest."

Al rubbed the back of his neck and fell into the chair, "I felt the magic but it didn't work, like something blocked the magic."

Sherry rubbed his back. "Sit down, Brainiac."

Marvin walked toward the bar shaking his head, "Get me an ale, too good to be true. These aren't the ones."

The large man said, "Fifteen years of oppression and I thought here is our salvation." He walked back to the table, "Bring another ale."

Carl placed a mug of ale in front of the large man who chugged the drink and pounded the empty pewter mug on the table. Then the large man shuffled to the kids' table. He grabbed Al by the collar and brought the teenager within inches of his face. "Buddy, if I ever catch you in this village again, you better run, because I don't like being made a fool. Go home. Wherever Montana is, go back, and never darken this tavern with your lies and pranks." He pushed Al into the chair and walked out the door.

CHAPTER 7

An hour later, Erik walked with Al, listening to him babble about magic. He rubbed his hands together in the cold mountain air.

"I'm telling you; I felt the force." Al said. "I have magical energies."

"The force like Star Wars?" Erik smiled at his friend.

"Tingling in my hands and energy flowed from my fingers."

Erik had a strange foreboding about this place. "If you felt the force then why weren't you able to light the torch or the fire?"

"My powers need training. I'm gonna find a wizard school and learn magic."

"Give it up, you don't have magical powers." Erik headed down the snow-covered mountain. "Where are we?"

"I'm not sure, see the volcano in the northeast? Sometimes a wisp of smoke and ash shoot out. There aren't any active volcanoes in the States."

Erik stopped walking for a moment and stared at the volcano. Mountains surrounded them with glaciers and snow blanketing the peaks. "I don't recognize these mountain ranges."

"That girl, Zita, say's we're in the Velidred Province. I don't trust her." Al said.

Erik glanced down the trail where Sherry and Zita walked together. "Zita is pretty. Have you noticed her eyes and the way she walks? Familiar."

"Familiar? Are you serious?"

"What?"

"Except for the black hair, Zita resembles Lily. Remember Lily, the girl we're attempting to rescue."

"No way. Zita has black hair; Lily has blonde hair. Lily has that small birth mark an inch from her nose and is taller. These girls are different," Erik said.

Al pointed to the mountains, "There, see the puff of smoke from the volcano?"

Erik glanced over his right shoulder, and far in the distance, the volcano puffed ash. The snow below the peak was a dirty gray from the fallen ash. "The Velidred Province, does that sound Russian to you?"

"We're in Russia? How did we reach Russia? How would we travel under the ocean and walk hundreds of miles to Russia? And have you noticed it's still light out? My phone says it's eight at night, but the sun is high. It appears to be around noon."

Erik said, "No cars. My cell phone can't pick up a signal anywhere. No Wi-Fi in the village."

"Were we transported to the sixteen-hundreds in Europe?" Al asked.

"You laugh at me because I say we're in Russia and now we're in seventeenth century Europe? Are we time travelers? Next, we'll be running from the Eloi."

Erik kicked a clump of snow and watched it explode into a million tiny snowballs. "There should be roads near a tourist attraction, so why is Zita taking us on this mountain cow path?"

"Stop walking like two old ladies." Sherry stopped to wait for Erik and Al to reach her. "We need to catch up with Billy and Lily.

"How far to the castle?" Erik walked faster.

"Seven days walk or more," Zita said.

"Seven days?" Al's eyebrows lifted in disbelief. "Where are the cars, buses, horses, cows or something we can ride? We don't have seven days."

"Maybe a cart to ride, but most people walk faster than a donkey and cart." Zita said.

Sherry said, "We can't be out here for seven days. Our parents will kill us. My mom is probably wondering where I am right now. I just told her we were playing D&D, but I didn't tell her where."

"If Mom knew I was anywhere near the mountains her head would explode. Mom believes it's dangerous in the mountains." Al said.

"Are we getting close to a larger village where our phones might have cell coverage so we can call our parents?" Sherry asked.

"We are coming close to a village." Zita said.

A few minutes later, they came upon a group of women dressed in thin white dresses dancing around an enormous tree.

"Are these women crazy?" Erik asked. "It's freezing out here and they'll freeze with what they're wearing."

Zita's lip curled. "These women are members of the Order of Nature's Love, a religion run by the priestess, Forest River Blossom. They believe nature has religious significance and are dancing around a stupid tree. For them spring arrives earlier in the mountains because of their dancing. When we get a warm day on the same day they dance, they take credit for the warm day."

Erik watched the women weaving and flowing around the tree. They ranged in ages from girls his age to older women his mother's age. Watching the dancing reminded him of Lily. "It isn't even winter yet, and they are already working on spring?"

"What do you mean, we are just getting out of a brutal winter." Zita said.

"Winter isn't here, yet," Erik muttered, "I raked leaves last weekend."

"Does the religion have a chapel?" Sherry asked.

"No, just the stupid tree."

Three men banged out a rhythm on drums.

"No building, they dance around trees and set up boulders in a ring. That's their religion."

"Like Stonehenge in England?"

"Stonehenge? England?" Zita asked.

"Okay that's it," Erik said. "Enough of this rubbish, where are we? What state, what country, what year? Tell me now. I'm tired and want to find Lily and go home."

"Come on you guys are smart, we're on the outskirts of Tanuku in the province of Velidred."

Al said, "What planet?"

"These are subjects we teach eight-year-olds. The next question you'll ask is how many moons we have."

"What planet?" Sherry stopped walking and stared at Zita.

"How many moons?" Al asked.

"I should leave you in the mountains and let the animals eat you."

"Is this planet Earth?"

"No, it's not planet Earth. At least try one of the six planets that circle the sun." Zita said.

Erik seized Zita's shoulder and spun her around. "What planet?"

She slapped Erik across the face, her nails drawing blood. "The name of the planet is Aloheno with three moons and if you touch me once more, you'll lose the hand. No one touches me."

"I'm sorry." Erik said rubbing his face. "This morning we were on Earth, walked through a cave and now … bizarre."

"She's lying," Al said.

"It isn't possible for us to be on another planet," Sherry said. "We should go home; our parents have to be worried."

"I'm not lying," Zita said, "and yes you should go home. Now."

"Why are you telling us this bizarre tale of being on a different planet, what's in it for you? Did Billy put you up to this?" Sherry stood in front of Zita.

"Go home, I don't want to be here with you. I have somewhere else I would rather be, just leave."

The women stopped dancing around the tree and raced barefoot in the melting snow toward the village. They shouted to the teens, "Peace and Love. Be kind to nature and nature will be nice to you."

"Get away," Zita yelled at the women.

Al rubbed his hands, "Three moons? That means the cave is an interplanetary portal."

"No, it isn't a portal, something else is going on here." Sherry said. "We gotta go back through the cave. Let's go home. Our parents must be worried, and we didn't call them to tell them where we are."

"Something strange is happening no doubt about it," Erik said. He tried to find a logical reason for it all. These bizarre occurrences, the strange light in the cave, the fact the cave wasn't just a small hole in the rock, it's all wrong. "I know something isn't right, but let's go on another hour."

They kept walking and entered the village of Tanuku. The people there, dressed in bright tunics of blues, yellows and red. Most had red or green tattoo patterns, composed of hundreds of dots, on their noses.

A group of giggling children ran past and Sherry said, "This is a happy village."

Zita said, "The king uses the priestess, Forest River Blossom, as a seer or prophetess and leaves the village alone. These houses are garish colors." She waved toward the lime green house across the street.

"A fortune teller?" Al asked.

Drumming sounded in the distance, "This village is noisy compared to the mountains."

"Week-long festivals every month celebrate the sun, stars and the moons," Zita said. "A new tree sprouts in the dirt, they celebrate. They're happy and don't trouble the king, so he lets them do whatever they choose."

"How do you know so much about the king?" Erik asked.

Zita stumbled and paused. "I used to work as a handmaid for the princess."

The drums grew louder as a large crowd of people marched up the street following a woman in green robes. "Who's that?"

Zita shook her head. "Forest River Blossom, self-proclaimed priestess of the Order of Nature's Love. Quick, in here to get warm." She grabbed Erik by the sleeve and tugged him into a gloomy tavern.

Sherry said, "Erik where are you going? I want to meet this woman."

Erik shook his arm from Zita's grasp and hurried back into the sunshine. He glowered at Zita who stayed in the tavern.

Erik felt genuine excitement as the group approached. Drums followed the procession and flutes played a cheerful melody. Forty men and women trailed a small woman. She appeared young from a distance, but coming closer, Erik thought her older than his mom. Reaching the teens, Forest River Blossom raised her hands silencing the drums, flutes and the entourage.

The priestess said to Erik and his friends. "Why are you here?"

"I'm Erik —"

"I know who you are. Why are you here?"

"We're searching for our friend, Lily."

The priestess stepped closer to Erik, assessing him with her brown eyes, "Show me your hands."

Erik jabbed his hands into his pockets. "No."

She stood with out-stretched hands. Bells dangled from her ear lobes and a diadem of silver bells flashed in the sunlight. Her hair cascaded to the middle of her back.

Sherry said, "Go ahead, Erik. It'll be okay."

Forest River Blossom moved closer.

Erik pulled his hands from his pockets and pressed them in her palms. Her hands felt warm despite the cold. She turned his hands palms up and bent to study them. She mumbled something unintelligible to Erik, and he inhaled an aroma of lilacs. The priestess squeezed his hands and shook her head.

She said, "The others." One by one, she examined his friend's hands while mumbling words and shaking her head. She cupped Sherry's face and announced, "You're not prepared, go home. Staying here means certain death."

Erik murmured, "We're searching for Lily."

"No, go home. She doesn't need you, and you don't need her. The runes have cried to me all week, and if you stay on this planet Al will die."

Erik's knees felt weak, and he almost collapsed to the street. Would Al truly die if they stayed on this planet?

Sherry put her hand in Al's hand. "You better not die on me, Brainiac."

Erik reeled from the news. He had known Al his entire life; would this foolish D&D quest put his close friend in peril?

"You've ruined everything that was setup fifteen years ago." Forest River Blossom held Erik's arm. "You aren't due for four years and your presence is fatal to plans made to safeguard our people. Go, the cave closes before the sun sets." She pointed back toward the mountain, turned and strode away, her long flowing gown dragging in the snow. The drums began a somber beat and her entourage followed.

CHAPTER 8

l said, "You heard the woman, we must go home. We can't stay on this planet. Don't you agree with me, Sherry?"

Sherry said, "Al's right, it sounds dangerous to us and the people of this planet."

Erik said, "I agree. Sherry, take Al back to Earth while I travel to the castle with Zita. Maybe if we aren't all here, we'll be okay."

"No," Sherry said. "I'm sure we all need to leave. That lady sounded serious."

Erik struggled between the desire to find his friend and not wanting his friends killed. "The priestess read our palms. You're the smartest woman I know. Do you believe that mumble jumble?"

Sherry said, "The whole situation weirds me out. If we're on another planet, is this our only chance to escape and return to Earth? It's better to let adults solve this problem."

"No, I'm rescuing Lily."

Zita approached the group, "What did the priestess say?"

Erik remained quiet and stared into Zita's green eyes. Could he trust Zita? What was her role in this intrigue? *Her eyes are amazing.*

Zita said, "Are you leaving like Forest River Blossom told you?"

"How do you know what the priestess told us?" Sherry asked. "You stayed in the tavern."

"I needed warming but stood by the door listening."

"Why are you hiding from Forest River Blossom?"

"She's been at festivals, and her fortune telling scares me. Her fortunes seem to announce bad things. Three years ago, she read my future with tea leaves and told me I would fall through ice and drown."

Sherry said, "Yeah, that sounds scary, and yet, here you are. What aren't you telling us, Zita? You've wanted us to go home this whole time. Why?"

"You don't belong here. You aren't dressed right, and ten-year-olds know more. It's a dangerous world."

"Would you take me to the castle if I send the rest home?" Erik asked.

Sherry said, "No, you can't stay. Erik, you have to come home with us."

"I don't care what you do. I'm going with Zita to the castle to find Lily."

Sherry said, "I beg you, don't do this. Zita is right, we're ignorant of the dangers of this planet. If we say something wrong or commit a social blunder, we could get into serious trouble. Remember what happened to the indigenous people in Central and South America when the Spanish conquered them? Many died of illnesses brought from Spain. What if we're bringing a disease that these people can't resist, or we catch a bug our bodies can't fight? The food is different and is the water safe? No hospitals in the villages. No cars. Will you let a witch doctor handle your wounds if injured or sick? Blood-letting was standard practice two hundred years ago. Find the wrong doctor and you die."

Erik walked away from his friends. *Would it be the right thing to continue to chase after Lily, or should we go home and let professionals handle it? Is it possible Lily is safe with Billy— or Kestrel the Falcon Prince— or whatever stupid name he calls himself?*

"Come back Erik, we need to talk," Sherry said.

"I'm done talking, I'm rescuing Lily." Erik remained focused on the road that led to the castle.

Sherry said, "Al, stop him."

"What can I do?"

"You're his best friend. He's gonna get hurt if he does this."

"Erik, that lady said the cave closes soon," Al said. "We have to turn back, now. Stop being stupid."

Erik faced Sherry, Al and Zita. "I want to do the right thing. I want to go home, but I want to save Lily, too. What if we get back to the cave and it's closed? Then we'll lose all the time it takes to get back here."

"We need professionals to handle this situation." Sherry grabbed Erik's arm. "Please; what if the spiritualist, fortune-teller lady is right? Do you want to lose both Al and Lily?"

Erik ran his hands through his hair, blew his cheeks out and released the air through pursed lips. What should he do?

Zita said, "If you want to leave through the cave, it will be dark in an hour and Forest River Blossom said the cave closes at dusk. We'll have to hurry to get there in time."

Erik lowered his chin to his chest and shook his head. "Okay let's go back."

# # # #

Fifty-five minutes later they stood next to the stone warriors, a few hundred feet from the cave entrance. The setting sun shone red against strips of clouds in the distance.

"We better hurry to get to the cave in time." Sherry said.

"I can't breathe, let's take a second." Al grabbed his knees, and his whole rib cage heaved as he struggled to catch his breath.

"Come on, Sherry," Erik said, "let him rest, we traveled all uphill for the last thirty minutes."

"We can't let the cave close. We have to keep moving. Look the sun is setting." She pointed at the hazy red sun setting over the mountain peaks.

Al took an inhaler out of his jeans' pockets, put the tube in his mouth, pressed down and breathed in the medicine. His wheezing instantly became less distressed.

The cave entrance was hidden from this location, but Erik hoped it remained opened. Zita had stayed with the teens the whole way back to the portal. Would she come through the portal with them?

"Come on Al, we gotta keep moving." Sherry said.

"Okay," He gasped.

They followed their footprints through the snow back down the slope. How would the cave close? Would a big metal door plop over it? Maybe they were wooden doors? They could break wooden doors. This civilization appeared primitive to Erik.

"Who or what closes the cave, and how does Forest River Blossom know what time the cave is closing?"

"I didn't know about the cave before I met you." Zita said.

"How long have you lived in the village but not known about the cave?" Sherry asked.

Zita raised a single eyebrow, opened her mouth to say something but said nothing and stared at Sherry with a glassy gaze.

"Well?"

"I'm visiting a sick cousin in town and we haven't done any sightseeing."

Sherry pressed. "You've left your sick cousin to spend all this time with us? And you're planning on taking us to the castle which takes seven days. That doesn't sound right to me."

Zita let out a noisy sigh, "The reason I'm willing to show you to the castle is I live in Velidred, and I decided to go home today. You met me at an opportune time."

Erik listened to the conversation between Zita and Sherry while thinking about the footprints in the snow. Would they be able to find the footprints if they came back another day? If the cave closed, how would they get back to Earth?

Al said, "There's the cave, is it still open?"

"I can't tell in this dim light." The setting sun threw dark shadows on the cave entrance.

"What's that noise?" Sherry stopped.

"It must be the rocks moving. Hurry." Erik said.

They all ran down the incline toward the closing cave. Giant boulders hovered in air. Then with a smooth movement they fit together, closing up the space.

They had fifty yards to run, maybe ten seconds or so. A gap remained for the teens to squeeze through, but they had to hurry.

Al wheezed behind Erik. His friend had used his inhaler when they stopped last time. Could he make it to the cave?

"Faster," Erik yelled.

With twenty feet to go Al said, "I can't—," and collapsed in the snow.

Sherry stopped. "Al, no!"

Erik slid to a stop and hurried back to his friend.

"Al, are you okay?" Sherry lay in the snow next to Al's limp body patting his hand. "Talk to me."

Erik's breathing came in short gasps as he alternately looked at the cave and Al lying in the snow. *Was the spiritualist right? Would Al die on this planet?*

"Is he dead?"

"He's still breathing. He passed out. His big ole body can't draw enough oxygen to run that fast." Sherry patted Al's hand.

Erik sat down next to Al and watched the last two boulders fly into place blocking the cave entrance.

CHAPTER 9

The next day they walked for hours up and down the mountain. Erik felt happy getting through Tanuku without running into Forest River Blossom. He didn't know what to say to his friends about not making it to the cave in time.

"I'm tired of walking, where's a bus stop?" Al asked.

Erik lowered his gaze and grimaced. *Is Al in real peril? Will we get back to Earth or die on Aloheno?*

They walked up a mountain path toward flowering plants with large leaves. The field awash with large purple and pink flowers. They were five feet high like wild sunflowers waving in the wind, a beautiful view against a backdrop of snowy mountains in the distance.

Sherry ignored Al's question. "There are hundreds of animals in the flowers."

Erik asked, "What animals, where?"

"Keep watching the flowers, every once in a while, an animal jumps over the flowers" Sherry pointed.

"Are they dangerous?"

"They're eating flowers."

"Why did you stop?" asked Zita.

"Animals in the flowers." Erik gestured up the hill.

Zita said. "Those are anouora."

Erik responded with a blank expression.

"Frogs. Frog legs."

"Frogs?"

"Yeah, come on, anouora aren't dangerous."

The teens approached the flowers and Erik spied a bright, pink frog the size of a large pig. The animal bent the plant stem toward its mouth and chewed the pink blossom. "I've never seen a pink frog."

Zita said, "Their color comes from the flowers they eat. The pink frogs eat pink blooms and the purple frogs eat purple flowers. A mating technique, spring season." She winked at Erik.

A purple frog made a powerful jump over another frog among the flowers. "Did you see how high it jumped?"

Zita said, "Saw one in town that was captured to be eaten and it escaped by jumping a twelve-foot wall. The frogs prefer to stay near the flowers. I'm surprised the wildflowers are blooming so early with snow on the ground."

Suddenly a terrible noise emanated from the frogs like the thunder of a motorcycle, so loud Erik covered his ears. "Why are they making that racket?"

"What?" Sherry said holding her ears.

"There's danger nearby." Zita yelled.

The frogs leaped from the flowers into the clear field, each leap carrying them ten feet.

Zita shook her head and pointed west toward a mountain top in the distance.

A strange beast the size of a grizzly bear walked out of the forest brush. The animal's body was large and wide with a long narrow face. Two straight horns stuck out behind its ears. From the eyes to the end of its snout were two wide, white stripes on black fur. The beast roared.

"A stegox," Zita yelled, "run."

"Wait, I want to watch." Erik said.

"You mean you want to get eaten, because they eat humans."

The anouora came from the flowers and formed a circle in the open field. The stegox chased around the frogs.

Zita grabbed Erik's hand and pulled him toward high grasses away from the frogs.

"Where are you taking me?"

"Safe from the stegox."

"Sherry. Al. Follow us."

When they reached the tall grasses, Zita pulled him down and they watched the beast and frogs.

The stegox searched for a delicate spot in the frog's defense, skirting the frogs as the frogs voiced the deep croaking sound. Purple frogs in the inner circle while pink frogs were three ranks deep on the exterior edges.

The stegox snapped at the frogs, rushing in, opening its jaw wide and struggling to snag a frog. Frogs closest to danger spit a white substance at the attacking beast. It snarled, backed off, and with its long blue tongue wiped its eyes. The stegox re-attempted this strategy three or four times with no result other than leaving large scratches on the frogs.

The stegox backed up, cleared its eyes with its tongue, roared and charged. Frogs five ranks deep bunched closer at the point of impact. When the bear came within ten feet the frogs expectorated large amounts of the white substance. Spit irritated the bear, causing it to lose balance moments before reaching the frogs. The beast crashed to the earth. The frogs croaked louder.

Frogs jumped on the struggling beast. Then the stegox roared, struggled to its paws, shook off the frogs, howled and hobbled toward the forest.

When the beast disappeared between the trees, the frogs quieted and dispersed through the flowers.

Erik said, "It's incredible that frogs could win this battle."

Al said, "It reminded me of old westerns on television and the wagon train would circle the wagons when in danger. The anouora were circling the wagons."

Zita said, "I've witnessed anouora kill a person by pouncing on them multiple times. But we're even luckier the stegox didn't find us." She caressed Erik's shoulder with one hand and with the other hand brushed hair from her face.

Erik licked his lips as euphoria pulsed through his body.

"What is that substance they spit?" Sherry asked.

"A liquid which causes burning in your eyes. Too much will poison you."

"You told us they were harmless."

Zita shrugged.

They viewed the anouora several minutes then renewed their journey to the castle. They walked for six more hours until all complained of sore feet.

The trail led them up a steep path through a pine forest. Erik, in the lead, crested the hill and entered a meadow. He rested in the grass while waiting for the other three. In the distance, a crimson moon rose over the horizon.

When Zita came close, Erik said, "You told us three moons. What's the name of the red moon?"

"Velidred, the Red Devil," Zita said, "same as the province name, because of volcanoes that flare up in the kingdom."

Sherry approached panting, "Did she say we're walking toward active volcanoes?"

"Don't fret. They aren't harmful. They don't explode," Zita said. "Sometimes the sky flames up red when the volcano has flowing magma, but the lava never reaches the castle."

"The smallest moon, Pantaleon, is known as the lazy moon taking one hundred days to revolve around the planet. The third moon, Anticletus, not as big as Velidred, takes six days to orbit the planet. Anticletus has a blue glow because it has water."

"People believed the Earth's moon had water," Sherry said. "Then we sent a space craft to the moon and found it was nothing but rock."

"A space craft?" asked Zita.

"On our world we send rockets into space to explore other moons and planets," Sherry said.

They stopped for the night at a small country inn. The dining area contained six tables with benches around the tables, and a small stage was set in the corner.

The teens plopped down on benches and ordered dinner. Erik asked the serving woman, "Can I have an omelet?"

"What kind of egg?"

He raised his eyebrows toward Zita. "A chicken egg."

"We have three different birds we harvest eggs from, some people like the small variety, pink robin eggs, which get a little slimy. The ratchet bird lays a green egg that when you crack the egg the yolk comes out blue. I hate the color of those eggs, so I eat the larger teracop eggs. They tend to be sweeter and are a pretty peach color."

Erik said to the waitress, "I'll have the teracop egg."

They talked for an hour teaching Zita about spacecraft and the Earth's moon until a bard picked up a lute. He mounted the small stage and sang, playing music and telling stories.

An hour into the entertainment, Al whispered across the table to Erik, "Check out the two guys sitting by the door. I've seen them before."

Two men sat at a bench near the door. "These same guys were in the tavern last night at the Village of the Stone Warriors. They wore blue and yellow tunics.

"Are they following us?" Al asked.

"Maybe they're just going in the same direction. Might be coincidence."

After the show, they headed to their rooms. The teens from earth shared one room, and Zita had her own.

"Hey guys, watch." Al picked up a lighted candle and blew out the flame.

"Come on Al, that's our only candle, now what are we going to do?"

Al placed his hands over the candlestick, whispered some words, and then the wick sparked. A bright flame brought the candle to life, providing light in the room once more. "On this planet I have magic. I need to find someone to train me."

He blew out the flame, waited a second and re-kindled the candle.

"We aren't planning on being on this planet that long," Sherry said, "We'll find Lily and return to Earth."

"How? The cave is closed." Al extinguished the flame once again. "I have magic capabilities, and the first chance I get I'll find someone to teach me how to sharpen my magic skills."

Sherry shook her head. "Then what will you do? How do you know if the skills will work on Earth?"

"Doesn't matter, I plan to stay on Aloheno." The flame re-appeared on the candle.

"No, you're not, because you're taking me to homecoming, and that's on Earth. So, vanquish any dreams of staying on this planet."

CHAPTER 10

The long day of walking wore on Erik who hadn't slept well the previous nights. Sherry slept in a bed by herself and Al shared the other bed with Erik. Al wrestled with the blankets for an hour until Sherry convinced him to be quiet, but Erik gave up and bunked on a narrow wooden bench in the corner and woke sore and tired.

On the fourth day of being on Aloheno they woke early to a bright sun, but it provided little warmth. The inn had primitive facilities.

"This place is horrible, yucky and dirty." Sherry said after visiting the outhouse. We need to catch up with Billy and Lily today and then figure out how to get home. If I don't get a real shower in the next two days, I'm gonna scream."

They walked for two hours until reaching a village named Crossroads, the largest village they'd encountered yet on their journey. A ten-foot-high wooden fence surrounded the village. The path led to a gate flanked by guards.

Erik said, "Why is there a fence?"

Zita said, "To protect their village from dangerous wild animals."

"Dangerous? Birds, deer and squirrels?" Al asked.

"This time of year, a wolf or stegox might rampage into the village and abduct a child or sometimes a small adult. Aggressive animals with babies will make multiple trips. Don't stay out at dark."

"Should we worry about the sentries?" Erik asked.

"Let me do the talking," Zita said.

Upon reaching the gate, two guards dressed in blue and yellow tunics and holding spears stopped them. "Why are you coming into this village?"

"We're just passing through and want to get something to eat, then we'll continue our journey."

Al said, "We're going to Velidred Castle."

The dark-skinned guards took a defensive stance pointing spears at Al and Erik. "You're not allowed into the village."

Erik's stomach tightened as he stepped back. The guards were small men, but they brandished spears, and he had no way to disarm them.

Zita laughed, "Don't listen to my friend. We're stopping for food and we'll be on our way."

The larger guard held his spear tip inches from Erik's abdomen. "The people of the mountain king are forbidden entry into the village. Search for weapons."

Erik put his hands into the air. "We don't have weapons, and we aren't people of the mountain king."

"Quiet," the sentry said.

One guard frisked the teens. When the guard got to Zita, she touched the gold chain hanging from her neck and said, "We're not here to make trouble."

"That gold chain might convince me to let you into the village, otherwise, we'll arrest you as spies of the mountain king."

"This was a gift from my mother and you'll never have it." She backed away from the guard.

"Don't do anything stupid little lady. A week in the dungeon will change your mind." The guard moved closer.

Zita moved her arm from right to left across her body.

Erik felt a strong wind blow. The spears flew out of the guard's hands, impaling themselves in the ground two hundred yards away.

The guards said, "Stay here," and ran across the field after their spears.

Zita hustled through the gate, "Let's go!"

The teens ran with Zita through the city streets until they couldn't see the guards. The village was a thriving hub with many people doing business. As they slowed, they passed small shops where merchants hawked their wares. Erik smiled at a shopkeeper and found her following him trying to sell him a scarf.

Zita said, "Don't interact with the shopkeepers, otherwise they'll follow you. There's better silk closer to the castle."

Sherry stopped and handled a multicolored scarf, "The large blue butterflies are gorgeous."

Al pointed to a sign across the street, "Hey, The King's Magic Shoppe. I'm going in for a magic book."

"We aren't here to shop." Erik tried to grab Al's arm.

Al bolted into the store, and the teens followed. The room, gloomy and dark, glowed red with red candlelight, and a small fire burned in the fireplace.

An older gentleman with gray, thinning hair approached Al, "What do you want?"

Al said, "I need something to help with my magic."

"Do you seek a scroll, potion, staff or wand?" The shopkeeper asked.

"A wand or staff would look cool."

"Staffs are over here." the shopkeeper led Al to a display with a handful of staffs. "A staff for protection or attacking?"

"Is there a staff with a dual purpose?"

"These are specialized. The others are out of stock," The old man selected the longest staff. "This one is the right size for your tall body. It puts a ring of protection around you. Depending on your magical abilities and range of power it will shield your friends, too."

The wooden staff extended a foot taller than Al with an image of a wolf face carved near the top. Al held the staff and strutted up and down the little aisle. "How can I tell if it works?"

"You bond with the staff which takes a few hours. After bonding, say a few words and the staff provides protection. Do you have a wizard's license?"

Al laughed. "A wizard license, are you joking?"

The man put his hand on the staff. "I can't sell magic items to strangers without a license. We worry about black market selling to wizards banned from owning magical items. Your license, please."

"Where do I get a license?" Al asked.

"You must apprentice under a master wizard. Were you born under the path of Pantaleon?"

Erik stared at a cabinet containing large jars of dead animals in liquid. "Born under the path of what?"

"The moon of Pantaleon. Wizards must prove birth within its path. You can't become an apprentice without that proof."

Al said, "What if I show signs of magic, isn't that proof enough?"

"Many years ago, before the mountain king came to power, we didn't have these restrictions. But the king wants to limit the number of wizards, so we have restrictions. It's difficult to arrange a birth in the path of the moon, not like the old days when there were huge celebrations. The king prevents mothers from having babies in those areas, a great loss to my business. Today it's difficult to become a qualified wizard."

"I don't have a license and wasn't born on this planet." Al released the staff to the old man and picked up a gold key from a table. "What does this do?"

"If you have magical abilities, hold onto it for a few seconds and it will whisper its secrets."

Al held the key a moment. "It unlocks the door to the dungeon of the Velidred castle."

"Brilliant, Brainiac," Sherry said, "a key unlocks locks. Did they teach you that in third grade?"

"I'm not kidding. It opens the dungeon door in a specific castle. Amazing."

The old man took the key from Al, "The boy is correct. That is the key's purpose. What do you mean you weren't born on this planet?"

Erik stepped closer. "He's joking sir. His mother dropped him on his head a few times." Erik grabbed Al by the elbow and tried to re-direct him to the door. "Time to go."

Sherry took Al's other arm and helped. "Yeah, we should leave."

The shopkeeper stepped in front of the door. "Your friend has talent. Stop at Master Wizard Ishwa's school. He may take you as an apprentice."

The old man whispered to Al, "He will help you … find your proof of birth."

CHAPTER 11

At Al's insistence, the old shopkeeper gave the teens instructions to find Master Wizard Ishwa. They walked two blocks and turned right and then veered left into a smaller alley. The last alley was so narrow it forced the group to walk single file. The two-story high buildings in this neighborhood produced dark shadows.

Erik said, "Pretty dicey neighborhood, graffiti everywhere." Images of skulls on the wooden walls made him think eyes were watching. "These people dislike the mountain king."

He pointed to script, "Down with the mountain king. Restore the Kalluri Kingdom."

Sherry said, "Al are you sure these directions are correct?"

"The wizard dude said, 'Right at the yellow skull.'"

"There is no yellow skull," Sherry said.

"The lighting is poor, and the image is fading." Al pointed to a yellow skull painted on the wall.

"We don't have time for this foolishness. We need to go to the castle," Erik said.

Al said. "You know I've always craved to do real magic not mere sleight of hand. Here's my chance to be a wizard. I have talent. How many times have we played Dungeon and Dragons and I played the wizard? I've wanted this my entire life and this might be my only opportunity."

"We can't split up on this planet," Sherry said. "Why would a respectable wizard be in this section of town? Somebody at the castle can teach you."

Erik threw up his hands. "How will you eat or pay for lessons? We don't even know what kind of money they use here. Where will you live? Zita, talk to him."

Zita said, "Don't speak my name. Call me Carlotta."

"Why?" asked Sherry.

"I have qualms about the neighborhood."

"What are you concealing?" Sherry asked.

"Nothing."

"We have company, guys." Erik pointed to a group of teenagers coming up the alley.

Sherry pushed Al in the back, "Lead the way to Wizard Ishwa."

Erik peered around the corner. "This is stupid; there's no exit from this alley. If we go there, we will be trapped. Better we leave this neighborhood and head to the main road."

Al turned into the alley anyway.

Heaps of rubbish lay along the building walls, and small animals scurried among the debris. Al stopped at the fifth door along the wall and knocked.

Erik, trailing the group, looked back at the alley entrance, "Al, knock again. Hurry."

The gang, appearing more dangerous in the dim light, followed the teens into the alley.

Al knocked louder.

A small animal scurried over Erik's shoes. "Hurry, Al." The gang leader grabbed Erik's forearm. Erik studied the kid who was smaller and more muscular than Erik, but of a similar age.

The gang member said, "What chu doing in this neighborhood?"

"We're here to visit Master Ishwa," Erik glanced back at Al.

The other gang members laughed. The leader said, "That old man? The washed-up blind man can't help you. Show me your arm." He jerked Erik's left wrist, pushed up the jacket sleeve and twisted the arm side to side. "Clean. Why are you here?"

"We're here for the wizard, now get away." Erik thought, this is bad. We have no protection against these jerks. There are ten of them and they look stronger than us.

The alley darkened as clouds shrouded the sun.

The gang leader moved closer to Erik, "You want me to hurt you?" He pushed Erik back against the wall holding him by the jacket. "Hand over your money."

Adrenaline coursed through Erik's body and he tensed his muscles. *This adventure is out of control. Our money isn't valuable on this planet anyway, but they aren't getting anything from us.* Erik's anger grew as he wondered what these ruffians would do? He wrestled and pull one arm free.

The boy holding Erik shouted, "Stop that. Grab him."

Two gang members grabbed Erik's arms and held him while the leader struck Erik across the face.

Erik moaned from the blow, shook his head, and felt pain spread through his jaw. He struggled against one of the guys holding his arms and freed one arm. He pushed the other boy to the ground and pressed the leader against the opposite wall. The boy's throat was pinned behind Erik's arm. "Listen, we don't want trouble. Leave us alone."

Another gang member hit Erik in the kidneys and Erik fell to his knees in pain.

A deafening explosion ripped the air like a thunderclap, and everyone froze.

A frail old man came through the doorway and paused next to Al. The short dark-skinned man hadn't shaved recently and wore a week's growth of gray beard, "I told you, stop knocking on my door." He aimed a staff at all the teens.

Al said, "I'm searching for Master Wizard Ishwa. The man at the Magic Shoppe sent me."

"Who are you?" The elderly man asked.

"I'm, I'm, I'm Alpherge. Al."

"Alpherge. I remember that name from ages ago." The man stroked his beard and spoke, "I had a colleague, Alpherge the Great. Come, let's talk. Leave the rabble rousers in the street."

Erik said, "Al, get us inside."

"Can my friends come?" Al said.

"Yes. Yes." The man signaled with his staff to come in as he held the door. The gang members attempted to follow, but the old man stopped them with his staff, "Jyothi, I told you not to disturb my guests."

"They're different sir. They aren't Kallurians. Be careful, sir. They're spies."

"Thanks, Jyothi. Get on home."

"Yes sir." Jyothi hung his head and the gang members walked back into the alley.

"Come." The elderly man shuffled into the building.

CHAPTER 12

Dark drapes covered the windows letting little light into a large room. Benches lined the walls, and the teens huddled on one bench.

Al said, "It's dark in here."

"Oh, where are my manners?" said Ishwa. Waving his hands twelve candles ignited.

Books lay in a jumble on the bench next to Erik. He picked up a book, blew off a thick film of dust and read the title, "*Magic through the Centuries*." He thumbed through the book, hand lettered and bound in leather.

A staircase led upstairs, and a grandfather clock stood in the corner. The room smelled musty.

Master Ishwa held a staff, seven feet tall, which towered over the short man. A rugged face with a long beard was carved near the top of the wooden staff and above the face a row of five bright colored arrows in red, orange, yellow, green and blue and an intricate decoration of three moons in various phases hovered above the arrows. Two other faces were carved lower on the staff.

"Who is with you Alpherge?"

Al said, "Friends, Sherry and Erik."

One of the faces on the staff, a female said, "One more, a female."

"Carlotta from Cascadia," Zita said and took a deep breath. "I'm showing the others the kingdom as we travel to the Velidred Castle."

"Velidred castle? Not everyone in this town will be happy to know that is your destination," said Ishwa.

Erik spoke, "Our friend, Lily, is being taken there by a classmate, Billy Cutter. We're traveling to the castle to rescue her."

"Billy Cutter? I'm not familiar with that name."

"He calls himself, Kestrel the Falcon Prince," Al explained.

"Ah, Kestrel, Prince of Acadia, a sneaky, power-hungry young man. Your friend, Lily, does she have a last name?"

"Goodwin."

"Yes, part of the families with children we sent to Earth.

"You know of Earth?" Erik asked. He wondered how everybody on this planet knew of Earth while Erik and his friends knew nothing of Aloheno.

"Never heard this story?" Ishwa asked. "No, they wouldn't tell you. I suggest you go home. The prophecies—" His body heaved in great coughing spasms.

"Can I bring you water?" Sherry asked.

"No, fine," he waved his hand.

"Sir, we're finding my friend first and then going home." Erik said.

"Not that straightforward, the gateway opens for a limited period when the three moons come near alignment. If you don't go back now, the gateway will close and trap you on this planet for four years."

"The cave is already closed. We tried, but failed to reach the entrance in time." Erik stared at the floor, knowing it was his fault they were trapped on this planet.

Al said, "I want to stay. Can you teach me magic, Master Ishwa?"

Sherry grabbed Al's hand. "Al, continue with us. We must stay together."

"I'm not going back to Earth without learning magic."

"Ah, reminds me of your grandfather. I studied in school with Alpherge, a headstrong and impulsive young man always investigating new magic, dangerous magic."

Ishwa said. "I don't know if I can teach you, young Alpherge. I'm a frail old man." Ishwa coughed.

Erik thought Ishwa is a weak, elderly man with no strength. This decrepit wizard will perish from old age soon. There's no way Al can study magic under this man.

A boy came bounding down the staircase waving a small piece of paper. "Master Ishwa, communication from Captain Arun. He is prepared—" The boy trailed off.

Ishwa said, "Fine. Go upstairs and we'll discuss the message when I'm finished with our visitors."

"If you notice, Alpherge, I'm a busy man. You and your friends should leave. Hide in the mountains for four years, and stay away from the Velidred castle." Ishwa took a deep breath and leaned on his staff.

"But sir, I'm eager to learn anything you might teach me. I can work for you. Just share a little of your knowledge." Al stood and approached the blind master wizard. "Please teach me."

Sherry said, "No, you must stay with us. Everybody says it's unsafe. Make him leave with us."

"The young lady is right, Alpherge," Ishwa said, "Hold out your hands."

Al raised his hands.

The old wizard held the boy's wrists. Time passed, and Ishwa said, "I'm wrong, Alpherge must remain."

Sherry said, "No! Al can't stay." She began to cry. "We need you. I need you." She stood behind Al and placed her arms around his waist laying her head on his back. "Brainiac, come home with me."

A second face on the staff spoke with a high-pitched nasal male voice, "The resonance is disturbing, Master."

Ishwa said, "Carlotta come."

A bright red glow bloomed on Zita's face as she said, "No sir, I'm fine right here as I have no wish to study magic."

Ishwa said, "Oh I don't want to teach you magic. Your jewelry resonates. Please, may I?" He held out his palm.

"I would rather not, sir, it's a present from my deceased mother." Zita moved toward the exit. "Should we go, Erik?"

"Permit me to touch it," Ishwa demanded.

Erik said, "Z . . . Carlotta let him touch it."

"No one touches the necklace. It's my connection to my mom." Zita clung to the small, emerald turtle hanging from the serpentine golden chain, but the chain rose from her chest. "No, don't, please."

Ishwa walked over and placed frail fingers on the floating chain.

The grandfather clock ticked in the silent room.

Zita's fingers trembled as Ishwa held the turtle. Her face showed worry and panic.

Ishwa released the chain which descended like a feather to Zita's chest. "A nice focusing device. Did you say the object is a gift from your mother?"

"Yes sir, a present for my seventh birthday." Zita placed her hand on the necklace and rubbed the chain.

"You need not do that young lady," Ishwa said. "I won't harm you. Your father has done plenty to last a lifetime."

"Stay away from me." She pushed the shorter man. "We must leave."

Ishwa said, "As you wish, child. No one will keep you here against your will. Listen, you and Lily have a connection, by family and fate."

Zita rushed from the room.

CHAPTER 13

Sherry blew her nose and said for the hundredth time, "Why let Al stay with the wizard? Al can't take care of himself. He will die on this horrible planet."

Erik said, "It's what he wanted. All those hours playing Dungeons and Dragons at home, Al portrayed the wizard character. He memorized spells and exhibited great strategies as a wizard. I had to let him try."

"It's not fair. We expect your protection and commonsense. Instead, you let Al stay with that old wizard."

Erik lowered his gaze and grimaced.

"Zita, what did the old wizard mean when he said, you and Lily have a family connection?"

"I don't know anything about Lily."

"Who are your mom and dad?" Sherry asked.

"No one special, my mom's name was Noreen and my dad's name is Haskell. They're just simple peasants like me."

Sherry said, "Erik, why do all these people know us or know about us? Are we somehow connected with this planet? Did your mom ever tell you about this place?"

"No, I grew up in Montana and Dad served in the military and died serving the country. I don't know a lot about Dad because I was so young when he died."

"I remember paintings in Mom's bedroom closet years ago that showed a night sky with three moons." Sherry said, "I asked Mom about the moons and she grabbed the paintings, and I never saw them again."

# # # #

Erik sat on the rocky shore of a lake skipping rocks as they rested. Erik's legs were heavy, and he felt a blister forming on his left foot from walking all day. But in the late afternoon sun, the tension and stress oozed from his body.

Without a sound, a creature emerged from the water and chomped on Erik's right leg. Erik fell to the ground screaming. The creature's face looked like a fish, and it had fins on its body. But it also had legs making it look part alligator. The monster dragged Erik toward the lake.

Sherry ran and grabbed Erik's arm pulling him up the shore.

The monster, with powerful legs, backed toward the water. It was winning the tug of war with Erik as the rope.

Erik's heart raced, he tried planting his free foot, but the shore was all loose pebbles. Despite his dry mouth, he shouted at Zita, "Throw a rock at it."

Zita threw stones and pebbles at the creature. The beast dragged Erik across the rocky beach taking no notice of the flying stones striking its reptilian body.

"Do something different!" Sherry screamed.

"Like what?"

The creature kept walking backward, and Erik's left leg entered the water.

Sherry said, "Al would use magic."

Zita removed a bobby pin from her hair.

Erik's body ached from stress and walking, and despite the adrenaline rushing through his body, fatigue crashed his strength. They were no match for the water creature who had now dragged Erik waist deep into the lake. Erik tired from the struggle. He had visions of alligators submerging their prey in deep water, drowning them and feasting on their victim over many days. Erik fought harder, "Come on Sherry. Zita, what're you doing?"

Sherry struggled knee deep in water pulling harder. The extra effort helped, but the creature also strengthened, and the water rose to Erik's chest.

Zita ran to the lake and threw a bobby pin into the water.

Erik yelled, "No time for your hair. Help us."

Zita shouted over the splashing, "Nykkjen, Nykkjen, we have copper, we have protection, sink into the abyss hopper."

The beast thrashed through the water dragging Erik deeper, then, unexpectedly, the creature released. Sherry and Erik ran back to the rocky beach and fell to the ground.

Chills ran up and down Erik's spine as he rocked back and forth. Bile crept into his mouth and he struggled to swallow.

"Do you know magic, Zita?" Sherry asked.

"That isn't magic. That's an old wives' tale I learned from handmaids. We're lucky I recalled what to say. I believed it peasant superstition. This saying will work for anyone."

"Even me?" Sherry said.

"Yes. Not only copper, any metal will work. Say the words, throw the metal into the lake and the Nykkjen slinks back to the water."

Erik examined his leg. "Are these creatures in all lakes?" Erik asked.

"Lakes and wide rivers contain these Nykkjen and other vicious beasts. Don't cross wide rivers at night. How's the leg?"

"I'll be okay," Erik examined the puncture wound on his leg and other scratches sustained while being dragged across the rocks. "Is there a village nearby? Night is coming."

CHAPTER 14

arkness descended before the teens reached the village, forcing them to walk in the dark. Two moons were in the sky, the waning red Velidred was near full moon and blue Anticletus, a waxing Gibbous moon. The mingling of crimson and blue moonlight threw strange shadows upon the path.

Erik said, "Zita, in Montana when walking a trail where grizzly bears might be near, we make noise. The bears won't approach the humans. Will making noise keep the stegox away?"

"No, they're attracted to sound. Their eyesight is poor, and they hunt by sound."

"Wonderful." Sherry said.

Erik asked, "Are you okay?"

Sherry pushed her hands into her jacket pockets. "No, I'm not okay. I'm exhausted and my feet ache. I long for a hot meal, hot shower and a warm bed. My warm bed. I want Al back, and I want to go home."

The temperature dropped fast after sunset, and they hiked in silence until coming upon a modest village. They walked the abandoned dirt lane until they reached a tall building with candlelit windows. A sign hung from the wall, bearing a hand-painted picture of the building and a lake, with the words, "Seeley Lake Village Inn." Underneath the sign a note was tacked, "No Vacancy."

Sherry said, "No Vacancy? Are we supposed to trudge through wilderness all night getting eaten by beasts?"

"Relax," Erik said.

"Relax? Reeelaxxx? You have us tramping through the back country on this strange planet. You lost my soul mate and your friend, Al, and you want me to relax."

"Easy." Erik tried to comfort her.

She parked on the stoop of the inn. "I want a hot shower and cocoa. I'm numb."

Erik sat next to Sherry and placed his arm around her. "We'll manage. It's okay."

Zita stepped around them and entered the inn.

Sherry wiped a tear from her eye. "It's not okay. I'm miserable, cold and don't want to get attacked by wild beasts and never go home."

Erik ran out of ideas. His wet tennis shoes had been okay during the sunny day, but when the temperature plummeted the shoes no longer kept his toes warm. But he still had to think about Sherry. "Go inside, warm up and get food. Then I'll knock on doors. Someone in the village will allow three teenagers to stay the night in their home."

"Are you listening to what you're suggesting? We're different from these people. They'll glance at your clothes and hairstyle, and when they hear your accent, they will send you to the forest." Sherry's shoulders slumped to her knees. "Doomed."

Erik felt energy drain from his body, and mental fatigue made him ache to give up, but Sherry needed hope. "Come on, let's eat. Then we'll decide." Erik lifted her chin. "Please?"

Erik helped Sherry stand, and they stepped into the inn.

Zita greeted them. "I spoke to the innkeeper." She pointed to a gaunt man with a nose like a bird of prey. "He's removing families from two bedrooms and giving us the rooms."

Erik said. "What innkeeper does that? Did you pay him a large sum of money?"

"No. They're lower caste Kallurians. Velidredians are superior and are entitled to the rooms first."

"Superior? Who or what determines that? Are you implying they don't deserve warm beds, but we do?" Erik asked.

"Yes. Watch them come from our rooms." Zita beamed.

A few minutes passed, and the innkeeper shepherded a Kallurian man, his pregnant wife and a sleepy toddler down the steps. The little girl dragged a blanket while sucking her thumb.

Sherry gasped. "Where will they sleep?"

Zita said, "What do I care? Barn or next village doesn't matter as long as we enjoy nice accommodations." To the innkeeper she commanded. "The bedrooms will be heated and clean."

Erik thought. What manner of society forces a pregnant mother and family from their lodgings into the darkness filled with stegox? "Zita, this family can keep the room, and we'll bed in the barn."

"No, you're royalty and deserve the best."

"Royalty? We aren't royalty, just ordinary teenagers from Montana."

Zita sat at a table in the common room. Sherry moved near to Erik and whispered, "Even though I'm beat, we can't permit them to sleep in the freezing barn."

"Don't worry, let Zita go to her room and then we go to the barn and switch places with them."

The innkeeper descended the stairs again, leading an older man and woman, fragile and thin, embracing each other tight while walking with care down the stairs. Erik's eyes watered, watching the couple be escorted into the frigid night air.

The teens ate dinner and warmed themselves by the fire. Two hours later the host led them to the bedrooms.

Zita said, "Sherry sleep in my room tonight. We can share girl talk and get to know each other better." She winked at Erik and placed her hand on Sherry's elbow.

Sherry pulled her arm away and stepped behind Erik. "Tonight, I'll sleep in Erik's room."

"Tomorrow night then." Zita entered the room the innkeeper had prepared.

The innkeeper ushered the other two to a bedroom with a fire blazing in the hearth.

"Wonderful, so warm." Sherry rushed to the fire, rubbing her hands together near the burning logs.

Erik pulled the innkeeper into the room. "Kind sir," Erik whispered. "Where did you send the other family that held this room before we arrived?"

"Into the barn as prescribed by law."

"Shhh." Erik placed a forefinger over his lips. "We'll sleep in the barn tonight."

"No sir. Not allowed. I'll get in trouble with the law and lose my inn license." He scanned the room as if the town police waited in the corner for him to break the law. "I have four young children to feed and can't risk impropriety." He bowed and backed to the doorway.

"Please sir. We're from Montana, sleeping in a barn is like camping in the park."

The host stepped into the hallway and shut the door.

"Now what?" Sherry asked.

A half hour later, Erik and Sherry snuck down the dark back stairs where no candles illuminated the passage. They reached the ground floor and opened the back door. Erik feared the innkeeper might lose his license, but he feared Zita discovering their plan even more.

They arrived at the barn without incident. The Pantaleon moon was a sliver in the sky above the horizon with the other two moons still riding high. The blue Anticletus moon had passed the red moon. An animal howled in the distance, and Sherry moved nearer to Erik. The barn sat thirty yards behind the inn, and Erik felt the piercing cold on his nose and ears. Erik opened the barn door causing a shrill squeak of the rusty hinges, and he stepped into the barn.

A man pushed Erik against the wall. "What do you want?"

"No, No. Let me go." Erik pushed the man, realizing the father they had seen forced out held him.

Sherry said, "The family with the pregnant mother and little daughter should sleep in the bedroom."

"Why? Are you attempting to get us arrested?" The father asked.

Two torches glowed, and in a stable next to sheep, the expectant mother clung to her daughter in a tender embrace.

Erik said, "Sir, I beg you. Take the room. Your child and wife are freezing, and there's a warm fire blazing in the room."

Sherry approached the elderly couple lying on a bundle of hay. Sherry said, "Please go with the young couple and share the room."

The woman shook her head no.

Erik moved to them, took the woman's frigid hand and eased the venerable woman to her feet. "You remind me of my grandparents, and I would never allow my grandparents to sleep outside in this weather. Please take the room."

The old man stared at his wife. "No. It's against the law of the mountain king."

"Ignore the mountain king," Erik said.

The aged man shuffled back a pace and his mouth dropped opened while the old lady's hand moved to her bosom.

Erik pleaded, "It's too cold here, take the room. I'm wearing this warm coat, nice and warm."

The woman shared a brief glance with her husband giving an unspoken comment and the old man relented.

Erik said, "Quiet. No trouble. Take the back staircase."

Sherry helped the pregnant mother and daughter from the sheep pen.

Erik walked to the back entry and helped them into the inn. He returned to the barn and found Sherry in the hayloft stacking hay forming a small room.

Sherry said, "This will keep our body heat in the tiny room. We won't freeze to death."

Erik said, "Stinks of sheep and cows — not quite the warm room you requested."

CHAPTER 15

Erik woke in agony from pain in his feet, ankles, calves, hips and back. He wasn't used to walking miles upon miles, and he had slept all night in an awkward position. He roused Sherry early to get to the common room before Zita woke. They ate a bowl of mash that tasted like wet cardboard mixed in sawdust. Additions from a jar of honey on the table helped Erik manage the horrible flavor of the mash.

Erik rubbed his leg where the creature from the lake had bitten him. The blue jeans had averted the puncture wound from being deep, but he limped this morning walking into the inn.

The elderly couple shuffled into the common room and came straight to the table bowing to Erik. "Praise you for your hospitality last night, Lord."

Erik placed his forefinger to his lips. "Shh. I'm not a Lord."

"If I can be of service." The man said.

"Can you recommend a doctor for my leg?" Erik pointed to his injured leg.

"I can help." The man descended to one knee and pulled up Erik's trousers leg. "What happened young fellow?"

Erik said. "A creature in the lake yesterday chomped on my leg and attempted to yank me into the water."

"Nasty creatures." The man said. Erik's skin was bright red. "The leg is infected."

The elderly man shuffled into the kitchen, returning with a tin can stuffed with a substance smelling of bacon grease. He took a metal object from his pocket and waved the object over the substance mumbling an incantation. He kneeled and spread the fatty substance onto Erik's leg.

Erik flinched on the initial touch. "It's cold."

Sherry said, "Smells like bacon grease."

The man said, "Yes, it's a mixture of pig fat and magic. Rub the paste on the leg three times a day for three days to drive out the infection."

Erik laughed, "Very well, but we'll be hounded by dogs wanting to lick my leg."

The elderly couple laughed.

Zita walked into the room. "What's going on here?" She pointed to the old couple. "Get away from us you filthy vermin."

The man bowed to Erik and said, "Thank you for your kindness."

The woman whispered to her husband., "You shouldn't use magic. We're supposed to be hiding."

Zita said to the teens, "You have to act like royalty. In Velidred we'll get you proper garments and treat you with the respect you deserve. If not for me, you would have slept in the barn last night."

# # # #

Late that morning, after walking an hour, Erik heard the screech of a bird of prey. He stopped and scanned the surroundings. They were walking on a path in a forest of old growth hardwood trees and had passed rocky areas with giant boulders. Looking up into the trees he saw a large shadow glide across the landscape reminding him of an airplane passing overhead in Montana. He couldn't see the bird, but knew it must be close from the size of the shadow.

Then he heard a noise behind him on the path. A branch broke as if someone stepped on it. Looking behind, he saw no signs of movement; no one came into view.

"Not good." Erik said.

"What's not good?" Sherry asked.

"We're being followed."

Zita asked, "A crowd of people?"

"No, well maybe not a crowd, but I think one person." Erik bent to adjust his shoelace.

"We should hide, and when he walks by, we can decide whether to attack." Zita said.

"Attack?" Sherry asked. "With what? How do we know they aren't people walking to a destination, the same as us?"

Erik pointed to nearby boulders. "I'll hide behind those boulders. You two keep walking the path and when the person passes, I'll question him."

Sherry said, "Frightful idea. You stay with me, and Zita hides behind the boulders."

"Fine." Zita lifted her nose in the air. "I can take care of myself. Go."

The two walked on, but Erik sneaked a glance over his shoulder. The trail behind was empty.

An explosion shattered the silence and a harsh crack followed as a tree toppled to the forest floor.

Erik pushed Sherry to the ground, jumped down beside her. "What was that?"

"It sounded like lightning striking a tree." Sherry said.

After a second explosion, Erik rose to his feet. "Somebody is shooting at Zita. Find a safe place to hide." He pushed Sherry toward a grouping of huge boulders and rushed back to where they left Zita.

A young man wearing a hoodie that partially covered his long black hair shot lightning bolts from his hands toward Zita's position behind the rocks. Erik ran toward the stranger.

The caped man turned slightly and gestured toward Erik

A lightning bolt flew within inches of Erik causing his hair to stand on end. Erik stopped running and fell to the ground. Adrenaline rushed through his body and his heart pounded in his chest.

The young man sauntered toward Erik.

Erik felt the blood drain from his face. He knew he would die. Time slowed, and in slow motion he rose and hurried to his right toward the trees. The man threw another bolt at Erik.

A tree toppled, forcing Erik toward Zita's position.

Zita yelled over the racket generated by the lightning strikes. "Stop it right now."

Erik dove behind the rocks next to Zita, just missing getting struck by another bolt. "Do you know this guy?"

"Yeah, I attended school with him and we dated."

"Bad ending?" Erik peeked around the boulder, and an explosion struck the rock inches from his face, shards of rock scratching his face. Erik ran fingers through his hair and felt a tightness in his rib cage.

Zita tried to stand, and the assailant fired another bolt toward her, missing by inches.

"Assuming he is your boyfriend, why is he attacking us? What did you do to him?"

"Nothing."

"How do we stop him?" Erik searched for an object to throw, but he needed to get nearer to this maniac. Another group of boulders was ten feet nearer the attacker, and Erik wondered if he could make it there before being struck by the magic fire bolts.

"His magic isn't that strong. You notice he hasn't managed to hit either one of us yet. He must have a focusing device."

"What do you mean focusing device?"

"A wand, staff or piece of jewelry."

Erik ran toward the rocks, and the attacker fired at him three times. On the final blast, Erik's left heel was hit knocking the shoe off his foot. He dove to the ground behind the boulders.

He grabbed his shoe and put it on, pondering a strategy. Erik moved again, running to hide behind a tree. A blast smashed the tree and it began to topple. He dove behind a boulder as the tree fell toward him. Erik hunkered down behind the rock, and the tree smashed over the top of the boulder. Small branches scraped his arms and face, but the boulder prevented him from being seriously hurt.

Zita stood and drew the attention of the attacker.

Erik sprinted toward the man in black, hoping Zita was keeping his attention diverted. He tackled the guy, driving him to the woodland carpet. They grappled in the mud and leaves.

Zita stood over them. "Kestrel. Stop right now."

Kestrel relaxed and Erik asked, "Billy Cutter?"

Zita said, "Erik meet Kestrel."

Billy still wore the black cape with an image of a red exploding volcano embroidered on the back and the falcon on the front.

"Where's Lily? What did you do with her?"

"She's at the Velidred castle visiting with the mountain king."

"I want her back." Erik pummeled Billy.

"Stop it, Erik. Let's talk to him." Zita tried to pull Erik off of the other boy.

Erik said, "Why are you stalking us and hurling lightning bolts?"

"Orders from the mountain king to keep surveillance over you and Zita."

"The mountain king knows about us? Why does he care?"

"The proph —."

"Shut up, Kestrel. You're stalking me, despite me telling you the romance is over between us. How long have you been watching us?"

"I ... found you yesterday."

"Well, it's shameful what you're doing." Zita gestured to Erik. "Go back to Sherry so Kestrel and I can talk alone for a few minutes."

"Alone? He attempted to kill you. Are you certain you want to be alone?"

"Yes, I'll be fine. Right Kestrel?"

Erik found Sherry hiding behind a tree and they walked farther down the path.

Sherry asked, "Why go back after Zita?"

"Well, she's helping us and I wanted to protect her."

"You can protect me by leading us home and getting off the planet."

"That won't happen because the cave is closed, but trust me, I'll protect you."

"Billy knows magic and will make you look like blackened chicken at a barbeque. How can you protect us? What's going on with you and Zita?"

"Nothing."

"She likes you."

"What?"

"She asked me questions. Who you're dating? How long? What interests you have. The questions girls ask when they like a guy."

Erik, speechless for a moment said, "You mentioned I'm rescuing Lily?"

"Perhaps."

CHAPTER 16

Master Ishwa led Al upstairs after his friends said goodbye. Three flights of stairs opened to the top of the building.

Master Ishwa said, "The trainees practice on the rooftop."

The kids were divided into five groups. Students Al's age threw fireballs at a sketch of a human drawn on a low wall around the building rooftop. The younger children, in a circle, tossed rocks at a ten-year-old in the center, but the rocks bounced off an invisible shield. Al passed a group of girls. One girl was chanting a spell which caused the other to change in appearance. The transformed kid's clothing and skin changed chameleon-like, to match the wall behind her as she walked.

Al said, "Will you train me to throw fireballs?" This would be impressive. He'd always day-dreamed of magical powers and shooting fireballs at monsters.

Ishwa said, "First you learn to defend. You will train with the youngest pupils. After mastering basic skills, we'll teach you more advanced techniques."

"I will learn defense fast, and then you'll teach me how to throw fireballs?"

"Time and patience, young Alpherge. Many students never master the shield. We cannot permit novices to proceed if they cannot defend."

"The shield will be a breeze." Al laughed. "I learn everything fast." In high school, classmates struggled with calculus while Al finished half the book within two weeks. *Magic will be a breeze.*

Ishwa introduced Al to Wizard Jayanti, a petite woman with short cropped black hair.

Jayanti said, "Master Ishwa, I can't accept this new student. These trainees," she motioned at the younger children, "are a week from advancing to the next level."

"I have confidence Alpherge can learn in one week with your class." Ishwa put his hand on Al's shoulder.

"But sir, it's not fair to the other pupils. I can't spend time with them if I go to the first exercise for this student."

"Train him. He needs to learn fast. We're preparing to launch an attack."

She bowed her head, "Yes sir." She peered at Al. "In this group we're training to shield our bodies from attacks. Watch Gopal." She pointed to a short, rather chubby kid. "He clears his mind and imagines a small bubble forming. The bubble grows, protecting him as the others throw rocks. Proceed Gopal."

Al watched Gopal concentrate with closed eyes. No visible bubble formed.

Jayanti told the trainees. "Throw your rocks."

They lobbed rocks which bounced off an invisible shield two feet from Gopal's body.

Jayanti said. "Al, are you ready to try?"

"Yes."

"Say, 'yes Sergeant.' I'm your sergeant."

"Yes Sergeant, I'm ready."

Al stood in the center of the circle and imagined a bubble, but he had no confidence about how to create the bubble or what type of bubble to create. Should he create a soap bubble, a bubble gum bubble or a spit bubble made with your lips? He had created nothing by the time Jayanti told the trainees to throw rocks.

The students didn't lob the rocks like they did for Gopal. They hurled rocks hard which ricocheted off Al's temples and forehead.

"Ouch, how come they threw the rocks so hard? They only lobbed the rocks at Gopal."

Gopal said, "You're tall; we needed to reach your head."

The other students laughed.

Jayanti raised a hand and the students quieted. "You aren't concentrating. I will give you more time to create the bubble. Begin."

Al thought of a gigantic soap bubble, but a breeze blew, and the bubble floated over the rooftop wall.

"Concentrate Al."

The kids threw rocks again, but Al had no protecting shield.

Jayanti told the trainees to stop. "Al, go to the corner and practice creating a shield. When you can produce a shield, we'll try again."

Al shuffled to the rooftop corner. Would he fail this simple task? These children can't be older than ten-year-olds. I'm expected to be a great wizard and these children are better wizards. Al practiced making a shield. Sometimes he produced no bubble while other times a small bubble appeared which burst as he increased its size. Several flimsy bubbles flew over the rooftop edge. Once he built a protecting shield, but when he brought it toward his body, the bubble covered only half the length of his long frame. It popped, covering him with liquid soap.

At sundown, Jayanti said, "Al, time to try a shield again."

Al rubbed his hands on his pants legs and felt nauseated, his body bruised from rocks thrown on the previous attempts. He stood in the proper spot and the children picked up rocks.

"Form the shield."

Al formed a bubble, watching it grow in volume.

Before getting the shield around his body, Jayanti said, "Attack."

The kids threw their rocks, the bubble dissipated, and Al raised his arms to safeguard his head.

Jayanti said. "No, no, no, not your arms, let the bubble shield you. Stop." She raised her hand and with magic shielded Al from the remaining flying rocks. "We'll work more tomorrow. Let's go to supper."

After dinner, Gopal led Al to the bedroom. It was a cramped room with two sets of bunk beds, shared with trainees, Gopal and two other boys. The bed, too short for Al's tall frame, forced him to bend his knees to fit. Exhaustion set in from walking and the mental concentration required making the magic shield.

Al lay staring at the ceiling thinking of Sherry and Erik. *Should I have stayed with my friends? Will Sherry still like me when we get back together?* He hadn't thought about any consequences of his actions when he had made the decision to stay and learn magic.

A mosquito bit him, and he slapped his left leg. Then another mosquito bit his right arm, and the boys in the room snickered with the sound of Al slapping his leg.

Al said, "Come on, boys, let me sleep."

Gopal said, "Make a shield, Alpherge the Great."

"Don't call me that." A flurry of mosquitoes attacked and he slapped at his arms and legs and moved the blankets to defend against the onslaught. He tried forming a shield, but it blew up when a mosquito made contact.

The boys were relentless with the attacking mosquitoes, and Al sometimes succeeded in creating a bubble with shielding capability, but most of the time the bubble dissipated or didn't cover his entire body.

"I'm gonna get you Gopal." Al said.

"Fat chance, Al the giant stick boy."

The boys relented when the grandfather clock downstairs chimed twelve times. Al lay in bed nursing mosquito bites and bruises while thinking of home and the homecoming dance two weeks away in Earth time. Where are Sherry and Erik, and what can we do anyway since the cave is closed for four years or more?

Al practiced creating a shield while the boys slept. Toward daybreak he could establish a shield large enough to encompass his body on every attempt. With confidence that he could repeat the skill later in the day, he dropped asleep.

Al woke exhausted. He was bruised and bloody scratches covered his arms and legs. Breakfast consisted of meager, unpalatable mush. After washing dishes, the pupils trooped upstairs to the practice court. Clouds prevented the sun from shining through, leaving the rooftop chilly and damp. Al yawned.

Jayanti said, "Al, get in the spot. Master Ishwa informed me that if you can't form a shield today, I can send you home."

"Yes, Sergeant." Al thought, *I can do this. I managed it last night. It's easy.* A bubble formed and as it grew Al gained confidence.

Jayanti gave the command. "Toss the stones."

Even though the bubble shield covered him, Al's bubble burst when the first rock struck, and Gopal mercilessly released three stones in succession, hitting Al above the eye with the last stone. The other students pummeled Al's arms and chest with rocks.

Jayanti said, "Al, concentrate. You must master the body shield, first your own body and then to also shield five other individuals. These small stones are nothing. In a few days we will attack you with sticky fruit and fireballs. Concentrate."

Al struggled to form a shield and maintain control, but bubbles flew around him without serving as protection.

Jayanti raised her arms. "Stop." She strode to Al.

Al didn't like the look in her eyes.

"I'm sorry, but you can't make a defensive shield. You aren't right for this school. Hire a private tutor and try again in two years. Sometimes students study magic too late in life and can't train their bodies to control the power. Ishwa felt your great potential, but you can't remain part of this organization."

Al's shoulders slouched, and his head dropped to his chest. Everything he desired was lost in a few short hours. He felt devastated at being told he didn't have magical skill. Could he face his friends after making a big deal of becoming a wizard and failing in one day?

Gopal pitched one more rock, hitting Al in the ear.

Al had reached his limit. He never became angry with classmates on Earth, but fatigue, pain and failure were too much. He chased Gopal. The small boy laughed and ran around the roof top staying just out of reach.

Jayanti said, "Gopal, Al, stop it."

Gopal stopped, picked up a stone and hurled it at Al.

In an instant, a shield appeared and swelled to surround Al. The shield protected his body, the bubble held, and the rock bounced to the rooftop.

Did Jayanti notice? Had she protected Al, or did Al create the shield? For a moment Al wasn't sure. Then euphoria spread through his body because he knew he had controlled the magic. He crossed his arms, raised his head and widened his stance.

Jayanti studied Al for a moment then stared off into the distance.

Al felt she disliked him and wanted to send him away from training whether he succeeded or not.

Jayanti shook her head, pressing her lips into a fine line. Then she sighed and said in a monotone voice, "Can you reproduce the shield?"

"Yes Sergeant," Al gazed into almond shaped eyes.

Jayanti said, "Gopal, retrieve all the stones and stockpile them in the corner. The rest of you pick up one stone each and throw it at Al to confirm his shield building abilities."

CHAPTER 17

Al and the other students sat on benches in a classroom as their instructor, tall, muscular, blonde-haired Blayze, described military maneuvers.

Blayze pointed to the chalkboard. "Teams operate in small groups of four to eight with one person shielding while others attack. Move as a group with the scout leads coming in and out of the shield to reconnoiter the battlefield." He outlined the maneuver on a chalkboard. "The group leader gets feedback from the scout and signals from the field captain. Then the swarm moves to a different position to attack or stand by for directives."

One of the older girls said, "What happens if the individuals operating the shields get injured, aren't prepared to create a large shield or can't maintain their shields?" She glanced at Al.

"That happens, but each of you can produce shields, and there will be times you must prepare your own individual shield. We'll find the strongest shield wielders to protect the swarms."

Al said, "Who will we fight?"

Blayze said, "Do you not recognize the anguish and suffering of the Kallurian people? We're a conquered people placed into slavery at the hands of the Mountain King."

Jayanti stood. "Our families are starving. The Mountain King executed the king of the Kallurians and butchered the queen. Our enemy steals our food, taxes our families and kidnaps the children to be slaves."

Al thought of his friends, heading straight to the mountain king to find Lily. Should he leave this group and find his friends? Would Sherry be captured? His stomach clenched at the word Jayanti had just used, "butchered." Al said, "Who's fighting this war?"

Blayze walked over to Al. "Everybody in this room is fighting. We require as many wizards as possible. The Mountain King is a mighty wizard with a well-trained group of warrior wizards. Many of our own wizards have been captured and recruited to battle against us."

"You're sending ten-year-olds to fight trained wizards?"

"When they're ready, they'll fight the enemy."

"They won't be ready for six to eight years. You're sending these boys and girls to their deaths. How long will this war last?" Al hoped to study magic and have quests against orcs and dragons. He wanted an opportunity to impress Sherry. Warring against other humans hadn't been in his plan.

Blayze said, "We'll fight this war as long as necessary to defeat the mountain king and win back our kingdom, friends and family members. The war has raged for fifteen years. I've been training wizards since the king's warriors killed my father, mother and two brothers. I'll never surrender or stop fighting."

Master Ishwa stood in the doorway and shuffled into the room. "A crucial opportunity comes with the eclipse of the triple moons. Major celebrations occurred during past eclipses, and we're training to strike while the king is weak and distracted."

"An eclipse of three moons would be fantastic to observe and record," Al said. "Will it occur within our geographic area?"

Ishwa replied, "The squads will be busy besieging the castle and driving out the king's army. Develop your wizardry skills to join the assault on the castle."

Al never imagined wizards becoming war weapons. He pictured himself as a scientist and engineer. Magic was fun and challenging and carried the prospect of danger, but he hadn't thought of it as a combat weapon. *Did I make the wrong decision?*

Ishwa said, "Three other resistance armies will accompany us when we assault the castle. Listen to the commanders, and sharpen your magic because you'll need skill and craft to win."

# # # #

Eight hours later, after dinner, Al stood on the roof feeling a slight breeze in the cold night air. He had survived the day's exercises. The young wizard trainees had worked on defensive techniques to protect swarms, multiple small groups of wizards, from injury or capture.

Gopal stood next to Al, "I'm able to make a larger fog cloud than you."

"Your fog cloud lasted ten seconds while my cloud lasted a full minute." Al said.

"Yeah, and your goofy head showed above the cloud the whole time like a volcano in the morning mist."

"I need more practice." Al had noticed the fog grew faster and thicker after the sun set. He grinned and spoke the incantation to create a cloud. Soon Gopal disappeared in the dense fog. The big red moon hovered in the sky as the fog shrouded Al's shoulders.

Gopal kicked Al in the shin.

"Hey, stop that." The fog finally covered his head and Al moved away from Gopal's last position on the rooftop.

Gopal feet shuffled on the rooftop and his clothing swished as he moved. Noises that helped Al find Gopal's location in the murky fog.

Al created a mosquito and launched the insect at Gopal.

Gopal slapped his skin, a loud sharp clap. Then he slapped again. "Quit it."

"Make a shield."

"I can't, the mosquito is too big."

"Too big?"

"It's gripping my arms and flying. Help."

Al hurried to where he last heard Gopal's voice. "Where are you?"

Gopal's voice moved across the rooftop. "Hurry, it's lifting me off the roof."

Al followed Gopal's cries for help in the thick fog.

"Al, help me." Gopal's voice moved in the opposite direction.

Al got close, then the voice changed direction again. "Where—"

Gopal kicked Al's shin.

"Got you." Gopal said.

Al and Gopal laughed.

They worked on their fog making abilities, and Al thought the fog shrouded the entire rooftop. He speculated the cloud became easier to create at night when the sun didn't dissipate the fog.

Then the boys heard voices in the fog. Al whispered, "Quiet."

"How are the young children doing on defensive skills?" Blayze asked.

The thick fog amplified and disoriented the sounds.

Jayanti said, "They don't stand a chance. We should tell Master Ishwa to leave them here."

Blayze said. "The strategy is to overwhelm them with large numbers of wizards."

"That's the same approach the stone warriors tried, and they ended up as stone statues."

The leaders seemed to move away from Al and Gopal. Al followed at a distance trying to listen to the conversation.

"We didn't realize the Mountain King's power at that time, now we know to fight magic with magic." Blayze said. "The Mountain King's magic is depleted and Ishwa wants to attack before the eclipse. Ishwa thinks the king will recover his magic during the eclipse celebration and Ishwa wants to attack the castle while the king is at the volcano, but before he can increase his powers."

Jayanti said, "But sending ten-year-olds against mature wizards? We're supposed to train the children for the future, instead of sending them to their death. If we're killed or captured, then no one is left, and if the king gets stronger. . ."

Jayanti began to cry, and Al thought Blayze hugged her because the sobs became muffled.

What can I do to stop this war? Erik could talk to these guys and give them a better strategy than sending ten-year-olds to their deaths. How can I contact Erik? Al had tried his phone a few times, but never found a signal and knew that mobile phone technology didn't exist on Aloheno. He didn't know how far Erik and Sherry had traveled each day or even the distance to the castle.

Gopal grabbed Al's arm and whispered. "The fog is lifting, time for bed."

CHAPTER 18

Erik and the others entered the small town of Kavilly in mid-afternoon. Dark clouds formed in the western sky. At home he would say a storm brewed, here he wasn't sure what it meant.

Sherry pointed at the villagers sitting next to their homes. "These people look like they haven't eaten a meal in a month."

Erik felt heartbroken gazing at the emaciated residents sitting around their houses. Their arms were bones draped with withered skin. He didn't expect their legs had sufficient muscle to support the frail skeletal structure.

Erik said, "Zita why doesn't the mountain king help these people? Why is he allowing them to starve?"

Zita said, "They are the dregs of society and should get off their butts and work for their food."

"They don't have the vitality to work. They're near death, can't we do anything for them?"

"What can we do, sleep outside with stegox each night?" Zita said. "Perhaps we sell your jacket and shoes to feed these families. Then you can freeze to death at night. Is that what you want? Listen, this time of year many communities run out of food. This village didn't manage their winter stores now they have nothing to last them until the first summer harvest."

They walked past the hungry families.

Zita pointed to a building with a small sign, "On the Wing Messaging." "I need to tell my dad where I am. You guys stay out of trouble."

Sherry and Erik walked farther down the lane. They saw log cabins which had holes stuffed with cloth to keep out the weather. How did these houses keep a family warm? Little children sat outside the homes staring with hollow eyes into the road. This village had no merriment of children playing in the streets and no chatter of street peddlers.

Sherry said, "We should send a message to Al."

"What will you say?"

"Brainiac, we need you."

Erik missed his tall friend and the banter between Sherry and Al. "Al is busy becoming a wizard, he's forgotten us by now."

Sherry said, "Al could practice wizardry on Billy."

"That's the point of Al going to wizard school, so, he can practice magic." Erik placed his hand on Sherry's shoulder. "He doesn't have the wisdom to stop Kestrel. In fact, Al might die using magic if he's un-trained."

Erik pointed to a queue of people in the road. "What's going on?"

"I'm not sure. They're standing in line for something."

A man with a booming voice shouted to the people. "Come, bread and soup for everyone."

Erik and Sherry approached the line of people.

A large red-haired man ladled soup into a wooden bowl held by a tiny old woman.

Sherry asked. "Would you like help?"

"Yes. The wagon behind me has bread, grab loaves, slice it and hand two slices to each person in line."

"You, young fellow," he pointed his ladle at Erik. "Stoke the fire below the pot so the soup stays hot. These people need warm food."

Erik took logs off a wagon, arranging them in the fire pit underneath a large, cast-iron cauldron. After getting a roaring blaze going, he stood next to Sherry and handed out bread.

The tall beefy man stood in contrast to the short-emaciated locals. Erik asked, "Where did you get this food?"

"Loving friends of the people contribute money and supplies so I can feed poor communities. My name is Cugbert, third braid of the Pankratios." He flipped his long hair which hung to his shoulders and showed them three braids. "And you, my friends, who are you?"

Sherry said, "Oh we aren't from here."

Cugbert said, "I presume with that bright red hair you are from my home territory of Torgony."

Sherry smiled at a young family as she passed out bread. "I have red hair, but I'm not from Torgony."

"Ah yes, the accent is unusual. And your fellow there with the growth of beard reminds me of a young Sergeant, John Anderson. I remember fighting in many battles with him."

"My name is Erik Anderson, and my father's name was John. He was a soldier, but not around here." Wow, it would be nice to talk with someone who remembered my dad, thought Erik. But no one on this planet knew his father.

Sherry said, "If you were a soldier, how did you become a monk or a third braid or whatever you mentioned?"

"Ah, the Pankratios is a church of peace. I was a great soldier and my size helped me dominate battlefields." He stroked a magnificent red beard that reached to his chest. "But then I learned the story of the Pankratios. Their philosophy is help others and win friends loyal for a lifetime instead of forcing people to fear you, always hoping they won't stab you in the back. I chose peace, and now I travel through communities baking bread and cooking soup to nourish the hungry."

"That's an impressive transformation," Erik said.

"Would you care to accompany me?"

"We can't as we're seeking my friend, Lily. She is supposed to be at the Velidred Castle, and we want to bring her home."

"That is a noble quest, lad. You appear well traveled with unusual dress, have you seen the ancient city of Pankratios?"

Erik asked, "A city goes with the religion?"

"The ancient city of Pankratios is the monastery training ground for new seminarians."

Cugbert smiled at a villager as he ladled soup into the man's bowl.

"Is it far from here?"

"An evil spirit penetrated the city, and she vanquished the monastery. As monks, we search for the city and ask everyone if they know its location. There exist many seminarians in the monastery and we fear they may have turned to evil."

Erik handed bread to a young boy who stood next to his mother. "Where is this place?"

"We hear rumors and stories, but upon reaching the location, Pankratios vanishes. The monks search far and wide on wild rumors while feeding the people and listening for stories."

"Does the evil spirit move the monastery and everyone in it, or is it invisible?"

"There is nothing but weeds and jungle where the building once stood." Cugbert raised his voice to the people in line. "Tell your friends we have food."

Erik stood amazed at this strange world. In many respects it resembled Earth. But this was a planet with magic, strange frogs and a city that changes location.

Thunder boomed in the distance, and storm clouds approached with huge streaks of lightning flashing through the sky.

Zita marched toward them. She said, "What are you doing?"

She pointed at the huge red headed man. "We're helping Cugbert feed the people. He's a Pankratios monk."

"I know what he is. He gives these people hope."

Thunder sounded nearer now.

Cugbert said, "Zita you've grown since I last beheld you. Is your father well?"

Lightning struck close.

Zita said, "We gotta go." She grasped Sherry's arm.

Thunder drowned out Sherry's response, and large raindrops splashed on the dirt road.

CHAPTER 19

The raindrops came faster and harder and soon
became a drenching rainstorm. The kids weren't
dressed for this weather. Zita ran down the muddy
path refusing to slow the brisk pace.

Zita said, "Keep moving, we'll find shelter in Mahasini
tonight."

Erik asked, "Can't we find shelter here until the
downpour stops?"

"No." Zita slipped in the muck then resumed running
allowing the unrelenting rain to hide her tears. Seeing
Cugbert had brought back many memories.

"What are you running from, Zita? Or who?" Sherry
asked. "Do you know Cugbert?"

"I knew him when I was a child, back when my mother
was alive. Because of him my mother died." *Cugbert didn't
intend harm, and I was only a child when I told Dad the
plan.*

"Did Cugbert kill your mother when he was a warrior?"
Sherry asked.

"No, he was a peaceful monk when we met. He tried to
help my mother." Zita ran faster. *Cugbert had developed a
plan to remove Mother from the castle. My only
responsibility was to keep my mouth shut and not tell Dad.*

"Can't you run any faster?" Zita asked.

"No, I have a bad leg." Erik limped through the
drenching rain.

Zita remembered being seven-years-old. Cugbert
fascinated young Zita because the mighty man made her
feel secure, and she liked his gentle personality. Cugbert
and Mom were talking. Mom thought Zita was asleep, but

Zita overheard the conversation as the two planned an escape from the Mountain King.

Lightning flashed overhead and struck a nearby tree, sending it crashing to the forest floor.

"How did Cugbert kill your mother?" Sherry asked.

"Shut up. He killed her."

The weather that night reminded her of today's nasty storm. The night before the escape Father had read a book to Zita, a rare treat. Then Zita told her father, "I will miss you Daddy," and she told her father all about the scheme.

Another flash of lightning lit the surrounding path and exposed a village, "That should be Mahasini where we can find rooms."

Zita stepped into the foyer of the first inn they encountered where a roaring blaze burned in the fireplace in the common room. She craved the warmth and comfort the fire afforded. In the crowded room, several men sat eating and laughing at the tables. The room was noisy with several loud conversations and she worried they wouldn't get rooms.

A severe looking woman approached Zita and the teens. "Whatta ya want?"

"We need two bedrooms." Zita said.

The woman replied, "Those guys," and pointed to the fireplace, "don't wanna give ya a room."

Conversation in the room eased.

"The men by the fireplace don't like you or your companions. I suggest you continue down the road." The woman wiped her hands on her apron.

Zita thought the apron put more filth on the woman's hands. "You must give us lodging by decree of the Mountain King." Her dad taught her to talk and act tough to get what she wanted.

"Honey, I don't have to give you anything." The woman waved toward the fireplace.

Two short wide men got off their stools next to the fireplace. Conversation stopped as the two bouncers picked up large clubs and approached.

This process is easier in the high mountain region. The men in this room were miners waiting for the snow to clear before digging for gold and silver in the mountains. A rough bunch. Zita felt a hollowness in her belly and eyed the exit. *She could avoid them with magic but had resolved not to use magic in Erik's presence.*

The guards closed within five feet.

Zita touched her gold necklace.

Erik stepped in front of the men and put up his hands, "Stop."

They stopped. The taller of the two said, "Leave. Now."

Erik said, "Come on, Zita. Let's go. We won't sleep in this flea-bitten hole. There are other inns in this village."

"The other inns don't want ya either. Go back to Velidred Province."

The wider fella said, "Hey Jack, that name, Zita? That mean something to ya?"

"Yeah, I recognize that name."

Zita clinched her fists and her legs trembled. *If these miners figure out my identity, I won't be safe.* She grabbed Erik's jacket collar pulling him toward the entrance. "Time to leave."

"No, I'm not gonna let these goons take advantage of us." Erik stepped closer to the men and delivered a punch.

Jack caught Erik's fist and held on. "Whose gonna stop us 'goons?' You punk?" He pushed Erik to the floor.

Erik rose, preparing to go back into the melee.

Adrenaline pulsed through Zita's body and she shoved Erik toward the doorway. "Let's go." They tore out the door, retreating into the torrential downpour and down the street.

The bouncers stood on the inn porch, holding clubs on their shoulders.

The teens passed two inns but hurried on until one inn remained on the outskirts of the village. Zita slowed, "We'll try this one." *This village might be too powerful in the resistance, and we might not get a room.*

They walked up the steps of the porch where a thin man in shabby clothes with an unkempt beard slept on a bench. The inn was maintained well on the outside. This led Zita to speculate why the innkeeper let this destitute man sleep on the porch. The teens entered and shook rain off their jackets, their clothing was soaked through as if they'd been trudging through a pond.

A young woman with a clean white apron approached. "How may I help you?"

"A hot supper and two bedrooms." Zita said.

"Oh, that will be fine. Take off your coats and sit by the fire. You must be freezing; I will bring you hot soup."

They found a table near the hearth. The inn's common room was small, and there were few people sitting at the tables. Zita felt better about this place. As long as Jack didn't get a message to the inn keeper that revealed her secret, they might survive the night.

Erik moved his stool closer to the large stone fireplace, applying salve on his injured leg.

Sherry said, "Why were those guys at the last inn familiar with your name, Zita?"

Zita shifted in her chair, cleared her throat and spoke in a whisper. "Please call me Carlotta. The King Haskell, the mountain king has a daughter, Zita, and people in this territory get excited hearing the name."

Sherry gave Zita a suspicious look, and asked, "Are you the daughter of the Mountain King?"

"If I was the daughter of the Mountain King, would I be here, tired, with rain soaking my clothes and near death with hunger? No, I would be snug and warm in a castle with servants caring for my every desire, and I would visit with friends." Instead, she thought, I'm here with the riffraff commoners. She carefully took a sip of the hot apple cider the serving maid brought to the table.

"Why have you taken care of us? You buy food and give us rooms each night. What's in it for you?"

"My mom taught me to be nice to strangers."

Sherry huffed. "You aren't nice to strangers. You're only nice to us."

Zita answered, "It's obvious you don't belong here, so I resolved to help." She feared these teens might discover her intentions, she leaned nearer to Sherry. "Your friend Erik is cute; tell me more about him."

"Erik's searching for his girlfriend and isn't interested in you."

Zita tensed her jaw and furrowed her brow at Sherry. The red-haired know it all isn't being very nice. "He might not care about his sweetheart by the time we arrive at the castle." Zita pushed hair back from her face, raised her eyebrows and winked at Erik.

The front door opened, letting in an icy breeze as the homeless guy from the porch stumbled into the common room. He swayed and peered around the room, focusing on the teens an instant. Then he moved to the bar and slurred the words, "Give me a drink."

The serving lady addressed the destitute man. "Prince Krunal, come to a table and I will serve you a bowl of hot soup. After eating we will offer you another drink." She spoke to the man like a caring sister talking to an ill brother. She steered the man to a table near the teens.

Can this day get any worse? Prince Krunal is here? Where are his army and bodyguards? Zita had heard the Mountain King's armies had Prince Krunal on the run, but this fellow was a filthy, homeless drunk.

He lurched to the table and fell in a chair facing the teens. He tried to concentrate on the teens but his eyes wouldn't focus. He dropped his head onto the table.

I guess if he doesn't sober up and discover who he's watching I'll be all right, Zita thought.

The serving woman brought hot soup, and they ate. Erik slurped the soup into his mouth.

Sherry leaned close to Erik. "Why did you take a swing at that guy at the other inn? Do you want to die?"

"Yeah, stupid, wasn't it? I didn't care for the way the innkeeper treated Zita." Erik grinned at Zita and raised his eyebrows.

Zita put her forefinger to her lips and said with clenched teeth. "Call me Carlotta." She peeked at the homeless guy asleep with his head on the table.

# # # #

They talked into the night, warming themselves by the fire as their clothes dried.

Erik yawned, "I'm ready for bed. How much farther till we reach the castle?"

Zita said, "A few more days and we'll be there."

The destitute guy, Prince Krunal, woke up, rose to his feet and wobbled in their direction, falling into Zita.

Zita screamed, "Get off me," and pushed him.

He grabbed Zita's left arm exposing a tattoo. She shoved him again and covered her arm with the garment sleeve.

"You!" the homeless man said. "You belong to the Mountain King." He stumbled toward her, grabbed Zita's forearm and rolled up her sleeve exposing the tattoo once more.

"Get away from me," Zita tried wrestling her arm away, but the thin man had strength in his hands. He stank of wine and sweat.

Prince Krunal shouted, "These youngsters are from the Mountain King."

Erik rose from his chair to help Zita.

Two men appeared and blocked Erik's way.

Zita clenched her jaw and felt her heartbeat increase. She attempted to rise, but the homeless man held tight. The familiar family crest of an erupting volcano, tattooed on her arm at age sixteen, was revealed for all to see. More men advanced toward their table. She touched her necklace with her free hand and produced a magic shield around her body. She forced an electric jolt to the destitute man.

The man slumped backward.

Zita raced toward the door, snagged her jacket from the hook and hurried off into the night.

CHAPTER 20

When Zita left the room Erik felt like somebody had slapped his face. He fell into the chair with opened mouth in stunned silence. Two men tied his arms and legs while other men bound Sherry.

Erik struggled against the coarse ropes. "Why are you doing this?"

"We don't care for your kind in this town, Punk." A tall swarthy man, smelling of garlic, pressed a hand against Erik's chest. "You're from the Mountain King, aren't you?"

"No, we're searching for our friend, Lily." Erik struggled against the tight ropes. "Carlotta is leading us to rescue Lily."

The man drew his face near Erik. "Or you're spies sent to inform the Mountain King about our defenses."

Two guys helped the destitute man to the chair Zita had vacated. He stared with vacant eyes, blinked several times and rocked back and forth.

"What's the name of the girl that ran?" The man bunched up the front of Erik's shirt.

Erik struggled against the binding ropes, squirmed in the chair and peered into the man's dark brown eyes. "Carlotta."

"Heat the fireplace poker in the fire and we'll loosen his tongue."

Sherry said, "Erik tell them the truth. Her name's Zita."

"Somebody has common sense. Okay, little missy, tell us more." He motioned for the man to bring the heated poker, which he brandished at Erik. The end of the iron glowed bright red. "Talk."

Erik struggled, backing from the heat of the poker. "We aren't with . . . Zita. She was leading us to the castle to find our friend."

"What will the boy do with one eye?" The man held the iron rod close to Erik's cheek beneath his left eye.

Sherry yelled, "Stop threatening him. We're speaking the truth, and we aren't from the castle. We don't even know the its location. That's why Zita was helping."

"Then why travel away from Velidred Castle and toward the Kallurian castle?" The man moved the poker closer to Erik. "They're spies; I say hang them."

Erik squeezed his eyes shut in shock, a sudden coldness enveloping his body. Zita had tricked them. *We aren't even traveling toward the castle where Lily is held captive.*

"What do you mean, away from the castle?" Sherry asked.

Erik shifted his head to avoid the poker. The glowing rod was so close he smelled the hair of his four-day beard burning.

A gray-haired man smoking a pipe near the fireplace said, "Gavin, check their arms for the Velidred tattoos."

Gavin pulled up Erik's sleeves. "Nothing here."

Others checked Sherry. "These are clean."

Erik bounced up and down in his chair as a man tried to hold him still.

"Listen." Erik said, "We aren't from here and aren't from the mountain king." *Duped by Zita. She's right, this world isn't safe, and at every step we're in peril from our stupidity and ignorance.*

The homeless man stood, and the people in the room grew quiet. "Where are you from?" he commanded.

What could Erik say? We're from another world; we walked through a portal and arrived by accident. Who would believe that story? "I can't tell you."

The fellow with the poker said, "Stop lying, you filth." He touched the hot iron rod to Erik's cheek.

Erik screamed.

Sherry shouted, "Please, we aren't from this province. This is difficult to understand, but we're from a different planet."

"They be angels from the celestial heavens." One man mocked.

The room erupted in laughter.

"Listen," Sherry said. "We're from Cullerton, Montana on the planet, Earth."

Even Erik didn't believe it. How outrageous did that sound?

Gavin pulled Erik close. "There be hangings tonight."

Blood drained from Erik's face, and beads of sweat collected on his forehead. He felt numb, distant and dizzy. They were going to die, and Mom didn't know he was on this planet. Sherry and Al trusted him, and he had led them to death. Excruciating pain bubbled below his eye and the smell of burning flesh filled his nostrils.

"Hang them." A man in the back of the room shouted, and a chant erupted in the room, "Hang em, Hang em. Hang em"

The homeless man wobbling on unsteady feet, held up his hand and in a whisper said, "Wait."

The men nearest the shabbily-clothed man repeated the word, "Stop," raising their hands to silence the others.

Prince Krunal asked, "Where are you from?"

Sherry repeated, "Earth."

"I remember that name, Earth." The destitute man shuffled to Erik and regarded him. "How old are you, boy?"

"I'm sixteen. Now let me go."

A man slapped Erik. "Shut up."

A cut opened above Erik's eyebrow and blood dripped into his eye.

The homeless man, who was perhaps a prince, examined Erik. "Years ago, a friend tried to convince me to go to Earth, but I refused. At age sixteen, full of myself, I desired to destroy the mountain king, avenge my father's death and save my Kallurian people." The man sat on the floor in front of Erik.

Erik said, "We're from Earth."

The muscular man slapped Erik. "I'll tell you when to speak."

"Stop it." The destitute man rose to his feet without help, but placed a hand on the table for support, standing to face Erik.

Erik watched the man's eyes as the unfocused drunkenness vanished. His eyes grew sharp, and purpose built in his manner and bearing.

Prince Krunal said, "Tell me about Earth."

"I don't know what to tell you, sir." Erik struggled against the ropes.

"Wrong answer." Gavin raised his beefy palm to strike Erik.

CHAPTER 21

Prince Krunal seized Gavin's arm, preventing him from striking Erik. "Enough violence. Untie them."

The brawny man released Erik who let out a deep sigh. The room's built-up tension relaxed. Erik rubbed his arms where the rope had chafed. He pondered the incongruity of this rag-tag man commanding these unkempt men. They hadn't washed in recent days and looked as if they were living in the streets. Why were the men in this inn?

The man who had emerged as the leader bowed. "I am Prince Krunal Kalluri, prince of the Kalluri kingdom."

"Wow," Erik said. *A prince, and I thought he was a vagrant. But if Zita lied, this guy could too.*

"I'm the leader of the resistance, a group of Kallurians and others who want to defeat the mountain king. We are disorganized and not much of a force, but we are many in number waiting for the opportunity to conquer the king." A serving lady offered the prince a mug of ale, but he refused.

Erik mused, that this rag-tag hodgepodge of bums couldn't conquer anyone. "What are your plans? Do you have battlefield strategies and strengths and know the vulnerabilities of the enemy?"

"The king's forces assassinated our military intelligence commander three days ago, and we retreated, arriving in Mahasini at daylight." Prince Krunal ran his fingers through a greasy beard. "We need a new commander and more foot soldiers. Will you help the resistance defeat the mountain king?"

"No, we need to find and rescue my friend, Lily. We can't join a war." Erik rubbed his eyes. He felt exhausted from walking, mad at being deceived by Zita, and he would not join the weak Kalluri resistance. "You want me to join a military group with no tactics and no captain?" He shook his head in disbelief.

The prince glanced at the bar as if regretting refusing the mug of ale.

"Where's the castle of the mountain king?" Erik thought it was time to continue his mission. "We'll sleep here tonight and at first daylight head to the castle."

"No, that isn't permissible." Prince Krunal gestured to the guards.

Gavin and two stalwart men stood next to the prince.

"Two options," the prince said. "Join the resistance or we hold you captive until we defeat the mountain king."

"We aren't joining an unorganized group that prevents me from rescuing Lily." Erik rose from the chair.

Two guards, each of them twice as wide as Erik, pushed him into the chair.

"Should we tie you again?" Prince Krunal had a quiet but commanding presence. "You know of the resistance now, so we can't release you and risk exposing our plans."

Erik felt his chest tighten and gritted his teeth. "Have you captured Zita? Didn't you tell me she's the daughter of the mountain king? Worry about her. We promise not to tell the mountain king about the resistance." They were wasting precious time talking to these yahoos.

"Our patrols are searching for Zita." The prince spit on the wooden floor.

Sherry said, "That's disgusting. Why do you keep spitting on the floor when you mention Zita's name?"

"She's the offspring of a loathsome, destructive man."

Erik decided on a course of action. "Is there a map of the Velidred castle and the surrounding area? I can help with military strategy. I've played many online games and appreciate the skill needed for battle planning."

The prince clicked his fingers and a skinny fellow produced a rolled-up paper. Prince Krunal un-rolled the map flat on the table using empty mugs to hold down the corners. "What do you mean 'online games'?"

Erik prepared to tell the prince about the internet when Sherry shook her head. "Board games like chess, but these are military strategy games."

"Was Commander John Anderson your father?"

The prince's question sliced through Erik. *Is Dad from this world? Is that why Mom never answered questions about Dad?* "Father died when I was young and he served in the US Air Force." Erik repeated the words Mom had always told him. There were no photographs of his father.

Erik said, "Let's examine the map." He wanted to find the location of the Velidred castle to help set their bearings.

They discussed strategies for how to attack the castle and deploy the troops. Erik gave Krunal some new ideas. The resistance army of five thousand men expected more would join while marching to the castle. But the king had a large military with trained wizard warriors.

Erik said, "How many wizard warriors are in your resistance?" He studied the prince.

"A modest group trained by a master wizard. Wizards are scarce since the mountain king came to power. Many wizard warriors died during raids on the castle."

Sherry said, "Are you referring to Master Ishwa?"

Prince Krunal's eyebrows lifted.

Erik determined from the prince's reaction that Ishwa was the trainer. How would Sherry take the news that Al was studying with Ishwa to attack the mountain king as a wizard warrior?

Sherry stared with widening eyes as she spread her fingers in a fan against her breastbone. "Forest River Blossom predicted Al's death, and Al is in peril. We have to get him to leave the magic school. That big ole Brainiac won't have the wits to leave even when he comprehends the danger."

The prince said, "If you know of Ishwa and the resistance, there is no alternative but to imprison you."

Sherry grasped Erik's forearm with a trembling hand, "That lady," she hesitated in a restrained sob, "said Al might die. Was the fifty percent whether he joined the battle or returned home?" Tears rolled down her cheeks.

Erik said, "What if we pick up our friend from the magic school and promise to go home?"

"Give me three or four days." Prince Krunal said.

Erik's voice rose, "We don't have days, and I've given you solid strategies for how to attack the castle. We won't rat you out to the enemy. If the king thinks we're part of the resistance, we're in danger in his presence."

"We'll discuss this in the morning." The prince signaled to his men. "We're going to bed. Put them in a room on the third floor and put a guard at their door."

CHAPTER 22

S herry and Erik waited in the bedroom on the third floor of the inn for an hour. Erik said, "We'll sneak out the door when everyone is asleep."

"If they catch us escaping, they'll hang us."

"That's a risk I'm willing to take." The frustration percolated through Erik's body. Something had to be done, but exhaustion clung to his mind like a greasy film.

Erik pulled the door open a crack, praying the hinges wouldn't screech. Down the corridor, two stout men stood watch. Erik re-locked the door. Any hope of escape vanished; his breath rushed from his lungs, deflated like a toddler's balloon at the zoo. "There's a complication."

"What kind of complication?"

"Two soldiers guard the door."

"Just as the prince said. Now what will we do?" Sherry sat on the bed closest to the window.

"I don't know."

Sherry put her hands on her face. "I told you to let the adults resolve the situation. This is your fault." She punched Erik in the chest.

"I'm sorry," he placed his arm around her shoulders.

"Don't touch me." Sherry pushed his arm aside and moved to sit on the opposite bed. "Al's gonna die. As far as I can tell, we're all gonna die."

Erik lashed out. "Don't blame me. I commanded you to go home after we spoke with Forest River Blossom."

"I am blaming you." Her voice rose. "We'll 'follow the footprints.' you said. Keep running after Lily even though we're on another planet. Disregard the seer who prophesied your friend's death. Doesn't any of this upset you?"

Erik hung his head. *Sherry is right and everything that happened to my friends is my fault. If Al dies, it's my responsibility. Now as a wizard warrior, Al's life hangs in the balance. How many wrong choices have I made to this point? And now we're immersed in a no-win situation where we must join the resistance.*

"Here's a plan," he said, "I'll walk through the hallway, hit the guards, and race down the stairs. When they follow, go the opposite direction and out the door."

Sherry shook her head. "Dumbest thing ever. You'll be captured and hanged. I won't get further than a quarter of a mile before they catch me and hang me too. Do you have a death wish?"

"Well, what do you suggest?"

"I. Don't. Know." Sherry emphasized each word, one at a time. "Sit here and cry. I'm exhausted and could sleep three days straight."

"We just need to get out of this building without being observed," Erik said. "We can't leave through the hallway because of the guards. Can we escape out the window?"

Sherry raised her head and smiled. "Remember those old, black-and-white TV shows where people escaped by climbing out of windows using bed sheets knotted together? Would that work?"

Erik opened the shutters. They screeched and banged against the wall.

A knock sounded on the door, and a deep voice said, "What's that noise? What's going on in there?"

Erik jumped at the sound of the knock. *Oh no, busted.* "Sherry get into the bed and pull up the blankets."

Erik replied, "Just a minute." He messed up the bed sheets then opened the door.

The large man, Gavin, who had smacked him around downstairs, stood at the door. "What's going on here?" Gavin stepped into the bedroom and peered at Sherry in the bed.

"I'm sorry to disturb you, sir, I fell out of bed," Erik lied.

Gavin closed the shutters.

"Hey, we prefer fresh air when we sleep. Leave them open."

Gavin grabbed Erik by the front of his tee shirt. "Like fresh air? What if I drag you outside and tie you to a tree? Will that be enough fresh air for you? Three stegox were in the village last night. They get a smell of you and you won't need fresh air."

Gavin pushed Erik onto the bed. "Don't make me come in here again. Leave this door unlatched." Then he left the room.

Erik's heart pounded, and he waited several seconds then gestured for Sherry. Erik said, "Quick, tie up these sheets. Are there enough?"

Sherry said, "We need twenty-one to twenty-four feet. There's a sheet and blanket on each bed. We should be close." She gathered the bedding off her mattress while Erik cleared his bed.

Erik tied the bedding together and secured one end to the bed post. They lost three feet for fear the sound of shifting the bed would bring Gavin back. Erik opened the shutters, this time lifting the wooden shutter up and out to prevent it scraping against the window sill. He tossed the handmade rope out the window.

Would they reach the ground before Gavin heard them? Were there other guards patrolling the property around the inn?

Sherry grasped the bedsheets and hesitantly climbed out the window. As she reached the first window below, she bounced, causing a slight rattle to the shutters.

Despite the cool outside air, Erik's palms sweated as he held fast to the bed sheets and watched Sherry's descent while praying the door didn't open.

Sherry's clothes caught on the first-floor shutter.

Erik's fingers and toes tingled as he watched with heightened awareness of Sherry's every movement. He wanted to shout, "Be quiet." Erik closed his eyes and drew a deep breath, the rope swaying in his hands.

But, within a minute she shimmied to the ground and gave a tug on the rope.

Erik glanced at the door and climbed out the window.

As Erik descended, his weight dragged the bed across the floor, causing a shrill screeching noise ending with a deafening thud when it bumped against the inside wall.

Passing the second story window, Erik heard the door to his bedroom open and Gavin yell, "What's going on here?"

Adrenaline surged through Erik's body and Gavin yelled out the window. "They're escaping."

"Hurry Erik."

A man flung open the shutters at the second story window and reached for Erik.

CHAPTER 23

Twelve feet from the ground Erik released his grip on the sheets and fell hard to the dirt. His knees buckled, and an intense pain shot through his right ankle. He was injured, but his desire to escape was greater than the discomfort.

Erik pointed to the forest and yelled, "Run!"

Sherry sprinted toward the trees.

Inside, Gavin shouted, "Get moving you lazy pigs before they get away."

Pain radiated from his ankle as Erik stood and placed weight on it, but he forced himself to run.

Doors slammed in the inn, and men shouted as Erik limped into the forest. One moon glowed in the night sky, but the moonlight didn't penetrate the darkness of the pine forest. In the dark, Erik had difficulty finding Sherry.

When Erik caught Sherry, she asked, "Which direction should we go?"

It was early spring, and the underbrush wasn't thick, but they tripped over downed limbs, and low hanging branches slapped their faces.

Erik breathed heavily, and when he looked back, torchlights bobbed up and down through the trees. They needed to run faster. "Keep moving in this direction. Go, go, go."

They ran, but the men gained on the teens. A diversion might help, and Erik thought about letting Sherry run ahead while he circled back, but he decided getting separated was too risky. The roar of rushing water came to them through the trees.

Sherry said, "Stop!"

Erik caught at Sherry's arm to stop himself before flying off the cliff. Even so, he slid down the steep slope for five feet. He struggled to stop his descent with his legs, and his injured ankle caught on a broken tree trunk and twisted. Suppressing a wail, he came to a halt in a patch of dirt. Far below, a swift running creek gurgled in a deep canyon. Overhead, a large blue moon shone full in the firmament.

Sherry helped Erik climb back up the slope. Men's shouts came nearer.

Sherry had a peculiar iridescence around her as if the moon light reflected off her clothing and hair.

Erik was tired of making the decisions and asked, "Should we risk going into the ravine?"

She responded, "We can't risk the river without knowing how sheer the canyon is. There might be a sharp drop off and we'd be caught in water so cold we'd freeze to death before we could get out."

"Well, we can't stay here. Get into the forest out of this bright moon light."

Animals howled in the distance.

"What's that?" Sherry asked. "Those animals sound like that stegox that attacked the frogs. And they're close."

"Sounds like coyotes baying at the moon in Montana. Coyotes are leery of people." Erik felt trapped between the river and canyon on one side while men from the resistance pursued. Torchlights flickered through the trees. "Let's take our chances with the coyotes."

Sherry held his forearm, "You can't tell those howls are coyotes. They might be wolves or those horrible stegox creatures. And not just one. Two or more."

"Trust me, those aren't stegox. Keep moving." He moved toward the animals' howls, but agonizing pain coursed through his leg. Erik pushed on Sherry's arm. "Back in the forest before we're spotted."

The teenagers tripped and plunged through the woods trying to outrun the men from the resistance.

They crashed through the forest for another minute. Then Erik stopped. "Quiet."

The men from the resistance had stopped at the ravine, and the chatter of voices carried far in the still night air.

Gavin said, "Did they go into the canyon?"

"That's certain death. It drops one hundred feet. They would never survive."

"Check to make sure."

The men stuck torches over the side of the canyon.

Erik whispered, "Move slow and try to be quiet, so we can gain a lead while they search the ravine." He pressed onward.

A ray of hope bloomed in Erik's mind as they widened their distance from the group of men. His goal was to find a safe spot to hide. Erik searched trees for places to shimmy up and hide in a thick patch of conifers. The best idea he came up with was hiding underneath a couple of spruces—too obvious. There were oak trees here and there, but none of the oak trees had leaves yet and there was no place suitable for hiding.

The friends moved and reached the edge of the forest, stopping before they entered an open grassy meadow. The full moon shone bright, and Erik spied large rocks fifty feet away. "Can we run to those rocks to hide?"

Sherry said, "We can't risk the meadow, because the moon is so bright it's like a gigantic search-light. And what if the stegox are on the opposite side of that boulder."

"I haven't heard howling for a while—maybe the animals moved on. We gotta try for the boulders, it's our only hope."

Erik moved toward the boulders at the same time a large stegox and two smaller ones moved out from behind the boulder. They sniffed the air walking at a lazy pace toward the teens.

Sherry said, "We gotta leave now." She rushed into the meadow away from the stegox.

Erik followed, but running in the meadow became difficult because the grasses from the preceding summer were thick and stood six inches in large bunches.

The teens were thirty feet from the forest when five men from the resistance burst out of the woods. "Get them," one shouted.

Adrenaline surged through Erik's veins. He sped up disregarding the pain in his ankle. "Run faster."

Sherry breathed hard beside him as Erik checked the distance from their pursuers. He stumbled on a hummock of grass and fell flat on his face.

Sherry stopped. "Get up."

"No, don't worry about me, keep running."

A fourth stegox appeared in front of Sherry. It stood on its hind legs and roared.

She stopped and backed to where Erik had fallen.

Erik pounded the ground in rage and wanted to shout profanities at the beast, but his throat constricted and he couldn't make a sound.

The animal smelled like rotten garbage. It displayed menacing teeth and drooled as it sniffed the air.

The men walked backward toward the forest, laughing. One said, "We don't have to chase these two anymore."

The mother stegox roared from behind the teens and advanced toward them.

Erik and Sherry were trapped between the two sets of stegox, the brown mother and her babies and this larger cream-colored beast. Sherry was a mere eight feet from the cream stegox. Sherry was emitting a blue glow.

The blue aura grew around her body. The large stegox walked on two legs toward Sherry as she stood gawking at the beast.

"Run to me, Sherry. Move." Erik yelled. An iridescent blue crown appeared over her head. Erik, transfixed by Sherry's pulsating blue glow, stopped talking.

The stegox towered over Sherry's small body. The bright moonlight illuminated the surrounding area to appear like day. The large mammal snarled and showed fifty teeth or more in its long snout. Long, bear-like claws reached out for Sherry, and Erik knew she would die.

Everything moved in slow motion. The glow emanating from Sherry grew brighter than the moonlight. Sherry didn't move and although Erik tried yelling, his mouth was too dry.

The stegox stopped growling, paused and sniffed the air. It turned its head as if embarrassed to look at Sherry, and dropped down to stand on four feet.

Sherry stood motionless as stone.

Erik watched the animals lumber toward the men who were still watching from the forest's edge. The men ran.

After the stegox and resistance fighters left, Erik and Sherry wandered without any sense of direction the rest of the night. The stegox scared the men from the resistance, and the teens were not harassed by men or bear.

After three hours of variously running, walking and resting, the teens stopped moving when the blue moon set for the night.

Sherry said, "Get some firewood." She stopped in a little clearing that offered a place to build a fire, sheltered from the road by pine trees.

"Did you bring matches?" Erik asked.

"No, I didn't, but I'm a Girl Scout. I've camped with my mom for ages and can kindle a fire without matches. Get wood, and I will get a little fire going. Hurry. I'm cold."

Erik had trouble finding dry wood in the mountain forest. The logs lay in patches of snow and were too wet to burn. He came back with an armload of branches and small logs. Sherry sat on a log next to a fire.

Sherry grabbed a log from Erik's arms, adding it to the fire. "Perfect, just what we need. Well, most of what we need. A warm bath and a nice bed would help." She stacked the wood Erik had scrounged next to the fire to dry, and stretched her hands to the fire.

They warmed themselves for a while, and Erik asked, "Sherry, what happened to you in the meadow when the stegox rose in front of you? Did you do that?"

"Did I do what?" Sherry asked.

"Tell the creatures to go. Can you talk to animals?"

"What are you talking about? I did nothing. The big, bear-like, possum, mammal creature was two feet away, and I thought I was going to die. Then the animal dropped to its feet or paws and chased after the guys in the forest. I stood petrified."

"You didn't just stand there. You were all blue, and an iridescent crown glowed above your head. Are you a queen on this planet?" Erik arranged another log on the fire. Sparks exploded from the burning logs.

"Ha, a queen. That's perfect, Mom and I have had little all these years. I doubt I'm a queen on this planet or in any other dimension you want to mention. If I wasn't so tired, I would laugh. Be careful with that wet log, we don't want the fire to smoke too much."

They sat in the silence, a million stars shining in the clear night sky.

Sherry asked, "What's gonna happen to us?"

CHAPTER 24

That same night Al and Gopal sat on the rooftop of the wizard training school staring at the stars and the large, blue moon.

Al said, "Are you saying my talent at magic is controlled by whether I am born in the five-day window when the new moon of Pantaleon passes over head?"

"Yes, that's the way to gain magical power," Gopal said.

"What determines who is stronger in their magic? Does genetics play a role?"

"What's genetics?"

"You know, my grandfather is Alpherge the Great. As his grandson, he passes ability to his genetic offspring, the way you have brown eyes because your mother and father have brown eyes."

Master Ishwa joined the two boys and spoke. "Gopal time for bed. Al, I can answer your questions."

A chance to talk with Master Ishwa excited Al. "Can you tell me about my grandfather?"

"Yes, we were friends and had great adventures over the years, I remember the time we snuck two unicorns to Earth. What a blast. Even though magic doesn't work on Earth, Alpherge arranged an illusion that made the unicorns appear magical." Ishwa rubbed a hand over his bare scalp.

"Unicorns are real?"

"Yes, yes, but not native to Earth, just Aloheno."

"Is my power with magic determined by my parents?" Al wanted to listen to tales of his grandfather, but his stronger desire was for information about his abilities.

"Yes, yes. There is a line of wizards whose progeny display natural magical powers enhanced when born under

Pantaleon. You have stronger than normal powers, but you're learning magic late which is problematic and dangerous. Many who start training late are foolish and burn out their magical talents. Disciplined training will keep you safe."

Al gazed upon the blue moon. "How did my grandfather die?"

"Hmmm, your mother never told you the story?"

"Mom never mentioned this world." Al had always felt frustrated by his mother's refusal to answer his numerous questions about Dad.

Ishwa said, "Three or four years before sending you and your friends to Earth, Alpherge the Great and I searched for the Crystal of Zaraboth."

"The Crystal of Zaraboth?"

"Yes, yes. An object of extraordinary energy. The Mountain King had conquered many villages, which worried us that he desired to conquer the entire planet. A rumor surfaced that the Crystal of Zaraboth had the capacity to defeat the king. We investigated for two years then traced it to the province of Qasim."

"I told your grandfather which magical items were required to capture the Crystal, including the Rod of Paralysis, the Mantle of Optics and the Tankard of Charming. He found the rod and tankard and acquired the Mantle of Optics in a shrewd trade with a drunken wizard.

"Alpherge thought he had prepared well, but I argued to include the Crown of Anticletus.

"Your grandfather responded, 'I don't need the Crown of Anticletus; that's a myth perpetrated by spiritualists who claim when Anticletus is in the sky, a pure and innocent woman will glow, imbued with an aura of celestial influence. All creatures are compelled to obey her commands. Nonsense.'"

"Despite arguing for days, I can still hear his response in his deep, gruff voice, 'Folklore, don't need it.'" Master

Ishwa sat next to Al, "That stubborn wizard would stroke his long, gray beard and declare, 'legend.'

"After months of preparation we embarked on the journey, traveling for weeks through jungles, swamps, deserts and the northern ice fields. We reached Qasim, a hot, disagreeable place with a stench of death."

Al asked, "Were others with you?"

"Other wizards and baggage handlers traveled with the group. We didn't know if the territories we traveled through could supply food. A man wearies of scorpion stew in the wasteland and desert. Darlutle snake is tough and unpalatable.

"The time came when we discovered the palace, towering on a plateau. It took three days through harsh weather to climb the steep cliffs. The gear we had chosen and magical weapons were perfect. The Rod of Paralysis helped defeat the Giant Augean Leopards at the gates of the palace."

Al watched the man scratch his thin, white whiskers. "Giant Augean Leopards? And what is the Rod of Paralysis?"

"Yes, yes. The Rod of Paralysis is a rod made from the bones of a mastodon, created centuries ago by a great and mighty wizard. He combined ashes from a bat, legs of a spider and venom from a Darlutle snake and embedded the mixture in the bone. With a simple incantation you point it at your prey, and it paralyzes, producing powerful magic. It worked perfectly on the archaic leopard brains.

"At the door to the king's antechamber sat an ancient woman wearing a shawl of magic-laden, chain mail. She appeared easy to defeat, but we were mistaken. We thought the Tankard of Charming would be for a young prince or a warrior. But that tankard proved pivotal to get past the old woman. We endured hours to weaken her and beguile her to allow access. The woman drank tankard after tankard of magical drinks finally falling asleep in a drunken stupor in the early dawn.

"That left us to defeat the king, who had lived in the palace for centuries, guarding his daughter. We offered him a gift of the Mantle of Optics, a magical cape covered in different colored eyes, that enables the wearer to visualize their body in three dimensions and pass-through obstructions. The king put the cape over his garments and rushed from the room. Rumors still circulate that the crazy king runs through the province attempting to escape the eyes, which he believes are chasing him."

Master Ishwa remained quiet and Al thought he had fallen asleep.

Al said, "Sir, my grandfather and the Crystal of Zaraboth?"

"Yes, yes. There we stood in a barren chamber with a door in each wall. We had entered through the east door. I opened the door on the west wall and found the room stripped bare. Master Wizard Beckindorf opened the door on the north wall. That room was empty and painted solid white.

Alpherge the Great opened the door on the south side, and a drift globe attacked."

"A drift globe?"

"Yes, yes. Not important to the tale, banished easily with Alpherge's staff, this staff." Master Ishwa shook the long, wooden object he held. "Your grandfather carved the staff from a branch of a swamp tree and captured the two wizards whose faces are carved into the wood."

Al stared at the staff noticing three extremely realistic faces. The moons at the top matched the moon's positions in the sky. "I see three faces are carved into the staff, sir."

"Ah yes, we'll save the story of the third for another day after your experience in magic is honed.

"The sweet Crystal of Zaraboth shone in the center of the south room. Alpherge approached and extended his hands. Lightning spread from his fingers as he probed the magic surrounding the object and an enormous magical field formed around him. Flashes of blue light bounced from the wizard to the Crystal of Zaraboth and ricocheted off the stone walls and ceilings. The other wizards weren't able to extricate Alpherge from the mysterious magnetic current, and the great wizard burned to ash."

Al was devastated; his grandfather was incinerated by magic? One second alive and then burned to ashes. How horrible.

"We weren't able to penetrate the chamber and his ashes remain with the Crystal of Zaraboth. Someday we'll try again. But we all fear the Mountain King will capture the Crystal."

Master Ishwa added. "Your parents blame me for killing your grandfather, though he would have searched without me. That wizard was a remarkable but headstrong man."

"Is my dad still alive?" Al asked.

"Your father believed it more important that we fight the Mountain King. When the Velidred king became too powerful, we hatched a plan to send you kids to Earth for protection. A difficult debate ensued to persuade your mother into allowing our group to take you. When she saw the devastation, the king inflicted on the planet and the wizards, she consented to protect you and your friends. She begged your father to leave with you, but he refused and died in a battle against the king."

Al felt heartbroken to learn that Dad had remained on Aloheno to resist the mountain king. "What are the chances the Velidred king will retrieve the Crystal of Zaraboth?"

"The Mountain King is weak, which explains why we are training you and your classmates. His magical power is frail, but it prevents possession of the Crystal at this time. But someday, we fear he will take the Crystal to Earth, use it to make Earth a magical planet like Aloheno and become a wizard so powerful no one will stop him. People in the wizarding community believe the Crystal of Zaraboth has potential for immortality."

Al thought having magic on Earth would be cool. "Why can't magic work on Earth?"

"The magnetic fields around the planet prevent magic. Your father, grandfather and I attempted magic on Earth, but the presence of magic is too weak except for petty tricks. But, the Crystal of Zaraboth can alter the magnetic fields.

"I must warn you, even though the mountain king is weak, he is still a formidable force with great magic compared to yours. Don't battle him by yourself without years of study and experience. A triple eclipse of the moons, is coming and if the king can complete the immolation at the precise time, he will regain his powers."

"Immolation? A blood sacrifice to the gods?" Al stopped breathing for a moment and then sprang to his feet. "I must tell Erik. We believe our friend is at the Mountain King's fortress. Will she be the one sacrificed?"

"It's disastrous to stop your training. I came tonight to notify you of your advancement to the next level of training. You will study in Blayze's group. You have remarkable talent, don't be foolish and headstrong…"

Like my grandfather.

CHAPTER 25

Erik stayed awake the rest of the night, letting Sherry sleep. He woke her an hour after the sun rose. "We need to get moving before the resistance finds us. Let's find Al and go hide in the mountains."

Erik and Sherry arrived in the poor village of Kavilly without having eaten all morning. Erik empathized with the people they helped Cugbert feed the previous day. Had it only been a day? They stopped at a shop and watched a group of women walking through the village.

Sherry said, "Half those women are pregnant. Where are they going?"

The storekeeper pointed to an announcement posted on his shop wall.

Erik read aloud,

By Decree of the Velidred King
Celebration of the Triple Eclipse in three days. Pregnant women invited to the magical path of the Pantaleon Moon. Attend the celebration at the Velidred Volcano. Special sacrifice and worship to Velidred King's moratorium lifted for pregnant mothers.

"What does that mean?" Erik asked.

"Why would pregnant women walk to a volcano? These women will give birth any day now. Are they mad?" Sherry asked.

Erik pointed at the traveling women. "This entire world is crazy. Children traveling with the mothers aren't even two years old. Where are the girl's parents or husbands?"

One woman sank to the dirt and wailed.

Sherry rushed to her. "Can I help you?"

The woman screamed again and clutched Sherry's arm.

Sherry called to Erik, "This woman is in labor and needs our help."

The birthing pangs subsided, and the woman panted in long deep breaths.

The woman struggled to stand, and Sherry lifted her to her feet. "Do you want help? Let's walk to one of these…," she motioned her hand toward some dilapidated shacks, "houses, and we can help you deliver your baby."

The pregnant woman pushed Sherry away and staggered down the dirt path. "Leave me alone, I must get to the volcano and the path of the Pantaleon moon.

Erik's jaw dropped. He peered off toward the mountains rising in the distance. "The closest volcano is miles away. She won't make it."

"This is bizarro," Sherry said. "Oh no!"

The woman dropped to the ground screaming, clutching her swollen belly.

"We've gotta help." Sherry moved toward the crumpled woman.

Erik's stomach clinched as he followed Sherry, "Have you delivered a baby? Do they teach you that in Girl Scouts?"

"I was also in the 4H group. We delivered lambs and goats. Babies should be similar, but we can't allow this woman to walk wherever she's going, because she will die." Sherry ran to the fallen woman. She checked her watch. "Contractions are about a minute a-part." Pointing to an emaciated lady sitting next to a cabin, Sherry said. "Ma'am, can we take this mother into your home?"

The woman stared at Sherry and shook her head no.

"Please help, or this mother and baby will die." Sherry said.

A man charged from a nearby shop, confronting Sherry, "Get away; you cannot help her as she must walk alone to the volcano."

"She will die."

"Then she dies." the man said.

Erik shoved the man. *These people are bonkers. Who wouldn't help a woman in labor?* "Move aside, we'll take care of her."

Sherry helped make the woman comfortable.

Erik imagined this was similar to life in the twelfth century or maybe worse. No sanitary operating rooms in this little village. No EMTs would come help this lady. No phones to call an ambulance. No clean hospitals with competent doctors. But he knew women gave birth without clean hospitals long before he had been born.

He was so focused watching Sherry with the pregnant woman, Erik almost didn't notice the three guys brandishing clubs. One took a swing at Erik, missing his head by a fraction. Air whizzed by his ear.

"I told ya to leave the woman." The man swung the club once more at Erik.

Erik fell to the dirt to evade contact. Adrenaline flowed as he grabbed small stones from the road throwing them at his assailants. He jumped up, bracing for an attack.

The man swung the stick at Erik. Erik dodged and then ran and tackled the man, knocking him to the ground. He took the club from the man's hands.

Other men drew near Erik with their weapons swinging.

In the morning stillness, a booming voice resonated, "Peace my brothers. Peace."

"This is no place for you, priest," said one attacker. "Get."

"Lay down your weapons. These youngsters are guests, unaccustomed to our traditions." Cugbert towered over the men. "Let us educate them in our ways."

"Go away, priest. We'll educate them with blows to their heads."

The woman in labor screamed.

Sherry comforted her, "The baby is breached and this woman and the baby will die if we don't help."

"Forget her," the leader of the attackers moved toward Sherry with his weapon. "This is our tradition. Get."

Cugbert ran to plant himself between the attacker and Sherry. Cugbert raised his hands, "Peace my friend."

"Out of my way priest," He swung the club at Cugbert.

Cugbert caught the club, "Lloyd, I will not commit violence against you. Drop your weapon."

Erik's breaths came thick and heavy. He swung the stolen club, preventing the other two men from approaching Sherry. "Don't make me hurt you."

Sherry yelled, "I got the legs. He's coming out."

Erik glanced at Sherry and grimaced. Sherry held two tiny legs. He switched back to his assailants who hadn't moved.

A newborn baby cried.

"Wrong, it's a beautiful baby girl."

The leader of the attackers shouldered the weapon and retreated from Cugbert. "This is wrong, priest. This is not our custom."

"It's finished, peace my friend."

Sherry stayed with the mother until she delivered the afterbirth and became stable.

Erik asked Cugbert, "What's happening here? Are these people insane?"

"A thousand years of acquired superstition. No one can help a woman traveling to the path of the new moon to secure magical powers for her baby. Either she makes it, has the baby by herself or she dies. Without Sherry, this infant and mother would have died a long, painful death." Cugbert wrapped the tiny baby in a portion of his robe and held the infant in his arms. "This woman is fortunate you were here to help, but she may have problems when she goes home because she didn't deliver herself."

Erik felt tension in his rib cage. *Bad movies aren't this cruel.* "Is there something we can do?"

Cugbert said, "I will help persuade the mother to go home with the child. She has experienced shame and is humiliated and confused. She is young and doesn't know what to do with the newborn after your support."

Three pregnant women and four youngsters passed Erik, "Will these mothers experience the same fate?"

"Yes. Many will not survive; plus, hazards at the volcano will heighten the danger. It's an arduous task for the moms, but children born with magic will experience a more favorable future. The king lifted the taboo on these moon-blessed births for a reason which doesn't bode well for the mothers and their babies."

CHAPTER 26

Al studied under Blayze, learning the Blinding Spell known to Al as the Reflecting Spell. He partnered with Veer, a tiny Kallurian girl with long, straight, black hair. She was two years younger than Al, but more accomplished as a wizard.

Blayze instructed, "Concentrate on transferring power and light to the object you're using for reflection. Imagine you have a magnifying glass and you stick it between your light source, in this case the sun, and the object. This will focus the beam into one spot and reflect it at your foe."

Veer started, concentrating for a moment, and then light bounced off the tin pie pan lying on the roof and shone on the rooftop wall. Veer's attempt was not powerful enough to cause damage, plus the tin pan was dulled to prevent eye damage to other students.

"Not bad, Veer, but imagine a thicker more focused magnifying glass next time. Al, you try."

Al, excited to be in the older group because the pupils were nearer his age, still felt like a giant compared to his Kallurian peers.

Blayze rubbed his hand through his reddish-blonde hair and repeated his instruction, "Picture a large magnifying glass."

Al thought of a large six-inch refracting telescope. Not quite the equivalent of a magnifying glass, but he liked the concept. He struggled to focus the sunlight through the imaginary tube, then guided it toward the tin pan.

Nothing happened, and no reflection occurred. Then he spotted smoke rising from the pie pan.

Blayze yelled. "Al stop. Hold. Quit the spell."

Al stopped. "The pan isn't reflecting my light."

Blayze said, "No, it's absorbing energy because you created the focus so tight you've heated the tin past its melting point." Blayze picked up the pie pan showing an elongated hole in the center where melted tin had flowed before cooling. "Try to shine light into an enemy's eyes, don't melt the object."

Al raised his arms above his head like he scored a basketball three pointer because he melted a metal object with magic. How cool is that? "That's good though, isn't it? I can just magnify the light at my attacker." Wow, he thought, the melting point of tin had to be over four hundred degrees Fahrenheit. Awesome. *This is better than a laser.*

"You don't always wish to kill your attacker; sometimes you need to capture him. Blind him first and then capture, don't fry him for dinner. Or maybe you're seeking to signal your comrades, so learn control. Magic doesn't have to be full strength, next time, use lower magnification."

Blayze put a wet blanket on Al's enthusiasm as the teacher continued to correct Al more than any other apprentice. Sometimes the tasks didn't work the way they were intended. It brought back memories Al had of trying to play basketball in gym class. Classmates expected him to play better than others because of his height, but his coordination took holidays in a crowd of students.

Veer took another shot at the pie pan with the melted hole in the center. She increased her magnification, and light bounced from the metal object to shine faintly on the wall.

On his next attempt, Al imagined the family magnifying glass at home. He'd last used it to ignite tissue on fire in the backyard. With less risk of melting the pan, he concentrated the sunlight through the imagined glass. He aimed it at the pan, but light reached the pan without reflection. Too diffused. Al tightened the focus through the lens and produced a faint shine on the wall.

"Great Al," Blayze patted Al's shoulder.

Al, not satisfied, narrowed the focus. In his mind's eye, the beam focused a little more, then he gathered the light in a single beam toward the tin pan. Light flashed off the pan and a steady glow shone on the rooftop wall like a flashlight with fresh batteries.

Veer and Blayze slapped Al on the back.

Al said, "High five," elevating his hand above his head. The others did nothing. "You're gonna leave me hanging?"

"Okay, excellent progress for both of you, but remember, it's easy in the practice field. During the heat of battle, it evolves into a different experience. Learn to focus fast, then change your position and focus again. Then move into the shelter. Fire and move, attack and shelter." Blayze turned his attention to sounds by the rooftop door. "Do it another ten times each, as you must become proficient during battles."

A student ran through the doorway to the roof top practice ground. Breathing hard and heavy, he said, "The Mountain King's … wizard warriors … are marching toward us."

Blayze barked commands to the students on the flat rooftop, arranging students into battle swarms. He sent Al, Veer and three others to the west side of the building deputizing Veer as the team lead.

Is this a training exercise like a fire drill at school?

They reached their position, Veer said, "Al, provide a shield for the five of us. We will attack from the rooftop."

"A shield?" Al said. "I burned a hole in tin and you want me to shield?"

"You've been in magic class three days, now protect us."

Excitement coursed through Al's body with this opportunity to use real magic for more than practice. He attempted the shield, but the excitement of events and other students distracted him.

"Al, on my command create a shield adequate to cover and protect the team."

He struggled to calm his excitement and nervousness so he could form a shield. *Relax. Create the bubble.*

"I see the enemy marching toward the training school with wizard warriors in front. Al shield us." Veer signaled the other team members to prepare to attack.

The bubble grew in Al's mind, becoming larger and cohesive, then the bubble burst into soapy liquid, coating the five students.

"What are you doing? Give us shelter!" Veer shook her head and crossed her arms, while other students pulled at clothing or wiped soap off their faces.

A lightning bolt fired by the ground troops tore through a section of the rooftop wall near Al as the explosion threw debris across the rooftop.

Sweat beaded on Al's brow in the crisp, morning air. He drew a deep breath, exhaled and centered his mind. *Relax.* One more deep breath and he created the bubble, enlarged the size, and the shield formed.

A fire bolt struck the shield near Veer seconds after Al completed its creation. The bolt bounced off the shield.

Blayze yelled from the center of the roof. "In rotation, fire on them."

One by one, the pupils exited the sanctuary of the shield, selected a target, launched their shot and retreated to the shelter's protection.

The key, Al remembered from the classroom, is to fire in rotation. A student that kept firing without breaks between shots wearied faster and might risk burning out his magic, requiring months of rehabilitation.

Debris flew from the roof wall as the mountain king's forces fired bolts of lightning. The debris bounced off Al's shield, but the school building was suffering damage which exposed his classmates when they tried to exit the shelter to strike.

One student in the swarm stepped from the shield, and an intense flash erupted where she stood. When the smoke cleared, only her shoes remained on the spot.

Al smelled burning flesh and felt nauseated. He vomited on the rooftop, and the shield wavered.

Veer shouted, "Hold the shield, or we'll all die like Sasha. Hold the shield."

Sweat poured off Al as the attackers bombarded the defense with fire bolts. Focus, focus, focus he thought and closed his eyes to expel the vanquished girl from his mind. *Relax.* The shield strengthened.

The bombardment of the young wizards continued for an hour, and Al breathed hard, but the mental concentration required to maintain the shield this long was exhausting him. A headache pounded in his forehead.

Attacking wizards forced the apprentices from the crumbling wall. Other swarms, once strong with five students, were weakened with two or three surviving students.

"Gather to the middle of the roof. Hurry—" Blayze yelled while gesturing his swarm to follow him to the center.

Veer gave hand signals to retreat. "Hold the shield."

Blayze brought the swarms together and rearranged teams into groups of five, mixing younger pupils with older, advanced wizarding students. The students struggled to combat the older, experienced wizards, and the swarms of student wizards was finally reduced to eight. Students lay on the roof top, dead, dying or missing limbs. Gopal joined Al's swarm, and Veer led her team back to the edge of the rooftop.

Reaching the edge of the roof, Al noticed attackers gathering on the roof of the building across the alley from the school. Al and his swarm were sitting ducks for the attackers. The rapid-fire from the older attacking warrior wizards was too much for the school's wizards. The students under his protection weren't able to exit the shield to take a shot. The assault never let up, pounding the shield with multiple explosions. Al said, "Veer, we have to move, I can't continue holding this defense."

Veer raised her arms, signaling to fall back, and the swarm retreated to the rooftop door or at least what remained of it.

Veer's unit joined Blayze's swarm as he barked a command, "Retreat into the building, and try to battle through the windows."

The group descended the stairs and were met by students escaping hostilities below who were ascending the staircase.

One student said, "The attackers occupy the first two floors. Master Ishwa is holding them off and commanded us to come here."

Veer returned her swarm to the roof and stationed the group in position on the rooftop.

Al ached to release the shield, but knew his classmates would die. How long could he hold? He asked Gopal. "Can you create a shield for a minute? I need rest."

Gopal concentrated for a moment and the shield formed over Veer, Al and the other students.

Al relaxed his shield and rested on the rooftop. Exhaustion poured over him. Other students sat. *Is this how it will end? I won't be able to say goodbye to Sherry or Erik.* Gopal's grave expression and grim twist to his mouth betrayed his haggard and drained body. *What about my experiment with the tin pie pan? Can I do that against the king's wizards?* He targeted the building next door where the mountain king's troops gathered.

Al imagined the telescope again and stood squinting at the wooden building across the alley. Fifty or more trained wizards on the rooftop threw lightning bolts at the smaller group of students. He felt furious and exasperated by watching adult wizards attacking children, so he exited the group shield and formed a shield covering himself.

He concentrated on the telescope with the source of light behind him.

Three explosions pounded his shield.

The protection held. He imagined sunlight streaming through the telescope tube and pointed at a spot he believed might be a load bearing point on the opposite building wall.

A blinding flash exploded five feet in front of him and the rooftop swayed as chunks of timber fell to the floor below, and a hole formed in the rooftop.

He dropped the shield and discharged his magnified sunlight. A laser beam flickered, formed and shot toward the building target point.

Blasts from the attackers exploded near the unprotected Al.

Seconds slowed to milliseconds as the blue laser proceeded on its journey toward the assaulting forces. Al's eyes narrowed with intense focus as he willed the laser faster.

A fireball from the other building was moving toward Al, and he calculated it would strike him at the same time the laser reached its destination. He needed to form his shield before the fireball struck and disintegrated him. But the laser had to reach the target before he shielded or the laser would fail.

Al felt a craving to escape, his brain pounding like ten drummers hammering on his head and he peered back at Gopal. The young boy hollered at Al, but he heard nothing over the deafening throbbing of the blood in his temples.

Three seconds until the fireball strikes the wizard from Earth and my life as a wizard will end. Al's shoulder slumped and his jaw trembled, but he held the laser steady at the target.

Two seconds, the blue shaft of light was aimed true, but the clock in his mind kept ticking. Numbness enveloped Al, and he thought of Sherry Berry and wished to embrace her once more.

The oncoming fireball grew in size.

With one second remaining, the building occupied by the attackers erupted in fire and crumpled where the laser struck.

Al's vision filled with the fireball aimed toward his head and he closed his eyes as it exploded inches from his face. Light exploded through his closed eyelids.

Al opened his eyes, and in a daze, watched the building across the alley buckle and burn.

Gopal had established a shield in front of Al in the nick of time.

Distracted enough by the shifting structure and fire on the rooftop, the enemy warrior wizards stopped attacking. Wizarding students cheered for a moment and began firing lightning bolts.

Al pumped his fist with jubilation as adrenaline pumped through his body. This was like playing video games at home. He retreated to the safety of the group and recovered enough strength to form the shield to take over for the tiring Gopal.

The building supporting the attacking wizards collapsed. Wizards held onto whatever they could grab. The Mountain King's warrior wizards jumped off the roof as an explosion sounded, and the building tumbled into itself silencing the screams of dying wizards.

Master Ishwa came through the rooftop doorway. "Come together everyone." He waited for them to assemble around him. "We're outnumbered and their force is stronger, we will surrender."

The students groaned.

"We can't surrender."

"No."

"Not now. We must fight."

Ishwa said, "No. Rest. Relax." Come to the center of the rooftop and sit. "Your classmates." He pointed to the lifeless, dying or injured students on the rooftop.

They ceased firing and moved to a safe spot where Ishwa pointed.

Ishwa stood, clutching his staff in front of the tired, gasping students and waited.

A young man, his head covered by a hoodie approached through the splintered door frame. Long black hair hung around his face.

Ishwa relaxed, hands by his side, in an attitude of surrender.

Is this an opportunity to surprise the attackers?

The young man called out, "Master Ishwa, I condemn you to death for treason to the Mountain King." The young wizard raised his hands.

Al sat astonished, his eyes bulging. The wizard was about to attack Master Ishwa. Al yelled and jumped up, "Master Ishwa watch out."

With a wicked grin, the young man discharged a lightning bolt at Ishwa.

"No!" Al rushed toward Ishwa who made no effort to shield. Master Ishwa crumpled to the rooftop.

The young wizard moved his arms and turned toward Al.

Al quickly produced a shield just in time to bounce the fiery bolt away from his body.

An officer from the attackers walked onto the rooftop. "Kestrel. What did you do? They were surrendering."

Kestrel's malicious grin returned.

Al imagined the laser telescope and prepared to send a bolt at the attacker.

Five more wizards poured through the door to the rooftop.

Al felt numb and his limbs heavy. *What chance do I have against six attackers and probably more behind them?*

He dropped his plan to shoot the laser. He contemplated the other students and how they might be in jeopardy if he attacked. Color drained from his face as he hunched over in grief and fatigue and collapsed next to Master Ishwa's dead body.

CHAPTER 27

Erik stood next to Cugbert who cooed at the newborn baby. They walked with the child's mother toward the village of Crossroads.

Cugbert asked, "What are your plans?"

Sherry held the mother's hand. "We decided to go home and are traveling back to Crossroads to find our friend, Al. Then we'll hide in the mountains until it's safe to go home.

"That's a bold course of action. Don't you have a friend at the castle, what about her?"

Erik curled his fingers into fists, gripping them tight, as options tumbled over and over in his mind. He ached to rescue Lily, but understood he had to do everything possible to protect Al and Sherry. Would Al choose to stay here now that he was learning magic?

"We'll let the adults solve that problem. That spiritualist lady, Forest River Blossom, told us Al is in danger of death if we remain on this planet."

Cugbert laughed a loud rumbling, resounding laugh. "Forest River Blossom told you these things? Is she always right? No. Not by a long shot. If she tells one hundred people something dreadful will happen to them and misfortune falls on five, then people believe this woman can tell the future. Hogwash."

Erik and Sherry exchanged glances. Erik said, "You believe Al will be safe if we continue to the castle?"

"I'm not a fortune teller, but at the Velidred Castle, Lily's life is in jeopardy. The Mountain King can't be happy that you and your friends have escaped his grasp for so long."

Erik rubbed the back of his neck. "We shouldn't be here. We're mixed up in a crazy, political conflict that has spawned a war, and I want out."

"Okay," Cugbert sounded disappointed.

The baby cried a woeful noise, and Cugbert handed the infant back to her mother.

They reached the village of Crossroads in mid-afternoon. The town was quieter than when they had been there before. Smoke billowed in the distance.

"Do you remember how to get to the wizard school?" Sherry asked.

"I can get us close. I hope those thugs aren't around; we don't need another run in with them. Do you recall the name of the old guy at the school?"

"Master Ishwa."

"You've met Master Ishwa?" Cugbert asked.

"Yes, he's teaching our friend magic."

"A good man, past his prime these days, but the school teaches good wizards. Let me take you."

Five minutes later they reached the right location, only to find destruction everywhere with the wizard school in flames.

Sherry said, "What happened? Where's Al?"

Erik staggered backwards at the scene, speechless. Two buildings that had been standing yesterday were heaps of rubble. People hauled bodies from the collapsed buildings, most of them unmoving and caked with dried blood. The stench of burning flesh and death hung in the air.

Sherry grabbed Erik's arm. "Is Al okay? You don't think he's...."

"No, don't say it. Maybe he's injured. We'll find him." Erik thought, there was no way Al could have survived this disaster. What caused such total destruction, an earthquake or gas leak? Is natural gas flowing into these buildings? "Don't worry. I'll ask around, stay away from the buildings."

Sherry said, "I'm coming with you," and hurried toward the burning building.

Erik followed. "No, Sherry, don't go in there."

The entry door, blown off its hinges, rested on the ground. Flames licked the window frames and door way. Sherry stepped into the burning foyer, covering her hair with a forearm.

Erik tried to grab her but missed. "Don't go in there."

She moved toward the flames, shrieking, "Al!" But the intense heat forced her back.

Sherry ran toward forms of people who had been laid on the ground, their bodies covered with cloths. She pulled up sheet after sheet, searching for her friend. The figures, blackened from the fire, had missing limbs. All were dead.

Erik watched as Sherry uncovered corpses, and she cried at the sight. Then he noticed a cloth covering a thin, long body. Something about the way the sheet lay over the body concerned Erik.

Sherry must have noticed the figure, longer than the others, shrouded with the cloth. She ran, picked up the sheet then collapsed on the rubble-strewn ground and burst into tears.

Erik caught up, glancing at the corpse next to Sherry. The light-skinned body, scarred, burned in numerous places and headless, forced Erik to catch his breath, and any remaining strength left his muscles. He dropped on weakened legs next to Sherry. "I'm sorry."

She wept in his arms, inhaled a deep sob and pounded his rib cage with her fists. "You killed him. You murdered my best friend."

Erik sat paralyzed. Al was dead. Why hadn't they stayed on Earth? He comforted Sherry.

They sat hugging each other, the passing time forgotten, Sherry's eyes red and swollen. Erik stared at the dirt. "It's my fault."

Sherry said nothing.

"Can you ever forgive me?"

Sherry stared expressionless at the burning school.

Erik's nose dripped, and a lump filled his throat. *Why didn't I listen when my friends ordered me to leave this planet? Poor Sherry. We're children and shouldn't be facing this kind of danger.*

"We need to take the body home." Sherry said.

"What's his mother going to say?" *What could I say to Mrs. Greystone?*

The teens shuffled to a man caring for injured students.

Erik pointed at the destruction and carnage and asked, "What happened?"

The man bandaged a young woman's injuries. Her leg had a nasty gash from her knee to her ankle. "Go away, tomorrow we'll talk."

Erik felt blood pounding in his ears, "No, now. What happened?" He pulled the man's shoulders to force him to face Erik.

"A battle — the mountain king's warrior wizards attacked the school." The man wiped a bloodied rag across his forehead leaving a crimson smear.

"Are there still students in the building?"

"No, the ones not injured or killed were captured and taken to the Velidred Castle."

"How many captured?"

"We don't know. We hid when the fireballs started flying between the buildings. You take shelter when wizards throw fireballs."

The young woman with the ailing leg spoke. "I'm Jayanti. Your friend is the lanky boy, right?"

Sherry responded, "Yes, Al was his name."

"If not for Al we would all be dead, the warrior wizards trapped us from the building next door. Al shielded us longer than I've ever witnessed anyone maintain a shield. Then he fired a peculiar beam of light, not the usual fire bolt we're taught. The shaft of light blasted the building the enemy was using, shattering the structure to rubble."

Erik clenched his eyes tight and pulled Sherry to him, "He died helping the other wizards."

Jayanti's eyes opened wide, and she shook her head. "Al isn't dead. After a warrior wizard, named Kestrel, killed Master Ishwa, Al and the others surrendered and are being marched to the Velidred Castle. They left four hours ago."

Sherry wobbled in Erik's arms. He pressed her close, relief flooding through his body. "Al is okay! He's still alive."

CHAPTER 28

Erik patted Sherry's forehead with a rag soaked in lukewarm water. "Are you okay? It's been a stressful couple of days. Just relax."

Sherry's pale face made her red hair appear as a halo. She moaned, "Al is being taken to the castle of an evil wizard who doesn't like us and wants us dead. What are we going to do?" She drew her knees to her chest and hugged them while rocking in a gentle rhythm.

Erik didn't know what to do. He placed his arm around Sherry's shoulder, and she leaned into his chest.

Erik said, "I'm continuing to the castle. Now more than ever I'm mad, and I'm rescuing my friends."

"What can you do? These people are wizards with great power, we're simple people from Earth. Are you a wizard?"

"We can't let our friends die. Are they being tortured? Kestrel won't get away with hurting my friends because I will devise a plan to defeat him."

"Does the drinking water on this world make everybody crazy? We have no chance against these people. Al blew up a building, and even so, he's captured." Sherry crossed her arms over her breast, shook her head and glared at Erik with an expression of disbelief.

Erik stared at the ground. "I've been making horrible decisions, yes, but we have to rescue them."

"Al will hang, end up beheaded or receive some other fourteenth-century punishment. Who knows what the king will do with us if we're captured? Why go forward, do you wish to die too?"

"I can make a difference. Go back to Earth if you like, but I'm traveling to the castle and rescuing my friends." Erik rose and brushed dirt off his jeans.

Sherry climbed to her feet. "I'm going with you, because I can't allow my Al to rot in a torture chamber. Plus, you haven't got a chance to manage this without me."

They traveled for several miles on the roadway to the castle. By mid-afternoon, they passed more pregnant women with young children walking in the same direction.

Young men and women, attired in crimson robes with black trim, sang, danced and beat drums as they traveled. The group danced around Sherry as she trudged ahead of Erik.

One young fellow, with light skin and a dark, black mustache, said to Sherry, "Cheer up, a great festival is at the volcano. Come, dance and sing."

"No, I'm not interested in dancing and singing." Sherry pursed her lips.

The young man grabbed Sherry's arm and whirled her in a circle. "Come with us, be free and dance."

Sherry glared at the man.

Singing, red-clad women encircled the young man and Sherry, with drummers forming behind the circle beating a rhythm that invited one to dance.

Moving with the music, the young man waved his arms back and forth. He gripped one of Sherry's hands and forced it into rhythm with the music. He swayed back and forth holding her hand.

Sherry's body loosened and began to sway slightly.

The mustached young man urged her with a smile.

He put Sherry's hand on his shoulder and placed his palms on her hips, helping Sherry feel the beat.

Sherry licked her lips, and a slight smile broke across her face.

A spin move by the young man and a quick swirl to Sherry's hips and her hearty laugh filled the air.

"Travel with us to the festival, the biggest celebration in our lifetime." He danced with Sherry to the beat of the drums.

Sherry was still smiling but said, "I can't, because I'm searching for a friend."

"He's perhaps on his way to the celebration, we can meet him at the volcano."

"No, I'm positive he's not going to the celebration." Sherry emphasized the last word and released the young man's hands. She broke through the circle and returned to Erik's side.

The merry group proceeded down the road.

Erik shook his head in disbelief. "These people are crazy. They're walking with pregnant mothers who will die because of the journey. Plus, they're traveling to the volcano to watch a human sacrifice and yet celebrating and partying."

Sherry said, "Remember, we're in a different culture here. We're insulated in our little community in Montana. But, I agree, they're bonkers." She laughed.

"While you were dancing, I noticed two men from the resistance are following us."

"How can you tell with the number of people on this route?" Sherry stopped, twisted and scanned the crowd, "Hundreds of people are ahead and behind us."

"I recognize these guys from the inn where we escaped. They're the ones from the resistance who lingered at the edge of the forest when the stegox came after us."

"Are you sure? There's nobody I recognize back there."

Erik felt disheartened, Sherry was no longer being vigilant and now he had detected pursuers from the resistance.

They ducked behind nearby trees and shrubs by the road. Studying the passersby for fifteen minutes, no members of the resistance walked nearby. The stream of party goers seemed entirely comprised of young people and pregnant women.

Sherry said, "Is that them?" She pointed to two guys carrying bows with quivers of arrows over their shoulders. "They saw us hide behind these trees and stopped moving when we stopped."

"Should we give them the slip by taking the trail behind us that leads into the woods? We can sneak onto the trail and try to escape."

"Can you run? Isn't your leg still hurting?"

Erik trudged along the path today because of his swollen ankle. They had to avoid these guys if they wanted to reach the castle in time. The festivities, celebrations and crowds of people traveling to the volcano meant the sacrifice could happen any day. "Getting captured by the resistance and taken to Prince Krunal will prevent any rescue. Let's run."

Erik ran fast, the ankle pain intense enough to make his teeth hurt at every other step. He had trouble keeping pace with Sherry. The path twisted back and forth through the woods and up the mountain with large pine trees hiding their passage. His ankle throbbed with each step on rocks and tree roots on the irregular path.

For thirty minutes they ran and at last reached an outcrop on a broad exposed rock. They paused.

Sherry panted, "I have to stop… and catch my… breath."

Erik said. "Maybe we fooled them."

"It'll be temporary, they know we never came out of the trees." Sherry sat on a large rock.

Over the edge, four-hundred feet above the road, they saw thousands of pilgrims traveling to the volcano. Many people were dressed in red hues. "This is like football fans traveling to a game." He peered into the distance then signaled to Sherry. "Come here!"

Erik pointed to a black castle on the horizon.

"Is that Velidred castle?" Sherry asked.

Erik thrilled at the sight. They were close. "I guess so, but we still have five to ten miles to walk, and those look like rain clouds heading our way."

A branch cracked behind them.

"Run!" He pushed Sherry up the trail. Erik's ankle tightened, and the initial push off that foot caused terrible agony. He faltered, hopping on his good leg for three steps hoping he'd caused no further damage.

Arrows rained around Erik and one swooshed by with a thwack as it embedded in a tree.

A hollowness formed in his rib cage, the rescue now leaning toward hopelessness, ruin and doom. Erik confirmed two members of the resistance stood one-hundred yards away shooting the arrows.

An arrow unleashed from a bow, and Erik picked up the whirling sound of the arrow traveling two hundred miles an hour. Then he spied the arrow and struggled to turn, but he was too slow. The arrow pierced below his collarbone close to his left shoulder, forcing him to falter.

Erik swallowed hard at the intense pain. Blood oozed through the hole in his jacket, dripping along the arrow and down the jacket front. Adrenaline kicked in, and Erik ran. Now, he felt no pain in his ankle because of the panic racing through his brain. Death be swift, he thought, as warm liquid saturated his shirt. Running became problematic with the arrow stabbing through his shoulder. It hurt every time he pumped that arm.

He lost track of time, just pounding his legs against the irregular trail, advancing up the mountain. Then the first snowflake fell. Followed by more.

Erik stopped Sherry and scanned the landscape. "We'll be easy to track if it keeps snowing, we must hide right now." The mountain sloped up above them with the path being the single safe means to navigate through the dense, conifer forest. He peered over the side of the mountain at a blue spruce twenty feet below the trail. The tree grew on a flat patch of rock jutting fifteen feet away from the mountain.

"We can jump onto that tree and slide to the ground and hide."

Sherry stared at Erik with an incredulous expression. "Are you demented? If we miss the tree, we plunge hundreds of feet to our deaths. How will we climb back to the trail?"

"Go Sherry."

She studied him and the arrow protruding from his jacket. "You've got an arrow sticking through your body. We need to surrender and get you medical help."

Erik pushed her hard toward the tree.

Sherry tried to seize his arm, missed, drifted sideways, slipped over the edge and landed on her back and side on the tree. Its limbs bent downward from her speed.

He watched as if in slow motion. The tree trunk bent to the point of breaking, but sprang back as Sherry rolled to the ground with a big umph.

Erik glanced behind, then jumped to the tree, aiming as low in the branches as possible without landing on his ankle. The arrow in his shoulder snagged a branch and flesh tore as he tumbled down the tree. He bit his lip in agony and fell to his back on the rugged outcrop.

Sherry grabbed Erik's legs and dragged him to the side of the ridge where they were hidden from anyone above.

Darkness settled around Erik as sharp pain raged in his shoulder and blood soaked his jacket. He moaned.

Sherry said, "Quiet."

CHAPTER 29

Al, one of thirty-three young prisoners marching along the road to the Velidred Castle, wanted to sit, rest and eat. The captives hadn't received food or water since morning and had marched miles across valleys and plains. *Doesn't this planet and nation have rules and regulations for prisoners of war? They can't just let us die of starvation and thirst, can they?*

Gopal walked beside him. "Are we gonna die?"

"I don't know," Al whispered. "We might be valuable to the king; maybe he will re-purpose us."

"What does that mean?" Gopal stopped shuffling.

"Keep moving." Al tugged on the chain joining them. "It means nothing." Al's anger showed. *What could he tell the younger child? Yes, they would die a slow, excruciating death at the hands of an enemy.*

They trudged in silence. Al shuffled his feet along the dusty road trying not to stumble. Falling meant beatings and whippings, but the leg irons made maintaining balance difficult. His normal big steps with his typical long stride were impossible while chained to the smaller wizard. They rounded a bend in the road snaking through the dense pine forest.

Gopal said, "There is the black castle."

The Velidred Castle, home of the Mountain King, became visible. Visiting the castle at any other time might be a fascinating experience, but today Al felt weak from marching non-stop for over fifteen hours. He stopped walking a moment to view the impressive fortress. The town wall rose twenty-five feet, constructed with black stone. Al supposed the castle's color came from volcanic rock. Guard towers on the corners and around the entry gate deterred attackers. The castle rose behind the rampart.

One soldier guiding the captives stepped up to Al. "Beautiful, isn't it?"

Al nodded in agreement.

The guard whipped Al across the shoulders with the bull whip. "You aren't here to sightsee; keep marching."

The captives trudged another half-hour before reaching the fortress gate.

A voice yelled from one of the guard towers. "Lower the drawbridge."

The prisoners stopped while the drawbridge slowly descended toward them. Then the line of captives picked their tired legs from the ground as lashes rained across backs and shoulders. Al peeked over the edge to view the moat. Fifteen feet below, three immense reptiles floated under the bridge. A wooden gate blocked the prisoners from advancing.

A voice above yelled, "Raise the portcullis."

The wooden lattice grill lifted.

Kestrel led the captives through the city as townspeople stopped their routine tasks to cheer while banging pots and pans. Kestrel raised his hands in triumph, holding Ishwa's staff with two hands above his head. Horns blared victory from the castle walls.

Another horn bugled within the castle keep. Al felt pounding in his ears and closed his secured hands into fists. Kestrel reminded Al of the high school football players strutting around the field after a victory. "I'm gonna get you someday Kestrel," Al said. "You'll pay for killing Master Ishwa, and I'm getting my grandfather's staff from you."

# # # #

Zita, wearing an emerald, brocaded silk gown, relaxed in her chamber at Velidred castle, as a handmaid brushed Zita's hair.

Horns blared, trumpeting the victory of a conquering warrior campaign.

She rose and dashed downstairs to observe the returning war party.

Warrior wizards arrived, herding into the castle over thirty prisoners, including the tall, lanky boy, Al. Kestrel led the warrior wizards and paraded into the castle brandishing a wizard staff.

Zita stood before Kestrel and folded her palms over her heart. "You won."

"Won and slew the blind master wizard, Ishwa. Pathetic decrepit man." He raised the staff. "I have Ishwa's staff."

Zita approached Kestrel to offer a celebratory hug. "Congratulations."

Kestrel pushed Zita aside and walked pass.

Coldness pooled in Zita's abdomen as she sought answers for Kestrel's behavior. "How dare you shove me? I'm princess of Velidred Castle."

Kestrel ignored Zita, approached Lily and bowed. She wore a sky-blue cotehardie composed of velvet and silk, with yellow stars ringing the hem. Kestrel took her hand and kissed her wrist.

Zita's vision blurred as she stiffened her jaw. *What? Was I gone from the castle so long that this relationship could form?*

The king approached Kestrel and congratulated the young warrior wizard. Kestrel strutted like a peacock.

Zita mumbled, "I'm going to fix that little bimbo. Kestrel is mine."

The king waved to Zita. "Come, praise the conquering hero who crushed the Kallurians forever."

She crossed her arms beneath her bosom. "Yes, your majesty, based on knowledge I gave him concerning Master Ishwa's location."

"Is that one of the youngsters you were to follow?" The king pointed to the lanky boy while peering straight into his daughter's eyes.

Numb, she stammered, "Well yes, that's one of them."

"And the others? Kestrel tells me two more walk near the castle. Did you send them home?" The king lowered his voice to a paternal tone.

Zita couldn't lie to the king who always correctly interpreted her facial expressions and recognized her lies. "I left them in a village on the other side of Crossroads."

"Isn't that the territory where our spies last saw Prince Krunal and the resistance?" The king raised his voice. "You dropped the teens the prophecies predict will kill me in the domain of the resistance?"

"Yes, your majesty." Her stomach turned, she slouched and studied the floor. *How did this transpire? It's that witch's fault and her friends. That bimbo must die.*

"Go. This celebration is for people who follow my commands." King Haskell pointed to the stairs.

Zita's cheeks blazed. How dare Father embarrass me? She scowled at Kestrel and ascended the stairs, aching to deliver a curse on the foreign girl, but that might make Father angrier. *I need a plot to upset the troublemaker. How dare she steal Kestrel from me?*

# # # #

Al and the other prisoners proceeded to the castle. Inside, Al saw Zita approach Kestrel who pushed Zita away. *Why is Zita dressed like a princess? Didn't she tell us she's a handmaid?*

Al watched Kestrel continue walking toward a blond-haired woman, with flawless skin, attired like a princess. *Is that Lily?* He struggled to shout at her, "Lily, its Al. Lily, Lily." His parched voice croaked a little above a whisper.

Three guards beat Al with canes and he crumpled to the ground. "Silence!"

By the time Al struggled to his feet, Kestrel, Zita and Lily had disappeared. A short heavy man with a crimson cape and a crown approached the prisoners. He ambled around the young wizards and drew near Al.

"I recognize Alpherge the Great's grandson by his stature and prominent nose." The short man's beard, long, thin and white, moved up and down when he talked.

"Let me go," Al said.

The whips hit Al, but he maintained his stance. He set his jaw and studied the mountain king. Al ignored the pain radiating through his back and shoulders.

"I will not let you go. I have a special treatment planned for you and your friends. The blond one will travel to Velidred Volcano for the eclipse of the triple moons celebration and be sacrificed to make me a god. And after the eclipse, there will be another ceremony where you and your remaining friends are beheaded. You'll experience the same death as your father." The small king turned and strode to the castle interior. "Throw them into the dungeon."

Fatigue and despair hit Al across his shoulders and legs. He was unable to focus. *This is it. No return to Earth and no college. No magic. Pitched in the dungeon until we're beheaded. Sherry Berry where are you? Did Erik take you home? Please Erik, take Sherry home. Save her.*

Al and the prisoners shuffled down granite block stairs in single file. They ended in a gloomy basement space with sacks of supplies in the chamber. Al didn't see prison cells or holding rooms like he recalled from movies.

Four soldiers guarded the room and two opened a trapdoor in the floor. They snatched one wizard prisoner from the line, unshackled her, and thrust her into the hole.

A thump sounded as the wizard landed and people below said, "Quick, get her."

In rapid succession, the soldiers tossed the wizard prisoners into the dungeon. Al was left for last. His shoulders slumped, and he displayed no expression. He didn't care what they did because he knew he'd never see his friends again.

Two guards whipped his back and said, "Move to the pit."

Al moved, and the guards pitched him through the narrow opening, his back scraped the edges as he dropped. He landed on a soft pad which prevented a painful landing. People in the dungeon manhandled him off the stack of dirty, ragged clothing they had piled beneath the opening.

Then the trapdoor closed above, and darkness shrouded the prisoners. The only light entered from a tiny opening tunneled through the wall.

"The door is sealed, that's the last." A deep male voice spoke in the darkness.

# # # #

Entering her bed chamber, Zita removed her shoes and hurled them against the wall. She plucked the hair brush from the dressing table and heaved it at the door. Seizing her face cream jar, she aimed at the window, but halted. "Face cream. I can produce something with face ointment."

Zita smiled and touched her gold pendant and delivered an incantation, "Face so pleasant, cute as a dimple, apply this cream and you have pimples." She could manage worse, but Dad would yell and place her in more trouble.

She ordered the handmaid, "Doris come here."

A short Kallurian woman stepped into the chamber and bowed. "Yes, my lady?"

"A gift to the castle's guest, Lily." She passed the ointment jar to the servant.

"Excellent my princess, when should I present it?"

"Go now. If she has another jar of face cream, replace it with this. Mine is superior, and our honored guest deserves the best."

The handmaid bowed to leave.

"Wait. When you finish with the cream, put my shoes away and find my hairbrush."

"Yes, my lady."

"Scoot." Zita flicked her fingers as if shooing a fly.

CHAPTER 30

The snow swirled around Erik and Sherry. They listened for the pursuing resistance men. Would the goons pass or discover and massacre the teens?

Pain coursed through Erik's shoulder as he thought about why he forced them off the trail. Were they going to die here, pecked by birds and gnawed by forest animals?

Sherry placed her finger over her lips, "Quiet, I hear them above the ridge."

A high, whiney voice said, "Maybe they're on that ledge."

A rich, deep voice said, "No way they down there. How they get there? Where's the rope? Did they fly or jump twenty feet to the ledge?"

"Keep following the path?"

"Of course. The arrow landed, and we'll follow the trail of blood and find that young fella dead in the next quarter mile."

The voices became muffled as the men proceeded up the trail.

Erik said, "Now what? Will I die here."

"You won't die, because I'm gonna remove the arrow from your shoulder as soon as those goons move out of range."

"Are you serious?" Erik shook his head and lifted a single eyebrow, "Girl Scouts or 4H teach you how to remove arrows?"

She grinned. "I can pull it out, I watched an old black-and-white TV western once where they pulled an arrow from a guy's gut. Bet I can do it."

Erik struggled to turn, but the injury produced excruciating pain.

After waiting several minutes Sherry took a deep, slow breath. "Okay, the arrow didn't hit any major arteries or organs or you'd bled to death by now. It might have gone through your scapula. Once I remove the arrow, we have nothing to sanitize or cauterize the wound. Can't light a fire; even lighting an end of a stick might reveal our location."

She found a stick on the ground. "Clamp your teeth on this. That should muffle any screams."

"Oh terrific." Erik's body stiffened, anticipating the pain.

"I have to break the arrow first and pull the shaft through the back. It will be worse pulling through your shoulder the other way."

He ran a hand through his messy wet hair. "What if I bleed to death?"

"That's what you deserve for getting us in this mess. In fact, if you don't die, I may murder you."

Sherry gripped the arrow shaft near Erik's shoulder with both hands, and struggled to break it.

Erik moaned in pain.

"Be quiet and keep still." She applied more pressure and attempted to snap the arrow shaft again.

The agony was worse the second time, and Erik moaned. He pulled the stick from his mouth. "Just kill me. That will be less painful."

"Let me try something else." She retrieved two rocks from the ledge.

Erik muttered, "Great idea, knock me out first, so I won't scream."

"Put the stick back in your mouth, this will work." Placing the larger rock on the ground, she rotated Erik to his side so the arrow shaft lay on the rock. "Okay here goes." Sherry raised the other rock, forcefully smashing the shaft.

The pain, as the shaft moved in his muscle, almost caused Erik to faint. He let out one long, slow, deep gasp and peered at the split arrow shaft.

Sherry still had to complete the break, bending the shaft back and forth several times until a sharp snap sounded and the feathered part of the arrow came loose.

Erik wiped sweat off his brow. "Hope that's the painful part."

"This will hurt more. Remove your coat and shirt, so I can examine the damage." She pulled the zipper down on his jacket.

"Are you mad, I'll freeze to death?"

"Stop being a big baby." Sherry helped him remove the jacket and shirt.

Seeing the amount of blood soaked into his shirt, Erik emptied his stomach.

"Now onto your chest and put the broken shaft on the rock. You need to force the arrow through your shoulder. The arrowhead is stone, chipped into a point, but not enough of the arrowhead is showing to grasp. And there's sticky, slick blood everywhere. I don't think I can hold onto it."

"Nope, no can do, I will walk to the castle like this. No problem."

Sherry gave Erik an expression that his mother used to make when she wanted him do tasks at home. *Do they teach all women that look?*

He shifted onto his pink belly, the ground ice cold on his exposed skin. Gritting his teeth and rising like doing a pushup, Erik positioned the arrow shaft over the rock. He dropped his arms to the ground, but the arrow didn't move.

Sherry watched and said, "Okay try again. Put the stick back in your mouth. Now position the shaft over the rock and nod your head when you're ready."

Erik followed her orders and nodded his head. Sherry placed one foot on his shoulder blade, inches from the arrowhead, and stepped down hard. The shaft moved, and Erik muffled a scream.

"Be still a moment." Sherry grabbed the exposed arrowhead and yanked.

He felt the arrow shaft slide inch by inch through the shoulder muscle.

"I got it." She flung the arrow over the side of the cliff.

Erik's body shivered in the frigid weather as snow began to fall harder with larger flakes. The wind blew stronger. "Now what? Can I put on my shirt and coat? I'm freezing."

"Not yet, I want to stop the bleeding." Sherry pressed the shirt over the exposed hole in Erik's shoulder. "Leave your shirt and jacket off a few minutes, the cold will slow down the blood loss and help it clot."

He wrapped his chest with his arms. "Hey, how about putting the salve the old man gave us on the injury?"

"Let's try, you're gonna die without it."

"What's the plan to get off the ledge? Did you bring bed sheets?" She walked to the edge. "It's a steep drop to the bottom."

Erik rolled back and forth trying to find a comfortable position to rest while sprawled on his coat. The sheer rock face rose above him and they couldn't see the trail at the top. "There must be hand grips to use to climb to the path." He gritted his teeth and shivered as snow accumulated on his bare chest.

"Wait until the thugs return and they head back down the path. We don't want to reach the trail at the exact time they come back." Sherry said.

"I don't know. Can't I put on my shirt?"

"You need to think through situations and not act on impulse. Let me examine the wound." She poked around the injury. "Not bad. Roll over, let's inspect your back."

His whole body stiffened in the raw, icy wind and snow, making it arduous and painful to move. He rolled over to his belly which helped warm up his chest, but blood caked on his back dried ice-cold in the biting winter blast.

"It looks like the blood is clotting, you might be okay."

"Is it safe to put the magic bacon cream on the injury?"

She applied the cream on the arrow holes and saw immediate blood clotting.

Sherry walked to the edge of the cliff.

Erik fell in and out of consciousness as he lay in the snow. At one point he heard voices, but he wasn't sure if they were dream inspired or real. Then he bolted upright. *The resistance, they're here. Where's Sherry?* She stood looking out over the edge. *Didn't she hear the guys?*

Erik's breathing accelerated.

CHAPTER 31

Erik grabbed a pebble and tossed it at Sherry. The object missed, instead sailing off the mountain past her right ear. On the second try the pebble bounced once on the ground and rolled off the ledge.

Erik's heart galloped despite the bitter cold. *Come on Sherry, turn around.*

The next pitch flew too high, traveling over her head.

Erik wanted to stand and throw the stone, but he was so cold he couldn't move fast enough. He felt frozen to the ground.

On the fourth toss, the stone struck Sherry's neck below the left ear.

Sherry rubbed her neck and glared at Erik. Then the blood drained from Sherry's face.

Sherry lifted a foot to run toward the wall.

Erik noticed the snow accumulating between him and Sherry, a half-inch deep on the ground. He panicked and used hand motions to signal. "Stop. Hide behind the tree."

Sherry froze, not moving toward Erik or toward the tree.

Erik willed her to action. *Move, move, move. Go, go, go, go, go.*

She looked at Erik, then the tree.

Erik pointed at the tree and mouthed the words, "Go."

Then she stirred and disappeared beneath the spruce. Snow shook from the branches above helping to cover her.

"Hey, see that?"

A deep voice answered, "What?"

"I don't know." The whiney voice said. "Something moving on the ledge."

"Yeah, it looks like tracks in the snow. Is there an animal on the ledge?"

"Hard to tell—footprints, but are they human or animal? Throw a rock at the tree to scare the critter out from hiding."

The two men tossed large rocks at the tree, but Sherry didn't move. More snow from the spruce fell over Sherry covering her. The men stopped the assault and Erik heard the sound of someone striking steel together.

"This blizzard isn't letting up," said the deeper voice, "let's get back to a village and warm up before getting trapped up here."

The smell of tobacco smoke drifted with the snow.

The whiney voice said, "I'm gonna shoot arrows into the tree. I know something moved. Who knows, maybe we roast rabbit for supper tonight."

Erik shook and shivered, not knowing if from cold, anger or fear. Do we surrender or will the spruce slow the arrows before hitting her?

Erik held his breath to keep from making noise.

An arrow loosed from above hurtled and crashed through the tree then flew past the ledge.

"You won't kill anything shooting like that. You're horrible with a bow and arrow." A cigarette flew into the snow a short distance from Erik.

The next arrow came in low, hit the other side of the spruce from Sherry and rolled limb by limb till it caught on branches two feet above the ground. Another arrow sped through the tree and off the ledge.

"You're no better."

"Watch, I'll make that rabbit run."

The arrow slashed through the tree, ricocheting off branches, slashing and tearing through pine needles and landed on Sherry. She didn't move a muscle.

Erik felt the boom of his pulse pounding in his ears. The arrow stood on end, its point resting on or in Sherry's body. Erik's jaw clenched; it required every scrap of muscle control he could muster to keep from rushing to her.

"Ah, there's nothing there. If arrows didn't scare the varmint out of hiding nothing will. Let's go. Stop wasting arrows; I'm getting cold and need ale."

Erik waited, a nerve-wracking experience, for a proper amount of time before moving to check on his friend. *What if it's a trick, and the guys have pretended to leave? Is Sherry bleeding out while I'm waiting instead of helping?*

Erik didn't know how long he waited, it felt like an hour. His patience ran out. If the men still watched, then surrender would be the remaining option.

Moving to the tree as fast as possible given the pain in his ankle and shoulder and his chilled muscles, he studied his friend. Sherry lay like an angel, the arrow sticking through her back near her arm. "I'm so sorry, Sherry."

Sherry moved and slithered from under the spruce. The arrow poking through her back.

Erik searched for blood where the arrow had penetrated the jacket.

Sherry struggled to grab it with her free arm.

Erik said, "Let me remove the arrow. Are you in pain?"

"No."

"Raise your arm." The arrow poked through the front of Sherry's coat. He giggled. "It passed between your arm and back. The arrow is caught in your jacket."

Erik struggled to speak, eyes tearing as he pulled the arrow from Sherry's jacket.

Sherry poked her finger through the holes and grinned. "We gotta get off this ledge, we're gonna freeze."

Awareness of the cold rushed upon Erik. Blood was caked on his chest. His bloodstained shirt, frozen, inflexible and stiff, creaked as he forced it over his head, but the jacket was less frozen and provided warmth.

"What's your plan, big guy, to get us off this ledge?" Sherry shook her head.

Plan? He had no plan. The plan was to keep from being killed. "There're a few handholds. I'll boost you up on my shoulders."

Sherry snorted and placed her hands on her hips, "You're gonna help me? You can't stand, and you have one useful arm. How will you scale the wall?"

They needed to climb twenty feet or more to the trail. There were hand holds and places to secure your feet. But what were Erik's chances in his condition? Slim. "You go first. We should be able to climb this wall."

"No, you go first. I'm not climbing up then coming back down to help you. Look at you."

Erik rocked back and forth and rubbed his eyes; his legs were tired and unstable. "No, you first. I'll make it." He pushed Sherry toward the embankment. "Go."

Sherry didn't move when Erik pushed. She stood her ground, took a deep breath and exhaled.

"Hurry, Sherry. The snow is still falling, and it will be harder to find hand and foot holds the deeper it gets." Why did she have to be stubborn this way? "Please climb before it gets slippery."

She said nothing, and glared at Erik.

"Okay, okay. I'm freezing. I'll lead." Erik shuffled to the wall, found a satisfactory place for his foot, established his healthy hand in a crack in the granite wall and climbed like a sloth up the crag. He planted his injured foot on a tiny protuberance and winced at the pain shooting up his limb. The hurt shoulder and arm were useless. He found it impossible to lift the damaged arm above his chest, so he used it to bolster his weight until he could spot the next proper foot and hand holds.

Six feet from reaching the path, Erik placed his good foot on an oval rock protruding from the wall. He placed the foot in a favorable position and pushed off. The rock popped out of its position and Erik slid down the cliff face to within a few feet of Sherry.

Snow, rocks and ice fell on Sherry's head.

Sherry yelled, "Hey, stop that. Don't knock me off, I'm climbing."

Erik interrupted his fall with his wounded arm, agony flooding his senses. Searching for another foot hold, the first blows of doubt struck him hard in the stomach. How horrible would it be to settle on this ledge forever? They could build a fire to keep warm, and then in the morning after resting they could scale the wall.

Sherry struggled up next to Erik. She drew a deep lungful of air, her face rosy red from the effort of the climb. "Keep moving. Don't stop. Another ten feet and we'll be there."

"Yeah, keep going. I'm resting for a moment." His face, scratched during the fall, dripped fresh blood.

Sherry poked a hand in Erik's face. "Look at these fingernails. I've been growing them long and manicuring them for homecoming and now, oh, I want to shriek."

Erik stared at the ragged fingernails with edges like an animal chewed them. He snickered, which grew to a full belly laugh. *Here we are in the midst of nowhere, near death, and Sherry's worried about her nails?*

"You're laughing at me?"

Sherry climbed.

Erik didn't move. He was immobile, stuck, trapped, and wedged to the wall. He closed his eyes and hugged the wall with his body, wanting only the release of letting go and tumbling to the ledge. He had no strength to descend carefully. Just slide and fall asleep. So tired and cold.

Sherry yelled, "Come on. Snap out of it. I've made it. Do I need to come and get you?"

Numbness, like a sweet cocoon, held him in place. He wanted a nap, and he closed his eyes.

A pebble hit his head. "Hey, stop that."

"Move. You can't stay there. I'll keep throwing rocks until you move."

Erik grunted. "Okay." The wall above became a white blur in the falling, blowing snow. *Why can't I concentrate? Focus. I can accomplish this. No. I can't. I've failed. Lily will perish. Al is already dead. Sherry will die. I should just collapse, tumble off the wall and plunge over the edge of the mountain.*

A larger rock struck his head. "Earth to Erik. Are you climbing?"

He peered up. Sherry's red hair was billowing in the wind over the rim. Stinging sleet bit into the lacerations on his face.

CHAPTER 32

rik thought of his friends. *I'm supposed to protect these people. What am I doing? Come on, focus on finding toe holds and hand grips and climb.*

"Come on, move." Erik yelled to motivate himself, pounded the wall with his fist and then climbed.

When he reached the spot where he slipped, the displaced rock opened a nice foothold. With one powerful push off his good foot, he reached Sherry's out-stretched hands.

There was no celebration, no happy dance and no joy in reaching the trail. Sherry was panting hard from the effort of helping Erik. He lay in the snow with his eyes closed. His body demanded sleep, but he wanted to eat a juicy hamburger even more.

"Which way?" Sherry asked.

"We can't walk down the mountain. The resistance guys might be waiting at the bottom. But we can't linger here either, the snow is getting deeper."

"The trail will be unreadable in another hour. Does this take us farther up the mountain or run back to the road?" Sherry asked.

"We gotta walk up the trail. Let's go for an hour. It's growing dark. We'll find a cave or somewhere to sleep and follow the trail in the morning."

\#\#\#\#

The next day dawned brisk but sunny. The teens spent the night in a cave other people had obviously used. Sherry built a fire and they were able to warm themselves. Erik tossed and twisted all night, unable to find a position on the rough ground that didn't irritate his injuries. They woke with the morning sun.

For two hours they trudged upwards. The ascent was continuous but not impossibly steep. When the trail leveled and they entered a spindly pine forest, Erik said, "We're almost above the tree line. Look through that break in these twisted trees. We must be at least a thousand feet higher than where we camped."

They arrived at an outcrop devoid of trees, and the lowland widened into the distance. "The black castle is closer than what we saw yesterday." Erik pointed to the black castle. "We've covered a few miles."

"Have to get off this mountain first." Sherry tried to shake clumps of snow from her feet. "These are the wrong shoes to wear for trekking in the snow."

"I'm hungry and cold," he said. "There must be a village below with food and hot fires."

"We can't wait another hour or two to get to the village, we need nourishment now," Sherry said.

Erik taunted. "I know. Is there a McDonald's or a coffee shop nearby? We'll stop for food when we find it."

"Don't get irritable with me, or I'll leave you here to die." Sherry pounded down the path with enough determination that Erik almost believed she might leave him.

Erik limped along, making faces at her back. The trail, now steeply descending and rugged, caused him to stumble on a tree root and crash hard in the snow. A shock of pain coursed through his injured shoulder.

Behind his eyes a pounding pulsed in his skull. Erik struggled to get up. He wanted to chase Sherry and give her a piece of his mind, instead he stomped down the path in silence.

Sherry stopped upon reaching a level space where the snow lay only an inch deep. "Animal tracks, on Earth I'd say rabbits. We need food or we'll die of hypothermia."

Erik's brain, foggy from fatigue, hunger and loss of blood refused to function. His head pounded out an irregular beat like different drummers each performing a unique rhythm. "Okay, whatever."

They tracked the animal. The footprints showed two animals came together and then separated. Sherry followed one set.

Erik had trouble thinking. *Is something wrong? What am I supposed to be doing? Oh, find something to eat, follow the second set of tracks.* The sunshine warmed his frosty face. He paused, glanced at the sun, and a slight popping noise sounded to his left. *Oh yes, the animal. Follow the animal.* He found the set of tracks and proceeded along the narrow path.

Disfigured pine trees and deciduous shrubs with fresh shoots surrounded him. A pleasant scent like citrus wafted on the slight breeze and the fragrance drew him. The animal tracks headed in the same direction. A tree, only fifteen feet ahead, bore fruit, and he jumped for joy. That's what we need, fruit. The tree had no leaves, but big blue fruits, the size of softballs, with spines surrounding the exterior, dangled from the bare branches. He shouted, "Sherry!" Nothing but a croak came from his mouth.

The animal tracks headed to the tree and Erik caught a peculiar smell near the tree. It reminded him of the stench of dead ground squirrels which sometimes got trapped in his family's garage in the autumn. Something didn't appear normal, but he could not escape the maze in his befuddled mind. Fruit lay on the ground. Sunlight sparkled on the fruit, and a little squirrel-like creature stalked the giant spiny blue berry.

"Go away little squirrel, that's mine." Erik mumbled, but the squirrel didn't appear frightened of Erik. A quiet psst sound, like air escaping from a bike tire, emanated from the berry. The sun glistening on the fruit fascinated Erik as he stared at little droplets of water from snow-melt reflecting and refracting the sunlight.

Sherry's voice rang clear in the peaceful morning. "Erik where are you?"

"Over here," he squawked.

The squirrel reached the fruit first, and Erik moaned, "No, no that's mine, get away." Leaning forward to scare off the little rodent, he observed the sunlight on the berry. Now he became aware of other fruit on the ground, opened, exposing seeds and red flesh, and his brain registered danger.

Sherry yelled, "Erik get away; it's going to explode."

Too late. The sizzling stopped, and the fruit exploded over his face and neck. The squirrel jumped in the air, crashed to the ground and squirmed in agony.

One needle punctured Erik above his eyebrow. Three spines embedded in his cheek, and many barbs found his neck. Intense, hot pain shot through his face and shoulders. He swung toward Sherry's voice.

"Be careful, Erik; there's more fruit close to you." She didn't approach.

His face swelled rapidly. His eye was nearly shut and he had trouble keeping Sherry in focus. His throat numbed, and as he lurched toward his friend, more fruit exploded. Staggering into Sherry, they tumbled to the snow.

Erik's brain registered this as the end. He struggled to say something, but his brain searched in vain for words that made sense. His swollen face and throat wouldn't cooperate to say the few words he could find. The left side of his face was numb and his hands fumbled as he tried to loosen the collars on his coat and shirt. Breathing became difficult. He was light-headed, dull and groggy.

Sherry was speaking gibberish. He only heard a loud ringing in his ears. Someone pulled needles from his neck and face and piled cold snow onto his swollen face.

He attempted to rise, but hands forced his body to the ground. His brain reached the edge of hysteria. *Is this how it all ends?* His feet quivered, convulsed as if electrified. Then someone sat on his legs, but was it a daydream or real? Erik brought an arm toward his face and viewed three hands attached to his wrist.

The sunlight burned through red hair, and a three eyed woman studied him. He closed his eyes and drifted into darkness.

CHAPTER 33

Erik woke to the smell of brewing coffee, burning wood and the stink of unwashed clothing. He struggled to open his eyes, but one was swollen shut and the other was a slit. Someone touched his hand.

Sherry whispered, "How are you doing?" She squeezed his hand tight.

"Horrible." He mumbled.

"Don't say anything, just listen. We're in a home near the Velidred castle."

Erik attempted to rise. "Gotta go to castle."

"Be quiet and listen. I noticed the same flag here that hung at the resistance headquarters. Shut up if you want to live."

Sherry squeezed his hand until it hurt. He sought to loosen her clutch, but pain coursed through his shoulder when he moved.

Blurry movement behind Sherry caught his eye, and a stranger's voice said, "Is the boy awake? Good, means he might live."

Erik wasn't so sure he wanted to live. He had a monster headache and numb face. What had Sherry said?

A tall thin man wearing a stained leather apron sat on the bed next to Erik. "Young man, tell me what happened to your shoulder?"

"Men chas—."

Sherry interrupted, "Like I mentioned, a hunting accident, a friend shot him with an arrow."

"Not asking you little missy." The man scowled at Erik.

Concentrating on the question demanded focus, but his mind raced to recall what happened. *A hunting accident? Which friend of mine has a bow and arrow?* "What's the question?" He recognized his voice, which sounded slurred and echoed in the room.

The man softened his voice. "You're groggy from the poison in ruptured scatter fruit. A young fella your age should be wise enough to stay clear of scatter fruit in spring sunshine. Lucky to be alive."

What hurt more, his shoulder, pulsing ankle, or pounding headache? "Is this the hospital?" Felt like a hospital, but the thatch ceiling and wood cabin walls, seemed circa seventeen-hundred. The room smelled weird. Must be a clinic.

"You kids talk strange." The man touched and pressed the swollen skin over Erik's eye, causing him to flinch. "Had a friend poisoned by exploding scatter fruits, took a month for the swelling to recede. Where you from?"

Erik sat silent, not remembering. Words floated at the tip of his tongue and poof, gone.

The man pushed the swollen eye again.

"Stop, it hurts."

"Oh, I'm intrigued by the swelling. Lucky this little missy found me on the trail this morning, saved your life. Least you can do is answer questions."

"What did you do to me?" Erik attempted to focus on the man with two heads. "What trail? Who is little missy? Who are you?"

Sherry said, "He's talking about me. My name is Sherry, sir. Not Missy."

"Aren't you a bold little wench? A little past marrying age; must make you angry."

"I'm irritated because my friend needs rest. We have someplace to be."

"Where do you need to go, little missy? You mentioned that, but you aren't forthcoming with information. Why you hiding and from whom? I would expect you to be on the road to the volcano with the other young people going to the celebration not wandering in the mountains, hungry and cold."

"Go to castle." Erik felt elated to string together a sentence.

Sherry shook her head, waved a hand at him and placed a finger to her lips.

"Gotta run to the castle, do ya? Friends with the king?" The man faced Erik, planted a bear-paw sized grip on his injured shoulder and squeezed. "I don't like the king."

"Ouch, Lily's there."

"Who's that, your sweetheart, bride, a princess, friends with the king? I'd rather you boil in Velidred volcano than help you visit the king."

"Volcano? What volcano?"

"Sir, he's delirious with fever and doesn't know what he's saying. Let him rest. When he recovers, he'll answer your questions." Sherry pleaded. "Don't you have any fever medicine?"

"Might give him something, but don't like liars. Why you lying, little missy?"

Erik tried to sit but collapsed back in the bed. "Tell the nice man, little missy." *Who is Missy and why is she lying?*

"Erik snap out of it." Sherry sat and offered him a sip of brown water. "Sir he's sick. Please give him medicine, and then I will tell you the truth about everything."

A tear leaked from Erik's good eye, "Sherry, tell little missy to tell the truth. I need help."

"We're here, you're gonna be okay."

The man stood, "I'll go get something."

"Where's Al? Are we at the castle? Why is my face numb?" He struggled to recall what happened to his shoulder. *Head hurts. Focus.* "Will I lose my sight?"

"You gotta get better. We're losing time." Sherry helped him sit and gave him more of the brown liquid. "Drink, you've lost a lot of blood and have poison in your system from the exploding fruit."

Erik panicked, "Where's Al? I lost him on the mountain. Shot with an arrow and fell off the ledge, didn't he?"

"Relax. Al wasn't with us."

"Can't think straight."

"Right, which is why you need to shut your mouth." Sherry whispered.

With each degree of lucidity, Erik suffered a flutter of confusion. "Where are we? Can we go home? I can't drive. Can you drive?"

"Yes, I will drive, just be quiet."

The man returned with liquid medicine in a brown bottle with no pharmaceutical label. "This will help him sleep. It restored my son when he was sick. Before he died."

Erik blurted, "I don't want to die."

"You won't die," Sherry said. "The medicine will reduce the fever. You'll be able to concentrate if we reduce the fever."

"Yes, medication."

The man poured a reddish liquid from the bottle into a wooden spoon. He shoved the spoon into Erik's mouth. "That should help, young fellow."

Erik hoped the chaos cleared soon.

The man questioned Sherry, "So the truth, what are you two strangers doing in Velidred?"

Sherry said, "We aren't from this planet...."

Erik trailed off to sleep.

CHAPTER 34

Zita walked down the stairs in an elegant light blue ball gown. Her heart fluttered in anticipation of the largest party she'd ever seen at the castle. Astronomers stated the triple solar eclipse occurs once every hundred years, and the king planned a celebration at the castle before leaving for the volcano the next day. The musicians, fiddles, drums, flutes and tambourines played as she descended.

Local dignitaries crowded the floor wanting to schmooze with the king. She made nice with the old men and women as she strolled through the bright candlelit chamber, the hundred-candle crystal chandeliers polished to perfection.

Zita found Kestrel in the corner chatting with three older warrior wizards. "Kestrel, you look nice this evening." She curtsied as he bowed. Her body tingled with anticipation. What would Kestrel think when he saw Lily? The cream Zita created would turn her into a hideous monster.

"Did you make nicey-nice with the king yesterday?" Zita spoke in a flirting voice to her former boyfriend.

Kestrel expanded his chest. "The king told me to be proud of the conquest of the resistance wizards." He beamed at his buddies. "The king will promote me to general tonight, making me the youngest general in the kingdom." He pointed to a medal on his gold tunic. "For bravery and service to the king."

Zita opened her mouth to say she led Kestrel to the resistance hideout. But instead said, "You're so intelligent and powerful and will make a great general." *Where's Lily? I can't wait to watch the expression on Kestrel's face when he discovers the transformation.* She peered around the room imagining the girl's entrance.

Many young guests twirled on the ballroom floor in an intricate dance that Zita had never mastered. She delighted in a younger crowd at the party instead of traditional castle parties where old widowers harassed her to become their bride.

The music finished and a trumpet sounded. The official announcer boomed. "With extreme pleasure, the King Haskell announces his honored guests."

Zita watched as the local dignitaries and surrounding kingdom's royalty were introduced.

A woman with shoulder-length black hair, wearing a full-length navy dress appeared at the entrance, escorted by a tall, gray-haired man with a trimmed beard.

"Presenting King Estevan and Queen Valeria of the province of Acadia."

Ha, Kestrel's parents. Won't they be surprised when Kestrel introduces ugly, pockmarked Lily to them as his girlfriend?

Zita zoned out the announcements as she thought of Kestrel's reaction.

When it became time for the king's introduction, Zita quit daydreaming and listened in rapt attention. The girl had to be coming next. *Will she even show at all? Too embarrassed and maybe won't make an appearance at the celebration? Oh my, won't that be a shame?*

The king walked into the chamber. Standing beside him with a hand over the king's arm, Lily was dressed in a flowing gown of white satin and lace.

"The king presents special escort, the lady Lily Goodwin, princess of Thyattica province."

The king patted the girl's arm and strolled into the room. Zita focused her attention on Kestrel to revel in his expression when he noticed the young woman's ugliness. Zita's servant had rubbed the cream on Lily's perfect skin, and horrible pimples had manifested on the attendant's hands.

Kestrel nudged a male colleague. "That's the girl who has pledged forever love to me."

Zita pressed a palm against her breast, a tightness in her throat making it difficult to inhale. Lily and Kestrel have pledged forever love? Knowledge of how ugly Lily must be kept Zita from choking, instead she bounced with giddiness.

Kestrel waved.

Zita almost squealed with pleasure, wetting her lips. The music ebbed higher and flowed in a pleasurable rhythm, and she sashayed side to side with the beat.

Lily approached the group and Kestrel took her hand; with an affectionate touch he bowed and kissed her palm.

The moment had come. Zita examined the young lady, did a double take, stuttered and stammered. "Your skin is unblemished."

"I know. Right? Woke up with a million pimples all over my body. Didn't want to attend the celebration. The woman that cares for me suggested I visit Priest Varesh. He examined me, said an incantation, and 'poof' the pimples disappeared with no scars. Isn't it incredible?"

Zita squelched her first instinct to howl and rush from the chamber. But instead, she forced herself to be calm and find alternative ways to win this battle. Kestrel fawned over Lily for a while, and then Zita said to him, "Can I talk with you alone?"

Kestrel, acting like quite the gentleman tonight, said, "Pardon me, Lady Lily."

When they were alone, Zita whispered, "You realize Lady Lily will be sacrificed to the Velidred volcano? Does she know? Should I tell her?"

"Might not happen. We wanted Lily to bring the teens to this side of the cave. It was the best way to lure them to Aloheno. We don't have to sacrifice her, but if we do then that eliminates the youngest member of the Goodwin royal line. That's something the king has wanted for years." Kestrel grinned. "The Goodwin castle is then yours. Isn't that what you want?"

She said nothing.

I've discussed this with the king and have requested Lily's hand in marriage."

It felt like Kestrel punched her in the gut. "No way. What happened to us? Weren't we vowed to each other since my tenth birthday?"

"The king believes he found another young lady to sacrifice, a certain red head."

"The red head has been captured?"

"Not yet, but reports suggest they're in the village. The king ordered a house-to-house search for those kids you didn't send home. You should have sought my aid and you wouldn't be in trouble. If they don't find the red head, we'll sacrifice you."

"You're a dreadful person and I'm gonna murder you," Zita said through gritted teeth while rubbing her gold chain and pendant. A little pain for Kestrel right now would be appropriate. The incantation to fracture his leg formed in her mind. What would Dad say if she caused a scene? Instead, she walked away.

She steamed inside, but no tears tonight. Dad can sacrifice Kestrel and Lily; he'll do anything for me. Walking straight to her father, the king, and using her finest formality, curtsied and said, "Your Majesty."

The king scowled, placed hands on his hips and glanced at the ceiling. "What do you want Zita?"

"Can we have a private conversation?"

"Of course, my child. Please excuse us, Mr. Mayor, Lady Jane, and Lady Ava." They bowed and curtsied, and the king nodded.

Zita and her father walked to a secluded corner, "What's so urgent to interrupt my evening?"

"Dad." she whined.

"What did I tell you child? Not in public." He held her chin.

"Your Majesty, I spoke out of place."

"That's better."

"It's Kestrel. He's bothering me." Zita pointed at the young general.

"You're wasting time over Kestrel flirting with a new girlfriend? Do I have to send you to your room for the rest of the evening? It's a wonderful celebration. Dance, mingle with the guests, or retire to bed."

"But the sacrifice. Won't Lily be sacrificed?"

"Go. Now. No more discussion."

Her shoulders slumped. *It's true then, Kestrel will marry the stunning blonde and I will . . . what get assigned to the kitchen to scrub dishes?* Zita wandered across the dance floor bouncing off young men and women who were twisting and twirling with their partners. Immune to the music as the dancers laughed and pointed, she felt numb.

A servant woman pulled Zita from the dance floor and sat her in a chair along the wall. "Champagne, my lady?"

"Yes, yes. Bring me something." Cold and lightheaded, she rubbed her arms. The room, dancers and chandeliers spun out of control.

CHAPTER 35

Two dances later, drunk on two glasses of Champagne, Zita hurried up the stairs, hatching a plan to steal the staff of Ishwa to irritate Kestrel. The celebration would end soon and the guests would retire for the evening in anticipation of tomorrow's events. Reaching the top of the stairs, she veered right toward Kestrel's living quarters. She stalked toward the door to his room, moving with hurried but quiet steps.

Her heart thumped faster, and she felt the adrenaline pulse through her body. Touching the latch made her wonder if Kestrel had booby-trapped his room, putting her in danger? No guards stood in the hallway. She placed a hand on the door latch, examined the corridor once more, lifted the latch and stepped into the room. The light from blazing torches in the corridor disappeared when she closed the door, forcing her to stand in darkness until her eyes readjusted.

Every inch of her body focused on finding the staff. After each step she paused and listened for voices from the hallway. *Is it possible to light a candle, or is there a trap?*

Zita had never entered Kestrel's room before today. Shadows of a wardrobe and a bed loomed in the dark apartment, but there were few places to hide if Kestrel opened the door. The window was a narrow slit in the stone wall, only large enough to shoot arrows at attacking forces. She recalled as a child being able to fit into the slits and terrifying her mother.

Light from the Anticletus moon trickled in through a window slit. Biting her lip, she thought where Kestrel might place an object as large as a staff? In the corner of the apartment, the clothes cabinet, or under the bed? She urged herself to move faster to the first corner of the room nearest the door.

She found no staff in the first corner.

A prickling of her scalp, hairs on her arms rose, and a tingling wiggled down her back. Someone was watching. *Relax, it's just imagination and nerves. Keep searching.* The second corner of the room contained a pile of clothes.

Remorse, shame and eagerness to leave flowed through her body. *No, don't listen. Those are just nerves. Keep looking. Find the staff.*

Nothing was in the third corner and she reached the clothes cabinet. A minor tug on one door and it screeched as it opened.

She blinked and peered around the apartment. Did anyone hear? Then she stuck her hand in the wardrobe searching for the staff. Shoes lay on the bottom shelf, jackets hung from the rack, a wizard's robe, but no staff. *How much time have I spent here? A lighted candle might be my downfall. I must search in darkness.*

A groan emanated from the bed.

Then silence filled the room.

Who is on the bed? Zita didn't move for risk of being detected. She needed light, but light would also reveal her presence to the person on the bed.

Time stretched. *Must act, I won't leave the room without the staff because Kestrel must pay.* She crossed to the last corner, but the corner contained nothing. *That means the staff is under the bed; where else would that jerk put it?* Zita dropped to her hands and knees and crawled to the bed. Could the person or creature in the bed see her? The act of stealing the staff would be counterproductive if someone saw her and told Kestrel.

Under the bed the shadows deepened, but nothing except light showed from the other side. Nothing stopped the light, meaning nothing lay under the bed. *Does Kestrel know an invisibility spell? Everyone stores things under their beds.*

She moved her hand back and forth beneath the bed but discovered no staff. Kestrel must have handed the staff to the king. Disappointment and anger swept through her at being bested by Kestrel again.

A groan again from the top of the bed.

This whole evening is dreadful, the pimple fiasco, Kestrel's nuptials, and now this total muddle. Without caring, she stood next to the bed.

The groan grew louder and more insistent, as if the person were having a bad dream or just waking.

Reaching her hand to the bed she found no body, just a long wooden staff. The staff was moaning. Zita placed a hand on the wood.

"Is that you master?" the staff asked.

Zita whispered, "No, a colleague. I'm rescuing you."

The voice, deep and loud, said, "You're female. I cannot be wielded by a female."

She blew out two deep breaths. "Quiet. Can you be silent?"

"Master Kestrel will be angry if you remove me from his apartment. Should I notify him you wish to move me?"

Her heart throbbed. "Be calm and quiet my friend, and I will take you to Kestrel. Silence is needed for immense danger is near if you make noises."

"Take me to Master Kestrel."

Zita opened the door and peered into the corridor. Nobody wandered in the hallway, but she had to pass the stairs. Anybody there would notice her with the staff. She shifted it so the broader part of her gown hid some of the rod. She hoped to cross the head of the stairs unseen. She couldn't conceal the long staff completely, but she had no other choice.

"Don't like being upside down, too uncomfortable," the staff said.

"Be silent." Zita gritted her teeth and scurried through the corridor but paused before reaching the stairs. She needed to reach her own apartment.

"Master Kestrel is near and should be notified."

Zita closed her eyes and drew a deep breath. *This isn't working because this staff talks too much.* She peeked over the railing. Nobody stood on the stairs, and she rushed past, brushing her hair with a hand, hoping to look natural, sauntering down the corridor.

"You aren't taking me to my master. Master is down the stairs and I must apprise him of my movements."

She sweated profusely as she ran toward her room. "No, don't report to your master."

As she entered her apartment, the staff of Ishwa said, "I have informed my master of my new location and Master Kestrel comes."

CHAPTER 36

Zita's mouth felt parched. Kestrel would be in the apartment in moments, furious if she held the staff. She was no match for his magical ability in a firefight. Where to hide the staff and keep it from Kestrel's hands? Kestrel could detect it under the bed or in the clothes cabinet.

She peered around the room, searching for an answer. On the dressing table lay her little golden chest, a magical device linked with a storage trunk on a secondary plane. But was there time to retrieve the storage trunk, hide the staff and obscure the large chest? Time was short and she had no alternatives.

She snatched the golden chest. A brief stroke of her necklace and pendant, a short incantation and she felt the enchanted trunk move from the secondary plane where it resided. No rushing this step as it required calmness. She drew deep breaths to relax the nervous energy flooding her body.

A four-foot by three-foot trunk covered in jewels and gold appeared on the floor next to Zita bouncing twice upon landing. The length of the staff didn't matter as the large chest had extraordinary abilities to hold objects longer or broader than normal capacity. But first she had to unlock the magical lock on the trunk. This was a tedious task even when she was relaxed. Zita murmured the first incantation to unlock the chest.

Kestrel banged on the bolted door. "Zita, give me the staff."

Zita jumped at the commotion. Regaining focus, she spoke the second chant.

The staff cried out, "Master, I'm here."

One more chant and the chest would open, Zita concentrated using deep breaths.

Kestrel banged on the door. "Staff come."

She said the three words, and flung open the trunk lid. But magic was still required to fit the oversized staff into the chest.

The staff vibrated out of control in her hands, shaking, slithering, slipping and shifting toward the door. "Save me, Master Kestrel."

She shoved hard on the staff, pushing it into the box. "Get in the trunk." She pounded the lid to a closed position.

The staff bounced off the lid from inside the chest with a loud hammering, trying to ascend to Kestrel's magical commands.

Zita's mind grew paralyzed with anxiety and needed relaxation and concentration to deliver the gilded chest back to the astral plane. No time for relaxing; three deep breaths then transfer the object.

Kestrel banged on the door. "This door blows up in three seconds. One."

Magical words tumbled from Zita's lips as she gripped the little music box in her left fist and stroked the trunk.

"Two."

The jeweled trunk shook on the room floor.

"Faster, please faster." Whispered Zita.

"Three." Kestrel banged on the door.

The trunk disappeared in a cloud of smoke.

The door exploded off its hinges and Kestrel stepped in, demanding, "Where's the staff of Ishwa?"

Zita put the music box on the dressing table, pressing hands to her abdomen as tension released from her body.

Kestrel raced to her and grasped her shoulder. "The staff is in this apartment. Give it back now."

"Whatever are you talking about, my love? I'm preparing for bed and it's scandalous to be alone with me this time of night. Would your fiancé and the king approve?

Did you come for a good night kiss?" With seductive puckered lips she made a kissing sound.

He stumbled backward. "No, my staff, I won it in battle. It's mine."

She brushed hair from her face and straightened her posture. "You're bold to break into my room at night. It suggests you're unsure of your nuptials, and you shattered my door."

The door lay on the floor in smoldering pieces. "Yes, well, sorry about that. No wait, I'm not sorry. You stole something from me, and I want it back. Now. Do I have to wield magic to hear the truth?"

"The king doesn't like others using magic in the castle," she said in a pouty voice.

Glancing at the dressing table, he said, "There." He pointed at the little golden chest.

"You think I inserted a long staff in a tiny music box?" Zita picked up the golden chest and handed the music box to Kestrel. "Lift the lid, it plays a charming song even you might recognize."

Kestrel examined the music box in his hands inspecting all sides. "I sense magic." He raised the lid and listened to the song. "This is a lovely tune. I might take this as a gift for my bride."

She glanced out the open doorway and Lily stood in a dressing robe.

Zita resumed. "You're here to renew our relationship, but we shouldn't. No kiss tonight, save your kisses for your latest lady conquest."

He drew a deep breath and huffed in exasperation before speaking, "This conversation isn't about kisses."

"Help with my dress buttons then I promise the kiss you all you desire." She turned her back toward Kestrel.

"I'm not helping with your buttons. I'm no servant and not here for a kiss." His volume rose as his face turned red.

Zita's servant entered. "Can I help, Miss Zita?"

Zita faced Kestrel with a deep curtsy, "Oh yes, my audience with Prince Kestrel is finished. Oh, hi Lily, I didn't notice you there."

The girl raced from the doorway.

Guards appeared at the door to investigate the explosion.

Kestrel spun toward the door and raised a hand. "Lily!" But it was too late. He faced Zita. "This isn't over, and I'll get that staff before traveling to the volcano tomorrow."

She studied his eyes. "You'll have to search the castle because I don't know where the staff is."

He threw the golden musical chest hard against the wall and stomped from the apartment.

Five notes of melody played over and over from the damaged music box.

CHAPTER 37

Erik woke with a dreadful headache in a dark room. *What time is it? Where am I?* His head hurt, and rolling onto his side caused pain to shoot from his shoulder to his leg. He was blind in the blackness.

"Hey Sherry, are you awake?" he whispered.

He received no feedback.

"Sherry?"

No response.

His eyes adjusted to the darkness, but saw nothing. He rolled off the bed onto a dirt floor and groaned in pain as he tried standing on feeble legs.

A man entered the room with a candle. "Ah, you're awake and perhaps hungry."

The man helped Erik to his feet and bolstered him as they made their way into another room where Sherry dined at a narrow wooden table. On one wall, the place had a fireplace with a kettle dangling from a hook over burning logs. No clue what simmered in the pot but it smelled like heaven with spices and a hint of meat.

"Oh, my!" Sherry rose from the table and helped Erik sit on the bench. "You look lousy, like a zombie."

A slight woman with gray hair tied in a bun handed Erik a bowl of soup and a portion of bread.

"Eat this, it'll help you recover," she said.

"This is Mikah and her husband Jonathan," Sherry said. "I've told them everything about us, Erik."

Erik noticed no eating utensils, so he dipped a chunk of bread into the wooden bowl and popped the savory bite in his mouth.

"They're members of the resistance."

Erik looked back and forth at the two older people and searched for exits. The room contained a single window and the door. His muscles tensed.

Sherry touched his arm. "Take it easy, it's okay, they won't release us to the resistance. They'll let us continue on our way at dawn."

Erik didn't buy it. He whispered, "They're fooling you; people are coming right now to take us back to Prince Krunal."

"No. Relax. Eat." Sherry said, "They lost a son in the war, he's one of the stone warriors on the mountain. Mikah appreciates our predicament and agrees we should rescue our friends."

"I don't trust them." Fatigue made him jumpy and suspicious, and he had misgivings about these people.

A knock sounded at the door.

Erik jumped at the noise.

Mikah checked the one window in the room and moved the curtain aside. "Castle soldiers."

Jonathan helped Erik to his feet. "Quick, to the bedroom. Both of you. Close the door. Mikah pull the flag off the wall."

Erik said, "Now we're in trouble. These men from the resistance are ready to take us to Krunal."

"Don't worry, we'll be fine," Sherry said. "They promised to release us."

"Of course, they'll say that. Did one of them leave the house?"

"Yes, Mikah fetched water for the soup."

"Right, and informed the resistance of our location. Erik's skin itched and his nerves felt raw. "Can we escape through a window?" He glanced around the room. *No windows. No wonder the room is so dark. Maybe we can escape through the thatch roof.*

He heard deep voices on the other side of the door, two guys talking to the older couple. "Have you seen two children?"

"No. We're eating our supper. Are you cold and hungry? Would you like to sit by the fire and have soup and bread?"

"No time to eat; we need to search your house for criminals."

Sherry whispered, "We're criminals? Those aren't resistance men; they're castle soldiers."

"The king wants us as much as the resistance. It'll be worse with them. We must get into the castle on our own, not as hostages." Erik sat on the bed and struggled to clear his brain.

In the other room Mikah said, "Please sir, my sick mom shouldn't—"

"I don't care about your sick mom." The bedroom door flew open, exposing the teens.

A soldier shoved a torch into the room. "Here they are." "Just like the descriptions, one red-headed girl and an older boy in strange clothing. Come with us." He gestured to Erik and Sherry.

Erik needed to stop the soldiers from capturing Sherry. Despite his damaged shoulder and weakened condition he ran headlong to tackle one of the guards.

The second soldier pulled a bludgeon from his tunic waistband and whacked Erik on the back. He dropped to the floor like a sack of potatoes. The soldier kicked him in the face and stomach a few times and stomped on his hand.

The soldier held the club steady. "Any other heroes?"

Their hands were secured behind their backs, and along with Jonathan and Mikah were forced out into the cold night.

Sherry exclaimed, "No, not the older couple. They didn't know we were criminals. Please let them go."

"No chance of that since they are harboring fugitives and get the death penalty like you." He strong-armed the group forward.

It was late night and nobody else was in the road. The clear night sky showed the blue crescent Anticletus moon before the starry blackness of space beyond. The two soldiers herded their prisoners along the dirt road toward the black castle.

Erik, with bruised face and ribs, weaved, lumbered and stumbled down the street, and as he meandered, he fell over a rock in the road.

The soldier nearest him kicked Erik in the gut. "Get up!"

Sherry screamed, "Stop that, stop kicking him. He's recovering from stings of scatter fruit and doesn't grasp what he's doing."

"Gonna know not to do it again because I'll teach him to respect the castle soldiers. Do you want a piece of this boot?" He walked to Sherry and spit on the ground in front of her.

Erik clinched his tied hands into fists as he winced each time the boot found its way home in his stomach and ribs. Wanting to attack the soldier, Erik glared with his less swollen eye at the soldier who stared right back.

A blue glow formed around Sherry.

Everybody in the road stopped walking and gawked at the girl wrapped in a cocoon of blue fog with a silver crown above her head. She said nothing that Erik heard, but the soldiers responded by shaking their heads in agreement.

The soldiers untied Mikah and Jonathan's hands and released them. Then the soldier that kicked Erik kneeled. He was shaking and untied the ropes around Erik's wrists. Without speaking, the soldiers nodded to each other and marched back toward the castle leaving their prisoners in the night.

When the soldiers marched out of sight, the blue glow subsided.

Sherry said, "Why did they let us go?"

"You don't know? You changed into that weird blue glow and got that crown thing working. I guess you talked them into releasing us."

"Let's find someplace to hide the rest of the night and investigate the castle in the morning."

CHAPTER 38

Erik woke cold and hungry in a ditch. They figured it unsafe to stay in town, and Sherry talked him out of a warming fire for fear of being noticed by other guards. Erik's face showed purple and blue from the beatings the soldiers delivered. The sun shone but storm clouds built in the west.

Horns sounding a proclamation interrupted the morning silence followed by a steady beat of drums.

Sherry stood. "What's going on?"

"I'm not sure. There's activity at the castle. Do you think they're going to come back and search for us with a larger army?"

Sherry had dark circles under her eyes. She ran her hands through her ratty mess of hair. She had lost weight on this journey. She stared down at her hands checking her fingernails. "I can't do this anymore. All this running. Not eating. This isn't us."

Erik lowered his chin to his chest while staring at his feet. "We have to camouflage ourselves better. We are dressed so differently from everyone else. Maybe if we put on clothes the natives wear, we'll have a better chance to keep from being captured." He didn't know what to do. He swayed back and forth on his feet.

"You should be in a hospital in Billings. You're near death and your injury could be infected or gangrenous."

"If we surrender to the king, they're gonna kill us. That's what the soldiers said last night." He walked close to Sherry to keep from falling.

The drums and trumpets came closer.

"Quick, maybe someone left laundry up to dry last night." He bent down to tie his shoes.

They walked through a number of backyards where a couple of women were hanging wet clothes on the lines.

The beating of the drums drew nearer.

Erik said, "We gotta hide."

Sherry pointed to the locals walking toward the noise. "But the people are heading toward the beating drums. If we don't follow their lead, we'll seem different."

They followed a throng of people lining the route. Erik leaned on Sherry, for fear of falling.

Three men with long trumpets led the procession, blowing their horns every few steps, followed by forty soldiers wearing red tunics with leather armor over the top. They carried spears and wooden shields. Behind them walked ten rows of men dressed in the same red and leather. They carried bows with a quiver of arrows on their backs.

"Are they going to war?" Sherry asked.

"No, this is more for show than an actual army." Erik stood erect to inspect the procession.

The next group comprised a hundred men dressed in long, dark crimson robes.

"Who are those guys?"

"Are these guys the wizards?" Erik pointed to men carrying wands. There were ten in the back row with staves of varying sizes and shapes. All but one man in the back row had a long gray beard.

The crowd cheered and jeered as a caged wagon pulled by oxen came down the dirt road. The locals threw eggs, tomatoes and pebbles at the cage imprisoning three blonde women dressed in white.

Sherry gasped, "Who are those women in the cage?" She pulled on Erik's sleeve.

Erik's pulse increased and he inspected the blonde-haired girls in the cart. But closer scrutiny revealed to him that none were Lily.

Another hundred soldiers followed the cart. Erik watched as the group maintained the journey to the volcano. A sudden coldness hit him in the core.

Lily, dressed all in white with a gold crown upon her head, rode a large, white horse. Kestrel, attired in a red military uniform, rode on a similar sized black horse, holding Lily's hand.

The crowd cheered the couple as they passed.

Flashes of colored lights appeared behind Erik's eyes, and he felt near fainting. "What is she doing?" He muttered and sat down on the ground.

Sherry sat down with him and patted his hand.

"All this time I've been working so hard to save her. Is she a princess or something? And the way she gazed at Kestrel, has she forgotten me?"

Sherry said, "We don't know what she's been through maybe she has Stockholm syndrome."

"What's that?"

"You know, where the captive falls in love with the person who's holding her hostage. She doesn't love Kestrel."

"I have to rescue her right now before she does something stupid."

"Ignore this for a while. We'll fix it."

"How? I'm going to her right now." Erik tried to stand, but at that moment all the people along the parade route kneeled and bowed.

Sherry pulled him to the ground. "Bow you idiot." She whispered to him. "It's the king and you don't want to stand out. You'll end up with a hundred arrows through your chest."

They stayed on their knees for a full minute as the king passed.

Erik watched in silence as another two hundred soldiers trooped behind the king. The soldiers were followed by donkeys pulling carts of food, supplies and servants

The commoners dispersed to their homes, businesses and gardens.

Sherry said, "Now what?"

"We follow them. They must be going to the volcano for the sacrifice." He watched the procession continue through the city gates.

"What are we gonna do against all those soldiers? They'll put arrows in you like you're a pin cushion. We gotta have a strategy. We need Al."

"Are you suggesting we storm the castle?"

"No, we should be able to get in and talk with Al."

"Do you believe they're treating him like a guest? We can't rescue them both. Al can take care of himself, and after we get Lily then we come back for Al."

Sherry's tired expression showed a woman drained and lethargic. "No, I'm not going another step without him. We have to get Al first."

The pain in Erik's shoulder flared and he winced. "We don't have time. What's going to happen? It might take us two or three days to rescue Al. We have to act now. Kestrel and Lily might be getting married at the volcano, or maybe she will be sacrificed."

Sherry planted her feet in front of Erik and grabbed his forearms. She took a deep breath. "I don't care what you do Erik. You got us in this mess, but I'm going after my Al. We need him and I won't allow him to be hurt by these horrible people. I'm going to the castle to rescue him, and I don't care how long it takes."

Erik struggled to find the right words. "But you might end up in the same predicament as Al. They might capture you and throw you in the volcano. They're still searching for us."

She stood firm in her stance, her face showing determination to follow the course no matter what.

He moved his head back and forth in a definite no and grimaced. "We can't split up. We have to go together."

Sherry didn't move a muscle. She stood firm and said nothing.

Erik felt the world spinning out of control.

CHAPTER 39

Zita watched the procession out of the castle from her bedroom window. Watching Kestrel and Lily holding hands as they rode horses sickened her. Her frustration mounted, and she talked herself into relaxing. Dad, the king, had entered the apartment this morning and told her to remain in the castle during the eclipse celebration. The guards were ordered to prohibit her from leaving.

She wept for a while and felt like her ribs squeezed her heart. How could Dad refuse to let her go to the big celebration? She knew that during the sacrifices magical power flows to people with magical abilities. In the past, Dad had allowed her to participate. Why not today?

How to escape the castle and hurt both Kestrel and Dad? One way she knew from lore and legend, through the dungeon caverns, but the caves were treacherous with killer traps. Maybe she could release the young Earth wizard, Al, from the dungeon. Then let him help her bust out of the castle. That plan had provided an interesting twist and if she then gave Al the staff of Ishwa. Wouldn't that be sweet revenge?

She watched the procession from the castle window. *How far away does Kestrel need to be before I bring the staff back to this plane? Is past the castle grounds sufficient; do they need to travel beyond the city walls or farther?* The procession advanced in slow passage through town as she gazed through the window. When the parade reached the outside city walls, she paced back and forth in the narrow room.

Zita checked her hair in the mirror for the umpteenth time, studied her dress, brushed off lint and drummed fingernails on the dresser. *Don't get too excited. Just relax. Everything will be okay.* The next time she checked, the procession had passed out of sight.

Her hands trembled handling the damaged music box. Would it work after Kestrel threw the precious gift against the wall? She caressed it for a moment and lifted the lid to listen to the tune, it played the five broken notes. Then, eager to gain vengeance on Kestrel, she focused and attempted the incantation to transport the great trunk to her room.

The chest landed on the floor with smoke and a thundering thud. She delayed a minute for the smoke to dissipate then managed the lock, raised the lid and placed her hand on the staff.

"Oh, what a dreadful little place." The staff exclaimed in a female voice. "Where's my master?"

"Your master is on a long trip to the Velidred Volcano so I'm offering you to a new master." Zita gushed with giddiness.

"Master Kestrel is within reach of my touch."

"What do you mean he's near, I thought he was far past the castle walls?"

"He isn't close, but I can detect him from a distance and I signaled him."

"No. Don't call him. Be quiet or I'll force you back in the trunk." She leaned to place the staff back into the chest, but instead, closed the lid and rushed from the bedroom with staff in hand.

In moments she reached the floor above the dungeon pit and shouted to the guards. "I demand to speak with one of the prisoners."

"Not allowed." A tall, wide-shouldered guard blocked her way.

"I'm the king's daughter; how dare you refuse me?" She strode to the guard who towered a foot over her.

He struggled to back away but found himself backed against the wall. "I'm sorry, but the king gave explicit orders that no one is allowed out of the pit."

The staff said, "I have alerted my master, and Kestrel comes to re-claim me."

The guard raised his eyebrows at the sound of the staff.

Zita wanted to scream as she wiped sweat off her forehead. She shoved the head of the staff under his nose.

"I will transform you into a tiny, green lizard right here, right now, with this staff unless you bring a prisoner for me to interrogate." She shook the staff.

The staff chided her in a nasal male voice, "You can't manipulate me for magic. I informed you a female cannot wield my magic. My master will arrive soon and show you how to control my energies."

Blood pounded in her ears. This terrible staff is nothing but trouble. Why hadn't she found something else to steal? She kicked the guard in frustration.

The guard responded by slapping her across the face.

Zita touched her necklace and pendant and spoke a few phrases, casting the bane spell upon the guard, a spell designed to weaken the guard's morale and make him more willing to follow her instructions. "Now free the dungeon door and get the prisoner."

The guard quivered in fear. "Please don't hurt me. I have a family."

"The next spell will cause you to go blind. Do you want that?"

"No, no, no. I'm opening the dungeon door. Which prisoner do you want?" He unbolted the trap door, yanked upward pulling the door free and dropped a ladder into the dungeon pit.

Zita yelled, "Alpherge come up here now. Hurry."

A minute passed but Al didn't climb the ladder.

"Al get up here, I need your help." Zita glanced toward the stairs to the main castle floor. This must finish before Kestrel arrives. "Move Al. Hurry."

Al's geeky head popped above the floor. "Who calls for me?"

Zita stood over the dungeon door.

"Oh you. Are Erik and Sherry with you?"

"No."

"Where are they? Weren't they with you?" He clambered from the pit and stood, bending, stretching and undulating his back as if painful to stand erect.

"We got separated. Here hold this staff." She threw the staff at Alpherge.

The staff sailed between them and Al caught it. "The staff of Ishwa. Did you know this was my grandfather's staff?"

"It doesn't matter, you need to use it before Kestrel gets here." Zita glanced toward the stairs.

"The staff must be in my possession for at least six hours to a month before I attune to its magic. Even then the staff can reject me." He hefted the staff in his right hand and then the left.

Zita said, "Well we've got a problem because the staff notified Kestrel, and he's on his way to re-claim it so get chummy fast because you have five minutes."

"Three minutes." The staff murmured in a rich, low voice. "Hmmm, I sense familiarity."

"We have no magic down here. A spell prevents the prisoners from reaching the source of magic." He brandished the staff back and forth. "Let me bring the other guys out of the dungeon."

Al yelled into the dungeon. "Come up the ladder. Hurry. We're breaking out of here."

"You can't all leave. Just you Al." This plan isn't going well Zita thought.

"No, we're escaping. Do you know a 'dispel magic' spell?"

"I can do an area spell of ten feet. I'm not powerful in magic."

"Don't work it yet, wait for the rest of the captives."

"Master Kestrel will arrive in two minutes." The staff said in a female voice this time and vibrated in Al's hand.

"Feisty little magic item, aren't you? Come on hurry." Al encouraged the others.

"In one minute, my master arrives."

The last prisoner struggled up the ladder.

Zita said, "I have to get out of here, Kestrel can't discover me with you."

"Break the magic spell first. Can you do that for us?" Al moved his arms to bring the group of wizards together. "Huddle up everybody. Come on get close. Okay, disrupt the magic lock."

Zita backed away from Al raising her palms in surrender. "I changed my mind. The guard will inform the king I let you leave. Back to the pit."

"My master's presence is in the castle," said the female voice, as the staff shuddered in Al's grip.

Al stepped to Zita and seized her arm. "We need you. You're our friend, aren't you?"

Is Al my friend? Does he realize I told Kestrel the resistance headquarters location? Can he guess what I did to Erik and Sherry? She stared at Al and realized time was short and escape up the stairs impossible.

Zita pushed Al toward the rest of the wizards, clasped her pendant and declared the incantation needed to unblock the spell preventing the young wizards from using magic.

Gasps emitted from the wizards as the magic flowed through them.

"Master Blayze, should I bind Zita?" Gopal asked.

"Yes, encase her in rope." Blayze responded.

"No Gopal don't." Al stepped in front of Gopal. "She's our friend and we need her help to escape the castle. Zita is there a path out of here without using the stairs?"

"Yes, but it's a dangerous passage through caverns below the castle."

"Quick, lead the way." Al pointed the staff at Zita. The staff convulsed in his grip as it struggled to reach Kestrel.

"Master, liberate me!"

Kestrel clomped down the stairs to the dungeon, yelling, "Zita where's my staff?"

CHAPTER 40

A narrow opening appeared in the rock wall opposite the stairs as Al watched. He assumed Zita created the space with magic.

Zita and Al led the way into the opening as Blayze pushed the younger wizards through the escape cavern. The passageway became dark, and Zita produced a blue globe that hovered above her palm lighting the cavern as she walked.

Al noticed the chiseled rock as he hurried along. The passageway appeared created by humans using crude tools. The narrow cavern forced the group to walk in single file. Al walked stooped to keep from crashing his skull on the low, rough ceiling. He hated tunnels and caves because they never suited his height.

"Where does this cave go?" Al asked.

"Don't know," Zita said. "I remembered locals telling me myths, folklore and superstitions about the castle. It leads out of the castle, but we might encounter obstacles."

"Obstacles?" Al ducked a low hanging rock.

"Well, traps, nasty creatures and potential snares." The tunnel opened to a spacious natural cavern.

Al stood straight and spotted two tunnels leaving the chamber on the opposite side. Zita stopped as the wizards pushed into the cave. Explosions boomed as Blayze entered the chamber.

Blayze said, "Kestrel is pursuing and throwing fireballs. My magic isn't at one hundred percent. I'm still weak, Al, hand me the staff of Ishwa, maybe that will help."

"This is my grandfather's staff. I won't give it to you."

Blayze approached Al. "As commander of this group, I demand you hand over the staff."

Kestrel tossed a fireball into the cave, just missing two of the younger wizards.

"Give me the staff." Blayze said.

Al glanced around at the younger wizards. "Let's get clear of Kestrel first and then we can discuss the staff's owner."

He visualized the bubble for the shield, the magic rushing to fill his senses. While in the pit his powers had been blocked, but now the chains preventing him from handling the magic disappeared. The bubble transformed into a protecting shield, filling the cavern and shielding the young wizards.

A fireball Kestrel shot bounced off the shield, exploding in the tunnel. Rocks tumbled from the ceiling and partially blocked the way. The next fireball ricocheted off the shield, struck the tunnel top, exploding more rocks. They fell, completely obstructing the shaft with rubble.

Al laughed. "Kestrel just blocked his ability to follow us." The staff stopped vibrating in Al's hands. *What does that mean? Is Kestrel hurt or dead?*

Zita pushed Al on the back. "Let's move. Rocks won't stop him for long. Do you prefer right or left?"

Al said, "To the left."

Blayze said, "To the right," as he glared with a resolute expression at Al.

Al signaled Zita with his hand pointing to the right.

"To the right it is." Zita headed into the passage.

This shaft, larger than the preceding section, allowed Al more head space as Zita led the group, followed first by Gopal and then Al. The carved passage curved through the rock.

Al noticed rodent bones along the side of the path and the stench of rotting meat in pockets along the route. "Hey Zita, what are these animal bones and half eaten rodents doing here?"

"They are animals trapped in the tunnels when the men built the castle. I'm sure there's nothing to fear." She advanced through the passage.

Angst filled Al. The castle had to be a hundred years old or more. Zita wasn't telling the truth. These fresh rotting corpses meant something else, perhaps there is a larger predator in this tunnel killing these animals even today. Al became vigilant on the path ahead.

Clicking echoed off the walls. A small sound at first, ten clicks per minute. Then as the group traveled through the cavern, the sound increased in volume and the number of clicks per minute.

Clicks sounded nearby, and Al heard others farther away in the enclosed cave. Sound echoing through the passages hindered his ability to identify the location of the creatures creating the cacophony.

Zita slowed and glanced back at Al.

Gopal stepped ahead of Zita.

"Gopal, wait." Al said.

Gopal stopped and peered back at Al. "Why are we stopping?"

The clicking increased, sounding like a million cicadas on a summer's night.

"Get back here now." Al threw up his shield, but too late.

A giant beetle rushed from a side alcove, attached pinchers onto Gopal and dragged the young wizard back into its lair.

Gopal screamed.

"I'm coming," Al yelled over the din of the clicking.

Zita stayed back with the other wizards. "Careful, there's more than one."

A second beetle emerged from the left side of the cave passageway. The beetle, black head, with shiny, dark blue-green wings, stood four feet tall. Pinchers extended two feet in front of its mouth. The pinchers came to knife-sharp points at their ends.

Al's shield did not deter the beetle. It snatched at Al as he sought to rescue Gopal.

Al thrust the staff at the giant insect.

The beetle backed away from the jab of the staff but then attacked with speed.

Gopal screamed, "Help, it's trying to eat me."

Al thought about his limited magic. How would he be able to beat this critter? No sunlight reached into the dungeon so no magnifying light trick. He lowered himself to one knee and fixed the staff under the beetle's body, attempting to flip the beetle onto its back.

The beetle sliced Al's arm with a pincher and backed away. Blood trickled from the wound as the clicking increased.

Al shuffled back five steps in surprise at the insect's quickness. He examined the laceration on his arm, a mere scratch.

Blayze said. "Use the staff as a magic element, not a stick. Give me the staff." He held out a hand for the staff.

"No, it's my remembrance of my grandfather, I'm not giving it to you." In the back of Al's mind, he contemplated giving it to Blayze as the team leader. But Al ached for his father and grandfather. He threw up his arm with the staff to block the beetle's pinchers.

Blayze shot a fireball at the creature which caromed off the insect's glittering wings and sent rocks tumbling from the ceiling.

"Don't trap us here," Zita shouted.

"Magic doesn't work on these beetles," Al said.

The wizard leader fired another fireball that knocked more rocks from the ceiling.

Gopal cried out, "Help me."

Al thought of strategies he used playing Dungeons and Dragons at home. They created fun magic when playing the game, laughing at ridiculous situations they created. He pointed the staff at the beetle. "Diminish in Size."

The beetle snapped at Al with both pinchers then shrank, hopping at Al as it diminished.

Al stepped on the menacing bug squashing it into the rock floor. Blue ink blood splattered against the floor and walls. "That's the way to slay bugs."

He scrambled to where he last heard Gopal. The beetle held him in its pinchers struggling to put Gopal into its mouth. Gopal used his feet as leverage against the lower jaw to keep from certain death.

Al raised the staff, pointed at the beetle and said, "Diminish in Size."

The beetle shrunk, dropped Gopal and scurried away before Al could squash it.

He didn't know if the staff aided in the magic or not since he hadn't had time to attune to the magic object.

The cacophony of clicking persisted in the cavern passageway.

Al checked Gopal's wounds.

Blayze ripped the staff from Al's hand. "This is mine as commander of the group."

CHAPTER 41

Al watched Blayze walk down the dungeon cavern holding the staff while adopting the diminish spell to defeat the beetles.

Al gripped his fists against his sides and had trouble swallowing. His mind raced back to the memory of the school bully, Tom Gallush, taking the miniature glass figurine Al kept in his pocket. The figurine had been a birthday gift from his mother. She had told him the figurine contained the likeness of his father and was created by his grandfather. Al always considered it magical, and it led him to believe his father and grandfather loved him even though he didn't remember them.

Tom threw the figurine on the floor and stomped on it; the same way Blayze stomped on the beetles. He recalled the delicate figurine smashed into a hundred fragments. He stared at Blayze. The same situations that happened on Earth were happening to him here. Having magical ability seemed to make no difference. Once a loser always a loser.

The wizards cleared the last of the bugs and progress halted in front of a door. Blayze put a palm on the door.

Al yelled, "Check for magic, and verify it's not a trap."

Blayze chanted a spell. "Aura blue, aura near, report the secrets within here." He waved his palm over the door and waited. "A light resonance of a weak trap."

"Can I try? I want to enhance my magic skills." He wanted to seize the staff from the commander. Patience. Al waved his palms over the door. "Spirit within, presence without, advise truth, magic scout."

He leaned close to the door his eyes widening, and he grinned. He ignored everything and listened to the magic voice. The encounter brought euphoria.

Al shook his head. "It's a con. The door says it has little magic, but the trap is inside the room, there's no exit."

"No, I didn't sense that," Blayze said. "The door has an easy lock. We're going into the room. There might be treasure and other magical items we need."

"The chamber is empty with a chance we'll be trapped." Al didn't understand the magic that had spoken to him about the trap, but thought this might end in a less-than-ideal resolution. He decided not to second guess his commander.

Blayze didn't listen to Al and placed his hand on the lock, "Quia nunc mihi aperuit."

Seconds passed, the lock opened, and bolts came undone.

The commander smirked and opened the door.

Al stepped back. He had doubts about following this path. Nothing happened as Blayze entered. In a moment the lead wizard said, "Empty with a door on the opposite wall. We're entering."

They all followed, and Al entered a spacious square chamber forty feet by forty feet. The temperature of the room was noticeably cooler compared to the dungeon tunnel, and Al sensed an unusual, magical presence.

Zita whispered to Al, "We need to get out of here fast."

Al hurried across the room. "Blayze, free the other door and let's get out of here."

"Is big Alpherge scared of an empty room?" Blayze sneered and tapped the staff on the floor.

Al paused and listened to a tiny whispering. To the left was nothing but a twenty-foot-tall granite wall. Unlike the passageways they left behind with their rough-hewn surfaces, this chamber's walls were polished to glass perfection. They reminded Al of Earth's polished granite counter tops. "This doesn't feel right."

Blayze laughed. "Feels fine to me."

The younger wizards made sidelong glances at the walls of the room, experiencing a general discomfort.

Zita yelled, "Get that door opened fast."

The murmuring in the room became louder.

Blayze dashed to the door on the opposite wall of the room. Before reaching it, both doors disappeared.

The magic trap was sprung, and the chamber became quiet. A few of the wizards cleared their throats. Younger wizards sidled up to older, wiser wizards each staring at friends with questioning gazes.

Whispering walls renewed their chant and a slight cooling breeze penetrated the room. The hair rose on the back of Al's neck. "Are we being watched?"

Blayze heaved a fireball at the spot where the door used to be. It bounced off the surface, caromed off the ceiling and touched down without harm on a group of younger wizards.

"Stop that," Al yelled. "Sometimes you must finesse things. You can't always blow-up walls."

Blayze raced to Al. "Stop telling me what to do, because I'm the commander of this group and you'll do what I command." He shook the staff at Al.

Al drew back on himself and tried to make himself smaller. In an unsteady voice he said, "I know, I'm just trying to help." Al hated himself for saying that. He struggled with following Blayze's commands and trying to keep this maniac from killing everyone in the room.

"Everybody relax, I will get us out of here." Blayze rattled the staff at Al once more.

Al's pulse increased as he wanted to shake Blayze, recover the staff and escape the room.

The whispers from the walls became discernible to Al. "You crave the staff. Take the staff. It's yours. It belongs to you. Take it back."

Al walked over to the smiling Blayze. "I want my grandfather's staff back."

"Get away from me. The staff is mine." He poked Al in the stomach with the staff.

The voices hissed in Al's ears. "The staff is yours. Strike Blayze, and seize the staff."

Al stood next to Blayze and worked magic to double his height. No bullying this time. Al raised his hand. "It's mine, my grandfather's, and it is attuned to me."

Blayze backed away from the taller wizard. "That's not the way it works. When wizards seize magical elements the team leader or commanding wizard has the first opportunity to accept the magical object as their own. It's always been that way."

On the one hand, Al wanted to adhere to the rules of the wizarding community. He pressed his lips together in a grimace as he struggled to find words. On the other hand, he wanted the staff. When he held the staff, it felt a part of him, like his right arm. The staff knew him. He closed his eyes and rubbed the middle of his forehead with his fist.

Blayze argued, "It takes hours and days to attune to a magic item this size, you haven't attuned to the staff in an hour. But you wouldn't know that because you've been a wizard for less than a week."

The whispering sounded in Al's ears. "Seize the staff. Fight the other wizard. Use powerful magic on the bully."

"Come on." Blayze waved at the other wizards. "We won't let him have the staff, will we?"

Al wanted to explode a spell on the wizard leader and get the staff back. Al expanded his body to three times his size, his head near the chamber's ceiling. "Give it back."

The staff spoke. A deep, low male voice was clearly heard from the carved wizard at the top of the staff. "Give me to my master."

Blayze stopped in surprise. "I'm your master now."

Al raised his hands and said, "Come to me staff." His hands tingled with excitement.

Blayze's eyes widened, and he shook his head. The staff vibrated in his hands and his mouth opened in confusion. "There's no way to attune to the staff this fast."

"It's not a random magic item found on an adventure but my grandfather's staff. It knows my genetics and has been in my family for generations." He didn't know if it had been in his family that long, but he liked the way the phrase rolled off his tongue, like a natural adventure storyteller. "Come staff."

It became harder for Blayze to hold the staff as it quivered, shook, trembled and shuddered. His fingers loosened on the wooden staff.

"Come," Al commanded. The staff flew into Al's outstretched hands. He raised the staff with both hands. "The staff has chosen its master."

The room's voices responded with elation in their whispering tones. "Excellent. Now kill Blayze. Use the staff's energy and smash him like the bugs."

CHAPTER 42

Blayze loosed a fire bolt at Al. The air sizzled.

He blocked the bolt by creating a shield around his body. The fire bolt bounced off the shield, ricocheted off the granite wall and exploded on the ceiling. The spell of sulfur lingered in the stale air. He studied the scorch spot on the ceiling. "Stop. This isn't worth killing over."

The voices spoke to Al, "Kill Blayze. You don't need him. He seeks to steal the staff. Defeat him now. The staff gives you great power to kill."

The young wizards bunched in the center of the chamber and walked toward Blayze like a gang of juveniles on the street at night.

Blayze retreated toward the wall, grabbed Gopal and manhandled the young boy as a shield against the other wizards.

The whispers picked up a chant, "Kill Blayze, make him ache, we want blood, for Velidred's sake."

Al needed a way out of this room, and they needed Blayze as the most learned wizard in the group. Killing him wasn't going to help. Once they found their way out of the dungeons, they might need Blayze's wizarding to fight Kestrel and the king's warrior wizards. Al had to discover a solution to the problem but how to stop the voices and escape the chamber?

He used the staff to detect magic, casting the same spell used before they entered. Were exits in the room invisible? Al felt an aura permeating the place, meaning the whole room held magic. The spell found no doors.

The young wizards aligned in a battle formation against Blayze.

Blayze might do something stupid if forced to defend himself. If the commanding wizard fired on the young wizards most of them would perish. Even though there were more of them, the leader's superior skill would wipe out most before he died. *Does Blayze hear the same voices I do?*

Al's body shuddered as he grasped the tragedy of their situation. These young wizards were safer in the dungeon instead of this death trap.

The chant persisted, "Kill Blayze, force him anguish, we want bodies, soon extinguished."

Catastrophe loomed; Al ran in front of Blayze to save Gopal. "Release Gopal, use me as a shield."

The voices repeated their mantra and the youthful minds not able to resist took up the chant, "Kill Blayze, Kill Blayze."

Al placed a hand in his pants pocket and extracted his cell phone, unused the last two days. He hoped enough battery power remained for what he planned. He typed in the security code and found twenty-eight percent power left on the device. Scrolling through his music playlist, he chose a pop song and played the song amplified with magic. The song drowned out the whispering voices.

The young wizards stopped their progress and shook their heads in bewilderment.

He played the music so loud it gave Al a headache, but the kids stopped their advance and Blayze released Gopal.

Two wizards curious how the music worked came to Al to examine the device held in his palm. There wasn't time to teach them about cell phone technology or even phone technology. "Zita, how do we get out of here?"

"Don't know; this is an unfamiliar chamber."

Blayze seized Zita around the waist pinning her arms to her body. "She trapped us here to die. I say kill her, appease Velidred which will force the spirits to free us. Blast her Al."

Zita struggled, but her arms were secured. "Let me go. I'm trying to help you escape."

"Let her go." Al wondered if Blayze still heard the voices despite the music. "We need her to lead us out of the caverns. There might be other obstructions where we need her skills."

"She has been little help so far."

"Release her," Al commanded over the music. "Instead of sending fireballs and killing young students, let's figure out how to escape. Do you have any suggestions?" He held a hand in front of Blayze to stop him from performing another senseless act.

Al hated being forced into a leadership role. He just wanted to use magic and come up with funny ideas to get his friends to laugh. Now he felt responsible for all these young kids, several younger than Gopal. If Erik were here, he would have ten plans to try in less than a minute. Al shook his head hoping to shake out his light-headedness.

"Magic doesn't work to identify the door, but can we physically touch the door?" Zita rubbed her arms after Blayze released her. "Does the door move?"

"Let's investigate." Al got the young wizards' attention. "Split up, feel the walls and locate a door."

Ten minutes passed, and nobody found anything but flat surfaces.

Despite the massive size of the chamber around him Al felt claustrophobic. In one corner, three boys and a girl cowered. Another effect of the room? Since the whispering didn't work, were the evil Velidred spirits assaulting them this way?

Another young wizard joined the four in the corner.

The staff spoke in a female tone, "You should kill Zita because she is the one making you suffer."

The action shocked Al. Did Zita just lure us into this evil chamber on purpose? He stepped away from Zita and pointed the staff at her. "Is that true?"

"No, the spirits are making us paranoid. I want out as much as you." Zita moved farther from Al.

The spirits desire a victim before releasing us. But, will they be satisfied with one victim or only after all have died? Is that what the voices are, victims of earlier poor souls who wandered into the chamber?

He needed time and space to reflect on this. Three more kids joined the group that cowered in the corner. The room emanated fear, paranoia, bloodshed and death.

One boy howled, "Save me. They're reaching for me. Get them off."

Al examined the lad from a distance. Nothing crawled on the boy

The student wizard rubbed his arms and face in frantic gestures, scratching his face in the process. "Take them off me. Please help."

The other kids backed away from the screaming boy.

Al didn't know what to do. "Nothing's on you."

"Help me. Get them off. They're biting my skin; I don't want to die."

Al stared at the wild-eyed wizard as splotches formed on the young boy's face.

CHAPTER 43

A teenage girl shrieked, "They're on me now, take them off. Help me." She swiped at her arms, legs and back trying to remove the invisible vermin.

The music stopped playing and Al studied the mobile phone. *Out of juice, now what will happen?*

Voices grew louder. "You must kill Blayze. He is your enemy and craves the staff for himself."

Ten young wizards walked toward Blayze who sat by himself in another corner.

The kid next to Al brushed his arms, legs and body in an attempt to remove whatever seemed to be crawling on him.

Al's staff said, "Forget the kid, we must slay Blayze."

How did the voices influence the staff this way? All this negativity in the room. Al remembered his mom telling him not to be negative.

The splotches on the lad's face widened as he wailed in panic.

A thought ran through Al's mind, what's the opposite of negativity? Positivity? Love instead of hate, killing and death?

Al embraced the kid. "You're fine and among friends. You are loved."

Zita yelled, "Say that again." She pointed to the wall.

"Say what?" Al peered at the wall where Zita pointed and the wall shifted colors a little.

"Whatever you just told the kid."

"You're fine." Al repeated. The surface returned to its former state.

"That isn't it. Try something else."

"You're fine and among friends."

"No, those aren't the phrases you used."

"I don't know what I said." He embraced the kid again. "You're fine and among friends. You are loved."

The spot appeared on the wall again.

An older boy flung a magic spell at Blayze.

Blayze stepped out of the path of the spell and sent a fireball at the kid.

Al placed a shield over the boy before the fireball hit, which caused the fire bolt to bounce to the ceiling. Another burn mark scarred the ceiling.

Zita ran to the girl complaining about bugs crawling on her. "You are loved." She hugged the young wizard in a rigid embrace.

A fragment of the door appeared.

Zita said, "Everybody find a partner and tell them they are loved."

Girls standing in a group giggled. Gopal stood next to an older girl with long hair and large almond eyes. He approached her, hugged her and said, "You are loved."

"Ooh, Gopal has a sweetheart," two boys mocked Gopal.

The girl Gopal embraced responded, "You are loved."

Ten percent of the door became visible.

The voices became urgent and picked up the chant, "Kill Blayze, induce pain, we want blood and the leader slain."

Al's staff picked up the chant, the female voice said, "Kill Blayze, induce pain, we want blood and the leader slain."

Al yelled at the other wizards. "Stop standing there and hug someone. It's our means out of here, hug someone and say, 'You are loved,' Do it now."

The young wizards approached their classmates. Al remembered how difficult it was the first time he held Sherry's hand. Now, asking classmates to embrace and say the "L" word was a difficult task at these kids' age.

More students embraced exposing more of the door.

"Come on all of you embrace, it's difficult, but you must do it."

The kids snickered and mumbled, but most of them embraced and spoke the words.

Blayze and the boy still needed to embrace, and the youngster approached the commanding wizard. Al wondered what the boy thought. Was he under the influence of the room's whispering voices, or would he listen to Al and embrace the commander? Embrace Blayze or attack?

Blayze stood watching the boy get closer.

Al watched without a sound.

The female voice of the staff shouted, "Kill Blayze."

Blayze prepared to shoot a fire bolt at the approaching boy.

The fellow reached out to Blayze and embraced him. "You arc loved."

The door became visible. Zita opcned it, and the wizards rushed through the exit into a cavern corridor.

Al said, "Do we have everybody?" He quickly accounted for everyone.

The door closed, sealed and melted into the wall.

Al embraced Zita, "You saved us. Thanks." He held the hug longer than necessary, but she didn't end the embrace.

"We aren't out of the dungeon yet." Blayze pointed to a fork in the passage.

The left direction showed darkness, but the right tunnel revealed light at the far end.

Al said. "Which way?"

"At least there's light at that end. Let's go that way." Zita walked toward the lighted tunnel.

Blayze said, "That's the way they want you to escape. The path with guards waiting to take us captive. She's tricking us."

"It isn't a trick," Al said. "Zita wants out of here as bad as you. I say we go right." He lifted his staff in the cramped passageway.

The kids all cheered.

"I'll blame you when we're captured this way."

Blayze led into the tunnel followed by Al and the remaining wizards.

Al spotted brown mold growing on the surfaces but ignored it as the light source grew larger with each step. Freedom neared and his thoughts drifted to reuniting with Erik and Sherry. He had plenty to tell them. This experience, the adventure of a lifetime dreamed all those years playing Dungeons and Dragons at the kitchen table. He must find Sherry Berry.

He stepped on a large splat of brown mold and his foot stuck. "Hey what's going on here? Stop."

Blayze stopped, glanced at Al and pointed at Al's foot. "Ha, yeah, you don't want to step in that stuff."

Al struggled to pull his foot out, but it didn't budge. "Zita what is this substance?"

"It's the simple brown mold the servants clean with ammonia, except...." Zita paused.

"Except what?"

"There is a more virulent form called, marugotapa."

"What do you mean more virulent?"

"Means it spreads fast, itches, and kills within sixty minutes. I didn't know it grew in the castle."

Blayze said, "Don't worry, I'll blast it with a fireball."

"No, don't blast it with a fireball." Al raised his hands for Blayze to stop.

Too late. The leader sent a fire bolt into the brown mold.

Al chastised the commanding wizard. "You don't have to blast, sometimes try to find other solutions." Al stared at the brown mold which expanded at a rapid pace around his foot.

"Oh, that didn't work, not enough energy and heat. Let me blast it again." Blayze sent another volley of fire at the mold.

Al felt the warmth from this explosion as the mold climbed his leg and surged around his other foot. The marugotapa was building a barrier between Al, Zita and the remaining wizards.

"Zita, stand back. This stuff is spreading. Blayze don't do another fireball. The brown mold grows with heat." Both of Al's feet were stuck in the brown blob, and his leg itched. He wanted to scratch his leg, but feared getting his hand stuck in the gunk. He lifted his staff above his head as the brown mold reached his belly.

Blayze withdrew from the advancing mold and faced toward the light showing from the end of the shaft.

"Where are you going?" Al asked.

"I'm heading out of here before the mold attacks me." Blayze rubbed the back of his neck.

"It's attacking because you blasted it with fire."

Blayze walked down the tunnel and out into the light.

"Come back, you're our commander." Al wanted to run after Blayze, but his legs wouldn't move. The itching became unbearable as the brown mold grew into a little mound around him. He blew out a series of short breaths, looked at the light at the end of the tunnel and back at Zita and the other wizards. The wall of mold between him and Zita grew. The young wizards were trapped in the tunnel behind the mold. "Zita, got any ideas on how to beat this?"

CHAPTER 44

Erik explained to Mikah and Jonathon his need to get inside the castle. "Are there any entrances to sneak into the castle?"

Jonathon stood with his chin in his hand. "I studied sketches of the castle when the resistance planned their attack. On the west side of the castle is a drainage ditch. We sent three guys in to scope out the castle dungeons a week ago, but they never returned."

Erik shook his head.

Mikah returned with garments from neighboring friends for them to wear. Sherry looked like she was ready to attend the Renaissance fair, wearing a floor length green tunic made of wool. "I need something to cover my head."

Mikah said, "An eligible young woman should not be hiding her hair."

"My red hair makes me stand out and I need a disguise." Sherry ran her hand through her hair.

"Here's something that might work." Mikah brought out a pastel blue kerchief and helped Sherry arrange it on her hair.

Erik grinned. "One of the locals now. But, these pants itch."

How were they going to get to the volcano in time to save anyone? Erik wanted to punch something as everything he tried made things worse in this world. He gritted his teeth. "Let's get moving."

Sherry gave Mikah a hug and thanked her for the clothes.

They walked out of the cabin, and onto the road and Erik noticed imposing dark clouds approach. How would the clothes help in rain or snow? The teens headed toward the castle.

A black horse galloped down the dirt road, raising dust. Kestrel sat low in the saddle.

Erik poked Sherry. "Stare at the ground and appear disinterested in the rider. It's Kestrel and we don't want him to recognize us. Hopefully, these disguises will work."

The stallion slowed as it neared.

The teens kept their heads down and moved off the dirt road.

Kestrel and the horse passed and swung back toward the youngsters. He rode back to Erik and let the horse walk beside the teens.

Erik grated his teeth stopping all rash desires to pull Kestrel off the horse and pummel him. He ignored the horse and rider. Erik lowered his head, sweat streaking down his back.

Kestrel and the black stallion walked beside them a few strides.

Erik thought about Lily. Would attacking Kestrel help him win Lily back? Were they an item?

The horse bumped Erik, and Kestrel kicked Erik in the ear.

Erik hardened his abdomen. It was difficult to keep from reacting, but it would be suicide to fight Kestrel without Al's help. Fatigue plagued Erik's mind and body as he fought the urge of muscle and sinew that wanted to pull Kestrel off the horse. His anger rose to the point of action. He had never been able to resist hitting someone, his trigger anger had caused problems in the past.

With another blow to Erik's skull, Kestrel yelled to the horse. "Go Cloud." Kestrel kicked the horse's sides and galloped from the teens.

They walked with a measured pace and Erik forced himself to stay calm. The blows to his head would leave bruises, and confidence to rescue Al or Lily leaked from him like water in a bucket with holes. They were all going to die, including Sherry. Erik didn't know if he detested himself or Kestrel more.

"I hate that boy," Sherry said. "How did you keep from striking him?"

"Mom taught me," Erik said. "Attack from a position of strength because anything else will make matters worse. But I wanted to yank him off the horse."

"Yeah, me too."

"So, how do we get inside the castle?" They walked a hundred yards toward the entrance.

Sherry pointed to a thatch roofed building. "Jonathon told us to veer left at the last street before the castle which should be this next row of buildings. I don't know how we'll keep from being spotted by the sentries." She glanced at the castle walls.

"Jonathon said there's a ditch not visible by the patrols on the castle walls. I hope he's right."

They turned left where instructed. The buildings served a dual purpose with the ground floors as businesses and the upper floors living quarters. At one shop, they passed a noisy blacksmith's forge with a strong smell of sulfur. Next to the blacksmith, a man worked on armor, pounding heated metal with a large hammer. The blacksmith and armor maker worked together using the same fire to soften their materials. Two houses later he noticed a tailor's shop with three men hand sewing red cloth. It was a bustling little village to serve the king and his court.

Thirty feet past the last house, they found the ditch. Erik expected a grassy ditch, but instead found mud and dirt. Even though Jonathon said it wasn't visible by the castle guards, Erik suspected soldiers watched the ditch. The patrols would observe every person who entered the ditch and verify they left the ditch. Their chances would be better to reach the castle after the sun set. Taller than most in this community, his head protruded above the sides of the small gully.

Lightning flashed in the distance and a few seconds later, thunder sounded.

"Keep your head down." Sherry waved at him to crouch lower.

"They already know I'm in the ditch. The easiest way for us to get captured is to make them suspect we're trying to sneak into the castle. We're workers traveling to the garden area, so remember the goal is to be like the locals." The soft sole moccasins he wore made his feet sore. He missed his sneakers for their greater comfort and thicker soles. "Do you expect we'll find Al?"

"Yes, we have to find him because we're going to homecoming next week. I've already bought my dress and we're going out to eat at that new Italian restaurant in town. I'm gonna give him such a hug when we free him."

Erik didn't want to acknowledge the elephant in the conversation. *The portal is closed. Is Al still alive? Did Al's capture increase his risk of death? Why isn't Al in the cart heading to the volcano? Instead of following Lily to the volcano, I have to wander through the castle, avoid notice, locate Al and then spring him free. What were we expecting?*

"I remember when Al first asked me to homecoming." Sherry stopped walking and a wistful expression came over her face. "He was so nervous. I didn't know what he planned to do and even thought he might throw up on me." She resumed walking and reminiscing. "Al stammered, stuttered and stumbled, but said those magic words, 'Will you go to homecoming with me?'"

They reached the garden space where rakes and hoes lay on the ground. "Okay, pick up a tool and pretend to garden. Scope out the area and we'll sneak in after dark."

They raked and hoed while sneaking glances at the castle walls. A smaller ditch ran from the castle wall to the garden.

Erik said, "The ditch to the castle wall is what Jonathan referred to as our entry point."

Lightning flashed in the sky and rain poured in the distance. He smelled the rainfall in the air as the sound of thunder rolled across the countryside.

He pretended to rake the garden area. "Still want to go through with this? Remember Jonathon said three guys entered and never came out."

"I will for my Al. We have to rescue him because I believe he would rescue me." She leaned on her hoe, staring at the castle wall.

"Stop gawking at the castle because the guard on the watchtower is interested in us." He pointed back to the garden. "Get back to work."

"Wait, there's activity in the hole in the wall."

CHAPTER 45

Zita watched the brown mold grow higher around Al. The barrier between Al and Zita expanded up and along the ground, blocking the route to the exit. She was trapped in here with the young wizards. What else lurked in the shafts?

Zita stepped back from the rising wall of brown mold.

Al sounded alarmed. "Where are you going? Will you leave me too?"

She had to decide fast, and she must make the right choice. Guessing wrong, Al would die, just as she started to like the geeky boy. That embrace in the magic chamber was more than just happiness at escaping. Hooking up with Alpherge the Great's grandson would fry Dad.

"Why are you smiling?" The mold reached Al's shoulders.

"I have two ideas. One, create a sword, but I don't know what a sword will do. Might make it worse."

Al said, "I don't like the notion of a sword near my legs. What's the second idea?"

"Well, if fire is bad, I'm guessing water will make it go away."

Gopal, standing behind Zita, said, "Not water, you need to freeze the mold. In the mountains in winter, the mold stops growing and we scrape it off the walls after it freezes."

"Well, it's still advancing although slower. Want to make a decision?" Al shifted the staff in his hands above his head.

"Don't panic." Zita stared into the little wizard's eyes. "Freezing will work?"

Gopal nodded. "Yeah sure."

"How old are you kid?" *Do I have faith a ten-year-old has the right answers?*

"I'm eleven years old and I've been a student wizard for six months. I know this is the right answer. It's not magic, just common sense." Gopal put his shoulders back like he had just slayed a dragon.

Zita touched her gold chain and pendant and opened her mouth to say the phrases to freeze the mold, but hesitated. She knew the spell for water, but never attempted a freeze spell. What effect could it have on Al? Could she injure him?

"Come on, are you gonna do it or not? Do you want me to say the words? What's the incantation?" Gopal touched Zita on the shoulder.

"I'll manage it, give me a second. It's important to chant the proper incantation." *Water first and then freeze the water on the mold or just freeze the mold using the water in the fungus?* She lifted her hands. "Hot, cold, rain, snow." She faltered. Could Al freeze into a block of ice along with the mold? Concentrate and relax. "Wind will blow with temperatures low."

Wind blew over Zita from outside the tunnel. A breeze, cold compared to the warmth in the shaft from Blayze's fireballs and the hot growing fungus, that enveloped them.

"Keep going, finish the chant, it's growing colder." Al smiled.

"Fall's sneezes lead to winter's freezes. Ice, ice, ice!" Her voice rose to the end and resounded in the shaft.

Everyone remained silent for a moment. Zita felt cool, much cooler, but had anything happened to the mold? Afraid to touch the fungus mound, and become stuck, she thought to lift the little Gopal kid and make him touch it.

Gopal, standing behind Zita chanted, "Hammer blows, hammer thrice, crush the mold, and break the ice."

Resembling a bell ringing in a bell tower, a hammer struck the surface of the brown mold causing a noise so deafening it pained her ears. The sound reverberated through her body three times. The wall of fungus shattered into dust with mold dust flying everywhere. She shut her eyes and mouth and didn't breathe.

Time stretched like following an autumn leaf drop from a tree. Zita feared to inhale, not wanting the brown fungus in her lungs. Were these kids going to kill her?

Al said, "Well that was an impressive solution, Gopal. Nice job."

Everything sounded muffled to Zita, her ears still ringing from the noise. Had they freed Al of the mold? Did she dare open her eyes as dust cleared from the air? The brisk breeze drove the dust back into the shaft away from the wizards.

The young wizards sneezed.

Al sneezed.

Zita sneezed. "Get out of here. Fast!"

"Why?" Al sneezed again.

"We need to remove this dust from our clothes and drink water to wash it from our bodies." She brushed off her clothing.

"Will the mold grow inside us?" Al sneezed again. "I'm still stuck here, and the fungus is cold, but Gopal broke down the barrier between us."

Zita viewed the sneezing wizards behind her and shouted, "All of you, out of the tunnel right now. Walk around Al and watch out for the mold on the floor and walls. Eat grass when you get outside so you will vomit. Get this stuff off your bodies. Roll around on the ground."

Zita noticed the light at the end of the shaft getting darker. "Hurry. The tunnel exit is closing." She craved a drink of water and wanted to bathe. Her stomach churned with fear of the mold growing inside her lungs. Would her lungs rupture? She raised hands to the tunnel ceiling shaking them. "I will get you, Dad, for leaving me in the castle."

The wizards bounded past Al racing to freedom outside the dungeon tunnels.

Zita watched them leave the tunnel as the hole became dimmer and gloomier. A thought ran through Zita's mind, she could perish here in the castle tunnels, or she could walk out of the tunnel and leave the big dork to die.

"Okay Zita, what's your plan? I'm freezing here."

She mumbled under her breath, "The plan is to leave you here to die."

"What did you say? I thought you said leave me to die." Al sputtered and sneezed.

Zita licked her lips and spit on the tunnel floor. "No, I will use a lighter hammer than the kid to kick up less dust." She touched her pendant, chanted a spell and a small hammer tapped on the lump of mold that entrapped Al. "This will take a while."

Al sneezed as Zita knocked dust into the air. In time, she freed his abdomen, and he twisted at the waist. "Ah better." He sneezed two more times and coughed. "Is my eyesight going? It's getting dark."

"No, we must get out, the shaft is closing, and we'll be trapped."

"We won't be trapped because the tunnel isn't closing." Al coughed a long hacking cough.

Lightning lit the shaft as thunder boomed, the sound carrying on the chilled wind.

"Hurry Zita," Al coughed. "I'm having trouble breathing and want to get out of here."

"Yeah, me too." She stared up at Al. In the tunnel darkness he appeared hideous with green spots splotching his skin, and the whites of his eyes were blood red.

Zita worked faster but reached the limit of her magic using three hammers on the mold mound. She released Al's left foot.

He lifted the foot, almost fell and placed his hand on her shoulders and coughed.

Blood dripped onto Zita's hand. "Al what's happening?"

Al slumped onto Zita.

What did he expect? She wasn't a nurse and didn't know how to care for injured people. "Al don't do this to me." Should she leave him? She might as well because he wouldn't survive. The mold worked too fast as it grew inside his warm body.

Blood trickled onto her arm. Not this. The blood reminded her too much of her mother that fateful night when the arrows flew from the tower walls. The first couple of arrows injured Zita's mom. Then when Zita ran to discover why Mommy stopped, blood dripped over Zita and her little cloth doll. Reliving these memories. Too much.

Zita stood.

Al stumbled to one knee; his right foot was still firmly held by the fungus. Cracks on his skin show red with pooling blood.

She ran toward the shaft exit.

CHAPTER 46

Al begged, "Zita help, don't leave me here to die. My friends don't know where I am. Help me get out of the tunnel, please?"

Zita paused, glanced back at Al and shook her head. "No, I can't, you don't understand." He had never experienced suffering and couldn't possibly understand the way she felt right now. "Don't condemn me for this, but I can't watch you die. It's not my fault." Blood puddled on the rock floor around Al as his wounds worsened. She stared at the blood on her arms and hands.

"Find my friends, and tell them where I am." He hacked up blood.

Zita felt numb, and a knot formed in her throat. "Why did you do this to me?" She had to get out, now.

"Help."

She dashed from the tunnel into the tumult of a raging storm with heavy, driving rain. Lightning flashed, highlighting young wizards rolling in the grass, as arrows flew from the castle walls.

Zita yelled over the roar of the storm. "What are you guys doing? Move, get out of here, run toward the mountains."

The wizards moved. *Where's Blayze? I'm not a wet nurse to young kids.* She prepared to run when she noticed Erik and Sherry pressed against the castle wall.

Sherry approached Zita. "Where's Al?"

"I don't know." Zita lied.

Sherry clasped Zita's forearm. "Where's my friend?"

Zita pointed to the tunnel. "He's dead."

Sherry's arms dropped to her side, and her mouth hung open as she stared dumbfounded at Zita.

Erik pushed Zita into the tunnel. "Show me where Al is."

"No, I can't go in there." She recoiled toward Erik as she struggled to wipe dried blood off her arms. This whole experience had brought back too many memories and nightmares, re-living that fatal night years ago.

"Show me, maybe I can help. What happened?" Erik forced the struggling Zita into the tunnel.

She jerked her arm aside and walked toward Al's unmoving body. She puffed out her cheeks and shook her head. "It's not my fault, I tried helping, but he died."

Reaching Al's body, she covered her mouth. Blood pooled on the ground around the fallen wizard. Her throat burned, and she had the dry heaves. She felt dirty, wanting to leave, and she pushed at Erik as she sought to flee.

"No, wait, I may need your aid." Erik kneeled next to Al, touching his friend's body. "Buddy, are you okay? Are you conscious?"

Al mumbled, "Help."

"Zita, help me pick him off this floor and out of the tunnel. What happened?"

"He inhaled mold dust when it shattered." She compelled herself closer to the body.

"Grab the other arm. Come on, he's still alive."

She stumbled closer to the prone body but kept her arms by her sides. *Is that Mommy on the floor? I didn't intend to hurt you Mommy. Daddy was delighted when I told him the plan.* She inched closer to the body on the floor. *Why won't Mommy get up and hug me? I'm scared Mommy.*

"Get down here and help." Erik toiled to bring Al to his feet.

Zita came back to the present, stooped and hoisted one side, helping Al stand. She used magic to free his other foot.

Al had no strength and acted like a dead weight to Zita. The three stumbled to the tunnel exit avoiding the mold.

When they reached the tunnel opening, Al leaned to Zita and kissed her cheek. "You came back."

Zita stared up at Al and bit her lip. A jolt of happiness surged through her body, and Al's weight felt lighter until she found Sherry standing at the tunnel exit.

Sherry pushed Zita against the castle wall and seized the unsupported Al. "Take your hands off my Al. What did you do to him?"

Erik said, "She did nothing, he inhaled mold dust and is having an allergic reaction."

Al wheezed with troubled breathing.

"The inhaler in his pocket." Sherry fumbled through his front pockets and pulled out the inhaler. "Al, use the inhaler. Can you hear me? Do you understand what to do?"

He whispered, "Yes."

Sherry placed the plastic mouthpiece in his mouth and squeezed the device.

"Didn't get much." Al undulated back and forth, "Again."

Sherry repeated the steps, but after pressing the canister, she said, "It didn't work."

"Yeah, almost empty when I left home," Al took the inhaler and stuck it back in his pocket. "Where's my staff?"

"What staff?" asked Sherry?

"My grandfather's staff … in the tunnel … must go back." He twisted and slipped to the ground. Rain poured down on his fallen body.

Erik said, "Forget the staff."

"No, it's my grandfather's."

Sherry fell to the soggy ground and wiped Al's face with the hem of her dress, wiping off blood and splotches of mold covering his face.

Zita wondered what to do next, should she leave these teenagers from another planet? Let them fend for themselves. She had lost Kestrel, and Dad didn't display much love these days. Go elsewhere to a fresh new life? Glancing for an escape route, she spotted wizards on the ground with arrows protruding from their lifeless bodies. The others had fled.

She turned to Erik. "Now you've found your friend, where will you go?"

Erik didn't hesitate. "Lily is on her way to be sacrificed, so we're traveling to the volcano."

Zita fell silent and studied her feet. Then she blurted, "Lily is engaged to Kestrel … to be married." She felt blood rushing to her face.

Erik ignored the comment and bent to Al. "Let's get him up and head to the volcano."

They struggled to get Al to his feet. His face, was green and blackened where mold had splotched it, but the blood had stopped dripping from his mouth and nose. Al coughed. "I need my staff before we leave."

"Can you make it to the volcano?" Erik asked the swaying Al.

"May I join you?" Zita asked and moved toward Erik as a sense of destiny coursed through her body. She needed Erik; she desired him to hug her but feared getting that close.

"That witch is not coming with us." Sherry held Al and pointed at Zita. "She made us wander around the mountains for days, dropping us in the control of the resistance and now—"

"Halt, what are you doing here?" Castle soldiers surrounded them.

Erik whispered, "Zita can you use your influence in this situation?"

"No, I'm supposed to be in the castle under house arrest."

"Any chance you and Al can use magic?" Erik drifted closer to Zita.

"Who are you people, and what are you doing near the castle? Are you helping these criminals escape?" The soldier pointed to the dead wizards lying on the ground.

"We're just farmers working the land for the king." Sherry stepped near the man. The rain had matted her hair, kerchief and clothing. Her tunic was muddy from helping Al and she looked every part the farmer. "When the storm broke, we took shelter in this shaft."

The guard peered at Sherry and the others. "Yeah, they aren't with these criminals."

"Okay, go home, but stay away from this wall. We better never catch you by the castle wall again. Go back to your home when it rains."

He trudged back to the other soldiers. "They're a bunch of simple peasants."

Sherry said, "Wait, the other girl, Zita, escaped from the tunnel with the wizards."

Blood rushed from Zita's face. "Are you kidding me? You little brat."

Sherry stuck her tongue out at Zita.

Erik stared at Sherry as if dumbstruck.

A soldier recognized Zita and seized her. "Come with me. You're supposed to be in the castle under house detention. How did you get out? Were you helping these wizards escape?"

Zita's mind scrambled to take control of the transpiring situation, "No, no, no, no, no!" She lifted her hands. "Don't touch me, and I'm not going back to the castle." She raised her voice. "Anyone who touches me will clean out the cesspit tonight." She needed time. So close to escaping she wasn't going to get pulled back into the castle.

"Come with me, my princess. We won't touch you if you cooperate, but don't force us to get rough with you." Three guards surrounded Zita.

Zita thought of her choices. Let Sherry go or tell the guards Sherry is part of the breakout plan? Let the little brat be flung into the dungeon. That'll soften her up, but dorky Al won't be too happy.

The soldiers poked Zita to leave.

Al said, "Staff come."

A soldier said, "What did he say?"

The staff flew from the tunnel into Al's hands.

In a deep voice, the staff said, "Master."

"My staff." And raised it to the sky.

The soldiers spun. "They're with the wizards, grab them."

The soldiers tossed the teens to the ground, and took the staff from Al. "Don't let him touch the staff, he must be a wizard. Find our wizards to restrict his magic."

Lightning flashed, and the rain stopped as the storm lessened. Zita must stop the soldiers from capturing them. I have to escape the castle and go to the volcano to enjoy the ecstasy of the magic of Velidred.

CHAPTER 47

Al felt dizzy from the loss of blood, the allergic reaction to the mold and the wretched conditions in the dungeon. The rain refreshed him, yet the whole situation confused him. They marched toward the castle entryway with three soldiers surrounding each of the teens. No wizards prevented Al from using magic to aid their escape, but one soldier carried the staff of Ishwa.

Zita pushed a soldier and took off sprinting.

Three soldiers chased after her. A soldier caught up and ran next to Zita for ten strides, then lunged for her legs at the same moment she changed directions. The soldier slid in the soggy field.

All the captives and soldiers stopped to view the chase.

Al wanted his staff, but feared calling it would make the guards aware of his intentions. He ran through a list of magic spells capable of helping the group escape. Fireballs were always a possibility, but required too much energy and he worried he didn't have the strength. Plus, the noise and time will give warrior wizards from the castle more time to join in the fight. He needed something quiet and effective.

Zita ran into a ditch, and a soldier yelled as he tripped and plunged headfirst down the steep side. Two other soldiers ran from the castle gate to capture the fleeing princess.

What do I know well enough to help them escape that uses the least amount of magic and power? He reflected back to his training sessions with Gopal. Yes, the night where he mastered the skill of hiding.

He watched Zita's long hair bounce and bob in the ditch as two soldiers invaded the gully farther upstream to block her route. She slowed.

Al noticed the humidity in the air after the storm, and the low, dark clouds. The wind had ceased and nighttime loomed, making the fields gloomy.

The princess bounded out of the ditch returning in the direction of the teens as the soldiers grappled with their burdens of swords and heavy uniforms to mount the gully walls.

Yes, Zita, run toward us. We all need to be near each other to escape without harm. He thought of the incantation needed. The timing had to be perfect, with the precise measure of magic coinciding with Zita reaching their position.

A nimble runner, with her hands holding up her skirt, Zita closed the distance to the teens to less than a hundred yards.

Al believed a football fan would cheer Zita's footwork, her ability to feint and uninterrupted movement toward the goal line. Once she was forty yards from them, he could recite the incantation.

Zita ran. Seventy yards to go, she pivoted right to dodge a diving soldier then sped onward to the teens. She reached sixty yards, and eluded the outstretched arms of two soldiers who smashed into each other. The next ten yards became a dash with a sweating soldier gaining ground at each step.

Al prepared the incantation, urging Zita in his mind. *Continue straight toward us Zita. Just another five yards to go before I commence the spell.*

She veered left toward the ditch and poured on the speed.

Al yelled, "No, Zita, this way, run toward us."

A soldier bopped Al in the head causing him to waver, "Shut up or I'll thrust this spear in you."

As Zita looked over her shoulder toward Al, she slipped on the soggy grass, tumbled head first and slid face and chest first through the mud.

The young soldier chasing Zita didn't expect her to fall. He tried to slow, struggled to stoop low to seize her, but hurtled by, and plunged headlong into the ditch.

Zita jumped to her feet and broke back toward Al and the teens.

Ten soldiers gathered to block the princess as they stood between Al and Zita. She would be trapped, with no way to beat that many.

Al whispered the enchantment. "Cool air, scorched earth, moisture high in the sky, waterlog, pollywog, clouds drop low, form the fog."

"I ordered you to shut your trap." A guard struck Al against the back of his skull with a club.

Al crumpled to the ground.

The soldier struck the new wizard thrice more.

Sherry ran to his defense. "Stop beating him, he's injured."

She shoved the guard away from Al.

Fog rose from the ground covering everyone's knees.

Al's head buzzed from the blows, ending his concentration and causing the mist to quit expanding. He lifted his head off the ground as Zita stopped twelve feet from the soldiers who encircled her.

Al launched a fireball into the sky producing a massive concussive explosion reminding him of Fourth of July fireworks that generate a loud bang with little flickering sparkles.

Everyone gawked at the fireworks.

Al stood, repeating the incantation, "Cool air, scorched earth, moisture high in the sky, waterlog, pollywog, clouds come low, form the fog."

Sherry scolded the guard with the Billy club and Erik jumped on the man's back.

Al lifted his arms and yelled, "Come staff."

Confusion rang among the soldiers. "Hold them."

The men surrounding Zita stopped advancing toward her and twisted to glance at the teens.

Zita, her face and dress covered in mud, sprinted between two of the soldiers heading straight for Al and the others.

One guard said, "Help me, the staff is trying to fly."

A soldier leapt to the man's side, grabbing the staff with both hands.

"Come staff."

"We can't hold it, help."

Fog swept across the ground covering his friends, soldiers and the sprinting Zita. He felt the staff move toward him in the air and settle in his palms. Raising the staff with one hand he shouted, "I am Alpherge the Mighty."

Sherry and Erik grabbed Al and hauled him in the opposite direction of the castle gate.

Al created a shield to protect from arrows, spears and soldiers as the fog covered their escape.

Zita crashed into the shield and slumped to the ground. Erik dragged her under the defensive enclosure and carried her in his arms as they snuck off in the fog, hidden from the soldiers.

CHAPTER 48

Al rested in a gully two miles from the village. He tried to relax but adrenaline pumped through his body after using magic and the dungeon adventure.

Erik said, "Is everybody okay?"

Al noticed for the first time that Sherry wore clothing matching the locals. Sherry's drawn face showed fatigue, her hair was frizzy and the wet tunic clung to her body, but Al felt safe and whole. He hugged her. "I love you."

"Love you back, Brainiac."

Both laughed. Al said, "I haven't been called that nickname in a week. Missed you, Sherry Berry."

"Can I break up this love fest?" Erik climbed out of the ditch. "I'm going to the volcano, are any of you coming with me?"

"I'll go with you." Al attempted to walk out of the gulley, slipped and collapsed face forward into the muck.

Erik slid back down the slippery terrain and helped Sherry push Al out of the gulley.

Al wiped his clothing, removing muck and the previous year's autumn leaves.

Reaching the trail leading to the volcano, Sherry pulled Zita to the side. The conversation started as a whisper, but escalated in volume.

Sherry squeezed Zita's arm. "If you touch or kiss Al again, I will make you hurt so bad you'll wish you remained at the castle."

"I'm a princess. I do what I wish, and you can't stop me."

Sherry spun Zita around. "I can stop you. And if you give us wrong directions to the volcano, I will throw you into the volcano even if I have to drag you a hundred miles."

Zita pushed Sherry.

Sherry came back into Zita's face ready for the challenge.

Erik stepped between them. "Stop it, both of you. Zita agreed to take us to the sacrifice and promised to travel the quickest way possible. I trust her." He pushed the girls apart.

They walked in silence for two hours in the dark. The arduous, uphill path, a combination of clay, slate and granite, contained dangerous slippery sections. The pathway was worn smooth in the clay and mud from the multitude of people traveling to the volcano. Al pulled himself up the muddy mountain using rocks as handholds and grasping shrubs, saplings and trees to keep from sliding.

Al, exhausted, when they halted for supper at a modest tavern, collapsed onto a bench at a table near the fireplace.

He devoured a hearty, spiced meat and vegetable soup from a wooden bowl and found his head jerking as he almost dropped asleep in the half eaten second bowl of soup.

When Sherry left the table to freshen up, Zita slid in beside Al and handed him a glass vial.

"Listen, this vial contains a magic potion. There will come a time when you want extra magic. Drink the vial's contents till it's empty. The elixir gives you about fifteen minutes of double your current magical powers."

"Does it have any side effects?"

"Nothing serious."

"What does that mean, nothing serious? Will it kill me? That's like those drug commercials on TV, medication might cause baldness, diarrhea, constipation, loss of appetite, convulsions, death, don't take if you're allergic to any ingredients."

"No, some wizards experience a little queasiness, but my dad uses it. In fact, I swiped it from his supply, and he uses the potion with no bad side effects." Zita brushed hair from her eyes.

Al lifted the glass stopper and sniffed. "Smells like apple juice. Drink it and receive fifteen minutes of added magic power?"

"Yes. Here comes Sherry, put it away." Zita slid back to her spot on the bench.

Al slipped the vial into his pocket as Sherry sat on the bench between him and Zita.

"What did the horrid witch say to you? I noticed her talking to you." Sherry crossed her arms in front of her chest and stared at Zita.

"Nothing." Not good at deception, Al felt sure Sherry would disapprove of the vial of magic. "She noticed I almost fell asleep in my bowl of soup and wanted to make certain I was okay."

"She's not to talk to you." Sherry glared at the other woman.

When they came out of the tavern, stars crowded the clear night sky. Al felt refreshed by the soup, but after an hour of walking, his eyelids became heavy and he swayed from side to side. He slurred, "Are those torches ahead?"

Zita said, "Yes, that should be the Velidred River Bridge. After crossing the bridge, we have ten miles to travel to the sacrifice altar. It's the largest and only bridge over the river in a hundred miles.

They found the bridge guarded by castle soldiers. When the teens tried to cross, a guard blocked their way.

"No one is allowed across this bridge." The guard held a sword in his hand and halted them with his shield.

"But we want to go to the triple eclipse celebration," Zita said.

"The celebration is closed, orders from the king are not to allow anyone else to the volcano."

"I'm the king's daughter, and he requested me to be there." Zita fiddled with her gold jewelry.

"Don't care who you are lady, because I gots orders and I'm following those orders."

Two soldiers stood behind the guard, one large with a long, bushy black beard and the second with a blonde pencil mustache.

The teens backed away and huddled.

Erik said, "Are there any other places to cross?"

"The next closest bridge to cross this river is one hundred miles north of here." Zita played with her pendant. "Requires walking two hundred miles or more in mountainous terrain to get back to the celebration."

Sherry said, "Stop calling it a celebration, my friend might be killed."

Al said, "I can blast the guards with a fireball." He wanted to sit and had trouble following the discussion because of his fatigue.

Zita said, "Let me knock them off the bridge with air."

"There might be a thousand soldiers on the other side of the river." Erik said, "Are there other places where the locals cross?"

"I recall as a child coming up here with Dad. Before the king built this bridge, we crossed a rope suspension bridge maybe a mile north. Maybe the soldiers aren't watching that bridge."

# # # #

They trekked for half an hour up the mountain, the terrain and path more hazardous and steeper with each step. Zita veered off the trail to a path heading toward the river. The teens followed.

Zita stopped. "No not this way, go back where we split off the trail."

Sherry stopped. "Do you know where you're leading or are we just meandering around the mountain at night? Is there danger of wolves, bears, stegox, mountain lions or some other nasty animal in these mountains? Are you hoping we get eaten?"

"It's been years since I came this way. I was a kid then, and it's dark now, so leave me alone until I get my bearings."

"Do you recognize anything?" Erik asked.

"Thought I did, but this area is different from how I remember it, the shrubs and trees have grown."

The wandering wearied Al. He had trouble breathing from the altitude and still suffered from effects of the brown mold allergy making it painful drawing in deep breaths. "Wait a second, I have to catch my breath."

"Listen, is that rushing water?" Zita asked.

"I've been hearing it a long time, because we've been walking next to the river for an hour," Erik said.

"No, a specific, unique sound coming from that next ridge. That's where the rope bridge is located." She pointed to a spot above. "I remember that sound, the bridge is there."

The teens followed the narrow-overgrown path to the ridge. Al wheezed the entire way and had nothing left upon reaching the ridge, collapsing to the granite ledge.

The all stopped on a rock outcropping next to Al.

Water cascaded off the mountain, and tiny droplets of moisture bounced off the rocks forming a mist on Al's arms. The opposite side lay in darkness. No bridge was in sight.

CHAPTER 49

$\mathbf{Z}$ita stood at the precipice of the rushing water. Abutments remained where a bridge had once been fastened, but no trace of the rope existed.

Erik shook his head and yelled across the river, "Noooooo." He collapsed to his knees in the muck.

Sherry came over and rubbed his shoulder. "We'll figure out something. We've beaten worse odds than this."

"Leave me alone, we lost the war. Go comfort Al because the quest is finished." He removed her hand from his shoulder. "It's over." He slammed his fist against his leg.

Zita had trouble breathing in the thin mountain air and smelled the sulfur coming from the volcano, glowing a dull red in the distance. Should she try to comfort Erik? "Is there anything I can do to help?"

He glared at Zita.

She smoothed Erik's hair back, disturbed from the wind, rain and storm. Her heart raced, touching Erik this way. Despite fatigue, she felt euphoria being with this man. She had never felt this way with Kestrel.

Erik pushed her hand off his head and said, "It's your fault. If you hadn't taken us in the wrong direction, we could have reached the castle earlier. We would have gotten away before the procession out of the village and before the soldiers closed the bridge. I wouldn't have an arrow wound in my shoulder and could have rescued Lily." He rose and pointed a finger at her. "It's your fault."

Her chest tightened, "What? No. Not m—"

"The spiritualist, Forest River Blossom, when she predicted Al's death … you arranged that didn't you?"

"No, what do you mean? I didn't." *Where is this coming from? I haven't seen Forest River Blossom in years.*

"Well, you almost succeeded, Al's over there near death."

Zita's body temperature rose, blood rising in her cheeks. "I had nothing to do with that prophecy."

"You arranged a meetup with that Prince Krunal character and the resistance. Trapping us with those guys."

"What are you talking about?"

"What am I talking about? Hah! The whole strategy to prevent us from rescuing our friend. You arranged it all. I'll bet you conceived this plan with Kestrel months ago."

"I didn't even know you existed ten days ago. There's no way I could have prepared all this." Zita raised her voice in pitch and volume.

"We wasted four days heading in the wrong direction."

It felt like Erik kept punching her in the stomach, and she waved a hand back and forth. "No, it's not like that."

"Did Kestrel cast a spell on Lily? Does she realize what she's doing?"

"Are you kidding? Kestrel knows how to make things explode and has no delicate touch of a true sorcerer to alter thoughts. Come on, we're all exhausted and need rest."

Al wheezed, "Erik, dude, chill."

Erik rubbed his hands through his hair. "Sure, that's what you want us to do. Rest and forget about what the king will do to our friend. Well, I'm not resting."

"Rest for a few minutes." *Why is Erik pushing so hard? I should have used magic on the bridge to get us across, then we wouldn't be in this position.*

"See the fire blazing in the volcano?" Erik pointed to the crimson glow in the night sky. "A girl I cherish is scheduled for sacrifice in the volcano."

Sherry put her hands on Erik's chest. "Come on, give her a break, we're all tired."

Zita said, "Please, just a little rest. There must be another way across the river."

Erik raised both hands and looked left and right. "Do you see any other bridge? Why did you lead us away from the castle?" He approached and raised his voice.

She backed up. "No. I didn't mean to hurt you and lead you astray. Someone forced me."

"What do you mean forced?"

"Why are you doing this to me?" She sought help from Al and Sherry.

"Tell me what you mean by forced."

"I, I, I don't know."

"Yeah, you do. Stop lying and tell me." Erik approached Zita, his jaw tight, as he stood over her.

"I followed orders." She maintained her position and stared into Erik's eyes in the shadowy light. The red glow of the volcano reflected in the boy's eyes.

"What orders?" Erik placed his hands on her upper arms.

Zita slapped Erik's hands. "Let's search for another way across the river. We don't have to cross here. The locals must have a canoe stashed somewhere along the river. I will lead." She walked away from Erik.

"Stop. No one's going anywhere until you explain who gave you orders. Why did you lead us all over the countryside? You didn't take us straight to the castle. Why?"

"Why are we wasting time here? We should find another bridge."

"We aren't moving until you answer."

"Okay, okay." She held up her hands in surrender. "Dad forced me to meet you and send you home."

"Well, you failed, because we didn't go home."

She approached Erik and placed her hands on his face. "I didn't know you then. I was just following orders. But now I like you and your friends."

He clutched both her wrists and removed her hands from his face. "You knew what you were doing and managed it well."

Al and Sherry stared at Zita.

"Please Erik." Her voice choked, and she reached for his face again.

"Don't touch me." He stretched back away from Zita. "You need to leave."

"I can still be helpful, because I know magic, the surrounding area and can—"

"No. Know what you can do? Leave." He pointed toward the trail.

She rubbed her arms with her hands, so cold, and in an unsteady voice said, "Please, let me help." She twisted from Erik and moved to Al. "I can coach you on magic."

Al sat on a large, black, volcanic rock, shoulders slumped, eyelids almost closed, head bending toward the ground, exhaustion oozing from his body. He wheezed, "Not my call."

Zita looked to Sherry.

Sherry put up her palm and turned her head away from Zita.

Zita's pleading expression didn't move Erik. He scowled, and she recognized the tension in his body, like a beast ready to pounce on an innocent meal. He approached Zita.

Should she use magic? "How could you accuse me of this? Don't you know how I feel about you?"

She studied Erik for a slow moment, examining the strain in his eyes. Zita broke eye contact, backed away and fled into the darkness.

CHAPTER 50

Zita walked down the path, her throat tight and strained from the stress. *I thought these kids were my friends, but Erik is just like Kestrel. At the first chance, they tread on me and grind me into the ground. Always shunned because I'm the king's daughter, people don't appreciate me for myself. They wanted me for my relationship to the king. What is wrong with me? Why do people always shove me aside or try to use me for their own purposes?*

She wandered without direction down the mountain. The gloom enveloped her, and her lungs felt so constricted they ached. Why did Erik expel her from the group?

The burning volcano glowed fiery red in the distance, and streaks of red showed where lava streamed down the hillside. That is how she felt, a hot, burning pain inside and fiery aches running through her body.

No stopping me now, time to take revenge on them. Throw Erik into the volcano and make sure Lily watches. Kestrel dies next. What to do about Sherry? Ah, special arrangements for the redhead. Dad showed me how to persecute, abuse and torture an individual and Sherry will scream with each painful cut, a minuscule slice at a time.

Zita walked back to the guarded, main bridge and hid in the darkness, devising a plan. If the soldiers didn't expect her, then a quick strike could cause a lot of damage. Then run across and hide in the cover of darkness. Reaching into the folds of her tunic, she brought out a vial like the one given to Al. These guys won't realize what struck them.

The bridge, was lit by torches, and their light revealed two guards standing at the entrance smoking cigarettes with another fifty soldiers sleeping on the bridge. None of the three moons were visible.

Removing the stopper from the vial, she swallowed the syrupy liquid. Although she'd told Al she knew what this would do, it was her first time taking the magic elixir. How fast did it work? Would it act right away or take just a moment? To be prudent, she waited two minutes. The tension in her body relaxed as warmth swept through tired muscles, and her fingers tingled.

The fast-acting potion kicked in and she knew it was time to charge across the bridge. She had to move fast before the time constraint of the potion kicked in. As her excitement built, she became light-headed.

Zita stepped to the two soldiers patrolling the bridge. Before they spoke, she cast a silence spell to prevent their shouts and used air to pitch the soldiers off the bridge into the river. Two splashes confirmed their fate.

The sleeping soldiers did not rouse. She navigated around them verifying the placement of each step before proceeding. The narrow wooden bridge was packed with sleeping soldiers. They lay, sprawled in random positions. A board squeaked as she stepped, which stopped her forward momentum.

A sleeping soldier grunted and curled onto his side.

She feared her pace was too slow. How long had it taken to get this far? Did she have five more minutes or ten, or maybe only two, before the potion's effectiveness diminished? Forty feet of bridge remained, and she didn't know how many soldiers waited on the other side ready to ambush her. She increased the pace but still placed her feet with precision to limit noise.

Not just fifty soldiers slept on the bridge, but a hundred or more. One group of six soldiers was packed so tightly that maneuvering without stepping on one or more was impossible.

Her heart pounded with abandon, from fear, excitement and the elixir. Sweat bubbled on her skin while she figured out how to traverse the heap of sleeping soldiers. *This is taking too long; the potion won't last forever and I might require more on the other side. Dad said fifteen minutes, but that was an estimate. The apothecary wizard wasn't exact in his measurements and the potion reacted differently for each individual. Size and weight probably matter too.*

Suddenly, she felt powerful and confident enough to accomplish any known magic. A thought burst into her mind. B*uild a plank of air over the sleeping soldiers. Then walk over them without waking a soul.* A murmur of incantation and Zita stepped up arranging a foot where she expected the plank. *It's there!*

Zita walked for five feet on air with one more soldier left in the group and she stepped where she thought the invisible plank would be. The platform was too short! Zita stepped on the soldier's skull and fell onto another sleeping soldier.

The soldier yelled, "Hey what's going on?" and shoved her off, "Get off me."

Shouts of waking men filled the air. Soldiers rose to their feet, bringing up shields and swords.

"We're under attack," one called.

"You're not under attack." Zita, surprised by her courage and calmness, felt giddy and said, "It's me, the king's daughter, crossing the bridge."

"No one may cross the bridge." A group of soldiers gathered between Zita and the escape route on the other side.

A glimpse behind her confirmed another ten soldiers approaching. "Well, I'm crossing." Zita raised her right hand above her head, outlining a huge circle like a baseball pitcher wind up. She touched the magic pendant around her neck with her left hand and sent a powerful breeze over the torches burning above the railings. She directed the breeze through the fire and toward the soldiers. The fire increased with the extra oxygen and blasted toward the soldiers.

The soldiers rushed from the fire to the opposite side of the river and Zita followed.

She closed her mouth and covered her head with her arms to protect herself from the flames flowing off the torches.

Behind her a soldier yelled, "The bridge is on fire, line up for a bucket brigade."

Another soldier in front of her yelled commands, "Archers to the ready, we're being attacked, close the bridge."

Zita sprinted as fast as possible and watched a row of soldiers assembling on the other side of the bridge. She raced through the fire and cast a spell, heaving a burst of air, flattening the forming soldiers. A hundred arrows launched at Zita.

CHAPTER 51

Morning broke with bright sunshine and a slight breeze. The sunlight felt delightful to Erik after trudging through rain the previous day. The sleep refreshed him, but he felt famished. His thoughts led to Zita. *Do we need Zita's knowledge if we find a way across the river? She has been to the volcano, and maybe I shouldn't have driven her away.*

Sherry woke and began asking questions. "Did you find a path for us to cross the river? Do you have food for us? Did you go to the drugstore and pick up allergy medication for Al?"

Erik shook his head and rubbed his hand back and forth over his chest. "How did Al sleep?"

"Look at him." Sherry pointed at Al.

Al opened bloodshot, swollen, puffy eyes. He wheezed and coughed, "Morning."

"What fresh pain do you have for us today?" Sherry asked.

Erik lowered his eyes. "I was wrong. This whole trip was a horrible mistake. If I could go back and change things, I would."

"Change things now by hiding in the mountains until the portal opens." Sherry said. "It isn't too late to make the right decision."

"But what about Lily?"

"One thing Mom taught me is you can study only so much, then you have to accept the results. We did everything, but now it's time to accept the results. We know nothing about this world."

Erik wrapped his arms across his middle. He felt a real hurt in his gut knowing Lily would die.

"Stay here, and I'll find something for us to eat. Give me ten minutes."

Erik walked along the river cliff, around several pine trees, and reached an opened area on a rock ridge. The remnants of an abandoned rope bridge hung across the river.

He grabbed a thick, cable rope knotted to a tree and shook it. The rope stretched seventy feet to the opposite cliff.

Erik examined the rope. It was only five feet above the water where it sagged in the middle. He assessed the situation.

The rope had slack and a little play to it. On this side the cliff was fifteen or more feet above the river. The middle was so low their weight might make it dip into the water. The far cliff was even higher. He studied the rope, squinting to see if there were frayed sections. Would it hold them?

He ran back to his friends. "I found a bridge that crosses the river. Follow me."

Sherry gave him an exasperated look.

"Come on." He helped Al to his feet.

They both supported Al as they walked to Erik's find.

When Sherry reached the rope she asked, "Do you expect us to climb that? Are you crazy? Al can't walk by himself and you think he's going to hang from a cable for two hundred feet?"

"It's not two hundred feet, no more than seventy feet, max." Erik thought the odds pretty good for getting to the other side.

"I won't allow Al to navigate that rope."

"Come on, that's not Al, that's Alpherge the Mighty, master of dungeons with a magical staff. Right old buddy?"

Al attempted to rise on his own feet without Sherry's and Erik's aid. He succeeded and stood tall.

"What are you doing, Brainiac? Are you as crazy as Erik? This isn't a fantasy game you two are playing at the kitchen table or on a computer. This is real life in a real world. See the flowing water with all the rain and melting snow? Can you imagine the river's speed and temperature of the water? Melting water from snow might be a degree or two above freezing. Spend less than a minute in the water you'll develop hypothermia. Just around that ridge is a waterfall with hundreds of rocks getting pounded by water." Sherry stood with crossed arms, a wide stance, and narrowed eyes, glaring at the boys.

Erik said, "We can do it. I'll go first to test whether the cable can bear our weight. If I get swept into the river, then let me drown. We can just use hands and legs to scoot across the rope. It'll be easy."

"Recall how much trouble we had getting Al across the bridge on Earth when we started this journey? A distance of ten feet. This is farther and more precarious, but you won't be satisfied until we're all dead, will you?"

Erik pursed his lips. *Is this foolishness?*

"I want to try." Al wheezed and wobbled, unsteady on his feet.

Sherry shook her head. "What are you doing? Erik how long will your shoulder last traversing the rope?"

"My shoulder is perfect."

"Yeah? You walk with your arm by your side. Show me, raise the arm in the air."

Erik lifted his injured arm and grimaced in pain, unable to move the arm above his shoulder. "I don't care, I'm going. Al, remember, keep your eyes focused above the ledge and you'll be great."

Erik stepped to the end of the rope shaking it up and down to judge its weight and strength to carry his body. The cable hung solid, attached to a mature oak tree on this side of the river, two feet above the rocks and a few feet from the edge. He settled on his back under the cable, head facing the river, and draped his legs around the rope. Then gripping it with both hands and clenching his jaw in pain, lifted his weight to the cable. "Easy."

Sherry rubbed her arms. "Are you kidding me, you're gonna go through with this? I'm not going into the river to save you."

Erik crossed the river moving his hands, then sliding his legs. The coarse rope felt rough on his palms and he wished he had gloves to wear. Descending the rope with his head leaning toward the river felt weird. Reaching the rope's low point, his body one foot above the rushing river, he watched fish swimming beneath him. He glanced at his friends on the cliff viewing the crossing. Al gave him a thumb up sign as Sherry turned her back.

The crossing became more difficult going up the other cliff. His legs didn't grip the cable well, he had minimal movement with his injured shoulder, which added more burden to his good shoulder, and his fingers ached for relief. He peered into the clear morning sky and wondered if the first eclipse was coming. Time was running out, and they had to hurry.

Over his left shoulder he noted the rock wall, not far, but a painful, strenuous climb. A few more feet of shimmying up the rope, then Erik was over the ridge, and he dropped hard to the ground. He breathed in deep gasps. The air smelled foul from the volcano. He rested a moment, rose and waved at Sherry and Al. He yelled over the rushing water, but didn't know if they heard him. "Okay, Sherry you're next."

Erik watched an animated conversation between Sherry and Al. Would Al convince her to cross?

She threw up her hands and walked to the cable. She lay on her back the same way Erik had. She paused often as she crossed, her dress seemed to bunch and fall making it difficult for her. At the low point of the crossing, she hung her hands in the water for a couple of minutes for each hand. Then she experienced problems as her dress soaked up water when the loose fabric fell into the river. It took her twice as long to navigate the span as it did Erik.

Erik glanced at the sky and imagined he saw a moon. Difficult to find, he felt it more a shadow than an actual visible object. *Hurry Sherry, because we're running out of time.*

Sherry reached the other side and fell hard on the rocky ridge. She lay on the ground panting and gasping.

Erik waved over at Al.

Al moved toward the rope, leaning on his staff.

"Oh no, the staff." Erik said.

"What?" Sherry asked.

"I should have taken the staff. Al will try to cross holding the cable and the staff."

Al arranged his frame on the rope with his feet going first.

Erik cupped his hands to his mouth and shouted, "Lead with your head not feet."

"He can't hear you over there, because the rushing water is too loud."

Erik tried to signal Al, getting no results as Al prepped for his journey. "Al won't have strength to climb up this cliff with his legs going first."

Al laid the staff over the top of his body, gripped the rope and slid across the rope, hand over hand gliding his feet along the rope. In control, switching hands, legs and feet in unison, sliding the lanky body, making quick work of the distance.

At the rope nadir, the staff slipped, and Al released one hand from the cable to re-position the staff.

It happened so fast. One moment Al was quickly moving forward. Now, he held the rope with one hand, and both feet dangled in the rushing water. He held the staff tightly in his other hand.

Sherry screamed, "You gotta save him!"

"Will the cable hold both of us?"

"Move. Save Al." She pushed Erik toward the rope.

Erik watched as Al struggled to lift his legs to the rope. Al didn't have the core muscle strength to raise his legs that far and flopped several times with his feet splashing back into the water.

Adrenaline surged through Erik's tired body as he settled himself on the rope, and descended to Al. The rope bounced from the added weight, but it held. He reached Al, but wasn't sure how to rescue his tall friend. The rope bounced back and forth every time Al tried to swing his legs upward.

"Stop bouncing." Erik yelled.

"Creatures are in the water." Al yelled back.

"What creatures?"

"I don't know, they're huge, with two legs, two fins and a tail. They look hungry."

Erik watched in horror as a huge reptilian creature jumped out of the water. Al, still gripping the cable with one hand, swung his legs up and away from the animal. The creature's mouth, full of ragged crocodile teeth, snapped broad, gaping jaws at Al's legs.

CHAPTER 52

Al had felt nervous making the passage across the cable. Then the staff shifted, and he lost his foot control on the rope. Now the creatures in the river were inspecting him for breakfast.

Three of the creatures swam in the river and one floated beneath Al. Two more creatures lifted their heads from the water as if to get a better view.

Erik's added mass dragged the cable lower allowing more of Al's legs into the frigid river. His jeans soaked up the water, the added weight making it even more laborious to raise his legs. His abdominal muscles ached each time he lifted his legs, and each breath came with effort.

"Hold on Al, I'm almost there," Erik said.

One creature jumped at Al and he stabbed him with the staff, but he felt his grasp slipping from the rope.

Erik reached Al. "Lift your legs out of the water, maybe I can reach them and help settle them on the cable for you."

Al raised his legs allowing Erik to seize one of Al's tennis shoes and lift. One creature jumped out of the water, its tail bumped Erik and forced him to release Al's foot, which splashed back in the river.

"Erik, buddy, hold on to my foot. I can't continue holding the cable if that creature clamps his mouth on my leg." Al wheezed. "The worst part is I have an itch in the middle of my back and I can't scratch it."

Another creature lined up in the water to jump at him. Al didn't have the strength to lift his legs anymore. It felt like he had fifteen-pound dumbbells on his legs because of the water in his shoes and jeans. His stomach muscles burned; his grip became weaker with each lift of his legs. *Protect myself, don't die here.* He prepared his staff to fend off the creature. Then he remembered what Blayze told him in the dungeon. "The staff isn't a bludgeon, use the staff for wizardry."

One creature swam upstream thirty feet then turned swinging its tail in large, powerful strokes. Nearing Al, it jumped.

Erik yelled, "Watch out Al, raise your legs."

Sherry's scream carried across the noise of the fast-moving river.

Al didn't move, but the creature stopped in mid-air, suspended for a moment, then slid down an invisible barrier. "Ah hah. It works."

"What happened?"

Adrenaline boosted Al's energy, "Magic my friend, from my grandfather, Alpherge the Great. That's an exercise on how to create a shield." Al grinned. "But I need your help. I can't hold on much longer."

Erik reached Al's legs. "Lift your legs. I promise not to drop them this time."

Al pulled his legs up using muscles he didn't expect would work. Every square inch of his core abdominal muscles shook from fatigue.

Erik grabbed and lifted Al's legs to the rope.

Al wrapped his legs around the cable just as his fingers lost their grip. His face splashed into the river. He lost the magic shield from the shock of the frigid water on his face and dropped the staff in the river.

He felt a tingling through his body, drew a small breath, swallowed water and choked, unable to breathe while underwater. No, he couldn't lose the staff, but how to signal it back with his mouth in the water?

Erik grabbed a fistful of the back of Al's shirt and hoisted him backwards out of the river.

Al hung in an awkward position, coughed and said, "I don't bend this way."

Two creatures flew out of the river and Al watched as they brushed their snouts against his belly and legs. His shirt and jeans ripped on the sharp edges of the horns on their snouts.

"I am Alpherge the Mighty," Al said. He planted a shield flat on the water below them. Now, the creatures had problems getting out of the water to reach the teens.

"Come staff." Al commanded.

The staff didn't appear.

"Come staff." Al yelled and searched the water. Where did it go? He had to retrieve it before it floated over the waterfall.

He couldn't see the staff.

Erik was getting low on patience.

"Can you reach the cable with those long arms of yours? Because I can hold you for about five more seconds."

"Come staff."

"Forget the staff, I'm losing my grip and you're gonna land head first back in the river."

Al located the staff, twirling in an eddy on the far side of the river, did water restrict the staff's response to his call?

Al reached for the cable and missed, which is when he understood death sought him. Sometimes on the journey he thought he would perish, but it worked out okay. This time he sensed his time had come to an end. With no physical strength remaining, his breathing shallow and eyes so swollen his vision was limited, he would die. Except he knew magic. He concentrated and chanted, "Rope is flexible, rope is strong, bend to me rope, I sing your song."

The rope curved in one spot, just in front of Al. He grasped the rope just as Erik's grip gave way. Al re-positioned himself and glanced at the creatures in the river.

One reptile swam back and forth, under and around the shield testing the shield with its horned snout.

The staff might be a valuable magic item, but to Al, the connection with his ancestors from this planet was the important feature. The staff must be retrieved. "Come staff."

The creature jumped from a non-shielded region, landed on the shield and didn't sink into the river.

Erik said, "Hey Al, we have a problem."

The creature moved with caution on the shield toward the teens. It roared like a lion and advanced. As it drew closer to the boys, it lifted its front claws off the shield and slid on its fins toward Al. Its mouth was on a level with the rope.

Al watched the staff as it rotated round and round in the swirling water, forced back each time by the speed of the river and debris captured in the eddy.

The creature moved closer, rising ever higher.

Al thought of ways to prevent the creature from killing him. The rope is the key. He extended the rope why not tighten it?

Al said, "Erik, hold on tight. It's gonna get bumpy."

"Yeah, why? We gotta move, we can't stay here."

"Hold on tight."

An incantation formed on Al's lips. "Multiple ropes, twisted right, squeeze the length, make the cable tight."

The cable contracted, jolting Al like a rubber band sending a spit ball. He held on tight, high above the disappointed creature. Al verified Erik was secure, then made the shield disappear forcing the creature into the water. "Climb Erik, I'm running out of energy."

They ascended to the ridge and dropped, first Erik, then Al onto the rocky ledge, drained from the effort.

Al stood and raced toward the rim of the cliff; his fear of heights dissipated as he searched for the staff. *Is it still trapped in the eddy? Please don't go over the waterfall which will crush you into a million splinters.*

Erik said, "Does the sky look peculiar?"

The sun shone, the sky was cloud free, but there was a hazy, lackluster shine. It appeared wrong. Al said, "The eclipse, the first occlusion is happening."

Erik said, "How much time do we have?"

"There's no telling." Sherry said. "It's supposed to be the celebration of the triple moons. Do they do the sacrifices when the first eclipse occurs or the last eclipse?"

"Or several sacrifices at each? Can you tell which moon is going first?" Al asked.

"What difference does it make?" Sherry asked.

"The king worships the Velidred moon, the red one. They will perform the principal sacrifice during that occlusion. All the symbolism I recall from the castle means we have to rescue everyone before the red moon eclipse." His shoes squished with every step as he searched the water. He found the staff again, still caught in the eddy. He dropped onto his belly and leaned over the ledge with a direct sight-line of the object, reached out his hand and said, "Come staff."

The water-saturated staff rushed into his hands, water dripping from the ends.

A deep male voice spoke, "Thank you, Master. I fear telling you, Wizard Isabel may have drowned. We'll know more when the timber dries."

Al's eyes moistened, his nose was runny, and a lump formed in the rear of his throat. *Did I drown Wizard Isabel when I dropped the staff? Why didn't I keep hold of the staff when I submerged? Why, why, why?*

Erik said, "Al, you okay buddy? We gotta leave. How far is it to the volcano?"

Sherry said, "Are you okay Al? Is something wrong?"

"No, nothing, let's go." He followed Sherry.

They walked away from the river and found a trail. After passing a wall of enormous boulders the sound of the river disappeared, and drums pounded a beat in the distance ahead.

Kenneth Brown

"Wherever the sound of the drums is coming from, that's where we're going," Erik said.

CHAPTER 53

The half-occluded sun shone weakly as the teens reached the celebration. The deafening sound of drums, flutes and celebrating irritated Erik. Many young people moved and danced with the pounding beat. Hundreds of women shrouded in red robes sang,

Come to me
Come to me
Turn to me
Turn to me

The beat pulsed as the singers swayed with unfocused eyes, staring into the distance, singing the melodic chant.

Shout to me
Shout to me
Shelter me
Shelter me

The earsplitting noise forced Erik to yell at Sherry and Al. "How do we get to the sacrifice area? Do you see Lily?"

Kneel to me
Kneel to me
Worship me
Worship me

Al, taller than the others, searched over the crowds and said, "Go in that direction." He pointed to the volcano rim five hundred feet higher than the festivities.

> *Praise the Mountain King*
> *Praise the Mountain King*
> *Praise Velidred*
> *Praise Velidred*

People attired in plum and red stood on the volcano's edge. Erik said, "Can we force our way to the rim?"

"No, there's a path in that direction, but soldiers guard the passage."

Several young men and women pressed the teens into the swarm of partiers and offered them refreshment from a wineskin.

Erik, parched, snagged the wineskin and hoisted it to his mouth squeezing the leather.

Al knocked it from his hands.

"Don't drink that elixir. It might contain a magic potion dangerous for us to consume. These people are under a spell or drug induced hypnotism."

Pregnant women screamed within the throng of partiers. Erik realized that many of the women were near their time to give birth. A woman nearby shrieked and sank to the ground.

"We don't have time to help all these mothers." Sherry pointed to a woman raising a newborn infant above her head. The surrounding mob cheered.

The volcano belched fire, and an acrid sulfur stench wafted to Erik. "I can't believe this many pregnant women survived the journey to the volcano. It's bizarre."

The teens pushed their way through partiers, pregnant women, drummers and singers, toward the guards. The thump of drums and singing of women filled the volcano's valley. Beneath their feet, the magma chamber heated the black rock so that it felt hot beneath their feet. A woman raised a newborn baby over her head and then handed the baby to the soldiers.

Sherry said, "Why did that woman hand her baby to a soldier?"

"What's wrong with that?" asked Al.

"What mom would abandon their infant to a soldier? Do you think it's his baby?"

A sudden coldness, despite the fiery heat, streaked through Erik's body, and he stared with open mouth. "No. Over there, that soldier is carrying two babies and is walking them up the mountain."

Sherry put her hands over her mouth. "They can't be taking the babies to the altar. These mothers have trudged many days and miles to have a magical child, and then they offer them up for sacrifice?"

"Use magic to stop them Al." Sherry tugged on his sleeve.

"What can I do? Do we want attention from these soldiers?" Al patted Sherry's arm.

"If you love me, you will do something," she pleaded.

"What am I supposed to do, dash over there and snatch the kids from the soldier's hands?"

"Work the staff. Doesn't that give you extra power?"

"It does, but I have to be careful or I can burn myself out grabbing too much energy. I'd literally burn to ashes. That's what killed my grandfather."

Sherry took deep breaths while tears formed in her eyes.

Hundreds of soldiers stood between them and the sacrifice altar. "We need a plan to get through these soldiers."

"Who are those people over there that aren't dancing or singing?" Al pointed to a spot away from the musicians and vocalists. "They're all dressed in shiny yellow robes. What does that mean?"

A woman near the teens screamed, and a group of celebrators ran to the mother and cheered. A man, clad in yellow, ran from his group to join the cheering spectators.

"This is too weird for me," Al said.

The woman wailed, and the throng of onlookers cheered with each cry. They chanted in unison with the beating drums, "Push for the mountain king, push for Velidred, push, push, push." The crowd cheered.

Then a man yelled, "It's a boy, present him to the god of Velidred!"

Sherry said, "Wait, what's happening? That guy with the yellow robe just rushed into the crowd and grabbed the baby. He's holding it above his head away from the hands of the mother and partiers." She grabbed Erik's shoulder. "That's Cugbert. What's he doing with the baby?"

The tall, broad priest stepped out of the throng and ran with the baby to the group dressed in yellow.

Two young men passed by the teens with a howling child and presented the child to the soldiers. "A wizard for the king. A wizard for Velidred."

"Maybe Cugbert can help us." Sherry followed the priest.

They caught up with Cugbert and the others attired in yellow. Men and women were tending about forty babies.

"Cugbert! Cugbert!" Sherry yelled and waved to draw his attention.

He scanned the crowd and noticed Sherry. "Ah, fantastic." He yelled, "I expected you."

Erik felt on edge. "What do you mean you expected us?"

"I knew you would come with innate talents to fulfill the prophecies."

"We don't have time to help you with the babies," Erik said.

"We don't need help with the babies."

"But ... they will be sacrificed ... and these poor moms." Sherry sobbed.

"No, the babies aren't sacrificed. The king will raise them to be wizards in his army. But the hour is coming for you to confront the king." Cugbert glanced at the cheering and dancing crowd. He pointed to a section and nodded his head to a guy dressed in yellow who raced to the cheering throng.

Erik said, "How's that gonna happen? We can't get through that many soldiers."

"I will show you a path to reach the king."

# # # #

Zita had a horrid night, waking to a headache that pounded like a hammer in the front of her brain. Was it caused by the potion or from sleeping in the woodland all night? She had escaped the archers within an inch of her life. Using wind, she drove the arrows back, causing the archers to scatter. She ran for an hour checking behind her for following soldiers, and then she hid the rest of the night. An hour after drinking her father's elixir, the potion quit working. Vitality and energy drained from her ragged body.

The sun shone bright in the dawn which hurt her mood and her headache. She woke with eyelids and a loud ringing in her ears. She had trouble focusing but knew the day required vigilance.

The goal today: get to the volcano rim and gain magical energy from each of the sacrifices. Her father performed the same rituals and repeated the same chants with each sacrifice. The magic flowed from the moon, from the sacrifice, from the volcano and from the blood. A stable position on the periphery should allow her to be a repository for the flowing magic.

The first challenge was to reach the rim without an invitation. She had to get past the soldiers guarding the trail. Dad hated having others consuming the magic. He craved it all for himself.

She walked for an hour before the music reached her ears the familiar drums pounding out the rhythm and the magic elixir used to numb the minds of the party goers. Zita had fond memories from past celebrations she attended, but today it had to be different. She must stay alert. The incessant drumming made her head throb.

The eclipse of the triple moons had attracted the largest crowd ever to attend one of these sacrificial events. So many dancing writhing bodies swaying with the rhythm of the drums. The first moon, Pantaleon, occluded the sun. Zita arrived in time to pick up a boost from the magical powers of the Pantaleon moon. She swayed with the music appreciating the surge of magic through her body.

Darkness rolled over the mountain as the moon occluded the sun. Silence filled the celebration. The volcano rim burst into flames, and fire danced fifty feet above the crater, exploding and raining droplets of lava into the caldera.

An immense cheer swelled from the crowd.

In front of the flames which shot high in the sky from the burning volcano, the shadow of a robed figure raising a knife turned toward the eclipse. He brought the knife down to the body on the altar. Brilliant red flashed toward a second shadow standing on a rock above the altar.

Erik felt the hair rise on his neck and arms. In a strident voice, he shouted, "Lily!" He huddled with his friends. "We gotta go."

Cugbert grabbed Erik's shoulder. "Not yet. The moment isn't ripe."

"But Lily is there." He wiped sweat from his brow.

More cheers erupted with each flare rising from the volcano.

Al said, "This whole volcano might explode. We have to move now."

"My friends, linger here and help us comfort the babies. We must save them."

Erik thought Cugbert too calm, like he didn't apprehend what was transpiring around him. "We can't delay. We need to rescue her now."

"Yes, and you must wait." Cugbert said with more conviction. "The time hasn't arrived. Wait for the second eclipse before your move."

Al said, "But, the king's magic gets stronger with each sacrifice to the volcano. We're hoping to rescue our friend while he's weak."

"As the mountain king grows stronger, your magical power increases too, giving you magic required to battle the king."

"Forget battling the king, I plan to rescue Lily and flee. In fact, Master Ishwa told me I required years of training and practice before battling the king."

"No, you must take action today against King Haskell." He studied the teens. "You will work together. Each of you has unique skills critical to the task."

Erik bit his bottom lip. "These guys have skills. Al has magic; Sherry has the strange glowing crown thing. I'm just a mope." He barked a nervous laugh.

Cugbert held Erik by the shoulders and bent near him. "You have more essential qualities, passion, patience, persistence and love. Persistence got you here. Patience will help you act at the proper time. Passion drives you to save your friend. Love will enhance you with wisdom and influence at the critical moment."

# # # #

Zita watched the first moon occlude the sunlight as darkness enveloped the volcano. The crowd became silent. No music. No pounding drums. No chanting and singing. Everyone paused in bewilderment. Closing her eyes, remarkable energy surged through her body. Warmth gushed through every inch, radiating her skin in a mellow, golden radiance, ecstasy and euphoria dancing through her muscles.

Then the wailing of the mothers giving birth crescendoed. The crowd chanted, "Push, push, push. Push for the Mountain King, push for Velidred." *Time to get to the rim.* She forced her way through the party goers.

Forest River Blossom came into Zita's line of view. Years ago, the spiritualist had predicted Zita's death by drowning, thus making Zita afraid of large bodies of water. She despised this woman.

Zita yelled over the swelling noise of the crowd, "Forest River Blossom." It always bothered Zita that the woman wasn't called by a single name.

The spiritualist stopped at the sound of her name and sought the source.

Zita slowly approached.

The spiritualist held her stomach as if in torment when she caught site of Zita.

"Come here." Zita moved her fingers in a signal to get the woman to come.

Forest River Blossom walked with head held high, stepping toward Zita with purpose on the rough volcanic rock.

Zita asked Forest River Blossom, "Why are you here?" Her pulse increased.

"What do you want from me?"

"Why you are here?" Zita's headache flared.

Forest River Blossom's eyes twinkled, and she smiled a playful grin. "I must serve my families and the king's subjects."

Why is that woman smiling when she knows I plan to kill her? "You are here to tell lies." Zita got close to the spiritualist, forcing the shorter woman to incline her neck.

"I reveal no lies, only what the future tells me. Why are you so angry, Zita?"

"I'm not angry," Zita shouted.

The spiritualist lowered her voice to a calming soothing timbre. "You are youthful, and young people don't always envision the larger picture. Relax and reflect on what is transpiring around you. Take your mind off your own problems and acknowledge the obstacles others face. Young women delivering babies on the side of an active volcano is more important than petty personal issues."

"You don't know my personal issues. Your life is hobbly-gobbly fluff, and you can't imagine my distress. I will show you pain." Zita closed her eyes, touched her pendant and let the magic flow, stronger magic, enhanced by the moon of Pantaleon.

"Zita, my child. Take a calming breath." The spiritualist put her palm on Zita's upper arm.

"Don't call me child, and don't use your mumbo jumbo on me."

"Where are your companions, Erik, Al and Sherry? You should be with them. They need you."

Zita rubbed the back of her neck. *Why am I so tense? My mouth is dry, too dry even to swallow.* "They aren't my companions or friends, I left them on the other side of the river and hope they're dead."

"They require your assistance to accomplish their task. You need them because you won't be complete until you make them a part of your life." She rubbed Zita's arm.

"They aren't my friends."

She recalled the image of Erik sending her away. Everybody she ever loved pushed her out of their lives. She adored Cugbert, but he let her down, and her mother left her forever. *Dad locked me in the castle. I hate Erik, Kestrel and that blonde witch, Lily.*

"Get out of my way." Zita, near tears, waved her hand and sent Forest River Blossom across the black rock with a blast of wind.

Zita pushed through a throng of partygoers as she headed toward the path that led up the volcano, hot tears in her eyes. She reached the column of soldiers guarding the route to the rim. With a wave of her hand, she created a gust of magical air and hurled the guards to the ground. She forced others back and stormed up the path.

Then she came to the grouping of wizards whose magic had been made impotent by her father. A favorite trick of her dad's was to bring the strongest wizards to the volcano with the magic flowing all around. But then Dad shielded them from obtaining the flowing magic by placing them in a powerful trance until the ceremony ended. A power play to demonstrate his authority over the fools. All the wizards watched in anguish as magic flowed out of the volcano and into the king. She walked through them with no trouble.

Zita looked for Kestrel in the wizard group, knowing Dad wouldn't allow him to be at the volcano rim with the magic flowing. *Kestrel is a threat to the king and Dad couldn't trust him to be unfettered.* But she didn't find Kestrel with the other wizards.

The trail became steep, and for the last hundred feet to the ledge, the path had steps carved in the volcanic rock. The stair wound in a serpentine shape, in clear view of the volcano rim, to be defended by guards. Pantaleon cleared the sun and sunlight shone on Zita's route.

Zita expected an attack. Guards were stationed to prevent anyone from going up the steps. She deployed a shield of air to protect her from archers. With ten steps remaining to reach the rim, she peered up. Arrows rained from the sky. Why had they waited so long? She hurried the last few steps under her shield as a barrage of arrows bounced and fell to the ground.

She breached the rim to behold Varesh, the chief priest, standing next to the altar. Her father, in red robes, with an expression of rapture on his face, stood on a section of rock above the altar. Kestrel stood next to Lily between the sacrifice victims and the altar. Two sacrifice offerings dressed in purple robes, stood next to the hot bubbling lava. Sweat streamed off of Zita's face. A strong, acrid stink of sulfur filled the air. Dad would be furious at her for leaving the castle and coming to the volcano, but she danced with delight for being here.

Kestrel noticed Zita and his eyes widened in incredulity as he mouthed the phrase, "Are you kidding?"

Sound roared from the lava which pounded in the volcano shaft. Eight soldiers approached and Zita threw half of them over the rim to the side of the volcano and the other half into the bubbling lava. Their weapons fell to the ground.

Zita felt all powerful at making it to the rim. She experienced all the ceremony, the singing, the drums, Dad standing over the ceremonial altar, the high priest handling the sacrifice and the chance to bask in the power of the magic flowing over the volcano. She was at the perfect age to receive the power from the incantations and ritual.

Should I go and confront Kestrel and find out why he isn't with the other wizards trapped from the magic? Maybe I'll visit Dad and see what his reaction might be. No, that idea is too dangerous, Dad might just throw me in the volcano or let Varesh sacrifice me.

More soldiers ran toward her and she dispatched them off the volcano peak.

CHAPTER 54

The Pantaleon moon maintained its pace around the planet exposing the sun. Another cheer rose from the crowd. The drums recommenced their rhythm, and the women resumed their song.

Come to me
Come to me
Turn to me
Turn to me

Shout to me
Shout to me
Shelter me
Shelter me

Kneel to me
Kneel to me
Worship me
Worship me

"When are we supposed to go to the king?" Erik asked.

"At the second eclipse," Cugbert said.

Tension built up in Erik's gut. He rubbed his arms as if cold, but sweat dripped off his forehead from the volcano heat. "What should we do?"

"Help us with the babies. There are still more to be collected."

As if on cue, a mother wailed, and a chant grew from a nearby group, "Push, push, push."

"Why is this society so crazy?" Sherry asked.

"It is our culture. Go over there, in that group where a woman is about to deliver. Save the baby." Cugbert pointed to a crowd surrounding a screaming woman. "And stay together."

The three teens ran to the circle of men and women surrounding the woman in labor. The group chanted and swayed with arms wrapped tight around shoulders.

"Let me through." Erik yelled. He tried pulling their arms to make room to penetrate the circle. But they didn't let him through.

Sherry tried to sneak between their legs, but the tight mass prevented access.

The circle became smaller and tighter.

Al approached the swaying huddle and poked his staff between two men. "Excuse me."

Two young people, their arms tight over each other's shoulders stopped chanting their mantra.

Al rose to his full height, planting his staff on the ground.

The circle opened, and Al and the others walked into the midst of the birthing circle.

The woman wailed, howled, whimpered and screamed as she experienced the pains of birth on the volcanic rock.

"I'm here to help you." Sherry kneeled next to the woman. "Al, hold her head and lift her torso like she's doing crunches. That will make it easier for her to push."

"Are you mad? I'm not doing that." Al backed away.

"Erik, get down here."

Erik dropped to the rocky surface.

"This girl isn't any older than I am." Sherry grasped the girl's hand. "So young to go through this agony. What's your name, sweetie?"

"Clarice." The girl tensed.

Sherry said, "Erik, hold up her body." She released the girl's hand. "Okay, Clarice, a nice big push for me."

The throng chanted, "Push, push, push, push for the mountain king, and push for Velidred."

Erik felt the surrounding bodies swaying to the music, the throng hot with excitement. The land shook with a small earthquake and the stink of sulfur wafted down the side of the volcano. The odor covered the smell of sweat, unwashed clothing and sour body odor from the crowd of men and women swaying around him. Volcanic ash floated by and beached on the sweaty bodies of bystanders and the young girl.

Erik squinted to keep the ash out of his eyes and tried to relax his facial muscles because he had clenched his jaw tight. Why did this crazy society allow these poor young women to give birth in this manner? He leaned over the mother to prevent ash from sticking to her sweaty face and arms.

Clarice pushed at Sherry's insistence. "You can do it, honey. One more big push."

The woman emitted a long low growl.

"That's it. You did it. Oh, Clarice it's a beautiful girl."

The baby's cry was drowned by the music and cheering from the dancing crowd.

Clarice reached for the baby.

Sherry extended the baby to give the child to its mother.

Clarice said, "I must take it to the king."

"Oh no, honey. You can't do that."

"Sherry don't hand over the baby to her." Erik laid the mother's head on the volcanic rock. "Al make room to get us out of here."

Al used his staff, and the huddle cleared a passage for the teens and the baby.

They brought the baby back to Cugbert's group, passing the infant to a woman dressed in a yellow tunic bloodied from handling the newborn babies. She took the child back to a makeshift nursery.

Cugbert waved at the teens and pointed to a circle of people assembling for another childbirth.

Three times they followed the same scenario. Al cleared an entrance into the throng using his magical staff. Erik and Sherry rushed in and helped the wailing mother deliver the child. Then they took the baby to the nursery.

Erik asked Al, "What spell are you using to get us to the mothers?"

Al grinned. "No spell at all. I'm dressed different, holding a staff, and they assume I'm someone important."

After the fourth delivery when bringing the baby back to the priests, Sherry said, "Look who's chatting with Cugbert. What's that woman doing here?"

The woman, Forest River Blossom, stood by Cugbert. Scratches covered her face and arms and a large bruise purpled on her forehead. She said, "Did you send them home?"

"No, we need them here. Today. Now." Cugbert towered over the spiritualist.

"Is Zita with them?"

"No."

"Where is she? I told you the whole plan will be ruined unless Zita helps them." She shifted toward the teens as they approached Cugbert.

Forest River Blossom stared at Erik. "You ignored my advice, I instructed you to leave a few days ago and yet, here you are."

Erik prepared a couple of snotty comments, but held back his anger and displeasure toward the woman. "Yes, we ignored your advice, because we preferred to rescue our friend."

"All isn't lost. The king's daughter, Zita, where is she?"

Erik said nothing.

Sherry said, "Go ahead tell her."

"Tell me what, dear?" Despite her stature she commanded attention.

Sherry said, "She was with us, but he," she pointed at Erik, "drove her away last night. We don't know where she is now."

"It's not my fault. I was tired and, and ...." Erik didn't have an excuse. *Yes, I drove Zita away. She trapped us, lied to us and caused our current bad situation instead of allowing us to head home with our loved ones. Zita didn't help us; she caused our troubles.* Fatigue racked his body from the heat, toil, and pounding drums.

Forest River Blossom said, "Zita is on this mountain, angry, scared, alone and in need of friends. I have proof of her presence here." She pointed to the scratches and bruises on her body.

Forest River Blossom touched Cugbert's arm. "Pull them off the volcano. No matter the loss today, preserve these three for another day. The spirits, the visions, the moons, the stars and the wind have predicted that we lose everything if we let them stay on the volcano without Zita. We had a chance if Zita was re-united with them. But now, we have nothing."

Cugbert answered in a calm voice, "Everything is in motion, and we fight our battles here. Now."

Erik glanced at the sun. "The second eclipse is coming. Cugbert, should we be moving up there?" He pointed to the lava bubbling up the volcano.

"Why are you like this, Cugbert? You're responsible for Zita's mother's death and now these four. How can you live with yourself?" The spiritualist waved her finger in Cugbert's face.

He seized her hand in motion and tugged her toward him. "I'm not a monster fighting machine anymore. I chose peace, and I sympathize with your worries and your prophecies. But times have changed. I believe their friends can be saved, without killing. We need to stop Haskell, but I don't believe death will result. We saved many babies." He motioned to the nursery.

Al whispered to Sherry, "Did the Blossom lady just claim we're all going to die?"

"Don't worry, Brainiac, I'll save you."

Forest River Blossom said, "If Zita had remained with you, maybe you had a slight chance. A poor chance. But Zita is upset, and she has no way to keep her anger at bay. I assure you, Zita is mad at you, livid at her father, and I bet she is furious with you, Cugbert. Watch yourself." She spun and strode from them.

"Does that woman ever have a conversation where she isn't frightening someone?" Sherry asked.

Cugbert watched Forest River Blossom walk away. He did not respond to Sherry's comment.

Al said, "Will we really die if we try to rescue Lily?"

Cugbert didn't answer and still stared at the retreating spiritualist.

Erik grabbed Cugbert's arm. "Should we climb to the rim now? Remember, we have to get through the soldiers." Erik pointed at the eclipse, the near occluded sun painting a dull glow on the mountain.

"Huh, what? Oh yeah. The second eclipse." Cugbert mopped sweat off his brow and issued commands to his colleagues in yellow. He faced the teens. "We aren't going toward the soldiers; there's another approach. A safer way."

CHAPTER 55

The teens walked with Cugbert toward the eastern part of the volcano. Their rapid pace carried them past people of all ages dancing to the music and around pregnant women. Erik thought it the craziest party he had ever witnessed. The drums pounded out the rhythm, and the women sang and chanted.

"Why are we going this direction?" Erik asked. "The path to the rim is over there."

"We will be safer going through the forest instead of walking over cooled volcanic rock. That is the roughest route to navigate. There is a pine forest a little farther, but it won't take as long."

"Won't the king notice we are coming this way and place soldiers in the forest to slaughter us?"

"Possibly — the last hundred yards is difficult to traverse, and the soldiers can defend from the ledge."

"So, a hundred yards unprotected against a band of soldiers with bows and arrows? That's your safe way?" Al asked.

"Yes. Because it's so simple to defend I don't expect the guards to be paying attention, allowing us to creep in undetected."

They reached the forest, and the path climbed the steep slope. The sun was ninety percent occluded. Stars appeared in the sky, and impending darkness created shadows in the pine trees.

Erik noticed strange circular shadows on the ground. "Hey Al, check this out."

Al stopped. "Oh, that's way cool. Wherever sunlight shines through a hole in the tree leaves the shadow shows the amount of the eclipse in the outline of the shadow's circle. Like using a pin hole in a piece of cardboard to let the sunlight shine on the ground to visualize the eclipse."

They persevered up the side of the volcano, the heat increasing with each stride in the forest. The sky darkened as total eclipse approached.

Cugbert said, "Hurry, we need to be near the open area when the full eclipse occurs. As we clear the forest, everyone has to be quiet. Expect total darkness. We have one minute to run one hundred yards."

Cugbert asked Al carrying the staff. "You know magic?"

"Yeah, a little."

"This mountain contains evil magic. The king extracts magical abilities from the Velidred moon, the sacrifices and the volcano." Cugbert stopped Al. "The magic will call to you, but you must resist. The more you draw from these evil sources the eviller you will become. Promise me you won't extract magic from the sacrifices."

"Yeah, okay, can I still use the magic I have?"

"Not a problem. But, remember, we don't want to kill anyone. I want us to defuse this situation with no bloodshed."

Erik asked Cugbert, "How about those birds soaring over the volcano rim? It looks like thirty or forty of them."

"Those are vultures."

"Vultures the size of single engine airplanes?"

"They have a thirty-five-foot wingspan and stand eight to fifteen feet high. The vultures feast on the babies or mothers that perish. They won't attack humans when we're still moving. You're safe for now."

"Wow, it's hot up here." Erik wiped sweat from his brow.

"The lava is near the surface with hundreds of micro fractures in the surface where heat is emanating." Al said. "Stand over here. Do you feel the heat and steam?"

A sliver of light shone from the sun. They still had a hundred feet or more to traverse before reaching the transition point from the forest to the volcanic wasteland.

Cugbert waved his arm. "Come on, hurry."

They picked up the pace, Al wheezing for air by the time they reached the transition point. Nothing remained between the teens and the rim but barren, cooled, volcanic rock. They stood behind pine trees hiding from the soldiers they expected were waiting for them.

Erik watched, mesmerized as the lava bubbled above the ridge. No soldiers were silhouetted against the blaze above the dark rim. The people below still danced and sang, the muted drumbeats almost drowned out from the roar and crash of the boiling lava.

"Okay, in thirty seconds, we run. It will be completely dark by then, but be quiet. Remember how everyone stopped, the drums, singing and cheering, during the last eclipse, the same thing will happen this time."

Al said, "Stay on your feet. The volcanic rock is like glass and can cut your skin to shreds. Be fast, but be careful."

Erik shook out his hands as if preparing to run a foot race in gym class. The higher stakes of this race caused a hollow throbbing in the pit of his gut.

Darkness descended over the volcano, the crowd and drums fell silent, and the gurgles of bubbling lava and sizzle of cooling lava hitting the ground filled the air.

"Now!" Cugbert charged up the hill.

Erik ran up the volcano. The mountain was so dark, but the red glow surrounding the rim illuminated his path. He shot upwards toward the seething lava. The cooled lava field undulated with uneven hills. They ran three feet up and four feet down making it challenging to keep from falling.

The ground shifted under Erik, and he stopped running. "What is that?" The ground shuddered, and Erik lost his balance.

"An earthquake," Al said. "The magma is flowing underneath us causing earthquakes. It might burst through the crust, so watch out for cracks in the surface. You don't want to fall into a lava pit."

Erik struggled as adrenaline poured through his veins. "Isn't this the safe way?"

The shaking ceased, and they ran again. Now Sherry nimbly led the race to the top, and the boys were slower. They lost Cugbert during the trembler.

Al looked back and wondered, *Did Cugbert keep running when the earthquake hit? He told us not to stop.*

It took forever to run up the slope. It might have been only a football field length as the crow flies, but with the ups and downs and zig-zagging, the distance increased. How long had it taken? How much time did they have left? Erik peered up at the eclipse. When he faced the path again, he lost his balance and stumbled down an eight-foot drop. He skidded across the solidified lava, pain coursing through his palm when he extended a hand to avoid landing on his face.

Erik struggled to his feet. The fall must have driven a volcanic sliver through his hand. The sharp pain made him reluctant to bend his thumb toward his fingers for fear of driving the sliver deeper.

A narrow crack formed in the volcanic rock, glowing red. Steam arose, then the crack widened to two feet in just a second. Incredible. *Lava bubbled up from the fracture. Should we try to jump the crack?* Small balls of bubbling lava jumped two feet and crashed back to the pit. If they tried to leap across, they might get struck by the heaving lava. *This is bad.* His leather shoes, more like moccasins, didn't provide much protection against the heated rock.

Erik and his friends raced left along the glowing crack. The ground split open in the same direction they ran. They weren't out-running it.

The same sequence happened over and over, the ground opening, glowing red, releasing smoke and steam and then bubbling lava. Erik could not get in front of the growing fissure.

Erik lost Sherry and Al. The fissure grew ten feet from side to side. Lava shot fifteen feet into the air and then flowed down the face of the slope. *I need to take a chance. If I don't get on the other side soon, I might die.*

He needed a chance to jump. At the next hill, he thought the time had arrived. When Erik crested the top of the hill, a fissure opened in the cool lava valley. He prepared to jump, but again, lava erupted out of the new-formed crack.

With time running out, Erik took the chance. *Take a running jump at the top of a hill and then keep running when I land. I can do it.* The stifling air slowed Erik, already parched from having no water to drink all day. Dehydrated, tired, and injured, he shouldn't be running over hot rocks and vaulting over lava pits.

Everything was going wrong. The angle of the growing fissure he'd been following was forcing him downhill away from his destination. His injured shoulder hurt from running. The scab from the arrow had opened and the bandage was loose inside his tunic. Blood or sweat, or both, trickled down his chest.

He knew it was now or never. Running up the next undulating hill, he saw the fracture form; the red glow brightened. Before losing his momentum, he hurled himself from the top of the mound and watched smoke stream out of the new-born fissure below his churning legs.

CHAPTER 56

Zita walked along the rim to Kestrel. The roar of the bubbling lava pounded like thunder in her head and the stink of rotten eggs permeated the air. Her headache throbbed behind her eyes, but she desired magic.

Varesh, the high priest, dressed in red robes and a black skull cap, stood at the blood-smeared sacrifice altar. He shouted an incantation but the noise from the volcano drowned out the words. Completing the spell, the high priest threw a sacrifice into the burning lava.

Fingers of magic flowed from the volcano straight to the king who stood cloaked in serenity. He looked like a man meditating with the warm summer sunlight on his face at the end of a harsh winter. Fingers of red magic flowed in swirling waves, whirling and twirling around the short man's body. A red glow surrounded the king's body.

Zita stood still for a moment, attracting the magic. She closed her eyes and whispered the incantation her father used on many occasions, "Soponfect momulanti quiducand." Then she relaxed and took a calming breath.

A hot wind from the blazing volcano flowed over her body. Upon opening her eyes, she saw a second red trail of magic leaving the volcano like aerosol lava and swirling in her direction. When the magic reached her, she sneezed. The magic from the Pantaleon moon had felt pure, like honey, but this magic was like stumbling into a mud puddle, dirty, unwashed and tainted. No matter, the magic strengthened her, and Zita moved in cadence with the swelling waves.

Kestrel came to Zita and shoved her away from the red flow. She fell to the ground.

"What are you doing?" Zita asked as she stood.

"This magic isn't for you. Only the king can consume the magic from the sacrifices. I'm here to prevent other wizards from absorbing the flows."

"Ha, that's a laugh. What's in it for you?"

"The king promised he wouldn't sacrifice Lily if I protect him and the magic."

"The king's a liar, and you better hope he doesn't sacrifice you when he sacrifices Lily. Don't you get it? There's no reason to keep her after the last eclipse." Zita stood and brushed volcanic dust off her clothing. She knew she was a mess, not that she cared what Kestrel thought of her appearance. "The king has sensed danger from the teens from Earth; it's about the prophecies. She will be sacrificed because she's from a family Dad wants to eradicate."

"Keep calling the king a liar, I'll sacrifice you myself." Kestrel moved closer to Zita.

Zita didn't move back. Kestrel had a puny little beard on his chin. It was as if he had tried to sprout facial hair to match the king. The look was ugly on the king and even more grotesque on Kestrel. Zita grabbed Kestrel's little chin hairs, and he cried out as she wrenched him to her. "Listen, I'm here, and I'm getting some of this magic. The king can't control all the magic. I'm going to consume some."

He shoved her to the ground again. "I'll throw a fireball at you if you try to seize the magic flows again."

Lily came to them dressed in white. Her pristine clothing protected from the flying volcanic ash by magic.

Zita said, "Try to stop me, and I'll throw you and your precious betrothed into the lava pit." This time Zita would not be bullied by Kestrel, she tired of his games of male dominance. What inducement had he received from this relationship with her dad?

Kestrel shot a fireball at Zita, just missing her right arm. She twisted to her side. "Stop it."

Another fireball whizzed by the other side of Zita, flames licking up her dress.

Zita controlled air and smothered the fire on her clothing. She called up a gust of wind and smashed Lily into Kestrel. "I told you, stop it."

Kestrel fell to the ground as Lily crashed on top of him.

"Okay, I sought the nice way." Kestrel struggled into a standing position.

"Yeah, what're you going to do?" The discharge of magic from the volcano and the moon that had flowed her way during the eclipse had dwindled as the sacrifice was consumed.

Kestrel said, "Hamdat gponli iptilv agerut."

A crystal barrier formed between Zita and the magic from the volcano. The red swirls pooled against the invisible wall, then caromed off the surface and swept toward the king.

Zita said, "No, stop it."

Kestrel didn't respond but used magic to send Zita flying to the far side of the rim.

Zita landed in a crumpled mess like the rag dolls she played with as a girl. Her befuddled brain and a sharp pain in her left side hampered her ability to move.

Darkness encompassed the volcano as the Anticletus moon, the second eclipse, concealed the sun, and the burning lava cast a red glow.

CHAPTER 57

Intense darkness surrounded Al and Sherry as they scrambled up the side of the volcano. They lost contact with Erik when the fractures started to develop in the volcano crust.

Al glanced at Sherry. "Are you okay?" He gasped for air. *Did Erik make it to the rim or is everything up to us?*

Sherry said, "We're almost there."

The sun breached the advancing moon and illuminated soldiers guarding the rim. Each soldier stood with drawn bow and an arrow pointing directly at Al.

Defeat encapsulated him, and Al did the first thing he thought of. He held his hands up in surrender. He slowed and staggered toward the soldiers. Then he reached out and helped Sherry the last few feet over the ledge. Lily's rescue team had failed.

Al's shoulders slumped. He placed one hand on a knee while supporting the other hand with the staff. He couldn't catch his breath. The hot, thin mountain air left him wheezing and gasping for oxygen. His body felt heavy as he feared a return to the dungeon.

To Al's left stood the sacrificial altar with a priest while the king stood on a ridge above the altar. Kestrel and Lily were near the altar. Two girls dressed in purple who appeared to be scheduled as a sacrifice were guarded by soldiers. He touched Sherry on the shoulder and pointed toward the hostages.

"Can we free them?" Sherry whispered.

"You ain't freeing nobody, Missy." A guard prodded her in the ribs with a spear. "Move over there with the other sacrificial offerings."

"Hey, the boy has a staff. Take it from him, before he casts a spell or something."

Three soldiers pounced on Al and seized the staff. "He doesn't look like a wizard. He's a dumb peasant, a sheepherder, not a wizard. Check out his clothes."

Al didn't care anymore. Why had he allowed Erik to talk him into this pipedream? *Go rescue Lily and discover you're on a strange world, with bizarre customs, sacrifices and now captured by soldiers. Would Sherry be sacrificed and tossed into the boiling lava?* His chest tightened. *How do I solve this problem? This isn't a simple problem like solving calculus and physics questions in school, but real-life evil guys.*

Then it struck him. Al, still so new to this magic stuff, forgot he had power to create a shield that prevented these soldiers from touching him.

Al stood straight, raised his hand and called the staff."

The staff vibrated in the soldier's hand.

A soldier said, "The boy's a wizard with magic. Take the staff to Kestrel. He's in charge of all magical items. Tell him we have a wizard here. He'll be interested in these two."

"Come staff."

"Trevor, help him with that staff, we can't let this boy take it back."

Another soldier helped carry the staff as they walked toward Kestrel.

Can't let Kestrel get his hands on the staff again or I might never get it back. "Staff burn hot."

The soldiers stopped as one released his grip on the staff. "Trevor, keep your grip."

"I can't; it's too hot."

"No, it's not. I can hold ... ouch. It's on fire."

"Staff come." The staff, flaming at its lower end, rushed into Al's outstretched palms. "Ouch it's hot." He dropped it to the ground.

"Master should instruct me to cool before catching me in his hands," the staff said in a deep male voice.

"Cool staff, and come."

The staff, charred at one end, said in a female voice. "Fire is a wretched choice of command for a wooden staff. Is it not enough you tried to drown me; now you want to incinerate me?"

"Way to go Brainiac; you got it back. Lily's over there, let's save her.

"Wizard Isabel is alive!"

A soldier poked Al with a spear. "I told ya, you ain't saving nobody."

A part of Anticletus still tempered the sunlight. Al said to Sherry, "What are you doing? You ... you're glowing and there's a crown on your head."

Sherry glowed even in the partial sunlight, causing the soldiers to quit poking her with the spear and move away from her.

Al said, "Sherry are you doing that on purpose?"

She didn't respond.

A short soldier said, "The Crown of Anticletus. Run."

Guards dropped their weapons and fled down the side of the volcano.

The Crown of Anticletus, Al shook his head in astonishment. *Is this what Master Ishwa and Alpherge the Great needed for their trip to obtain the Crystal of Zaraboth? They needed my ladylove; my girlfriend is the Crown of Anticletus. How awesome is that?*

Sherry's glow brightened, and she didn't speak to Al. She moved toward the sacrifice victims, and the soldiers let her pass unmolested.

Al talked rapidly. "This is so cool; you're the Crown of Anticletus. Did you know my grandfather searched for you? He tried to retrieve the Crystal of Zaraboth, but he needed the crown. He wanted you, and here you are and you are awesome."

Sherry stopped walking and kissed Al.

Blood rushed to Al's face, his nerve endings tingling, and he lost connection with the events on the volcano. He took Sherry's hand and thought, "Wow, our first kiss." They had dated a handful of weeks, but Al wasn't a fast-moving romantic guy. He hoped to kiss her the night of the homecoming dance. And here they were kissing on a volcano with death surrounding them. His troubles vanished, and he felt like he floated on air as he beamed at Sherry.

Then magic tugged at him and he noticed the king standing above the sacrificial altar. "Sherry, we're in trouble."

"What's wrong?"

"The king appears to be taking an interest in us."

CHAPTER 58

Erik landed hard just over the crest of the opposite lava hill and rolled to the bottom. He smacked his injured shoulder on the ground when he landed and lay still a moment as pain throbbed through his body. The increasing sunlight would expose him to being observed from the rim.

Too late. Cugbert said they had to reach the rim before the eclipse ended. He failed.

He searched around for Al and Sherry. *Are they safe?* The volcanic rock was so hot he needed to get up or be burned. To rise he had to push up with his impaired shoulder. He groaned out in pain with the effort. Blood soaked through the tunic from the arrow wound.

A voice said, "There's a person moving, prepare your arrows."

The little valley Erik fell into protected him somewhat from the soldiers on the rim. Crouching on his knees, he peeked over the mound of lava.

From above came the command, "Fire," and arrows whizzed toward him.

He ducked.

Where are Al and Sherry? Erik felt safe for the moment, but he scanned the undulating mounds of lava for his friends. *Are they alive, or did the soldiers capture or kill them? I ran left when getting around the lava fractures so I should go right.*

The archers stopped firing. He spotted another mound five feet away to hide behind. If he moved fast, he might not be seen. Should he dive and roll like the action scenes on television? Pain throbbed in his shoulder and the swelling hand from the volcanic splinter. *Nothing fancy, run fast and stay low.*

The sun brightened as the moon climbed and the second eclipse ended. Whatever needed doing had to be finished before the third eclipse.

He drew a deep breath and dashed to the next mound. This mound, smaller than the first, provided less protection, but he stayed flat as another volley of arrows flew above him. There was no sign of his friends.

A man yelled from the rim. "Hey buddy, we don't want to kill you. Just give yourself up, and we won't hurt ya."

Capture by the soldiers will not help the rescue effort, but how can I get to the rim? He had no method of attack available. Erik raced to the next mound, and a spent arrow bounced off the back of his leg. Too close. *Where are Al and Sherry, already at the rim or stuck in a trench?* If they were safe, Erik expected shouting of magical incantations and explosions firing back and forth between the wizards.

He darted to the next mound, moving closer to the top.

Then, as he prepared to run to the next mound two soldiers stuck their heads over the top of the very hill Erik hid behind.

They pointed spears at Erik. "Give it up young fella."

Erik grabbed one of the spears, pulled hard on it and the soldier fell down the volcanic hill, landing on his head. The other soldier poked at Erik, but Erik had time to block the thrust with the stolen spear. He ran uphill to another hiding place. The soldiers with the arrows didn't fire.

Erik found a flat spot, rotated the spear and faced the chasing soldier. He knew nothing about spears or defensive stances.

The soldier parried with the spear while Erik blocked the thrusts and backed away.

Erik worked through spear jousting scenarios in his head. Could he run at the guy and try to pierce the man's body armor? Why didn't they come at him with a sword?

He had watched TV and movie sword fights; he felt confident wielding a sword, but a spear?

A deep thrust by the soldier missed Erik's stomach by inches and Erik almost fell. Despite the deep lunge, the soldier had terrific balance and backed away from a half-hearted plunge by Erik.

Erik backed up to find two spears poking him in the back. He dropped his spear and raised his hands.

The soldiers marched Erik to the rim and Erik surveyed the scene. Al wrestled with soldiers as they pried the staff from his hands. *That staff is more trouble than it's worth.* Sherry glowed and even in the sunshine Erik spotted a slight crown gleaming above her head. The soldiers backed away from Sherry, dropped their weapons and dashed past Erik. Three of the soldiers guarding Erik glanced at Sherry and ran down the volcano hill.

Cugbert ran across Erik's field of vision heading toward two women knotted together.

Erik picked up a discarded sword and sparred with the remaining soldiers. His skills with a sword were worse than with the spear, but he managed to defend himself.

"Don't worry Lily, I'll save you."

He ran toward her using the sword to keep from being stabbed.

Lightness bloomed in his chest; calm and ease entered his body. *We are going to save Lily. Forty feet to go and victory will be mine. All the heartache, fear and pain on this blasted planet will be justified as we save Lily from the evil king.*

Time and space slowed, bubbling lava exploding into the sky. His focus was concentrated on reaching Lily. Find a steady rhythm: breathe in, breathe out, right foot forward, push off, and repeat with the left foot. The pain in his injured body was blocked out as endorphins raced through his body.

Without warning, Erik lifted off the ground and flew in the air toward the bubbling lava.

CHAPTER 59

As Erik ran to rescue the sacrificial captives, Zita's chance to strike arrived. She craved to make Erik suffer the same inner turmoil pulsing through her soul that made her feel helpless and unloved. She plucked him up with air and tossed him toward the bubbling lava, making sure he slid several feet on the volcanic rock. She wanted to take her time killing him.

Erik struggled to his feet, and as he looked her way, Zita whispered to herself, "Yes, it's me," Zita picked Erik up again and flung him toward certain death near the boiling magma beyond the volcano's brink.

Erik lay without stirring.

Zita's next target, Cugbert, slowed to a walk as he reached the sacrificial victims. "Cugbert come here, now." Zita's powers surged, her fingers tingling with magic potential, vitality stronger than she had ever enjoyed. The additional magic gained from the last sacrifice enhanced her power to this new level.

Cugbert flew in the air and landed at her feet.

"Cugbert, today is judgment day for killing my mother."

The peaceful priest rose, dusting off his clothing. "Zita, what happened to your mother was an accident."

"No accident. Mom and I were happy in the castle with Dad."

"Your mother wasn't happy."

"I was happy with Mom alive."

"Your mother, the Queen, begged me to liberate her and the child she adored."

"No, she wanted to leave Dad for love of you," Zita gazed into Cugbert's eyes remembering his gentle nature.

"The Queen didn't love me. I'm a priest and recognized the anguish, abuse and trials she experienced from your dad."

"You wanted to disrupt my wonderful life."

"Zita, the king learned of the escape plan and he provoked the tragedy to your mother. She loved you and wanted a better life for her child."

Zita's eyes watered, and she lowered her head.

Cugbert cupped her chin and lifted to face him. "It's okay. It's not your fault. You were young."

How was I supposed to know anything at that young age? It's all your fault, before you arrived, we were happy. Zita reacted with a blast of air, tossing the large priest fifteen feet.

Tears rolled down her cheeks and her nose dripped.

Cugbert walked back to Zita. "Help us today, and I can take care of you."

"I don't need you to take care of me." Her headache pounded like someone thumping on her skull with a hammer. "I want Mom, my mom."

Cugbert reached out and drew her into his chest wrapping his arms around her.

For a few moments Zita heard nothing and suffered no pain, feeling peace.

"Let us take care of you. We will protect you and show you a different path that includes love." Cugbert whispered.

That would be nice. To be cherished again. Strong emotions of safety and comfort she had felt as a child came rushing into her bosom.

She shoved the priest aside. "Dad will find me; I'll never be safe."

"I can hide and pro—."

"My father—" The world and anguish flooded into her head.

"We'll protect you."

He'll find me,"

"We'll take you far away from Velidred Castle and the local provinces."

"He—"

Cugbert tried to pull her to him again.

She forced him away. "There's no life without Dad."

"We'll break the spell your father has placed on you."

"He can track me. His magic is too powerful."

"We have wizards."

"Ishwa is dead."

"There are others."

The cacophony of the battle and the volcano roared in her ears. Never would there be peace in this life while Dad lived. No path for her to experience what Cugbert preached existed. Peace? Impossible. She touched the gold necklace, aching for the moments when she had felt peaceful with her mother. Everything slowed, and fiery, volcanic heat pulsed against her skin, pounding waves of woe, conflict and frustration.

She tossed Cugbert across the battleground.

This is my destiny. I am my father's daughter. Mom is dead. Zita walked toward Kestrel. She needed to break through the spell Kestrel was using to prevent her from attaining more magic. She touched the barricade, watched the magic strike the wall and glide away toward the king. The rage, the bitterness and despair she felt for her mother streaked inward; she wanted to flee.

Kestrel stood in her path.

She grabbed her pendant and discharged a blast of air at Kestrel causing him to crash hard to the ground.

The barrier blocking her from the magic broke as Kestrel lost his concentration. She absorbed magic from the volcano and the sacrifice as the tainted energy streamed toward her. The filthy magic feeding on the grief and hopelessness she felt stoked her rage.

She felt a delicate touch on her shoulder, and she spun. Cugbert.

"I told you to go."

"Listen. You need the other teenagers if you want to live."

"I don't need you or them. You are dead. The magic from the sacrifices is what I need. I choose magic."

"No, the tainted magic feeds on hate, rage, misery—."

She flung Cugbert toward the hot, burning lava.

CHAPTER 60

The king stood above the sacrificial altar as Sherry began walking toward him. She screamed, "Al help." She raised a hand in Al's direction.

Al said, "Where are you going?"

"The king is drawing me to him. Do something." Sherry reached for Al's arm.

Al formed a shield. The bubble held for a moment, but then it broke, splashing over them. "It's too hot and there's not enough moisture in the air. My shield won't hold."

Sherry still moved toward the king. Al walked beside her pondering how to disrupt the spell.

She stopped talking and glowed brighter. Whatever magic she possessed did not interrupt her forward momentum.

The moon moved away, allowing the sunlight to become brighter and brighter. Al brought out his magnifying spell and formed the telescope in his mind. He forced the sun through the scope and into the focusing glass. Then he pointed the weapon at the king.

A ray of blue light emitted through Al's hand and rocketed toward the king.

The king deflected the laser into the roaring volcano. The lava bubbled higher where the blue light struck.

Al rubbed the back of his neck. "He's too powerful for me, that's the best I've got."

"I'm not having any luck convincing him to let me go either," Sherry said. "Have you tried the staff?"

"I haven't had it long enough to know all its capabilities."

"Do something."

Al raised the staff and chanted. "formans murus ignis."

A towering barrier of fire formed ten feet from the king.

Sherry's trajectory now meant she would be sliding through fire.

"What is that?"

A tightness gripped Al's chest. "I hoped the wall of fire would stop the king's power from drawing us to him."

"Get rid of it, I'm not gonna die by fire."

"You're gonna die anyway if the king captures you."

"Get rid of it. I don't want to die by fire."

Al pointed his staff at the fire.

Witch Isabel of the staff said, "I don't want to burn anew master."

"You will not burn." Al wanted time to examine his options and determine possibilities to solve the problem. He wished for an opportunity to search the web for alternatives. Instead, he said, "mergit in igne."

Droplets of water fell from the sky and sprinkled on the wall of fire.

"That didn't work."

"Master, I don't do well with fire." The staff's female voice said.

"Relax about the fire, both of you. I'll quench the fire, but there isn't enough water in the sky this close to the volcano."

Sherry said, "Mom used salt on a kitchen fire once."

"Maybe..."

They moved closer to the flames.

Where do you find salt at the top of a volcano? "I hope this works. Ignis sale."

Salt spilled from the sky covering the flames, but still not adequate to snuff out the fire. The flame recovered and burned even higher.

Sherry moved closer to the flames.

Al hurled a fire ball at the king.

The king deflected it with ease.

"Is that a smile on the king's face?" Al asked.

"He's playing with you."

Al had trouble finding the right words and refused to look at Sherry. "The king's too powerful for me."

"Do something. Put the fire out first, we're too close to the flames."

He stumbled in a low spot as doubt creeped into his thoughts. Time was running out and his heart thudded in his chest. If this was a birthday candle, I would blow it out with air, Al waved his staff. "Cessat ventus, ignis."

A fierce breeze blew over the flames. The fire swirled and burst even higher advancing toward Al and Sherry.

"You're feeding the flames. Did you learn nothing in grade school? Less oxygen."

"Ah yes, a breeze, but reduce the oxygen, Nutrientibus dolor de igne."

The blaze dissipated.

"Great. Now, stop me from moving."

"This might work." From his pants pocket he withdrew the vial Zita gave him.

"What's that?"

"Zita gave me this potion and claimed it would strengthen my magic for a few minutes."

"It's ludicrous to drink that. She's not on our side in this battle. You know who her father is, don't you? What's in the vial?"

"Don't know, but what else can we do?"

"Even if you drank the contents, what spell would you throw? How fast does it work?"

"Works right away."

"Dangerous?"

"No. Well, maybe."

Al struggled to physically restrain Sherry with his body to no avail.

"I'm gonna drink it." He uncorked the stopper.

Sherry grabbed his wrist. "Don't drink it Al. I have a rotten feeling about this idea."

"Trust me. It'll work."

He brought the vial to his lips and tilted back his head. The sweet elixir flowed down his throat as warmth rushed through his body. He enjoyed the sweet flavor of the elixir. Then his brain went black and he collapsed.

CHAPTER 61

Erik felt the heat radiating from the bubbling lava as he struggled to stand, his body freshly bruised and scratched from being thrown around by Zita. Fatigue and pain wracked his body.

Cugbert flew toward Erik and landed next to him.

Erik said, "Are you okay?"

"Yes. We must release the prisoners. We're running out of time. The last eclipse has begun."

The murky cast of the sun returned, and Erik thought it weird to have three eclipses in one day, although he never experienced even one eclipse on Earth.

Surprisingly, they reached the prisoners without being hurled around the volcano rim by Zita.

Two women stared transfixed into the volcano.

Cugbert untied the ropes that held them. "Are you okay?"

He got no response.

Erik shook the women. "Wake up—"

"Cugbert, why won't she answer me? All I get is a vacant stare."

"She's in a magical trance," Cugbert said. "Sacrificial victims drink a charmed potion and slip into a trance, making them easy to manipulate. The potion keeps them from struggling when placed on the sacrificial altar."

Erik screamed at them. "You must wake up!"

Despite being untied, the women stood like statues.

Erik ran a hand through his hair. "What can I do? Should I attack the king?"

"No, that won't work." Cugbert said, "You would be useless against him."

Erik's chest tightened in dread "I must do something because I can't remain here and watch these women murdered by this maniac. Do you have a plan that will help?"

"Yes. But you won't like the plan." The priest spread his hands on Erik's shoulders.

The prisoners lined up and faced the altar. They stared straight ahead and shuffled forward.

"No! Stop." Erik ran in front of the women, and stretched out his arms, but the women shuffled around him.

"You can still save them." Cugbert grabbed Erik's arm.

"What? Tell me. Hurry."

"Zita is the key to preserving them all. Without her we lose the opportunity to save any of the victims, but she lacks something. Only you can provide what she needs."

Erik watched the prisoners walking toward certain death. "I'll do anything. Is there time to run and get the object before the eclipse?" The sky darkened.

"Oh, you don't have to travel anywhere, because you already have it," Cugbert said.

"Well tell me, already; what are you waiting for?" Erik's breathing became shallow. He panted. His fingers were tingling and numb and his heart throbbed.

The women shuffled toward the altar and death.

Cugbert put his left arm around Erik's shoulders. "Zita needs one of us to persuade her that she is loved."

"Okay, how do we manage that?" Erik flung out his arms in frustration. "Do you want me to pick some flowers or buy a box of chocolates?"

"No, we need drastic action, and you're the logical one for the task. Go to her and kiss her. On the lips."

Erik's mouth dropped open, and he gawked at Cugbert as if in a daze. "You want me to kiss Zita?" He laughed like a braying donkey. "Yeah, she's an attractive girl. But I don't know her. You want me to go and just sweep her off her feet and kiss her? Like a hero out of a fairy tale?"

Cugbert clasped Erik's head in his hands and peered deep into Erik's eyes.

Erik felt peaceful, and his body relaxed allowing him to breathe.

"Zita is our only hope. Throughout life she has endured suffering, fear and hate. We need to show her a different behavior. She desires love, passion and tenderness, and you can offer her physical love."

"But I can't just saunter up to a girl and kiss her. I've never done anything like that. And remember Zita hates me so much she tried to throw me in the volcano. Twice!"

"She is filled with hate, but can be shown a new way. Her whole life, she has experienced conflict, hate, abuse and manipulation. It's your duty to present her a contrasting choice. Instead of conflict, show her tranquility."

"I wanted to ask Lily to the high school homecoming dance. What will she say if I kiss Zita?"

"You can explain it to Lily later." Cugbert maintained his focus on Erik. "Zita needs the touch of love, not hate."

"What about Kestrel? That crazy wizard will be furious." Erik remembered the fireballs Kestrel sent toward him in the forest. "Kestrel will go ballistic if I kiss Zita. I thought they were a couple."

"You boasted you would do anything to save your friend, were those empty words? Did you not mean it? Aren't you here to save your friends, or do you wish to be a hero without performing the tough tasks?"

The sky dimmed as the eclipse countdown approached zero. The massive red Velidred moon drifted in front of the sun. As the sky darkened, the boiling lava cast a crimson glow across the rim.

"I shouldn't have come because I'm no hero. I wanted to impress Lily and go to the homecoming dance with her." He hung his head, and a knot formed in his throat.

Cugbert whispered, "Zita needs you now. You're here for a reason, with special skills which will amaze even you.

You're not here for Lily. You're here to shift Zita from evil, to teach her love. Go now." Cugbert pushed Erik to confront Zita.

CHAPTER 62

The Velidred moon blocked more of the sun. The barrier Kestrel had created was broken, and magic flowed into Zita. The source of the power stronger than ever, she stood enraptured by the intense glow as magic poured into her body.

So absorbed was she in acquiring the tainted magic, Zita didn't notice Erik at first. When she saw him, a flaming glow surrounded his hair. He approached with a peculiar expression on his face. Zita tried to determine what the expression meant, a smirk, a smile, a grin or a leer? A strange demeanor, what did he plan?

She grabbed the pendant preparing for the worst. Whatever Erik planned, she wanted no part of it and would dispatch him into the volcano this time. No more puny drama; she felt all powerful.

Without warning, Erik took her in his arms and kissed her. A head butt would have been less surprising, but she didn't have time to react. He hadn't said anything, and the kiss left a fluttery emotion in her stomach. *What is this?*

Zita pulled away from Erik and slapped his face. "What are you doing?"

"Cugbert thought it would work." Erik rubbed his face.

"I should have expected that scheming old priest would try some trick. Tell him those tactics will send you both into the volcano." Her whole body shuddered. Was it from the kiss or outrage at the trick?

"No wait. Zita, I do love you, and I shouldn't have yelled and blamed you on the other side of the river last night. We need you, and I'm sorry for my behavior."

"You say that you love me because you need me." She raised her eyebrows, peered skyward and shook her head. "Do you even know what love is?"

Erik grabbed her again and pressed his lips to hers.

She felt his body heat next to her. A glow spread through her body from the tenderness of the kiss as the ugly hold of sadness and anger dissipated. *Is this true or am I just being used? My father told me he loved me. Then he locked me in the castle instead of letting me receive this magic.*

Erik stopped kissing and hugged Zita tight.

Is he doing this because I'm a princess? Does he have an agenda and only wants to manipulate me for cooperation? Zita didn't trust the emotions racing through her body right now, and she tired of being exploited as a punching bag for others.

Erik whispered in her ear. "We require your help to free the captives."

She shoved him away. "I knew you didn't mean it. Like everyone else, you don't care for me, but wish to control me to gain an advantage."

Erik approached her. "I mean it, Zita, even before I knew you were a princess, I found you attractive. Yes, I came to this planet searching for Lily, so at first, I didn't think that way about you."

Zita crossed her arms. "Free the girls. Release Lily." Her eyes narrowed. "I don't care for you, and you resemble a one-eyed, wart hog." *That's not how I feel about him. I melt every time I peer into his eyes, and the kiss made my legs tremble. I don't care.*

He pinched his lips together, but made no action, either toward Zita or away.

"It stings to be rejected, doesn't it?" She wouldn't be used again.

"Zita let me—"

"Let you what? Use me and toss my spent body into the volcano after you take what you want? Lecherous old men demand to marry me so they can be powerful like my father. Young boys like Kestrel believe I'm their ticket to wealth. Which are you? Do you yearn for riches? Do you crave power?" She spoke in a high-pitched voice to mock Lily, "Do you want precious little Lily?" She shook out her hair.

The darkness became oppressive to Zita. The impending eclipse meant time was growing precious. When the next sacrifices began, she wanted to gain more magical energy. Despite being no match for Dad's power, she yearned to enhance her magic, to open up more opportunities in the future.

Erik said, "I want to be the friend you've never had. I grew up with Al, Sherry and Lily. We were close, playing together, and we attended the same school. Yes, we're poor, but we're happy together. Join us and aid us. Please?" He reached out his hand.

A deluge of warmth engulfed her body. *Is this true? Would he indeed be my friend?* "No, I don't need friends. I need more magic. That will satisfy me. You lust for wealth just like the other young boys."

"I don't care for wealth. We can help you. What do you want, Zita? Let me help you find it." He moved closer.

She tried to shake the stiffness from her neck. She wanted a friend and wanted Erik to love her.

Thoughts filled her mind. *This is my last chance to obtain more magic and I need to hold Erik off a few more minutes.*

The sacrificial victims lined up next to the altar.

Zita thought, the sacrifice will be brief. The sun will go dark. The priest will drive a blade into the women. The blood will spill, flowing toward the priest in channels cut into the altar. The priest will capture the blood, sprinkle blood on my father and into the volcano. The god of Velidred will release magic.

No more would she be her father's captive. Oh, he would still have more power and influence, but then she could disappear and distract any wizards Dad sent to locate her. Independence and freedom.

"Make a decision Zita. You can have love in your life, now. Peace, love and hope for the future. Let me hold you. Help us."

Zita noticed his eyes. They were different from Cugbert's, the only other person who had held her gently, but Erik's blue eyes had the same calm, strong, peaceful presence. A protecting presence. A loving, kind presence.

She said, "I can't."

Erik placed his arms around her and hugged her again.

So much peace and love in his touch. The influence, less than Cugbert's talent, but it felt sensational. She felt peace, never wanting Erik to let go.

Erik didn't move but held the embrace.

Wait, I'm not a love forlorn peasant girl, but the king's daughter, a mighty woman and wizard. Why be distracted by simple devotion and peace mumbo jumbo? Is this what Cugbert used on my mother? Peace, love and oh yeah, death?

Everything glowed red. She pushed Erik away, and the crimson glow altered the color of his eyes. They weren't bright blue and didn't sparkle anymore. They lost their attraction and power.

"If I help you, what will the king do? His rage will be devastating. He might not protect me anymore. I can't help you."

Erik grabbed her waist and hugged her tight. "I love you more than Earth." He kissed her.

Zita felt it, strong, passionate, intense and she knew Erik meant it this time. He wasn't just saying words. "Your remarks, 'I love you more than Earth,' what does that mean?

Are you going to remain on this planet with me? Aren't you going home?"

Erik said nothing.

She felt loved, but divided. "Dad will be angry with me." She sent a spell at the two girls shuffling toward the altar. They stopped walking, looked up startled and ran from the bubbling lava.

CHAPTER 63

Al opened his eyes with effort. The back of his skull felt like someone smashed it with a baseball bat. Darkness enveloped him with an evil red glow, and ominous shadows flickered over him. *What happened, and where am I?* Red fountains of lava burst above the shifting shadows, and reality sprinted into his mind. *Sherry.*

The volcano. He moved quickly trying to get to his feet. *Where is Sherry? What happened to her?* He remembered Sherry being pulled by magic toward the king. Al had tried to stop her. He drank something. Water? No, his lips were cracked and his mouth parched. The potion Zita gave him. It didn't contribute more magic; it knocked him unconscious and left behind a nasty headache. *Why didn't I listen to Sherry?*

"Captain, the boy is stirring."

"Seize him."

The soldiers were back. *Of course. If Sherry is captured by the king, she can't use her magic to continue to manipulate the soldiers. What will the king do with Sherry? Will she be sacrificed on the altar, too?*

"Hey, someone should grab his staff. Is the lad a wizard?"

The staff. Where did it land when I fell? He felt along the ground, but didn't find the staff with his hand. "Come staff."

"Here, master." A whiney male voice pleaded from the ground. "Someone is stepping on me."

Al spoke and lifted both arms. "Dispergimini in aera militibus."

A dozen soldiers whooshed into the air. Two screaming men catapulted into the boiling magma.

"Come staff." His grandfather's staff drifted into his opened hand. Around the volcano rim, many shadows ran in murky darkness, with several people near the altar of sacrifice. The final eclipse was in progress meaning the final sacrifices would begin. Would that be Sherry's fate?

Al searched for the platform where the king stood and found Sherry standing next to King Haskell. She shone blue, with the crown above her head. *Sherry, send me a message.*

Sherry's voice penetrated Al's mind. "Protect King Haskell. Do not harm the king."

Al said, "Are you talking to me? Are you instructing me not to harm the king?"

"Protect King Haskell. Do not harm the king."

Al heard Sherry's voice. Were these messages for him or the soldiers? The soldiers wouldn't attack the king. The king's risk of attack came from Al and his friends. Not just Al, Alpherge the Mighty. The king must be manipulating Sherry to broadcast the message to distract him. *No need to tune in to Sherry until after I rescue her.*

He had the staff and needed to save Sherry by using the added magic. Otherwise, Al and his friends were going to die. After cracking his knuckles, he tensed. *I will send a million droplets of lava at the king. No, that might injure Sherry too.* He needed time to rest and attune to the staff to learn its capabilities.

Sherry droned in a soothing voice, "Protect King Haskell. Do not harm the king."

Al uttered a spell he had used when playing games with his friends, "Thor de caelo fulmen." He pointed the staff at the king. This had to be exact, because if he missed the king and hit Sherry… *Let's hope that doesn't happen.*

A lightning bolt blew out of the staff and headed toward the king. The kickback of the lightning knocked Al down and the boom of thunder sounded as loud as if a lightning bolt landed right next to him.

Rising to his feet, Al knew he either missed the king, or the king had blocked the spell.

King Haskell had his own staff, and a crimson glow coalesced at the tip. A spell forming.

"No, no, no, no, no," muttered Al. His mouth was dry. *How can I avoid a spell from the king? Why did I attack the king?* "Help me!" He dove to the ground.

Heat rushed over him from fast-moving lava sailing above his head in a narrow-focused river. Drops of hot lava touched his legs and burned holes in his trousers. He rolled from the flaming stream.

Flying lava. How can I beat that?

The lava stopped flowing overhead. A red glow surrounded the volcano. It looked as he imagined the depths of hell. The unnatural darkness felt overwhelming to Al. He stood. His sole hope to save Sherry was to get closer to the king.

The king delivered a hail-storm of rocks at Al, knocking him to the ground and burying him with a small sheet of black, golf-ball-size gravel.

Al felt bruised all over, his temple was tender and blood dripped into his left eye.

Al thought he would perish. The Mountain King was getting stronger in his magic with each sacrifice. *Why did I ever let Sherry get away from me? I should protect her. I'm such a nerd to drink a potion from the king's daughter, and now what will I do against a wizard that's worked magic his entire life? This mountain top is my final opportunity to practice magic. I don't stand a chance.*

There had to be a spell to cast at the king and penetrate his defenses. He thought back to the Dungeons and Dragons games he played, searching his memories of strategies that should give him a chance. He combed his mind for any spell with possibilities of working. Nothing suitable bubbled up to his consciousness. The spells flashed through his brain, and Al laughed at the thought of the hat of camouflage and dust of sneezing and coughing. *Really? My plan is to slay the king by making him sneeze to death?*

Would Sherry be the final sacrifice, or would the king keep Sherry and go after the Crystal of Zaraboth? That prospect felt like a sword passing through Al's gut. He had to figure out something. *What other spells do I know? And even if they worked in the childish games at home, are they real here?*

Al gasped as a thousand shiny objects reflecting red light from the volcano flew toward him, and he hit the ground just in time as a thousand knives sailed over him. Three pierced the back of his right leg. He shut his eyes and yanked the knives from his leg.

This can't be happening; the king is just playing games with me. A bigger surprise must be coming, a life-ending surprise. Perspiration beaded on his forehead from the heat, exhaustion and fervent desire to live. Al coughed, breathing the acrid air. Fatigue sapped him. There had been too many days with inadequate food and proper sleep. His mind was shutting down from lack of nutrients and water, rational thought was futile. He felt emptiness. He closed his eyes. Numbness.

Sherry's voice penetrated Al's mind. "Protect King Haskell. Do not harm the king."

Sherry. He loved Sherry, so funny, smart and nice to be around. Al was determined to save her. With no plan and no special magic spell, he dashed toward the king.

CHAPTER 64

Erik watched the prisoners flee from the high priest and the altar.

Zita said, "Dad will be angry with me."

Great she released the prisoners. Does that mean she will help us defeat her father? The whole scene darkened as the third and final eclipse reached totality. A surreal landscape was revealed with soldiers rushing in disarray around the volcano rim. To Erik they were nothing more than shadows. The red lava danced overhead back-lighting the rim with an evil crimson glow.

Sherry, glowing with the crown on her head, stood next to the king. "Protect King Haskell. Do not harm the king."

How did the king capture Sherry? Where's Al? Is Al dead? Everything the spiritualist said is coming true. In fact, Lily stood next to the altar for the sacrifice. Why had the other sacrificial victims run, but Lily was still next to the altar? Erik watched in dismay as the priest lifted Lily's hand.

Black spots floated across Erik's vision and he felt dizzy. Is this the end for Lily? He swung to Zita. "Please help. Don't let her die."

Zita backed away, wringing her hands. Her head bobbed back and forth. Then her gaze settled to the ground.

"We're running out of time. The priest is taking Lily to the altar now."

Zita grimaced, and shook her head.

Erik felt the blood draining from his face. "Don't ponder, do something." He approached Zita and embraced her. "Please help."

"I ... I can't." She dashed into the darkness.

"Come back, Zita. I need you." Erik fell to his knees. What can I do now? Without Zita, hope is lost. He closed his eyes, and his hand shook as he mopped sweat from his brow. The red glow lit the volcanic rock. *Al is dead. Lily will die soon. Sherry is in the hands of the king. I have brought them here to die. My fault, I drove them to this.* He vomited green bile from his empty stomach.

A lightning bolt flew toward the king. Erik felt the thunder roll through his body. *Was that Zita? Has she agreed to help?* Then a torrent of lava discharged from the king toward the source of the lightning.

Erik felt hope. Zita will help. *What can I do? I can't fight the king, but I can save Lily.*

The high priest placed Lily on the altar. Why isn't she struggling? She isn't tied.

He passed his hand through his hair. *What to do? Too far to run to the altar with sufficient time to stop the sacrifice.* A hollow sensation rose in his gut. Not enough time, but he stumbled toward the altar anyway.

Erik had no energy left to run. Run? Standing and walking were difficult. At the altar, the conflict played out like a scene from a Dracula movie. Lily lay on her back on the altar, her hands by her side. The priest sprinkled water or oil or something over the body as he walked around the altar.

Erik's mouth dry, shoulders hunched, he watched the altar as he walked. Without warning, he crashed to the ground, tripping over a dead soldier. Erik fell hard onto his right hand, the crack of bone caused him to howl in pain.

He positioned the good hand beneath his body to help him get up and touched something. *Was that a bow? Are there arrows here?* Despite the pain he crawled on hands and knees, searching the ground in the sparse light. A quiver of arrows must be here. "Please, please let there be arrows." He examined the body and found nothing.

The priest stopped the sprinkling rite and walked around the sacrifice with an incense burner.

Am I too late? Erik licked his lips with cautious hope. *Still time if I find the arrows, but where are they?* He crawled in a circle around the soldier expanding the circle with each new trip.

He had to crawl around the body twice just to search six feet from the fallen soldier. Erik found nothing.

Where would a quiver of arrows be after someone is killed on the battlefield? Did someone else take them? They must be valuable to another archer, either for personal use or to sell.

On the third rotation, Erik expanded the investigation another three feet. He needed to hustle; the sacrifice would be over before he found the arrows.

He detected nothing.

On the fourth circuit as Erik finished the last half of the loop, he found a quiver with twelve arrows. They must have been kicked from the fallen soldier.

His limbs trembled with optimism. He gripped the bow in his healthy hand, but had trouble nocking the arrow with his splintered, broken hand. The hand swelled and became difficult to move, but time was running out; he had to rush. He secured the arrow to the bowstring and tried to pull back with the bad hand and injured shoulder, but lost his grip, and the arrow fluttered to the ground.

Erik glanced at the altar. The high priest stood with both hands raised over Lily's body and chanted.

Still time, but he had to hustle. But, not too fast. Picking up an arrow he tried again and succeeded nocking the second arrow. He lifted the bow and arrow and pointed it at the priest. Fighting through the pain he drew the arrow back. He knew he wasn't drawing it back far enough because his shoulder hurt and hand both ached. He took a breath and released. The arrow glided a few feet, not far.

He chewed his bottom lip and drew blood as he grabbed another arrow from the quiver and nocked it. His whole frame shook so much, how could he hit anything? Even if he had the fortitude to draw the arrow to the maximum extent, his body trembled with effort, fear, fatigue, and desperation. How would he be able to aim accurately?

The distance might be too significant, but he sighted the target and stretched the string back to his cheek. His body vibrated from the pain. He released. The string hit his arm on the release and the arrow flew for fifty feet, but not far enough.

His heart thundered in his rib cage. This won't work. Erik's only experience as an archer was on one summer outing at a renaissance fair. He thought about his father. Mom said Dad was a noble soldier and commander. What would Dad say to him? "Be steadfast in the face of adversity," Erik imagined.

A heightened tolerance for pain swept through his body. He nocked the next arrow and took a deep breath. "Relax." A calming breath. He drew back the string a little, pushed away the pain in his shoulder and hand and brought the arrow to his cheek. One more cleansing breath. He focused on the priest. The arrow released.

The arrow sped straight and true, feathers rotating on the shaft. It was difficult to track the entire journey in the darkness. The arrow flew far enough, but missed the priest by three feet.

A numbness flooded Erik's body. *I missed, was this my last chance?*

The priest lifted an enormous knife above his head.

"Hurry, hurry, hurry," Erik muttered. The next arrow nocked, and he raised the bow into position.

Cugbert said, "Stop Erik, don't do it."

"Are you kidding? What do you mean don't do it? I have to save her."

"Causing death of another individual is not the answer to your problems." Cugbert said.

Sure, Cugbert is saying this because that isn't his friend. "Al is dead, I'm saving my friends who are left."

"You have a destiny here but through peace. You possess great power, but not like this. Don't follow the path of anger, death and vengeance."

Erik's stomach clenched. "Stop talking! I'm doing this."

Cugbert placed his palm on Erik's shoulder. "At your age, I followed a path of anger, revenge and violence. It tore at me every day."

Peace flowed into Erik's body from Cugbert's touch.

"Let go your anger and bitterness. This is the way of things. Peace."

Peace, yes, peace. Calmness and love. Erik stared at the altar. The priest held the dagger above his head, ready to plunge the sharp steel into Lily's unmoving body.

Everything slowed. Erik drew back the arrow, pointing the bow at Varesh with the knife overhead.

Cugbert yelled, "No."

Erik drew the string and nocked the arrow to his cheek. Calmness flooded through his brain. A cleansing sigh, then a concentrated, focused sighting along the arrow shaft. Erik released.

Cugbert touched Erik. "You shouldn't have. It will make things worse."

Erik flicked Cugbert's hand off his shoulder. "She's my friend."

The arrow sped in a magnificent arc toward its target with the glow from the volcano glittering off the arrow shaft as it rotated on its passage.

The sacrificial priest extended hands one more time above his head and the arrow penetrated his chest. He arched his back, tottered and fell.

"I did it," Erik yelled.

Cugbert stared at the altar with his mouth dangling wide and shook his head.

Erik screamed. "No, no, no."

CHAPTER 65

Zita ran to the far edge of the volcano rim, away from Erik, the soldiers, and her dad and watched the sacrifice at the altar. The priest finished his incense burning.

Zita bounced on her toes with anticipation of the sacrifice. *Can't he perform the sacrifice faster? Why is it taking so long?* She swayed in rhythm to the splashing lava as the magma bubbled. She craved the rush of magic into her body.

Hurry Varesh. Hurry. I don't want Kestrel to stop me. I need that magic running through my soul. Okay, the incense part is complete.

The priest raised his hands over the individual on the altar.

Zita said, "Say the words you always speak. Why read it from a book when you repeat the same words every year? Get on with it." Her swaying gestures became more pronounced as the sacrifice moved toward its conclusion. She lifted her hands the same as the high priest and swung them side to side.

Varesh finished and seized the blade from the rock altar and held it over his head. A few more phrases before the final act of the sacrifice, plunging the knife into the victim.

Zita's pulse quickened, and she felt a lightness in her chest. A sneer spread across her face. "Yes, yes. Go ahead. Plunge the knife into the body, get on with it, man."

An arrow sped by Varesh, but the priest didn't notice.

Zita scanned the perimeter. *Who shot that arrow?* She spied a towering shadow of a man back-lit by the glowing lava. *Is that Cugbert with Erik? I thought Cugbert is a peaceful priest. Why is he allowing Erik to shoot arrows at*

Varesh? After this long wait, will Erik ruin the moment? "Plunge the knife," Zita yelled.

She faced the altar to determine the identity of the sacrifice victim. Lily?

Zita glanced at Erik who held a bow. He was nocking another arrow while having an intense argument with Cugbert. Varesh finished the words for the next step in the sacrifice sequence. *I shouldn't let Varesh kill Lily.* Yet, she lusted for the euphoria of the magic. Plus, to watch Lily be sacrificed must be killing Kestrel. She became less animated and rubbed the back of her neck.

Allow Erik to kill Varesh or let Varesh kill Lily? Zita wanted more time to ponder what to do and decide on whose side to fight. Her enthusiasm slipped from the sacrifice, replaced by heaviness in her body and tightness around her chest.

"I need that magic," she yelled. *If I help Erik with the arrow and Dad finds out, then I'll die. But I can't allow Varesh to kill Lily. It would be okay if Erik replaced Lily on the altar. Erik can die.* "Focus, focus."

Varesh raised the knife one last time, marking the moment the blade would slice into the sacrificial victim. Her vision blurred, and she blinked her eyes. She wanted to scream but nothing came out. *Can't someone interrupt the proceedings?*

Zita spotted the arrow a moment before it plummeted from the sky into Varesh's chest. He floundered as if he would fall backwards into the volcano. No, he slumped forward. Zita watched the knife plunge into the sacrificial victim and blood droplets splatter across the altar.

The altar contained a rock hewn drain where body fluids spilled into the volcano. But she knew Dad needed to touch the fluid. The sacrifice sequence included Varesh sprinkling blood on the king during the ceremony.

Zita observed the wave of magic pouring from the volcano. The magical blend of the Velidred Moon, the sacrifice and the Velidred volcano were perfect. The red magic streamed like a river during the spring thaw. It split into three streams, one flowed to the king, a branch trickled toward Al, but the largest current roared toward Zita.

She drifted closer to the gelatinous flow and welcomed the fervor of its magic. Zita's body tingled, and tension in her neck vanished. She tilted her head back and closed her eyes while enjoying the spirit, soul and magic. She wanted to live in this moment forever.

The magic stopped as if someone instantaneously had built a dam on a river. She grimaced in misery and searched the rim. *Who did that?*

The magic river struck a magical barrier and diverted to the king.

Zita yelled, "Kestrel." She spotted him not far from the altar and tossed a fireball at him.

He ducked, shielded and shot fire bolts at Zita.

Her body tensed and she deflected the fire bolt with air. It exploded in front of her, but she lost her night vision. *Dangerous to stay in the present location, I need to move to remain alive. Move closer to the altar, pick Kestrel up and plop him into the lava.*

Another fireball exploded near her, but she hid behind confused soldiers distracting Kestrel's line-of-sight view. *I need to get closer to smack him, trap him and toss him in the lava.*

She used air to extract arrows from a soldier's quiver. Lining them up, she launched them at Kestrel. That will get him. Not waiting to watch what happened, she ran closer to the altar. The barrier separating her from the flowing magic stayed with her as she moved.

Kestrel blocked the arrows and launched a shot high into the sky which flared up and lit the perimeter. The next fireball came right at the exposed Zita.

She narrowed her eyes and dove to the ground. The fireball missed by inches. She clenched her fists tight. The darkness became acute after the exploding fireball as she lost all night vision. The light was so bright, she knew Kestrel would lose her whereabouts for a few seconds. "You are so stupid Kestrel."

She stayed low to prevent detection as she dashed toward the altar. The volcano lit the altar, and she felt exposed. This was the wrong place to shelter. Another fireball cruised over her head, exploding a few feet from the king.

Is Kestrel this stupid? The king must think Kestrel is attacking. Zita smirked. I might not have to kill Kestrel; the king might do it for me.

Zita sent a puff of fire at Kestrel's backside. Dad always told her the simple attacks were the most successful. While your enemy is using up his magic power with large-scale spells, many small spells could be just as effective. The fire puff landed on Kestrel's uniform jacket and burst into flames.

Kestrel jumped and swung toward Zita as he ripped off the burning jacket.

She reached the altar, dipped her index finger in the flowing blood from the sacrifice and smeared it across her forehead. This shattered the magic barrier Kestrel had created and Zita felt the surge of magic again. This time the taint of evil felt stronger than before because she touched the blood allowing physical bonding to the magic.

Lily said, "Help me."

Zita brought a shaking hand to her forehead and her chest caved. Is she still alive? "What?" Zita stammered.

"Help me find Erik." Lily's breathing was raspy and irregular.

Zita tossed Varesh's corpse to the ground, pulled the blade from the sacrifice victim and put her hands on the wound to stop the gushing blood. It caused the tainted, greasy, foul and contaminated magic to grow stronger within Zita's body. She became lightheaded as magic raced through tingling fingers. *Must get away, must stay and absorb the magic. B*ut her legs felt unsteady.

Lily looked at Zita and placed her hand on Zita's hand. "You're a beautiful woman."

"You're gonna live. We can save you. Cugbert is here. He can help."

A fireball flew past Zita's head, exploding behind the king.

"Stop that, Kestrel." Zita felt powerful. She chanted magic at Kestrel, "Magicae murum aeris ad resiliunt inimici." A barricade of air formed between Zita and Kestrel.

Zita wedged her hands underneath Lily's shoulders and boosted her into a sitting position then brought a water skin to the victim's lips. "Drink this water. We need to get you to the ground before Kestrel kills both of us." She dragged Lily's bleeding body to the edge of the altar and they both tumbled to the ground. A fireball exploded against the wall of air. "That wall won't last."

CHAPTER 66

Erik hurried and found Lily sprawling in a pool of blood with her head on Zita's lap. Vultures flew close as they checked the dead soldiers on the volcano rim.

Erik raised his hands to scare off the birds. "Get away." He felt nauseated. "How is she? Will she live?"

Zita shook her head.

He wanted to holler and punch a wall. "Hold on, we'll take you to a hospital."

Lily smiled at Erik. "Come here." Blood and spittle trickled from her mouth.

Erik came closer as a lump formed in his throat.

"Can you do something for me?"

"Yes, anything, but you have to live so we can go home," Erik pleaded.

Lily opened her mouth to say something but coughed, and blood oozed down her chin.

Erik wiped her chin with his tunic. "Stay with us. Don't go."

Cugbert arrived and squatted next to Erik.

Erik touched Cugbert's arm. "You can help her. Heal her. Give her hope. Help me take her to the emergency room."

Cugbert examined the knife wound.

Erik stared at the murky spot spreading across Lily's white dress.

Cugbert touched Lily's forehead and gripped her head between his hands. "She's lost a lot of blood."

Pain coursed through Erik's head, and he had trouble breathing. "You have to save her. We can help, you and I together."

Cugbert shook his head. "I don't know if you're strong enough."

Erik's lips stretched back baring his teeth. "I'm not saying goodbye because we're gonna help her. Stitch her wound, then help her recuperate. Quick, find something to carry her down the mountain. We can use spears lying around and a soldier's tunic to make a litter. She can heal in the city."

Lily coughed up more blood.

"Don't die. If Cugbert can't help, maybe Al can. Do you believe it, Al is a wizard? Isn't that bizarre? And Sherry glows blue."

Cugbert grabbed Erik's hands. "Put your hands on her forehead."

"Can we save her?"

"I don't know; we'll try. You must have faith."

Blood pounded in Erik's brain. He placed his hands on Lily's forehead.

Zita said, "There's a problem. Kestrel is almost through the shield. We need to move."

Cugbert put his hands on the wound. "Faith my boy. Concentrate on healing."

Zita touched Erik on the shoulder. "We gotta move."

"Take your hands off me, we need to heal Lily."

"If you don't move right now, you're all going to die."

Cugbert lifted his hands from Lily's body. "We can leave her under the altar, she's stable, after this is all through, we can come back and help her. She should be safe there until we resolve this."

Erik kept reliving the shooting of the arrow that killed the priest and the resulting injury to Lily. He replayed the sequence in his mind and kept repeating it over and over while pounding his fist on his leg.

Cugbert helped Erik to his feet.

Erik said, "What have I done?"

A large vulture flew ten feet over their heads.

"Get away birds, she's still alive, leave her alone." Erik waved his hands over his head.

A fireball screamed above them.

Zita grabbed Erik's arm. "The shield's gone, let's move."

"I'm sorry Lily. I'll make it up to you. Please forgive me." He reached out to her.

"Move!" Cugbert pushed Erik away from the altar. "It's not safe here."

"We can't leave her here. We have to take her with us." Erik struggled against Cugbert. "She's lying next to the priest that plunged the knife in her body. That's not right."

Cugbert forced Erik away to get him moving. "We'll come back for your friend."

A fireball exploded five feet in front of them.

Zita said, "I protected you this time but can't guarantee I can keep doing that, keep moving."

Erik shuffled ahead of Cugbert who kept shoving him forward.

Kestrel threw fireball after fireball at the group, that Zita caused to glance into the sky. They weren't traveling fast enough to get to a safe distance. Zita stepped between the group and the next fireball. She touched her pendant, brought up her hands, and produced a shield. The fireballs hit the shield and ricocheted to the right and to the left. It was as if they were walking in a corridor between walls of fire.

"There's no place for us to hide," Zita said. "I will try something, but it might not work."

CHAPTER 67

Al ran toward the king. But he could make no progress because the king sent obstacles at Al, forcing him back. At first a swarm of bats attacked. The giant vultures ate those. Twice Al stopped to protect himself from sharp projectiles. He used a burning spell to slay thousands of rats the king sent at him.

Why didn't the king send him a single killing shot? He must have the power.

Al watched, horrified, when the priest fell onto Lily. Al lost his balance, but used the staff to keep himself from falling. He laughed inappropriately. "That crazy old spiritualist. She's right, if matters don't become better, I'm gonna die, too."

He crouched low when a bomb burst in the sky lighting the ground.

The king hurled a fire bolt, but Al had learned how to deflect those. He pointed the top of the staff at the fire bolt and visualized a Roman metal shield. Sometimes the fire bolt exploded on the shield, pushing Al back. Four times, the bolts deflected to the side of the volcano.

He felt the magic potion wearing thin. How long had it been since he drank the elixir? He had to establish a plan to weaken the king. Al watched the currents of magic flowing from the sacrifice. The king obtained a share, but another larger stream flowed to a smaller figure, perhaps Zita? And then a portion streamed his way.

He didn't know if he should participate in this feast of magic. It seemed wrong to gain at Lily's sacrifice. The torrent of magic flowed around Al's fingers, allowing him to touch the magic. It felt greasy and dirty, polluting his soul.

Al wanted to run away. *All these people want to kill me. Where's Erik?*

Sherry's voice spoke in his brain. "Protect King Haskell."

The focus returned. Sherry. The staff grew heavy in Al's tired arms. Who knew carrying a staff all day hurt your hands and shoulders this much? He wanted to text Sherry and tell her his progress. I'm coming for you. But texting was impossible on this planet.

"Focus. Focus." What's the problem? *We have to rescue Sherry. Who has Sherry? The king. Can I get to the king? No. I need support. Who? Erik can help.*

Al noticed a group of people running toward him despite being pummeled by fire bolts from Kestrel. Zita shielded the fire bolts from hitting his friends. Is she on our side after what Erik said to her?

Maybe I can help Zita. Al sent a fire bolt at Kestrel.

# # # #

Zita noticed the extra firepower and changed direction. "Everybody head toward Al and we'll combine forces."

They staggered toward Al. Kestrel's attacks lessened after the assault from Al bombarded the warrior wizard. Kestrel had to spend more time in defense.

The group traveling with Zita reached Al.

Erik said, "They killed Lily, Al, it's my fault."

The king dropped a truckload of rocks on the group. Al managed to shield against most of the rocks, but several hit Zita's feet.

Zita folded her arms across her breast. "You need a bigger shield." *Why am I teaming up with a wizard that has no skills and can't even shield a small group of us? This boy will be the death of me. I should flee while the tall guy is busy with Kestrel, just stroll off the volcano as far from these troublemakers as possible.*

"How about you make the king stop trying to kill us?"

"He won't slay you until the sacrifice is complete. For now, he's trying to keep you occupied. If he wished to kill you, well, you would be dead."

"What do you mean until after the sacrifice?" Al asked.

"The prophecies say Dad loses everything if you guys die before the sacrifice ends. Before the moon finishes the eclipse." A thousand darts pounded against the shield. "Why does your shield make so much noise?"

Al adjusted his grip on the staff. "We must kill the king in the next two minutes, because I'm pretty confident this eclipse will be over soon."

"You should practice a shield of air. The enemy will find your position with all that noise."

"No, these scorch marks on my shirt show that air shields don't work." Al tugged at his shirt revealing the burn marks.

"You can't kill my dad," shouted Zita.

"I'm rescuing Sherry, and if it means killing your dad, then I'll do it."

I want let them murder my father. I watched my own mother perish. Dad isn't a nice person, but I don't want him dead. "We should focus our attention on Kestrel. If we capture him, we'll have a better chance at the king."

Erik said, "Watch out, the king is moving toward the altar."

"No, you don't want him to do that. If he touches her blood, the king becomes stronger and he might try to finish the sacrifice." A headache pounded in Zita's skull.

\# \# \# \#

Al didn't like this setup and felt a nagging in the back of his brain that Zita was withholding information. *What isn't she telling us? If she had a chance for a kill shot at her father, would she take it? If Al had a kill shot, would Zita stop him?*

Darkness still encompassed the rim with the glowing molten lava casting shadows. Al took a brief glimpse at the sun and moon. How much time did they have? The soldiers still alive stood away from the battleground of magic as the vultures swooped toward their fallen comrades.

Erik said, "You should throw a grenade at Kestrel."

Al said, "That's brilliant. Zita, can you concentrate on Kestrel? What if we do this? You shoot a fire bolt at him. I launch the magic grenade."

"A what?"

Al laughed. "A grenade. Did you play army as a kid?"

Erik turned to Zita and smiled. "A grenade is something we have on Earth. A person throws it in the air and it'll explode when it strikes something."

"I will make it black and Kestrel won't expect it. Zita's fire bolt will light up his shield and I'll throw something over the top of the shield."

Al waited for Zita's fire bolt. Al liked the hypothetical plan to play army, an interesting out-of-the-box plan. Erik always thought of unique strategies. The fire bolt exploded. Al's pulse quickened as he saw Kestrel's shield unprotected at the top.

"Okay, send another fire bolt, but make it substantial and obvious so he sees it coming. Fire it at his feet and he shouldn't expect the grenade to come over the top."

Zita released a bright orange fire bolt.

Al used his staff like a World War I grenade launcher. Guessing at the angle required to clear the shield, he positioned the staff toward Kestrel. He planted the base of the staff on the volcanic rock and held the staff at the approximate angle to fire toward Kestrel. He discharged the grenade with a kerthump like he thought the sound a grenade launcher made as air launched the bomb out of a tube. He waited and watched with eagerness, not able to watch the path of the black grenade in the darkness.

Zita's fire bolt exploded in vivid reds, oranges and yellows but did not penetrate Kestrel's shield.

Al hoped the silent and invisible grenade flew in the correct direction. After launching the small bomb, he worried he might hit Lily. Why hadn't he contemplated that possibility?

He waited. Not long, but time dragged, a second felt a minute and two seconds an hour. But then the grenade landed twenty feet behind Kestrel.

His direction needed work. Change the angle of the staff by eight degrees. "Zita toss a fireball once more."

Al waited a moment, the kerthump sounding once more. Waiting for the landing required patience. It was horrible with the grenade virtually invisible and no way to track its direction. Zita's fireball hit low on Kestrel's shield, close to his feet. Zita did well using a lot of imagery, a bright explosion of reds, yellows and crimson to night-blind Kestrel, and then the long wait for the grenade to explode.

A second, maybe two seconds and the grenade landed three paces to Kestrel's right. This time Kestrel sensed something out of the ordinary happening to the right of his position, and the warrior wizard ducked to his left.

That worried Al. *If Kestrel knows it's coming, then he'll block the over-the-top shot.* Al knew math, but he had no practice with this magic missile.

Al readjusted the staff and waved at Zita. "We have to try again, load up another shot at his feet. No wait, go to his right a little, just off Kestrel's right shoulder. I will try to adjust my shot to the left."

Zita set her feet, placed her hands in the same position as before and prepared to shoot a fire bolt.

Too late, Kestrel sent a powerful fireball the size of a clock on a city clock tower. The fire bolt spun in a counter clockwise direction, a spinning mass of reds, yellows and oranges. Like a hurricane the spinning reds in the center rotated faster than the yellows on the edges.

The huge fire bolt traveled faster than anything Kestrel had sent before and Al threw up his metallic shield just milliseconds before the spinning fire struck. Upon striking the shield there was a sound similar to a person sanding a car body with an electric sander. Sparks flew off the edges of the shield like miniature lightning bolts.

The shield didn't cover everyone in the group and Zita yelled, "Make your shield larger." She patted out three fires on her dress.

"I'm tired of this Kestrel." Zita chanted the command to manipulate wind, blowing back sparks and fire that still peeled off Al's shield.

Al counted to three and launched another grenade, listening to the familiar kerthump as the cannon sent the three-inch, invisible egg-shaped object skyward.

In his mind Al counted out the time it took the grenade to land in Kestrel's general area. Three seconds, two seconds, Zita's wind aided sparks and fire grew and exploded to Kestrels right. Then count one more second. Kaboom. The grenade landed two paces left of Kestrel.

Al figured Kestrel knew what was going on now. He'd be ready to block the next attack no matter what. Should we do something different? Then he hatched the plan. "Zita, wait until I tell you to fire your bolt. I have an idea."

He made a quick calculation and re-positioned the staff. Al prepared the launch, this time without the noisy kerthump. *Keep the launch silent and send the grenade before Zita's attack.* "Zita, are you ready? Can you change the speed of the fireball to slow?"

"Yes."

Al launched the grenade, no noise, no sound, silent. "Okay Zita, in three, two, and one. Fire."

Zita sent a slow-moving bright fireball at Kestrel.

Kestrel waited for the attack, standing with both feet balanced, hands out-stretched, and watching for Zita's fireball. But Kestrel never saw the fireball strike because the grenade exploded next to Kestrel and he crumpled to the volcanic rock.

Al raised his hands in triumph.

Erik slapped Al's hands in a high five.

# # # #

Zita clapped her hands. *Yes. Kestrel is finished. He deserved everything he got.*

But Kestrel moved. He struggled to rise, pushing off the ground with one hand.

Erik pointed at the altar. "The king is almost to the altar. Can you attack him too?"

Zita didn't want to hear that. "Maybe we can leave the rim and hide. Then he won't get us."

Al said, "Sherry is alone, and I can free her. You watch my back, Zita, and keep your dad occupied."

Zita's belly fluttered, and she wanted to run. If she threw fire bolts at Dad, that would never do. *What if these kids from Earth drop me as soon as they get that red-headed witch Sherry? Then there's no way to get back into Dad's good graces.*

"Can you come with me, Erik?" Al asked.

"I'm not going with you. I'm going after Lily now that Kestrel's done."

"Come on, she's fine, we have to rescue Sherry."

Zita enjoyed watching them argue. That drew the pressure off her. Should she sneak away? These kids won't accept her as their friend despite her saving their lives today. Why should she make Dad angry for these mutts?

"Come on, Cugbert." Al grabbed a handful of Cugbert's tunic, and they trotted across the rim toward Sherry. "Zita, keep your dad busy until I rescue Sherry."

Erik said, "Kestrel is moving."

Kestrel grew wings, massive twelve-foot wings from tip to tip. He flapped. Then lifted.

"Kestrel looks like a falcon. Throw a fireball at him before he gets away."

"He won't stay around. Not like that. When he changes to a bird, he can't use magic."

She watched the large falcon with one injured wing fly from the volcano rim.

CHAPTER 68

Al and Cugbert made progress up the rocky bluff where Sherry stood with the crown glowing above her head broadcasting the message, "Do not harm the king. Protect King Haskell."

Al found himself three feet from Sherry, his pulse quickening. He felt excited to re-connect with Sherry and reached out to brush hair from her face. "Sherry." His hand bounced off an invisible barrier. "What is this?"

He walked around Sherry trying to find a way to reach her. The wall rebuffed him on four sides. "She's encapsulated in a box, an invisible box. No wonder the king left her here. Cugbert, help me get her out of this contraption."

Cugbert picked a rock off the ground and tried pounding and scratching the surface of the box with no effect. He threw the rock at the box. It bounced off and hit Al in the leg.

"Sherry, can you hear me?" Al pounded his fist on the wall.

Her expression didn't change as she stood staring into the distance with a vacant gaze. He pounded again and again, harder and harder.

Sherry said in the monotone voice, "Do not harm the king. Protect King Haskell."

"Why did I ever let her get away from me?" Al raised his staff. What's the correct method to remove a magical box? Melt the walls? This close to the volcano, the walls still stood, so melting won't work. How about the laser focus, but there is no sun?

The staff's high-pitch, nasal, male voice said, "Can you disintegrate the box, Master?"

"Are you crazy? That would disintegrate everything, even Sherry." He scrunched up his face and released a profound groan.

"May I touch the box, Master?"

"Okay, we can try that." Al pointed the bottom of the staff toward the box and touched the box with the charred wood."

"The other end, Master."

"Right." he held the staff head for a few moments against the barrier surface.

"This is dark magic from the ancient world, corrupt, evil magic."

Al grasped the neck of the staff with both hands and held it in front of him looking at the carved wizard faces. "Can't you do anything?"

"Don't get angry with me, Master. I'm not prepared ... we're not equipped to handle this."

"What do you mean, 'we're not equipped?'"

"When we have more time to bond, we'll have more power together, this takes months, maybe years. I don't know you well enough."

Al's body slumped. "We don't have time to connect now, the eclipse is almost over."

The king bent beneath the altar and touched Lily's limp body. The king rubbed his fingers across his forehead and cheeks.

"The king grows stronger." Al said, "Cugbert help me up on top of the invisible box. Maybe there's a hole in the top and I can lift Sherry out."

Cugbert stood with his back to the invisible wall, cupped both hands together and bent his knees. Al stepped on the cupped hands, crawled over Cugbert's shoulders and pulled himself on top of the ten-foot box. He walked on the top. "Total enclosure."

"Master?" The deep voice of the staff said, "You can solve the problem by removing the source of irritation like a pebble in a shoe. Can we deflect the situation with the priest?"

"What?"

"Hand me to the priest and send me away with him."

"I'm not giving you to the priest." *I've struggled too hard the last two days to allow anyone to handle my grandfather's staff that's now mine.*

"A few moments, Master. Only as a diversion for the king and a shield for Cugbert."

"A diversion for the king? What do you mean?"

"The priest can aid us by deflecting the king's anger."

"If I spend more time up here, the king will notice. Cugbert help me. Hurry!"

When Al reached the ground, he handed the staff to Cugbert. "Take this over near the boiling lava for a few moments. I need to check something." Al thought he understood what the staff suggested and Al lay on the ground while Cugbert left with the staff.

# # # #

Erik watched the king bend below the altar to touch his friend.

Heat built in Erik's face, as he yelled and shook his fist, "Get away from her. Zita, can't you do something?"

"I can't. He's my father."

Erik took her hands, held them together and kissed them. "Just a fireball to draw his attention. You don't have to send a killing shot, aim toward his feet."

She dropped her gaze. "I'm almost out of magic. I need to hold some back in case we need a shield."

"There's no reason to hold magic for later. The eclipse is almost over, and you told me when the sun reappears, King Haskell will slay us all.'"

Zita backed away from Erik.

He clasped her arm and yanked her close. "I don't know what your little game is, but I don't want that killer touching my friend. Now do something." He poked his finger to her chest.

She rubbed her pendant. "Why are you so callous to me? One minute you declare you love me. Now this? You're no better than my father."

Erik felt the pounding in his ears. "My friend almost died minutes ago. I need you to help me retrieve and heal her. What is your dad doing? Is he drinking her blood?"

"Eww, that's gross. He wouldn't do that. In the ceremony he puts blood on his face and palms which attracts and intensifies the magic."

"What can we do? What would you do if your dad killed your mother?"

"How dare you!" She slapped Erik across the face, spun and strode away.

Erik rubbed his face. When he swung toward the altar, Lily took the king's hand and stood.

Adrenaline surged through his body. "What is she doing? Lily stop, don't listen to the king."

Erik sprinted toward the altar.

# # # #

Zita wrapped her arms around her chest, chilled despite the volcano heat. She needed to get away from this place. These kids from Earth brought back memories, the wonderful and the sad, of her mother. She should flee the rim right now, and travel to another kingdom, a place where nobody would recognize her.

She glanced back at the altar and her father one more time. The girl lay on the altar again. The king raised the bloodstained knife. Erik ran toward the king. Why did he run in slow motion? He won't make it in time.

The king raised the blade above his head with both hands.

He recited the magic-laden sacrificial words.

\# \# \# \#

Al waited and watched Erik race toward the king. His injured friend couldn't reach Lily in time to free her. Erik's actions won't make a difference.

Sherry said, "Al be ready for an intense light."

Al's eyes widened; she's back. He placed a palm on the box surface and smiled at Sherry.

Sherry winked while reciting the mantra, "Do not harm the king. Protect King Haskell."

Al shifted back to face the king. Darkness cradled the volcano rim. The king's garments reflected the glowing furnace flames as the knife glistened red over his head.

"Now," Sherry said. She became a brilliant glow of light.

Al used the flash of light, guiding it through his inner mind forming a focused laser as he had practiced on the school roof many days earlier.

The king turned at the blaze of light from Sherry with a puzzled expression painted on his face.

Did the king assume the eclipse was over? Al's laser light developed as it traveled through the telescope magnifying device. It took seconds to produce, but the seconds dragged.

\# \# \# \#

Erik thought, *what is Al waiting for and why doesn't he send something at the king? The king must be vulnerable with his back to Al. Why did Al leave Sherry? Earlier, he stood next to Sherry, but now the young wizard stood with his staff next to the volcano.*

The king broke the ritual, shifted and loosed a fireball at Al.

Erik felt confused. Al didn't move; instead, he remained, gripping his staff.

The entire rim became bathed in bright blue light. Is that from Sherry or is the eclipse over?

Erik ran harder and picked up a spear lying in his path. If the eclipse is over, then the king didn't complete the sacrifice, and Lily might live.

This allowed more time for him to reach her. With fifteen yards to go he prepared to barrel through the king and take them both over the lip of the volcano into the churning lava. They would both perish, but Lily would live. His friends, Al and Sherry, would survive for a chance at romance and going home to Earth.

# # # #

Zita watched Erik racing toward the king. The luminous flash of light distracted Dad. Now, Erik might make it and kill her father. A simple push with the spear and Dad plunges into the magma. The king won't have time to react to Erik's speed. She must stop him.

Zita shot a fireball toward Erik.

# # # #

Al released the laser flow, pure magic not corrupted, and it rushed straight to where he aimed the beam. *The king must think that Cugbert with the staff is Al and isn't expecting the beam from Sherry's position.* Al saw Erik running fast and was close enough now to reach the king before the knife plunged into Lily.

Wait, Erik will arrive at the same moment as the laser, but it's too late to stop the beam. My friend will die when the laser penetrates his body.

# # # #

Erik drove through the pain in his legs and shoulder. Vultures flew among the soldiers lying on the ground. I must get to the king. But is there enough time? A vulture tried to land on a soldier on the ground in front of Erik. He swerved to avoid an impact with the large ugly bird that had no feathers on its neck and head. He heard a bird's "ker-reach" scream overhead.

I must plunge the spear into the king. Keep running faster.

Then Erik felt talons dig into his shoulders and he lifted off the ground.

# # # #

Zita wondered where the bird came from. *Why did it attack Erik? Those birds feast on dead carcasses not live humans. What is wrong with that vulture?*

Wait that isn't a vulture, it's Kestrel. He's back.

Zita's fireball missed Erik, missed the bird and rolled toward her father.

The king turned toward Zita with a surprised expression.

"I'm sorry Dad," she said. "I didn't plan to shoot a fire bolt at you, I aimed for the boy."

# # # #

The bird's talons dug into Erik's shoulders, ripping holes below his collar bones as pain tore through the injured shoulder.

Cugbert told me the vultures wouldn't bother live people.

The talons squeezed tight. It wasn't a vulture. A falcon. Kestrel.

I must make Kestrel release me before he drops me in the volcano.

The bird struggled with Erik's additional weight.

He poked the bird's belly with the spear.

Erik watched the fire bolt pass inches from his feet as it raced toward the king.

Kestrel veered to the left and dropped five feet, losing altitude as he adjusted to the additional weight.

Erik felt the heat from the volcano magma as the bird neared the vent.

Zita's fireball exploded in front of the king.

Erik poked Kestrel with the spear. He didn't have the strength to push it through the feathers because the talons gripped below his collar bones making his arms numb and weak.

Blue light danced in the sky, originating near Sherry. A figure lay on its belly next to Sherry. *Is that Al? Who holds the staff next to the volcano?* The person lying next to Sherry released a greenish-blue, pencil-thin light.

In a second, the blue-green laser beam hit the king. King Haskell didn't expect it, and the beam caught him on the back right shoulder while he glared at Zita. The king twisted, releasing a bolt of lightning at the figure standing with the staff.

King Haskell's fire bolt exploded in a burst of light as it struck the figure with the staff, but then ricocheted back at the king, creating an ear-splitting sound of thunder. The caromed bolt struck the king who flopped onto the altar and rolled off the slab, landing next to the bubbling magma.

One last shove with the spear, and Erik penetrated the bird's belly. Kestrel released Erik, sending him flying through the air toward the altar.

Erik hit the front of the altar hard, the spear broke, and the jolt knocked his breath away.

He lay still a moment but knew he had to move.

He brought the broken spear up over his head while jumping, falling, and flailing over Lily and the altar, ready to strike the king.

The king stood on shaking legs putting his hands in front of his face.

Erik plunged the broken spear into the king's shoulder.

CHAPTER 69

Erik hit the ground, falling hard on his injured shoulder. He howled in pain, afraid to open his eyes. Remembering the need to kill the king, he opened his eyes. muted sunlight shown. *The eclipse must be over, and I must strike the king before the king kills us all.* He searched above and below the altar. He raised the broken spear and walked around the altar, finding no sign of the king.

What happened to the king?

Lily lay unmoving on the altar. *No! Is she dead? She can't be.* He touched her hand. "Lily?" She moved her hand and looked at Erik.

She rose to a sitting position. "Where am I and what are you doing here?"

"You don't know?" Erik asked.

"Why am I dressed in this white bloody dress? Eww, there's blood on this table."

Erik helped Lily off the altar.

Cugbert, holding Al's staff, approached the altar from his position on the platform. He searched for the king on the other side of the altar. "Where's the king? I watched him tumble off the altar and expected his body right here. Did he slide into the volcano?"

"I don't know, I plunged the spear into his shoulder and now he's gone.

Cugbert and Erik healed Lily's wounds.

Erik searched the volcano rim in the hot sunshine looking for Zita, but didn't find her.

# # # #

Al put his hand on the box containing Sherry. He had watched the king get struck by the multiple explosions and Al prepared for another attack.

The sun burst in solar radiance as Velidred cleared the sun's edge. It blinded Al for a moment and he shut his eyes. Upon opening them, Erik stood over Lily. Then it looked like Cugbert and Erik were taking steps to heal Lily's wounds.

Al didn't see the king.

He touched the invisible box and stared at Sherry.

If the king died, why is the box still there? Have I failed?

Sherry shook her head, tugged at her right ear and touched the box.

Al placed his hand on the box, almost touching Sherry's hand but for the impenetrable magic barrier between them.

Cugbert came with the staff and handed it to Al.

"I can help, Master," said the staff from the topmost wizened image.

Placing the top of the staff to the barrier, Al wondered what might happen. He didn't have any words to remove this magic. The staff told him it was old magic, but did the staff know how to get rid of the box? Why didn't the staff do this before?

In a low, gruff voice, the staff said, "Velidred god, dark as night, evil demons release your prisoner, free her from your grasp."

The barrier disappeared, and Al touched Sherry's hand.

Sherry jumped into Al's arms. He kissed her and embraced her, never wanting to let her go.

Between kisses, Sherry said, "I guess the spiritualist was wrong."

# # # #

Zita sat below the rim of the Velidred volcano. She thought of her father. The last thing her father saw before he died was Zita sending a fireball at him. What must he have thought? She had dreamed of killing her dad as a young girl, after Mom died, but not like this. Her eyes watered. Why did I throw the fireball? How can I ever repay you Dad? Can you forgive me?

A high-pitched squeal, a screaming kee-eeeee-arr, sounded in her ears. Zita raised her right fist as Kestrel floated high overhead. "By the goddess of Velidred, I will destroy Erik Anderson for slaying my father."

The End

THANK YOU

Thank you for reading Eclipse of the Triple Moons. If you enjoyed it, won't you please take a moment to leave a review at your favorite retailer?

You may also enjoy book two in the Mountain King series, Zita's Revenge.

Book three, Rescue of the Stone Warriors will be available in late 2022.

GLOSSARY

Aldabert Greystone - King of the province of Ron-Salem. He is the father of Alpherge (Al) Greystone.

Aloheno - The name of the planet where the teens reach after going through the cave portal. The planet is part of a solar system that has six known planets. Three moons revolve around the planet.

Alpherge Greystone - Called Al by his friends. Grandson of Alpherge the Great. Rightful heir to the Province of Ron-Salem. Born on Aloheno, but sent to Earth as a child to live with his mother to protect him from the mountain king. Al can wield magic, but he must learn. He likes to be called Alpherge the Mighty.

Ancient City of Pankratio - A mythical city of the Pankratio religion. Priests that go to this city according to the legend never die. It is the goal of third-level priests within the religion to search for this city to gain immortality.

Anticletus - The middle-sized moon that circles the planet, Aloheno. This moon is blue. It is believed the moon has water on the surface because of the moon's color. Sherry can use the Crown of Anticletus when the moon is in the sky.

Anuoura - Large frogs on the Planet Aloheno. They come in pink and blue. They get their color from the flowers they eat. Humans find them delicious. They taste like chicken.

Bryce Goodwin II - His brother-in-law, Gerard, sells him and his family out to the mountain king. He is Lily's father. Bryce was the oldest of the Goodwin siblings, Carol and Noreen

Callahan the Curious - A wizard trapped in the staff of Ishwa. Alpherge didn't capture him in the staff. Callahan's nosy nature got the better of him and he found himself trapped.

Carol Goodwin - She is Lily Goodwin's Aunt. Carol comes from the royal bloodline of the Goodwin Kingdom. Carol and Lily are the two remaining members of the bloodline of the Goodwin royal family. Carol is the middle sister of Bryce Goodwin.

Crown of Anticletus - This is a person. When the moon is full, this person radiates a blue persona. It gives the person power over other's thoughts and they have to listen to the person. The person is imbued with a crown of righteousness, inspiring awe in all other creatures, human and animal. All creatures are duty-bound to pay attention.

Crystal of Zaraboth - Ancient legend of an object so powerful it could bring magic to Earth in the hands of a strong wizard. Legend believes it will give the holder immortality.

Cugbert - Priest of the Pankratios religion. He is searching for the Ancient City of Pankratio when he meets the teens from Earth. Cugbert wears his hair in three braids, a sign of his level in the Pankratio religious hierarchy. The Pankratio religion is a peaceful religion, vowing to do no harm.

Cullerton, Montana - A small town at the foothills of the Bitterroot National Forest.

Blayze - An instructor at Ishwa's school of magic. He is a leading warrior wizard commander for the Resistance.

Erik Anderson - Erik will take the role of leader to rescue Lily and help the teens during their struggle on the new planet.

Gerard Goodwin - Ambitious uncle of Lily Goodwin. He is not of the bloodline of the Goodwin Kingdom. He isnot a descendant of the Goodwin name, but takes his wife's name to provide him with more political power.

Irene Torkel - Queen of the Torgony Province and wife of King Oscar Torkel. Irene is Sherry's mother.

Isabel the Invidious - A witch trapped in the staff created by Alpherge the Great. Invidious means obnoxious or causing discontent, animosity, or envy. Alpherge the Great captured her in the staff when she caused havoc in a village.

Jayanti - Female wizard or witch that teaches at the school of wizards run by Ishwa.

Krunal Kalluri – He comes from the Royal Bloodline of the Kalluri Kingdom. Krunal refused a chance to go to Earth, choosing to stay on Aloheno, when The Mountain King conquered the Kalluri people.

Lily Goodwin - Daughter of Bryce and Milena Goodwin, King and Queen of the Province of Thyattica and the Goodwin Kingdom. Billy Cutter, aka Kestrel the Falcon Prince, kidnapped Lily, and places her in the hands of the mountain king. They will sacrifice her for a blood sacrifice during the Eclipse of the Triple Moons.

Marugotapa - A virulent form of Brown Mold that grows when exposed to heat. Al and Zita encounter the mold while escaping through the Velidred Castle dungeon.

Master Wizard Ishwa - He is the blind master wizard of the village of Crossroads and a leader of the resistance. He manages the school that teaches young wizards. Al goes to him to get a wizard's license and be tutored in magic.

Milena Goodwin - Queen of Goodwin Kingdom. She is Lily's mother and the wife of Bryce Goodwin.

Noreen Goodwin - Youngest sister of Bryce Goodwin and mother of Zita. She falls in love with a thief named Haskell, who becomes the Mountain King.

Oscar Torkel - He is the former king of Torgony. His daughter is Sherry. The mountain king killed Oscar in a battle.

Pantaleon - The smallest of the three moons circling the planet, Aloheno. The planet's inhabitants revere

Pantaleon for its ability to give magical abilities to babies born when it is in new moon status. They believe something on the moon sends out a signal that causes the magic. Pregnant moms travel to places where the signal is supposed to occur according to knowledgeable astrologers and astronomers. The Mountain King tries to prevent pregnant moms from reaching these destinations as he fears someone being born who can defeat him. The signal only lasts 5 days and is stronger or weaker depending on how close the moon is to the planet. Pantaleon is a white ice moon.

Patricia Greystone - She is Alpherge's (Al's) Mom. She is the queen and wife of King Aldabert Greystone of the province of Ron-Salem.

Prince Krunal Kalluri - See Krunal Kalluri.

Ron-Salem Province - A Province found north of the Velidred Mountains. This province is a major food producer for the continent.

Sherry Torkel - Former Girl Scout knows how to camp outside and camps with her mom, Irene, regularly. Not afraid of the big outdoors. Pet names for the Wizard (geek boy) (Brainiac). She is the daughter of King Oscar and Irene Torkel of the Torgony Province. She is the Crown of Anticletus.

Stegox - An animal with a body the size of a bear and the facial structure of an opossum. It has horns, massive paws and sharp claws. It has a top land speed of 30 miles an hour. It eats meat usually feeding on deer, small mammals, anuoura and some humans. The animal has a black body with a white stripe that goes from the eyes to the end of his nose.

Thyattica - Northern Province, where the Goodwin Kingdom is located.

Torgony Province - Located Northeast of the Velidred Mountains and east of the Haunted Forest.

Velidred - The largest of the three moons revolving around the planet Aloheno. Velidred is a blood-red moon that is worshiped by the Velo religion. The believers make blood sacrifices to the moon when it is in new moon status. Velidred is a name that means "Red Devil."

Zita - Daughter of the Mountain King and her mother is Noreen Goodwin. Has some magical ability. She looks very similar to Lily and comes from the same bloodline. Zita has black hair compared to Lily's blonde.

MAGIC SPELLS AND MEANINGS

Aura blue, aura near, report the secrets within here - Used by Blayze to determine traps and magic behind doors and walls.

Cessat ventus, ignis - Cease the fire with wind

Cool air, scorched earth, moisture high in the sky, waterlog, pollywog, clouds drop low, form the fog - When the conditions are right this spell forms fog.

Dispergimini in aera militibus - Disperse yourselves among the soldiers, in the air. Throw the soldiers into the air.

Formans murus ignis - Form a Wall of Fire

Hamdat gponli iptilv agerut - Barrier of Hamdat Shield this Magic

Hammer blows, hammer thrice, crush the mold, and break the ice. - A magic spell by Gopal to break the frozen brown mold.

Ignis sale - Salt the fire

Magicae murum aeris ad resiliunt inimici - Magic to account for the elasticity of the enemy, create a wall of air (Creates a wall of air)

Mergit in igne - Plunge into the fire - Al uses this to put the fire out with water.

Multiple ropes, twisted right, squeeze the length and make the cable tight - Tightens a rope

Nutrientibus dolor de igne - Nurse the pain of fire

Quia nunc mihi aperuit - Open the Door

Rope is flexible, rope is strong, bend to me rope, I sing your song. - Allows the user to form rope to their needs.

Soponfect momulanti quiducand - Capture the magic of the moment

Spirit within, presence without, advise the truth magic scout - Helps determine traps and magic behind doors and walls.

Thor de caelo fulmen - The lightning of Thor.

Velidred god dark as night, evil demons release your prisoner, free her from your grasp - A spell the Staff of Ishwa commands removing the invisible box where Sherry was entombed.

We need warmth, we require light, we want heat our desire is dire, where I point place this fire - First spell Al uses to start a fire.

Wind will blow with temperatures low. Fall's sneezes lead to winter's freezes. Ice, ice, ice. - Used by Zita to freeze the brown mold.

Get bonus content at https://kenbrownauthor.com

ACKNOWLEDGEMENTS

Thank you to my editor, who taught me so much about writing as she showed me how to improve the book.

Editor: Joan H Young
Author, Editor and famous Hiker

I want to give thanks to my friends who offered to be beta readers and helped make the book the best it could be. The writing group members challenged me to improve my writing, and I grew under their leadership.

Mary-Megan Kelvig
Brad Johnson
Sue Wells
Jeanette Baker
Theresa Brooks
Carol Ann Ray

Thank you all for pointing out when I was wrong, giving me hope and support when my confidence failed, finding errors I missed, and enjoying the story. All errors in the story are mine.

ABOUT KENNETH BROWN

Kenneth Brown is an application web developer by day and author by night. Over the years, he has written short stories for his own enjoyment and started a couple of other books, but never had the fortitude to finish the books.

But one day an idea came to him about a boy who wants to rescue a girl and finds that going through a cave, it transported him to another planet. A planet where magic is real and the dangers of wild animals, strange people and bizarre customs are just as real.

A photograph Ken found on the Glacier National Park's website inspired the book. It was a simple photograph from inside a tunnel in winter in Glacier National Park, Montana. The image showed icicles hanging from the tunnel exit with large boulders hugging the wall behind. Looking at the boulders and rocks, Ken saw images of people and horses and a story developed of a boy searching out the Mountain King.

A desire to write turned this fanciful world into a book, and it led three years later to Ken's first published novel, *Eclipse of the Triple Moons*.

May your life be filled with exciting adventures, great joy, amazing memories, and loving friends willing to go to the ends of the galaxy to save you.

BONUS MATERIAL

Thank you for purchasing this book. We hope you enjoyed *Eclipse of the Triple Moons* and will take the time to write a review on your favorite book buying site.

To find out more about the author, Ken Brown, and get advanced notification about future books, check out the website, https://kenbrownauthor.com. You will find ways to receive free books or discounted books.

The cover artwork for this book was created by Kenneth Brown, using images from Shutterstock and Unsplash. His creative director and wife, Mary Brown, helped to get the cover image into a format worth presenting to the world. We hope you like it.